SECRETS OF THE
disappearing

REBECCA S. PARKINSON

Helen,
Enjoy the mystery!
Rebecca Parkinson

Cover & interior design by Typewriter Creative Co.
Cover photo by frank mckenna on Unsplash.com.

ISBN 979-8-9855962-3-6 (Paperback)
ISBN 979-8-9855962-4-3 (eBook)

To the Lord God
from Whom comes
every good and perfect gift
and all wisdom and truth

A Few Thoughts

Writing a book is an adventure. Sharing it with friends and readers is a joy. In my travels around the globe, I've found two places I return to over and over: Nantucket and the Scottish Highlands. Some of you have been fortunate to experience the pristine beauty and spiritual quality of both. For others, I hope you will enjoy this armchair journey to Nantucket, a bit of Scotland that has floated to our side of the pond.

I have childhood roots in Nantucket. Standing in the middle of the moors or at the edge of a marsh or walking on the beaches of Nantucket refreshes my soul. I've yet to find a stretch of beach anywhere in the world more beautiful than those surrounding Nantucket. It saddens me to see its vistas disappearing and pristine beauty shrinking. Fortunately, there are places on the island that have been preserved. But I would like us all to consider the importance of continuing this preservation.

Reader, it's my greatest hope that you will enjoy not only the adventure of this book, but also the time you spend with the family of characters. We all have questions about who controls the universe. And increasingly, we face the presence of evil in our lives. The choices we make affect others. As readers, I hope to spark your search for what is essential in your life and in what you believe. Then ponder how you would make some of the moral choices facing the characters in this book. It is also my hope that you will consider just Who runs the universe and what is your part in that story.

One

no one on the island could have foreseen what would happen to the hillside above the marsh at Pocomo Meadows. Only the rising sun that first morning in June would reveal the truth.

Two birdwatchers, kayaking within the marsh's hidden recesses, saw the first disappearance.

"Josh, I think I need another cup of coffee."

"Marci, we just got started. Can't you wait until we're deeper into the marsh?"

"Well, if I wait until then, you'll fuss about me scaring the birds when I get out the thermos. I was so looking forward to sitting in the cool, still morning, holding my steaming cup of coffee and watching the world unfold before us. Guess I'll have to forsake that dream," she sighed playfully.

"Okay, okay. You win. Why do women insist on nesting every place they go?" Josh muttered into his fleece. "I'll watch for sharks coming in and out of the inlet. You get your coffee."

But turning to face his wife, Josh didn't see Marci contentedly holding her steaming cup of coffee. Instead, he saw his wife frozen with a look of horror on her face pointing toward the hillside above the marsh.

"Marci, what is it? Are you okay? Look at me."

"*No,* Josh. Look at the hillside!"

Pulling alongside Marci's kayak, Josh focused his attention on the hillside above the marsh. Then looking back at his wife, he heard a muffled groan. "Josh, I can't believe it."

"Marci, what is it?"

Gasping for breath, Marci scratched out in a trembling voice, "Josh, can't you see it? The houses are gone."

Sensing not just exasperation but fear in Marci's voice, Josh stared at the hillside once more. "Marci, that can't be. Check your binoculars. We just finished building that huge Pocomo house last week. I know they have first and second-floor views of the marsh and creeks.

"*Had views,* you mean. They're not waking up to any view this morning."

"But Marci, that's impossible. Maybe we're not close enough. It could be the mist rising off the water distorting our view or the steam off your coffee cup," he mumbled as he reached for his paddle. "Let's paddle closer. Maybe that will help."

"Josh," Marci pleaded.

"Okay, I believe you. How about we paddle into the salt pond for a better view?"

Turning north, Marci and Josh ran the tide with their kayaks and headed for the opening in the marsh that led to the salt pond just below the hillside.

"Marci, if the houses are gone, we need to tell someone right away."

"No, Josh. It's too weird. No one will believe us. We must be seeing things. Maybe we're not awake enough."

A long ten minutes passed before they reached the small pond's opening at the far end of the marsh. Both of them were silent. Only the birds heard their paddles slipping in and out of the saltwater. Alone in their thoughts, each was mentally running possible scenarios wishing they'd never left their warm bed and now dreading what the sun would reveal. The pleasant predawn light and their initial sense of adventure had vanished—just like the houses.

After a few minutes, Josh stopped paddling. Marci slowly pulled her kayak alongside his. Careful that the kayaks didn't bump and arouse the birds, they focused their attention on the far side of the pond, scanning in between the large patches of mist that were still rising off the water. The wildlife they loved had gathered along the edge of the marsh. Several snowy egrets were preening themselves on the lip of sand just above the high tide mark. One egret stood on alert while three others waded in the shallows. A stately blue heron and its mate were standing among the reeds at the water's edge. As still as the air, they waited patiently to catch their early morning breakfast.

"Josh, do you think those herons share breakfast when one catches a fish? They're so beautiful. I love their silky movement, slowly placing each foot down into the sand then pausing before they put down the other foot."

Focused on the herons, Marci didn't see that the mist shielding the Pocomo hillside was dissipating. Taking his binoculars, Josh surveyed the hillside, searching for the houses.

"Marci, I think you'd better take a look."

Scanning the hillside, Marci whispered, "Josh, the houses *aren't* there. How can that be?"

"I don't know. Something strange is happening to us."

"Not to *us,* to the hillside. *We* haven't disappeared. The houses have."

"Marci, maybe we should call Don and see if he's heard anything on the police radio."

"Wait. Think about what you're saying. It's five-thirty in the morning. You're in the middle of a marsh, and you call your buddy down at the station to report missing houses in Pocomo. You'll be the laughingstock of the force, let alone the island."

"Marci, play fair."

"I can hear Don now. Missing *herons*. Josh, you're calling me at this hour to report . . . oh, missing *houses,* now that makes more sense. Where are you calling from? And exactly where are these missing houses?"

"Marci, that's not funny. What do you want me to do?"

"Oh, right, they floated out to sea," Marci jested, still pretending to hold the phone up to her ear. She was enjoying play-acting Josh's friend at the police station. "Straight out of the harbor, behind the late ferry, in the dark of night."

"Marci, stop joking around."

"Well, if it's no joke, how did the houses disappear?" Marci snapped.

"Don's our friend. Maybe there's a logical explanation."

"Right, Josh. I can see it now, *The Inquirer and Mirror* Police Report: Josh and Marci Longmeadow, while bird watching in Pocomo Meadows, report-ed the disappearance of four McMansions on the Pocomo hillside above the marsh. Denying the presence of swamp mist as a factor, they insisted that some-one investigate the strange disappearance. Sergeant Don Moran took the call."

"Marci, stop. Pull yourself together. He'll think we're nuts," Josh pleaded.

"Okay, I see your point." But to crush the fear that was slowly creeping over both of them, Marci continued. "The report says the couple also claim they built some of the houses. Police are investigating."

"Marci, if we report this, people won't be saying we need new binoculars. They'll be saying we need a psychiatrist."

"Josh, even I'm starting to think we're crazy."

Now getting into the play, Josh fired back, "Yeah, I can see Sean at The Donut posting it on the *Hot News* blackboard, editorializing as he pours coffee, letting everyone know that we've gone stark raving mad."

"Wait a minute. All kidding aside, we both see it. Why don't we paddle across the pond until we're at the base of the hillside?"

"Okay. Maybe it's an illusion caused by the mist rolling up the hillside from the water. Let's keep paddling. Hopefully, when the sun burns off the mist, the houses will reappear. In any case, we're out here for fun. Right?"

"Okay. But can we break out the muffins before we go any further? I'm starting to feel lightheaded. Maybe this wasn't such a great idea after all."

"Hey, before the houses disappeared, we were having a great time. Let's allow the beauty of the morning to calm us and enjoy the quiet solitude with the herons."

"Maybe they'll start disappearing too."

But when the muffins were all consumed and the mist finally lifted, they faced an empty hillside.

Two

S weat poured down his face and onto his chest as Keta stepped into the placid Caribbean water. The tide was in, but the bottom sea life still gleamed through the water. Stepping carefully over the hundreds of pebbles, shells, and coral remnants, he dove into the aquamarine water. His lean, six-foot form was that of a swimmer, well-honed and already sporting a nice tan.

Out beyond the raft and moored snorkel boat, Lyrica was basking in the sun on a white foam raft, one hand dangling into the water, the other resting under her head. Her thick, auburn hair draped over the raft's pillow and dipped into the water.

Surfacing a few feet behind the moored snorkel boat, Keta looked over at his wife sunning on the mat, quietly talking. He could just make out some of the words. Deciding that she was focused on her musings, he dove again.

She's probably conversing with the Lord or singing, Keta thought, swimming underwater toward his target. Contemplating her surprise, he was about to surface behind her head when he checked himself. Lyrica was already skittish from the robbery. This wouldn't help. She might even scream and draw unwanted attention. Instead, he surfaced noisily about ten feet to the right of the sleeping beauty. Opening her eyes and pulling herself up on her elbows, Lyrica saw her husband quickly cover the distance between them.

"Better not let those pink toes dangle in the water too long. I hear the parrotfish nibble painted toes, especially hot pink."

"Hey, did you have a great run? Any bananas or papayas from the kids?"

"No, I didn't go into the rain forest. I pretty much stayed along the walking path that meanders through the fields and up to the bluff. Quite a view. But not as pretty as the one I have in front of me," Keta smiled as he rested his arms next to Lyrica's legs and looked tenderly at his wife of thirty years.

"How was your chat with the Lord this morning? Did He mention my name?"

"Well, I thanked Him for protecting me from the press, and He said to remember He's still in charge. He also likes the beach and the sun."

"Ah-ha, I see that sense of humor gaining on you. Guess all this pampering has had the desired effect," Keta said, smiling at his wife. "As for me, I need some tropical nourishment. Can I get you something?"

"Mmm. How about a pineapple crush and make sure—"

"They put in a cherry," finished Keta. "Do you want to drink it on the raft or the beach?"

"How about you grab a raft, and I'll paddle down to meet you by the bar?"

"Sure you're up to the exertion? Keeping this raft afloat can take a lot out of a gal," Keta teased.

"Yeah, those laps around the schooner Wind Swept did kind of wipe me out."

"Okay, mermaid, be back in a sec." Keta disappeared under the raft, surfaced, and swam toward the beach bar. Traveling the distance in less than a minute, Lyrica watched him wade through the shallows and sprint across the sand toward the bar.

"Ouch, I forget how hot the sand is this time of year," Keta growled, then quickly stepped into the shade of a large tree. "Ah, much better."

"What can I get you, sir?" Tezo asked as Keta approached the bamboo bar.

"One pineapple crush with a cherry and one coke, please." Mounting one of the polished teak barstools, Keta looked out at the water to check on his wife before he turned back toward the bartender.

"What's for lunch today? Any coconut ice cream?"

"Oh, I expect so. Marco stocked up, knowing that you both were coming. Can't run out of coconut ice cream when you're here, can we?" Tezo put the drinks in front of Keta. They were already sweating from the heat.

Sliding off the stool, Keta stepped carefully onto the hot sand and quickly headed toward the nearest raft. Soothing his burning soles in the cool sand of the tidal wash, Keta pulled a raft into the water with the drinks perched perilously on top. He then waded out until the water was deep enough to swim and headed for his wife. Lyrica had straddled her raft and was paddling toward Keta. She took the drinks from him and waited while he conquered the raft's slippery surface.

"Here's to paradise. May we always be this happy," toasted Keta.

"And may all our days be just like this one," added Lyrica. Both of them took long, slow sips of their drinks, letting the cool from the ice refresh their lips. Rolling the frosty glass across her forehead, Lyrica remarked, "This is the life. Presto, pineapple crusho. I didn't realize how hot it was out here. Do I look burned?"

"No, you look the same as you did when you walked out the door this morning. Beautiful."

"I think you've been out in the sun too long. Your eyesight is blurry," denied Lyrica. "So, tell me about your run this morning? Did any of the village kids tag along?"

"No, only a few goats, two dogs, and one donkey were out for the day. But the century plant is getting ready to bloom. I think it'll blossom while we're here. And there are some elegant flowering vines along the rocky shore," Keta responded. "Lots of birds, a few pelicans were enjoying breakfast, and a seagull was picking at a dead fish on the shore. I think the kids must still be in school."

"That reminds me. I want to see if the new plumeria bushes are in bloom. I'd like to finish photographing them. I just need a few more shots to finish the tropical exhibit. You didn't happen to notice if the red sword is bloom-ing, did you?"

"Uh, you're the one with the botanical bent, not me. You know the extent of my knowledge about flora and feathered fauna extends only to your photos. And I have to confess. I read the subtitles."

"We'll have to do something about that. Maybe an escorted tour of the grounds at sunrise covering the Latin and common names of the flowers?" teased Lyrica.

"Sounds good to me."

"No, what would you like to do? We have two weeks and no calendar to keep. Somewhere between reading on the beach, sleeping, and eating, we might be able to squeeze in a sports activity or two. Am I going in the right direction?" Lyrica hinted.

"When we start feeling rested, maybe a trip to the reef to add a few fish to our lifetime list," joked Keta.

"Hey, that's a great idea. I'll have my bird and flower lifetime lists. You can have a fish list."

"Does Chilean sea bass at dinner count?"

"Only in your case since you saw it when it was alive."

"How about the reef sharks?" Keta teased, knowing her dislike of them.

"One shark at the reef is enough for a lifetime. And it's not on my list for entrees either," Lyrica commented as she looked toward the beach bar. "Hon, do you know what time it is? We probably should have some lunch soon."

"I could go for that. Are you feeling up to eating down here, or would you rather eat on the terrace of our room?"

"Maybe we could make a foray to the beach restaurant. I'm feeling a lot more relaxed since we've had such privacy these last few days. Let's go for it,"

Lyrica said, turning her raft toward their beach chairs.

"Yeah, I'm ready for some adventure. Maybe I'll have the fried onion rings and coconut ice cream."

"Not together, I hope," Lyrica said, getting out of the water while Keta dragged the two rafts onto the sand.

"Looks like a lot of folks have already eaten," remarked Keta watching Lyrica put on her pareo, hat, and sunglasses.

"Here goes our first public appearance. How do I look?"

"Like a million dollars. Oops, sorry," said Keta grabbing her hand and pointing them toward a shaded area of sand. "Watch it. This sand is roasting. I barely made it to the beach bar to get our drinks."

"You know, I was thinking out on the raft. Maybe I'll do some freeform watercolors while we're here. See if I can break the mold a bit."

"That sounds kind of interesting." Keta raised his hand as if reading something written across the sky. "I can see it now. Famous photographer and artist stuns onlookers at her latest show in Boston. Freehand washes of color striking modern interpretations of Caribbean photographic work transform the walls into a melody of color. What will Lyrica Kea think of next?"

Stepping into the foot pool, Lyrica swished the sand off her feet and stepped onto the restaurant's blue-green tile floor. "Oh, that water felt good. They must dump the extra ice in there. I love making footprints on the tiles. I feel like a little girl."

"You know, going barefoot is wonderful. Although I have to admit, you have the prettiest toes between us. How about that table over there by the perimeter looking out over the water?"

"It looks fine. Order me some iced tea. I'll be right back," said Lyrica as she headed toward the ladies' room.

Seating himself, Keta surveyed the beach bar and restaurant, heaved a heavy sigh, and gazed out at the water. The sun was brilliant. The breeze was just enough to ruffle the water and keep the sailfish wanderers tacking back and forth in their little bay.

Man, I love this place, he mused to himself. For two weeks, we can sleep with cool breezes, wake up to brilliant sunshine, and stare endlessly out at the ocean. Keta was still happily taking in the scenery when Lyrica returned.

"Find anything good to eat?"

"Here comes your iced tea. Did you want a glass of wine? I haven't had a chance to ask about the coconut ice cream, but I did see some carrot cake on the dessert table."

"I'm proud of you thinking about dessert first. I'm going to have a grilled cheese to go with your fried onion rings," said Lyrica closing the menu.

"*My* onion rings? Who said anything about sharing? How about we get two orders?"

"Whatever your heart desires." Lyrica turned her head sideways to scan the restaurant's occupants.

"Not to worry, hon," said Keta, following Lyrica's gaze. I checked it out. No paparazzi, just sun-starved vacationers. You'd think we were in the witness protection program."

"Maybe that would be a good idea."

"Oh no. Lyrica, turn and face me. I just made a liar out of myself," Keta whispered urgently.

But Lyrica had already seen them, and her face showed it.

"Maybe we should go? We can slip out now like we just finished and go up to the terrace?" Keta suggested.

"Honey, I can't take this. I thought we were safe here. How did *they get in?*"

"I don't know. But I'm sure going to find out."

Three

"More coffee, Trish?" Becki asked as she took the pot from the coffeemaker and brought it to the kitchen table. She and her best friend were catching up after Becki's recent trip to Madeira.

"Mmm, yes. So, tell me what's been happening?" Trish asked, stirring warm milk into her brew. She loved having coffee with Becki. While living in Europe, the two of them had adopted the ritual of using warmed milk for coffee and tea as they sat in local cafes catching up on each other's day. She missed that daily friendship ritual now that both were living in busy downtown Boston.

"Oh, Trish, I don't even know where to start. This could take us more than one cup of coffee. Now that Mom and Dad are temporarily hiding away in the Caribbean, safe from the paparazzi, I feel like I can breathe again."

"Am I missing something? Has there been more adverse publicity about your mom?"

"Trish, sometimes I don't know whether this is a bad dream or a plot from one of your mystery novels." Becki pushed back from the 1950s aqua vinyl kitchen table and was rocking on the back legs of her chair. "What I know is that our family can't take many more of these lies."

"Help me out. What happened while you were in Madeira that set the press onto your folks again?"

"Trish, it happened so fast. One minute Stephen and I were cataloging a new orchid species enjoying the beauty of that island, and the next we were reading about ourselves in the tabloids." Becki hadn't even heard Trish's last question.

"Wait. I thought you and Stephen were, ah, just friends."

"Oh, it has nothing to do with Stephen and me. Not in that way. At least, I don't think so. Oh no, what if this does somehow affect Stephen? I couldn't face anything happening to him. Oh, I wish I'd never even heard of Madeira."

"Becki, stop. Can we go back to the beginning? I'm lost," Trish interrupted as Becki rambled.

"Okay."

"Maybe it would be better if we start after you both got back from Madeira when we had coffee at Poodles last week," Trish suggested. "All of this—whatever it is—has happened in the last four days?"

"Sort of. It all runs together now." Becki's eyes were welling up with tears.

"How about we start with Stephen? That seems to be what's upsetting you the most."

"Okay. Stephen went to work the day after we got back. He was all gung-ho about writing his report for Earsom on the land and the environmental statement for the company's development. He intended to propose they preserve the acreage with the tree orchids as part of protecting the ecosystem."

"Orchids?"

"Trish, Stephen's confident we discovered a new species of tree orchids. He's hoping he can name them," Becki said excitedly.

"Why would Justin Earsom care about the welfare of a few measly orchids? Can't the forest be part of the complex?"

"Trish, they're not just a bunch of *measly* orchids! Stephen thinks they are an undiscovered species. He's talking with some of his botany experts about the find to make sure."

"He didn't tell Justin Earsom that, did he?"

"No way would Stephen tell Justin anything important without witnesses. He's not that stupid."

"I'm sorry, Becki. I didn't mean to imply that Stephen wasn't a brilliant scientist. I'm just worried. You and I know Justin is a snake."

"It's okay. I said the same thing to Stephen on the phone when he told me about the briefing. He gets so excited. Sometimes I'm afraid he'll forget about corporate politics. You know how I feel about Justin and his crowd. But for now, Stephen thinks he can build his career at Earsom. They seem willing to give him the opportunity."

"Some opportunity. At what price?" said Trish, rolling her eyes.

"Stephen doesn't see it that way. For a land firm with an international reputation for environmental responsibility, it's hard for him to believe that economic gain is the sole motivator for the people around him. He's always believed that the top execs, other than Justin, really have a passion for environmental protection."

"Want more coffee?" Trish asked, reaching for the coffeepot.

"Yes, I'll take some more. But this will have to be my last."

"What happened after Stephen finished the briefing?"

"Justin wasn't thrilled with the proposal because it reduced the amount of land the hotel complex can develop."

"But didn't Justin send Stephen specifically because of his expertise in environmental land management? Isn't that what he does?"

"Yes, and no. Stephen knows that many of the top execs understand how ruthless and focused Justin is on profits. The word environment in the company's name is mostly for public relations. He hopes to persuade Justin to preserve the forest as part of the complex and not mention the orchids. It could be a corporate give back to the island."

"Yeah, right. Justin Earsom hasn't a benevolent cell in his body."

"Especially when it comes to money. He could destroy the entire ecosystem if he builds a hotel and market complex on that land."

"How is Stephen going to maneuver his way out of this one?"

"Trish, that's why I'm worried. Eventually, Stephen will have to tell Justin that the ecosystem and the orchids are in jeopardy. My botanical drawings will be part of his presentation. When he does, Justin's going to be angry that Stephen didn't tell him sooner. Plus, when he sees my name, he may associate it with stories in the press about my mom. It could jeopardize both the discovery and our jobs."

"Becki, how long can Stephen keep this discovery from Justin?"

"Stephen says that if he presents the preliminary findings to Justin without the other execs present, Justin will deep-six the information. He needs more time to check with his colleagues to see if there's a way to build the hotel complex and also protect the forest."

"So, Stephen didn't tell Justin his plans? And you're afraid that Stephen will lose his job when Justin finds out?"

"You got it," replied Becki. "But there's more. My job may now be in jeopardy."

Four

S oaked to the skin and both unusually quiet, Marci and Josh lifted the dripping kayaks onto their Jeep. The sun was up. Blue sky was pushing back the remaining clouds. They'd stayed in the marsh as long as they could without getting too cold. After settling the kayaks, Josh pulled out from the sandy landing, turned left, and headed up the Wauwinet Road. Stepping on the gas, he glanced at Marci. Neither wanted to break the chilling silence.

Turning onto the Pocomo Road, Josh slowed down to look for the new macadam road leading to the exclusive property where he and Jake had built the estate homes overlooking the marsh. Both Marci and Josh expected to see the Private Road sign a few yards after the Pocomo Road turned into the sandy washboard for which it was famous. But what they hoped for and what they expected were two very different things. What if the homes perched on that hillside overlooking the marsh had vanished?

"Josh, I think we've gone too far," Marci remarked. "The turnoff should have been before this. Maybe we should turn around."

"Let's keep going a little farther. Maybe we'll find the old construction road to the houses." Pressing on, both Marci and Josh silently scanned the roads leading off to the left, searching for the private development.

Arriving at Pocomo Point, Josh turned the car to face the harbor. The couple looked at each other. Each hoped the other would speak first.

"What are we going to do?" Marci asked. "Even the road leading to the homes is gone."

"I say we turn around and see how we missed it," Josh responded confidently. "Maybe we were talking and didn't see it with all the new scrub oak that has grown."

"Josh, we're not going to find the road. It's one thing to miss a dirt road. It's another to lose a macadam road and the houses we built."

"I know. But I think we owe it to ourselves to take a second look. Maybe we missed it."

"Yeah, right. Maybe we're not nuts. It's like our bumper sticker: Fog

Happens." Marci was not convinced. Josh wasn't either. But neither one wanted to contemplate what they would do if the homes had vanished.

"Josh, what about the people who own the houses? Are they missing too? How can bricks, shingles, and frames just disappear into thin air, let alone people?"

Josh didn't answer. Driving slowly back down the washboard road, he was still looking for the private paved road that led to the enormous estate homes. The early construction road was barely visible. The sandpile he dumped across the track to stop any traffic was now sprouting tall grasses, and the track itself was barely visible with the recent growth of scrub oak.

"No houses. No road. Not even a dirt driveway or a mailbox. Nothing. I don't get it," Josh moaned as he slowed the Jeep to a stop.

"Josh, something strange has happened to the houses, or maybe to us."

Heading back on the Wauwinet Road, both were quiet. Marci was the first to break the silence. "Josh, maybe we shouldn't say anything. See if anyone else reports the missing homes. If they've really disappeared, someone will notice. Why don't we wait and see what happens? I'm feeling overwhelmed."

"Yeah, I know. Not a great way to start our day, huh? Do you know what gets me? Why us? We're not exactly Mr. and Mrs. Excitement. What did your friend Kathy say? We're about as exciting as Squam Swamp on a rainy day. Things like this don't happen to people like us."

"Oh really? Thanks, Josh."

"Come on, Marci. You know what I mean. I didn't say we were boring, just that we find more creative outlets for our imagination than inventing headlines for the newspaper. The whole reason we came to Nantucket was to stay out of the limelight and pursue our passions without the world keeping tabs on our personal lives. That took too much of a toll on us."

"Sorry, Josh. I guess I'm hungry. Why don't we go home, have some hot chocolate, and wait for the paper to come out this afternoon? Maybe it'll be in the news. Then we can forget about reporting it. Let someone else be called the kook. Besides, we both have full schedules ahead of us today."

"Yeah, I can see it now," Josh joked. "Lost: Four McMansions, Pocomo hillside. If found, please return to the nearest real estate office. All leads investigated. Large Reward."

Five

"Lyrica, let's go. Maybe this wasn't such a good idea. We'll walk up the beach toward the sugar mill. Hopefully, they'll have left by the time we return," Keta said, looking at his wife's pained face.

"I feel as if I'm being watched," Lyrica whispered.

"Hopefully, they've not seen us." Just at that moment, Keta saw the two paparazzi get up from their table.

"Lyrica, stay where you are for just a minute. I think they may be leaving." Keta was watching the couple out of the corner of his eye.

"They're looking over this way. Just turn your head a little and—"

"What can I get you today?" the waiter asked.

A look of relief swept over Keta's face. Jonathan was perfectly blocking the paparazzi's view. Unfortunately, he was also blocking Keta's view. Stretching back a little, Keta glanced over at the other entrance to the beach restaurant where he'd seen the couple sitting. But Marco, the restaurant manager, had seen them and headed straight for the couple.

"What about you, darling? What are you going to have besides onion rings and coconut ice cream?" Lyrica asked.

"Well, I wasn't planning to have *both,* but now that you mention it, maybe I will. Jonathan, can you get the lady a grilled cheese sandwich with crisp bacon?" Keta replied.

"Sure thing, Mr. Kea—uh Sir," Jonathan replied, catching himself. "How about you?"

"Make mine a sirloin burger with the works, medium rare, please."

"Would you like anything from the bar?"

"No, I think the coke and iced tea will suffice. Maybe just two glasses of ice cubes with lemon. How's the family this year?" Keta asked, attempting to stall Jonathan a few minutes longer while he checked the other side of the restaurant.

Marco, however, had the situation under control. He had politely and calmly ushered the couple out of the restaurant's far entrance and pointed them toward the main house, where another restaurant served visitors. He stood watching them to make sure they didn't veer off the path.

Keta looked gratefully at Marco, thinking how gracious yet intimidating he was. He was six foot five, built like a Mercedes, with muscles practically bursting out of his tropical shirt. No one would casually refuse a suggestion from him. After seeing that the couple headed toward the main restaurant, Keta glimpsed Marco pulling out his cell phone.

"Robin, do me a favor? There are two paparazzi headed your way. I don't know how they got in, but I'm sending them up to the restaurant. Just make sure that's as far as they go. The Keas are down here eating lunch."

"Thanks, Marco. We were wondering where they went. The west gate security alerted us of two people on foot and no boat in sight. The guard told them it was private property, but they said they only wanted lunch. He'd told them to go to the main house. I guess they had other plans."

Marco pocketed his cell phone. Walking back toward Keta and Lyrica, he nodded and returned to his station where he could view the beach, the west gate, and the restaurant.

Lyrica watched her husband and noticed the change in his face but was temporarily distracted by Jonathan's four beautiful children smiling up from the wallet pictures he'd laid out on the table. Keta picked up the oldest child's photo, hoping to hear about the kids' latest soccer escapades.

"So, when will we see them competing internationally?" Keta asked, a twinkle in his eye. Jonathan's response was a delightful surprise. "My eldest child, whose picture you're holding, tried out for the Olympics this past year."

"Whoa. Tell them they're growing up too fast. Make sure you alert us when one of them makes it. We want to be there," said Keta, handing back the photo. "Say, any coconut ice cream down here?"

"Yes, we stocked up before you came. And chocolate sauce for your wife." Jonathan's smile was as engaging as his children's.

"Good," responded Lyrica. "I was craving chocolate on the beach this morning."

"I'm sure the house would put some chocolate in your minibar."

"They already have," said Lyrica. "Much to the benefit of our waistlines."

"Is there anything else I can get for you? We have two special salads today, one with greens and the other tropical fruit."

"That sounds great. Bring us one of each," Keta smiled.

"Gotcha." Jonathan disappeared toward the kitchen.

"Well, that was a pleasant appetizer for our lunch, wasn't it? How brazen can these paparazzi get, wandering into a private club? It doesn't make me feel very safe." Lyrica's face still had a pained look.

"Lyrica, they have it under control. I'm just grateful we were here and not on the beach. That could have been dicey."

"Now I know we agreed not to let paranoia spoil our time here, but that was alarming after being so relaxed the past few days," Lyrica said, brushing the hair out of her face after taking off her hat and sunglasses.

Recognizing that Lyrica was trying to cheer him up, Keta reached over and softly grabbed her hand. "God's still in charge, remember? Why don't we say grace and wait for our salads? At least we'll get our health food in before we hit the cholesterol."

"Thanks, hon. We both need a reminder occasionally of who is in charge of our lives." "Hungry?"

"Yes, but it seems like we just finished eating an enormous breakfast on the patio."

"Isn't that what we always say?" Keta was tenderly looking into his wife's soft brown eyes. Jonathan was now on his way back to their table, their glasses of ice cubes in his hands.

Six

"Becki, how can the status of Stephen's job threaten yours? You're an internationally known botanical artist wholly unconnected with Justin Earsom."

"Trish, I used some of my grant money from the Botanical Design Foundation to go to Madeira with Stephen to paint rare tree orchids. We plan to go to the Amazon next year to complete the grant. Now, because of all the publicity about Mom and Stephen clashing with Justin, the Foundation could withdraw my grant."

"That's ridiculous!" Trish exclaimed. "Who else would they give it to? You're one of the leading experts in botanical art and the *only* person who paints rare species. When they find out about Stephen's discovery, the Foundation should give you *more* money for all the publicity they'll get."

"Thanks for being my champion, Trish. But once the publicity hit about Mom, my credibility also took a hit. I was hoping this trip would boost my reputation." Becki gazed down at the table, shielding her teary eyes from Trish's view. "The Foundation called while I was away and moved up my presentation date. They've never even asked for samples this early in a project."

"Becki, try not to speculate. You don't know the motive behind their request. It may have nothing to do with your grant money."

"It's just not fair. Mom did nothing wrong. But the press convinced the world that she stole those photos." Becki had now let loose on the tears. "If my job falls into that same black hole, what will happen to my reputation? Oh, I wish Mom and Dad were here."

"Can it wait until they're back?"

"I don't have two weeks. Our discovery may not make the science section of *The Boston Globe,* but it's only a matter of days before Justin finds out about the orchids. If he gets to Earsom's execs before Stephen does, those orchids will never see the light of day, let alone make the discovery list."

"How soon do you think Stephen can find an ally in this?"

"He's trying to garner support from the environmental lawyers he knows, as well as his botany mentors. He wants to protect the forest. But Justin doesn't care about the ecosystem. He'll steal the discovery from Stephen or hide it so he can build his hotel complex. Everyone now assumes I come from an untrustworthy family. No one will believe Stephen or my botanicals, just like no one believed Mom."

"Becki, you're assuming that Justin will steal or crush the discovery before Stephen can get to the other execs."

"I think he may have already done so. Stephen told me this morning that he's off the Madeira project after next week. Justin wants him close to home for some new land deal."

"But Becki, you don't know that Justin reassigned Stephen to hide the discovery. Does Justin know about Stephen's field notes?"

"Yes, but the discovery isn't in his company notes, only in his personal journal. And he keys those notes to my drawings and descriptions of the endangered ecosystem."

"Does Justin know Stephen keeps two journals?"

"I'm not sure. Everyone who's traveled with him knows he keeps a personal journal and company field notes."

"So, the issue is, does Earsom own Stephen's personal notes and thus the discovery of the new orchids?"

"You got it. Stephen will have done all the work, and Justin will take credit for the discovery. Or even worse, he'll auction the ownership rights to orchid growers who will start propagating them in their hothouses. The poor islanders won't know what hit them."

"Who would have thought that a few tree orchids could cause all this trouble?"

"Trish, it's not just a few orchids. The entire ecosystem is at stake," Becki snapped.

"I'm sorry. I didn't mean it the way it sounded."

"Trish, I'm too tired to take on any more battles. Why does this have to happen now? Why can't God take out Earsom and some of the other creeps who are crushing the environment for private gain?"

"Becki, I'm so sorry. I know it's not fair, but let's not give up so fast. Can't you make your presentation without revealing the orchids as a discovery?"

"Yes. But either way, Justin plays this. I'm implicated. Besides, who needs proof to ruin a career? Look at Mom."

"Becki, they've not proven your mom stole those photos. Besides, the press will not connect the discovery of rare orchids—"

"Trish, you don't have to be guilty for the press to make you appear guilty.

They have diplomatic immunity, as well as being the judge and jury."

"Becki—"

"Why can't I have a normal life?" Becki was now holding her cat, Rollo, on her lap. "I want to be like Rollo, eat, sleep, and enjoy the sunshine on my back. How can you believe in a God who allows evil people to thrive and people like me suffer?"

"Becki, God's not causing the pain you are having."

"Trish, don't get religious on me. I need all the friends I can get. If God loved me, I wouldn't be in so much pain. He'd leave me alone."

"Okay. But remember, God is a gentleman. He doesn't interfere with our free will. Sometimes, as with your mom, people are victims of other people's wrongdoing. But God didn't cause that to happen—"

"Trish, get off it!"

"Becki, if you won't believe God, believe me. He loves you very much. You'll get through this, and so will your mom and dad. Remember, Paul and I will help you any way we can. I know it feels like the end of the world, but it's not. We've gotten through tough times before. You're not in this alone. Okay?"

"Thanks, Trish. Sometimes I get my life so aligned with Stephen I feel trapped. Other times, I feel as if I'm living Mom's life. I'm so tired of people giving me the cold shoulder or staring at me when they discover my last name. I just want to be an artist and work with plants and flowers, not people."

"So, do you still want to call your parents?" Trish asked hesitantly.

"No. But I really could use their advice. Besides, if I don't tell them, they'll be hurt."

"Then let's call. I'll stay for moral support."

"Now let's see, they're probably drinking pineapple crushes on the beach. Okay, here goes."

Seven

osh and Marci turned into the driveway that led to their secluded home. Their two vizslas, Mako and Sandi, came running down the rutted track, barking. Slowing down, each dog headed for a different side of the Jeep.

"Mako, off!" Josh yelled out the window. Mako was on her back feet, springing in the air, trying to leap through the window. On the other side, Sandi imitated Mako bobbing up and down, watching Marci.

"We never should have taught them to jump into the car through the windows. One of these days, they're going to kill us," Josh joked.

"Yeah, or kill each other as they collide inside the car," Marci laughed, watching Sandi. "This is as good as a circus act. Look at them."

"Okay, girls, off!" Josh shouted. "Go wait for mom and dad at the house." Slowing down their jumping, each dog watched the other, waiting to see who would break for the house, leaving the other to leap into the truck for a lap ride home.

"Mako, go get the ball," Josh shouted as he threw an old tennis ball up the track. Losing no time, Sandi cued up and leaped into Marci's waiting lap.

"Ha, ole girl, you fooled her again," Marci laughed.

"Look at Mako, go," Josh yelled as the dog disappeared around the bend and into the high grass and marsh that lined their driveway.

Mako bounced out of the grass like a gazelle every few minutes and then crashed down, splattering mud everywhere. When the grass stopped moving, her nose and head would cautiously appear above the reeds. Swiveling on her back feet, Mako rotated full circle to find Josh and Marci. Spotting them, she leaped out of the marsh and raced to the house.

Wet and muddy, Mako had to take the teasing from Sandi, who was stretched out on the front porch, pounding it with her tail. But Mako knew the routine. She went and sat patiently by the outside hose, waiting for Josh.

Leaving the kayaks on the Jeep, Josh and Marci filed into the house. Marci headed for the downstairs shower while Josh stopped briefly to hose down

Mako. Once inside, he headed straight for the cabinet that held the hot chocolate.

"Marci, sure you want chocolate and not tea?" he called down the hall to the bathroom.

"Chocolate, Josh, chocolate. Lots of it. Use the good kind. I need a bracer after that cold mist."

"A bracer? This sounds like one of Trish's Scottish mystery novels. Let's see, shaking off the cold beside their peat fire, Mr. and Mrs. Argyle drank their scotch whisky, savoring the taste as it warmed their bodies. Now, where are those scones? Maybe I should get out the clotted crème and marmalade. That way, when Inspector Holmes from Scotland Yard chats with us about the missing houses, we can properly entertain him."

Entering through the back of the kitchen, donned in her bright yellow bathrobe and a towel wrapped around her head, Marci took the scones from Josh's hands and popped them into the oven.

"Josh, what are you muttering about?"

"I'm creating the plot for Trish's next mystery."

Sidestepping this comment, Marci put her hand on Josh's shoulder. "Why don't you go jump in the shower? I'll heat the scones while the chocolate melts. Are the dogs on the deck? And Josh, throw your clothes in the wash with mine, please. Thanks."

Marci headed toward the stove to check the chocolate just as Josh's cell phone rang somewhere. "Great. Where did he leave it now?"

"Josh," Marci shouted at the bathroom door, "where's your cell?"

"On the deck, honey."

"That figures. Where else would it be at this hour?" she muttered to herself. Finding the phone, Marci saw Jake's number on the caller ID.

"Hey, Jake. What's up?"

"Hi, Marci."

"Jake, your partner in crime is in the shower. What can I do for you?"

"Well, that depends. Larry wants Josh and me to spec some property in Wauwinet. It seems he's got a hot buyer for Ole Man Taylor's estate. This guy wants to build a nice McMansion with several guest cottages."

"Oh," Marci replied softly.

"I thought it might be fun for us to work on the project together. It's way too much work for either of us alone. This guy's time schedule makes me think he's willing to go off-island if he can't find local builders. Larry was nice enough to recommend us. The buyer will pay cash for the rush."

"Oh, uh, let me go ask him. Hang on." Leaving the cell on the counter, Marci hurried down the hall and into the bathroom.

"Josh, Jake's on your cell."

"What's up with him so early?"

"He wants to talk with you about working together on a group of new houses."

"Where, hon? Does it sound good?"

"That depends on how you feel about going back to Wauwinet this morning."

"Oh man, wouldn't you know it? Which side of the road?" asked Josh.

"The Taylor property."

"What? You mean crazy man Taylor is letting go of his property? He must really be depressed. They haven't even called off the search for Priscilla."

"But Josh, it's Wauwinet. What if Jake wants to show the buyer the houses you guys built in Pocomo?"

"Oh yeah, right. I forgot."

"Forgot? Josh, how could you forget this morning?"

"Marci, calm down. Hand me the phone. I'll talk with him."

"Josh, you're in the shower. I left the cell in the kitchen. What should I tell him? He's going to wonder how far away our shower is if I don't get back soon."

"Why don't you ask him to come here? Then we both can meet Larry at the Taylor place."

"Josh, what if he asks us about this morning?"

"Marci, just tell him we saw a lot of birds and start naming them. When you think his eyes are glazing over, change the subject to food. Guaranteed, he won't remember what you said except the food."

"Right, Josh."

Walking back to the kitchen, Marci picked up the phone and took a deep breath. "Josh says that's great. But why don't you come over and join us for hot chocolate and scones?"

"Great, I'll be there in fifteen. Need anything downtown? I've got to pick up the survey work on the Taylor land. Where did the great explorers go this morning?"

"Nope, I think we're okay on food," Marci replied, ignoring Jake's question. "Thanks anyway, Jake."

Pressing the off-key, Marci muttered to herself, "Okay? What am I saying? *We're* not okay. *Nothing's* okay."

"Talking to yourself again, Marci?" Josh teased, entering the kitchen. Marci glowered back.

"Here, stir the chocolate. I need to whip the cream."

"Man, that shower felt good. I didn't realize how cold I was. I'm glad God didn't make me a heron. I'm not sure I'd like wading in cold water every time I got hungry. So, did Jake give any more details?"

"Not much. I guess the buyer wants to build some kind of family compound. And according to Jake, the buyer is confident the job will get approval quickly. My guess is he's got connections downtown by the way he's talking."

"Wow. That's a beautiful piece of property. Maybe we'll get to build a house that works with the land. Hopefully, we're not putting in a housing development."

Carrying their breakfast out to the deck, Marci handed Josh the marmalade. "Josh, what are we going to tell Jake about this morning?"

"Mmm, thanks. These scones are the best. Better eat up before Jake gets here," Josh said, ignoring his wife's question.

Eight

aving been ceremoniously escorted on a brief tour of the resort, Robin watched the cab go down the drive toward the gatehouse and then gasped as the man leaned out the window and shot photos of the beach restaurant. Pulling out her cell, she quickly rang the gatehouse.

"Mike, it's Robin. Please hold the gate until I get there. Tell the people in the cab, as nicely as possible, that they have to wait a moment. Ask them to please give you the digital camera they just used to photograph the beach restaurant. I'm afraid now we'll have to check their passports and find out who they are. This should only take a few minutes, providing they gave us the correct information up at the desk."

"Righto." Mike stepped out of the gatehouse to await the approaching cab. He saw the look of alarm on the woman's face when the gate didn't open.

"I'm sorry, sir, but because this is a private club, only members can take photos. Normally, we wouldn't allow you on the property. The front desk wants to see your passports and cameras."

"Look, we just wanted a place to eat and thought this would be perfect since we're in our beach clothes," said Jacks, leaning over his partner to talk with the guard. Opening the car door, Robin repeated Mike's instructions.

"We don't have our passports. We're at the beach," Jacks snapped. "It's a free country. We don't have to provide anyone with that information."

Recognizing an American accent, Robin proceeded politely. "You need passports to be on this island. And because you're on private property, you'll need to prove you entered as a tourist. This proof is on the entry stamp given you at the airport or dock."

The young woman was now conferring with the man in the car, but not loud enough to be heard. Robin tried again. "We can easily confirm your passports at the front desk. You can leave after we've checked your cameras. Just follow me back to reception."

A young, voluptuous blonde got out of the cab with her oversized beach bag. The man was right about being dressed for the beach. She wore only a short voile shift to cover her bikini. Her partner followed, carrying a camera and his backpack.

Handing Robin a different camera than the one he'd just used, Jacks hissed, "Satisfied now?"

The blonde was trying to appear innocent and terribly put out. "Can we please go now?"

Robin looked at Dimitri, the cab driver, and said, "I'm afraid not. We still need to look at the pictures from the camera you used and any other cameras you have."

"Look, those things are personal property. You can't take them."

"Oh, I'll return them to you. Don't worry."

"I'll also need your passports and the name of your hotel."

Jacks had not reckoned on this fresh development. Stepping off to the side, the couple conferred together in hushed tones; the woman gesturing in frustration. Oddly enough, a large group of sugar finches had gathered in the bougainvillea and were now "cheeting" loudly as the couple talked, flying above and around them. Noticing this activity, Dimitri walked over to Robin, still keeping a close eye on the couple.

"Look, even the birds know something's suspicious."

Turning to face Robin, Jacks stepped forward and spoke. "Look, I know it was inappropriate to come onto the grounds of a private club. But we didn't know that it was private when we walked up the beach. Isn't it enough if we just leave quietly?"

"No, I'm afraid not. Now that we know you were photographing the grounds, you'll have to surrender the photos you took, as well as provide your immigration status before we can let you go."

"What?" gasped Jacks. "Those cameras are private property. We have our rights. You can't do this to Americans."

"Your rights Mr.—I'm sorry I didn't get your name?"

"Jacks, Lucky Jacks," he retorted.

"And your friend, Mr. Jacks?"

"Oh, this is Wanton, my wife," Jacks replied, giving her a look to keep quiet.

"Mr. and Mrs. Jacks, you nullified your rights by trespassing on private property. On this island, you could go to jail for violating that law until they clear your charges."

"Don't American tourists have diplomatic immunity?" Wanton piped up.

"Mrs. Jacks, this is a tiny island. A good part of the land is privately owned. And we want it kept that way. Let's go." Robin directed them back up the driveway.

Jacks and his partner turned and followed her toward the main building. Out of hearing, Wanton whispered angrily, "What's this about me being your wife?"

"Babe, just play along. We're tourists, remember? You keep an eye on her while I drop the memory card into those blue flowers up ahead. We'll figure out how to retrieve it later." Strolling toward the main house, Jacks popped the memory card from his camera and dropped it into the blue phlox that lined the stone wall.

"It's too bad you didn't have a plan for when we got caught," Wanton whispered.

"Just play it cool. So far, all they have on us is trespassing."

"Lucky, when they find out who we are, they'll arrest us. I don't want to spend the rest of my vacation, let alone my life, in a Caribbean prison."

"Relax, babe. Just act confident and apologetic. We'll get out of this. Two ignorant tourists. That's all they have on us."

"Lucky, the cab driver probably saw you take the pictures and maybe the guard at the gate. We don't even know if the shots are any good."

"Oh, I got them all right. With a little magnification, it could be in the papers tomorrow. We'll just have to get it off the grounds later," said Lucky confidently. "We can take care of that with a little green paper downtown."

Nine

"Trish, doesn't it amaze you we can pick up a phone and talk with someone thousands of miles away just as if it was across town? I'll bet Dad answers. Hello, may I have the Kea's room, please? Thanks."

"I'm sorry, no one is answering. Would you like me to try the beach restaurant?"

"Yes, that would be great."

"Beach Bar, how can I help you?"

"Hi, this is Becki Kea. I'd like to speak with my parents, please."

"Sure thing. Let me go get them." Walking over to the Kea's table, Marco handed the phone to Keta, explaining that it was his daughter.

"Becki, are you okay?" Keta answered, concern crossing his forehead.

"I'm fine. I need to talk with you about something. I didn't wake you up from a beach nap, did I?"

"No, we're enjoying a little lunch with the birds and sunshine. Do you want to talk with your mother, or do I get some airtime too?"

"Dad, I hope you don't mind me calling. I know you guys want a break, but this really can't wait. I need some quick advice, or I would've waited until you were home. Do you think you're up to helping me solve a problem that's come up with Stephen and my work with the Foundation?"

"Of course we are. We've had three great days in the sun with no problems. Or let's say nothing we couldn't handle."

"What do you mean? Is Mom okay?"

"I'll let her talk with you," Keta replied as he handed the phone over to Lyrica, who was making faces at him, trying to discern what was Becki was saying.

"Baby, are you okay? You didn't pick up any strange illness in Madeira, did you? The trip was supposed to be work *and* vacation."

"Mom, I'm fine. But I have to make a decision that can't wait. I hope it's all right that I called. Trish seemed to think you wouldn't mind." Trish was now rolling her eyes for being named co-conspirator.

"Okay, baby. Tell me what's going on, and your dad and I will try to help as best we can."

But as soon as Becki started relating the story, tears began to fall.

"Mom, I don't want you to think this is happening because of the robbery. This is my own, entirely separate, personal nightmare. But Stephen is asking me for advice, and if his job situation blows up before I present to the Foundation, I might lose my funding."

"Whoa, Becki. What's going on? Why is Stephen's job connected to your Foundation work?"

Wiping away her tears, Becki told Lyrica about the rare orchid discovery, her new botanicals for the Foundation, and Stephen's fears about Justin Earsom deep-sixing their discovery. "My paintings and Stephen's personal field notes are inextricably tied together. If Justin hides the discovery to plow ahead with his development, my presentation to the Foundation will break the discovery. Then Stephen and I will look like we're hiding something. The press will have a field day with that. They'll pin dishonesty on me, just like they did on you. I won't stand a chance."

"Becki, are you having trouble with the Foundation because of the stolen photos and story coverage in the *Boston Flame?*" Lyrica asked hesitantly.

"Well, not exactly. But why else would the Foundation start to pull in the reigns? I've been working with them for over two years. Why do I suddenly get a phone call when they knew I was in Madeira and wouldn't be home?"

"Becki, do you think the accusations against me for stealing the Morston photos are damaging your credibility?"

"Mom, I'm not sure."

"Oh honey, I'm so sorry. I hoped things would settle down if we went out of town. Why don't your father and I talk about this and call you back a little later?" While trying to ease her daughter's fears, Lyrica knew she couldn't protect Becki against the inevitable.

Ten

"Morning, Ralph. How's the survey business?" Jake greeted his friend as he strode into the survey and architectural firm.

"Hey Jake. How's married life? Still working on the house?"

"We'll be working on that house for the rest of our lives. But it's a beauty. I love the Quaise area. It's like a small village all to itself. You should see Lovey and Marci. They're like two nesting birds. I think Lovey spent more money on paint and fabric than we did on wood trim for the entire house."

"That's what happens when women join forces. Ah, the bliss of newlyweds. It brings back wonderful memories."

"You better say that, or you know who will cook his own dinner tonight," retorted Charlotte, coming into the front office.

"Say, while I have you two together, what's the story behind Old Man Taylor letting his property go?"

"All I heard was that he got some outrageous price and was eager to sell since Priscilla was gone," responded Ralph.

"I think there are too many memories. Priscilla was such a spitfire, and they had such a great life. I don't think he ever really recovered from her disappearance."

"You mean her death, Charlotte," corrected Ralph.

"No, I mean disappearance. She might still be alive. The whole thing was strange, stranger than even Old Man Taylor himself," she laughed.

"So, Ralph, did you find anything mysterious when you surveyed the land?" Jake interrupted. "Any hidden treasure or bodies buried in the swamp—or wetlands, as they say now?"

"You know, Jake, that's one heck of a piece of a property. There aren't too many places on this island where you can find five ecosystems in one tract of land. Those hornbeams are some of the most beautiful trees I've ever seen. And did you know it was Priscilla's great-grandparents who planted them?"

"No kidding?"

"Yeah, apparently they planted them so they would have a special place to sit and watch the sunsets. Beautiful birds and wildflowers there."

"Uh, Ralph, other than the birds, what else did you see? Any excellent prospects for placing the house and cottages?"

"Good luck," Charlotte chided her friend. "Tell him, Ralph."

"Taylor wants a stipulation that the new owner can only put up three buildings on the land, and he's designated wild spaces to protect the vistas and the beauty."

"Why sell the land then?"

"You know, Charlotte and I can't figure that out. It's almost like he's doing this to find out if Priscilla really died or went off somewhere after a big fight," Ralph speculated. "There's something he's holding back."

"Well, if you ask me—" Charlotte chimed in.

"Here we go again, Agatha Christie herself."

"Ask you what?" Jake said, interrupting the banter.

"Oh, Charlotte thinks that Old Man Taylor isn't as crazy as people think. He just feigns senility and being ornery to keep people off his land."

"Sounds like it works."

"Yeah, well, it will not be his land much longer if this buyer gets his way. If Taylor is hiding something, he'd better cough it up soon," Ralph added.

"You mean like buried treasure?" Jake asked hopefully.

"I doubt that," Ralph replied. "But it feels like there *is* something he's hiding. Selling the land has come up in conversation several times when we've been with him at the Pub. We tried to get it out of him one night at dinner, but he wouldn't budge. He changes the subject every time we get near it."

"Frankly, I feel sorry for him," Charlotte added. "I hope he doesn't leave the island. That old codger is someone I'd miss. I love the smell of his pipe and hearing his ancestral stories of raising sheep on the island. He's like a comfortable old chair in your living room. The atmosphere changes when it's not there."

"Pretty soon, you'll be calling me the comfortable old chair." Ralph winked at Charlotte.

"Okay, I think that's my cue to go back to the drawing table. See ya, Jake. Stop by again when Ralph's out with his toys, and I'll fill you in on the actual story."

Using this slight pause in the conversation, Jake gathered up the survey, roughly scanning the topography before rolling it back up again.

"Jake, this buyer must be rolling in money to take on Old Man Taylor, the Historic District Commission, and town regulators together, as well as all the conservation organizations."

"I wonder who he knows that he thinks we'll be able to finish in a year," Jake laughed. "I guess money still talks, and big money buys bulldozers."

"Come on, Jake, we both need these wealthy off-islanders. How else would we feed our families?"

"Or furnish our homes and fill our closets with their contributions to the Take It or Leave It at the dump," finished Jake.

"You mean the Madaket Mall," corrected Charlotte.

"Whatever. But free stuff is sure cheaper than the stores here or on the mainland."

Putting the survey tube under his arm, Jake saluted Ralph and opened the door. "Don't draw anything I can't build, Charlotte. I'm sure Josh and I will see you soon."

"You got it, Jake. Say hi to Lovey and Marci for me."

"Will do. I'm heading to Josh's place now," Jake said, turning and heading down the old brick walk. I love being with those two, he thought, as he threw the tube on the front seat of his pickup. It's like standing on the shore, feeling the wind clear your head. I hope Lovey and I will have as long a marriage and life together.

"Oh, you too, Lucy," said Jake as he scratched the ears of his yellow lab. "Come on. We're off to see Mako and Sandi." Recognizing the two dogs' names, Lucy barked, stood up on the seat with her front paws balanced on the dashboard, and poked her head out the moon roof of Jake's pickup truck.

"Come on, Lucy, you've got to sit down before we can pull out into the rotary. Don't want you to be caught not wearing your seat belt," he laughed.

Fifteen minutes later, Jake was maneuvering the pickup along the rocky scrub track to Josh and Marci's home.

Eleven

"I guess we're at your mercy," said Jacks, still playing innocent.

Ushering the trespassers into the reception area, Robin continued her questions, hoping the findings would not confirm her uneasiness.

"You won't find us in the immigration and customs computer since we sailed in. We're day sailors from Montserrat," Jacks lied.

"Then where is your boat? Is that where your passports are?"

Stalling for some time, Jacks answered her, "Yes, they're on the boat with the rest of our things."

"Now, we can have this settled in no time. Would you please give me the camera you used to shoot the beach pictures and your other cameras?" Robin watched as Lucky took out two more cameras from his backpack.

"Look, we didn't even use these cameras on your grounds," Jacks pleaded again.

"Interesting that you would need three cameras for a beach walk."

"I'm an amateur photographer," Jacks responded quickly.

"At least that's one thing you're willing to admit. If you wait here, I'll be back shortly. You can stay here with Dimitri or in the bar over to your right."

"In which dockyard are you moored?"

"We're not," responded Jacks, cleverly weaving a plan in his head. "We're moored down the bay beyond that peninsula."

"I see. Well, that's unfortunate for you," responded Robin.

"Hey, you're not going to tamper with my photos, are you?" Jacks was pleading like a sad child for his confiscated toys.

"No, indeed. You can come with me if you'd like."

"Uh, no, we trust you."

"Mr. and Mrs. Jacks, I'll return in a moment. Dimitri, please have Marlon get them a drink at the bar while they wait."

"Oh, that would be great," piped up Wanton.

"What would you like, sir?" Marlon asked, coming briskly over to where the couple was seated.

"I'll have a double martini," Jacks kidded.

"And how would you like—"

"I was only kidding. I'll have a Miller Lite. And the missus will have iced tea."

"No, make that two Millers," Wanton retorted.

"Sir, we only have Australian and West Indian beer. I can bring you the light ones, and if you don't like them, you can try another."

"Fine," said Jacks, fluffing his T-shirt to cool the sweat on his chest. "Just make sure they're cold. This island is sweltering."

Within earshot of Dimitri, they limited their conversation. Noticing the sign marked Ladies' Room, Wanton headed toward the door. Jacks resigned himself to wait for Robin's verdict. It's a good thing I only used one camera, he thought, preparing what he would say when Robin returned.

Meanwhile, Robin had studiously examined the two cameras from Jacks's backpack. She was suspicious when the third camera was empty. He had removed the memory card. Her search was at a dead end. Legally, she couldn't look through their belongings. Seizing the cameras was a significant risk for the Club to take. Rather than pressing the point, Robin handed the three cameras back to Jacks. She thanked them for their cooperation and took a parting shot as she escorted them to the waiting cab.

"Next time, book a reservation at the main restaurant, and we'll be happy to serve you."

As the cab went through the gate, Jacks sat back with a smug look on his face.

"I don't know why you're so smug. We're no better off than when we arrived," Wanton griped.

"Not exactly. We now have an invitation to return."

"Yeah, right. Just try to make a reservation. I'll bet you a six-pack you can't. That woman was just being polite."

"Well, we'll just have to find out, won't we?" Jacks was already planning to get back onto the property before someone else found the memory card.

"Do you want to go back to your boat mooring, or shall I take you downtown?" Dimitri asked.

"Just let us off in town so we can get a bite to eat since we couldn't eat at the resort."

Dimitri let the remark go right on by. He was smart enough to stay businesslike. Maybe they would talk and reveal something that would help Robin. He'd driven cabs to and from the resort for thirty-five years and was astute at sizing up patrons and guests, invited or not. He didn't just make his living driving for the Bougainvillea Club. He was part of the family. The minute the two stepped into the cab, he suspected something was awry. Not everyone at the resort knew about the increased security set up to protect Keta and Lyrica. One of Dimitri's sons was working as an agent bartending for the guests. Even with the increased monitoring of the property's borders, these two had slipped in. He looked forward to hearing his son's version of today's excitement when he got off his shift.

The real question was, now that they'd removed the paparazzi from the Club, would they try to regain entry another way?

Twelve

inding down the dirt road to Taylors, Josh and Jake were swapping the latest building code revisions and bemoaning the shrinking number of buildable lots on the island.

"So, what's the story about the guy buying the Taylor land? You said he talked as if the Historic District Commission's hurdles and the other town requirements wouldn't phase his schedule. How in the world can he pull that off? Or did he just *say* he could?"

"I guess we'll find out later this afternoon. Larry is coming to talk with us."

"Does the new buyer know that our two companies are collaborating on this project? I don't want him to pit us against each other. Maybe it's time to establish our partnership formally, so there's no question in anyone's mind," Josh suggested for what seemed like the hundredth time.

"Yeah, just when the buildable lots run out," laughed Jake.

"Hey, it will be a long time before that ever happens. Do you know how much wild space is still family-owned?"

A loud thud and scraping sound issued from underneath the truck. "I think we're in one of those wild spaces," Jake groaned as he maneuvered the pickup, dodging rocks that sprouted up in the middle of the sandy track and then plunging wildly into the giant puddles that were still full from the recent rains.

"Whoever buys this land will have to travel this driveway. Maybe the first thing we do is bulldoze the road. We're going to need some maneuvering room for oversized trucks delivering cinderblock and wood."

"Ouch! That one hurt. We definitely need to bulldoze this driveway. How does Old Man Taylor's truck survive this beating?" Josh moaned.

"Maybe that's why he's so grumpy. Do you want to scout ahead of the truck?"

"No way. I wouldn't miss this time with you for the world. But I'm concerned about your dog in the flatbed back there," Josh added.

"Oh, Lucy can take it. Besides, there's still padding down from yesterday when I picked up an antique dresser for Lovey. How about we stop here for a minute?" Jake said, slowing down. "If we walk up that path, there's a three hundred sixty-degree view of the land and the island."

"What path? I don't see any path."

Jumping out of his truck, Jake motioned to Josh. "Well, it's sort of a path, a deer trail. You know how they wind through the scrub. It comes out in the meadow just below the hornbeams," Jake explained, pointing toward the top of a ridge.

"We didn't lose Lucy on one of those bumps, did we?"

"No, she knows the path and is probably chasing rabbits in the meadow by now."

Josh's mind was going a thousand places as they picked their way through the scrub oak, bayberry, and beach plum bushes. To call it a path was more than a slight exaggeration.

Emerging from the scrub, Jake pointed to the stand of hornbeams on a hill off to their right. "That's where we're heading."

"I thought we were going to the house site." Though muscular and tan, Josh's arms were now bleeding with scratches, and his enthusiasm was waning.

"We are. But first, I want you to view the land from its highest point. It's the easiest way to see where building sites are even possible."

"We're going to be moving a lot of scrub with the bulldozers. There doesn't appear to be much opportunity to find natural building lots. What do the plans say?"

"Oh, sorry, I left them in the truck. But they wouldn't make it through this scrub, anyway." Josh just rolled his eyes.

Out of the scrub and into the meadow, Josh and Jake made good time. A proud stand of hornbeams crowned the hilltop.

"Gosh, those trees are beautiful. I wonder why you don't see more of them," remarked Jake as they headed into the dense grove. Reaching the top of the hill, Josh looked for the promised three hundred sixty-degree views.

"Jake, how do you expect to see anything with all the trees and scrub? Hiring an airplane might have been a better idea. I wouldn't even know where the ocean is if I couldn't hear it."

"Not a problem. I found a great hornbeam for you to climb and look for us."

"Wait a minute, pal. You're the one who learned to climb coconut palms last year in the Caribbean."

"Actually," Jake said, pausing ever so slightly for effect, "I thought we both could climb up and look."

"What? In the same tree?"

"We're partners, aren't we?" Jake teased his friend. "Okay, you take that tree.

I'll take this one." Jake swung himself up onto the lowest branch and shinnied up to the next branch. Josh followed suit in the neighboring tree, but his heart wasn't in it. His morning in the marsh had satiated his appetite for adventure.

Leaning precariously against the top of the tree, Jake shouted, "Wow! This is beautiful."

Finally, reaching almost as high as his friend, Josh surveyed the land below. It was one of the choice tracts on the island. They could see nearly every ecosystem—woodland, meadows sloping into marsh and bog, and seagrass sweeping up to crest a dune overlooking the ocean.

"Jake, this is beautiful. Who in their right mind would ever let this land go for development?"

"That's a fair question. But Priscilla's the only one who could stop it, and she's gone."

"All kidding aside, I think we'll want an aerial view before we negotiate building sites. There are a few tricky topographical features we'll need to build around."

"I'll bet the buyer has a plane," Jake added.

"I hope this guy appreciates the gem he's getting, or this job could end up being one of our worst nightmares."

Thirteen

"What did you guys find at the beach?" asked the short, muscular man polishing teak on the seventy-five-foot yacht.

"Ask him," said Wanton, with a smirk on her face. "He's the one who failed the mission. I'm just his wife."

"What?" Guido stood up and looked at the pair stepping onto the yacht.

"Tell him, big boy. See if he can get *you* out of hot water."

"Now, wait a minute. You're in as deep as I am. Just because I covered for you as my wife—"

"No, Lucky. I may be in deep, but you're in over your head. I'm not getting you out of this jam. You're the one with no story. I'm leaving tonight on the plane."

"Oh, we have a story. But *when* I release it to the paper is my deal."

"Well then, deal the cards, Lucky. See if you can cheat your way out of this one. Remember, I'm not your wife in Boston either."

"You two might as well be married the way you bicker. Did you get photos of your celebs at the Club?"

"Yes, but I had to ditch the memory card into the bushes after we got caught trespassing on Club property. They confiscated and checked my cameras."

"What's the plan for getting the card back?"

"Ah, that's where you and the captain come in."

"Oh, we do, do we?" Guido replied suspiciously. "Remember, we only hired on as captain and mate. We've got a date with some celebs in St. Kitts tomorrow."

"Well, if you want a nice bonus, you and the captain may want to reconsider."

"And how do you think we can find a tiny memory card under some bushes after dark?"

"It won't be dark if you leave now."

"And what are you and your wife going to do during this time?"

"We'll grab dinner downtown. But you two might even get a free dinner at the Club if you play your cards right."

"Somebody mention dinner?" A deep voice boomed out of the cabin as the yacht's captain joined the group.

"Guess what, Hook. Tonight you and I are going to dine at the Bougainvillea Club, all expenses paid," his first mate said with a puckish grin on his face.

"Paid by whom?"

"The *Boston Flame*," Lucky answered.

"Jacks and Wanton didn't have too much luck today. As a matter of fact, they blew it. They want us to clean up their mess."

"I'm not cleaning up any mess Lucky makes just for the price of a dinner," snapped the captain.

"That's what I told him. As captain of this yacht, you get to make the executive decisions. The resort caught Lucky and his *wife* trespassing. They had to ditch a memory card into some bushes. He thinks we can retrieve it."

"Right. And the reward is?"

"I'll make it worthwhile." Jacks smiled as he pulled out a wad of hundred-dollar bills from his wallet.

"And while you two do the investigating, Wanton and I will be on the plane, headed for Boston. Just email me the photos tonight. That way, I'll have them when we arrive. We've got other fish to fry, as they say."

"Sounds as if we'd better be off if we're to make landfall by early evening," Guido said as he headed to untie the lines.

A half-hour later, they sailed into the Club's bay and dropped anchor near some other sailing yachts. Guido and Hook motored their Zodiac toward the dock near the stone breakwater.

The resort was landscaped with lush tropical plants and flowers, but it wasn't hard to find the restaurant and bar. The combination of outdoor lighting and Caribbean steel drums made it easy to identify the dining area, now framed by the sunset's glow.

"Guido, check those bushes by the bar and the foot washing pool and see what you can find. I'll find out if they still allow outsiders to dine here on Saturday night."

Hook walked up the landscaped stone steps onto a multi-tiered, open-air dining area. Soft candlelight and tropical plants separated the tables, creating an intimate atmosphere. One section overlooked the water where they'd moored their yacht. Other tables were perched even higher on the ridge, offering a spectacular one hundred eighty-degree view of the ocean surrounding the resort. There was even a tiny treehouse where the children could dine.

The high ceiling fans kept the trade winds constantly flowing through the dining area even on the hottest of evenings. Based on the glitz adorning the women, the crowd looked as if they could afford to buy the resort.

Walking up to the maître d', Hook felt the members eyeing him. *Guess they can quickly spot a stranger.* But he moved forward with confidence. The maître d' recognized the insignia on Hook's cap and approached in a friendly manner.

"Good to see you again. What celebs are on your vessel tonight that you're showing up here?"

"My partner and I hoped that we might have dinner. The celebrities left today for the mainland. They gave us both a generous tip, so we thought we'd spend it here. My first mate is probably at the bar by now. I'll go get him if you have a table available."

"Your money is as good as theirs," the maître d' said, pointing to the guests in a sweeping action. "Come back when you're ready to be seated."

"You bet."

But Guido wasn't in the bar. He was still outside looking for the missing memory card. After checking the foot-washing pool, he sat down on the stone wall and looked into the thick bushes. The landscape lighting helped him slowly work along the wall, gently peering into the bushes when Club members weren't present. Not finding anything from above, he got on his hands and knees near the foot pool and looked in the bushes at ground level.

Pulling out his lighter and placing it in his left hand, he maneuvered himself along the hedge. He was finishing up when he heard a voice say, "Lose something, sir?"

Guido was ready for the question. Pulling himself up to his full height, he turned innocently toward the voice. A tall man of equal stature wearing a Club polo shirt looked straight at him.

"Yes. I lost my cigarette lighter and thought it might have slipped off the ledge when I was sitting here earlier. I was trying to see if I could find it," Guido lied.

"You're not a member here, are you? I don't recognize you."

"No, I'm here with a friend who's trying to get us a table for dinner."

"Let me help you look. Someone is always dropping something into these bushes. Mostly it's keys or kids losing their toy cars and planes. But in this dry season, we don't want a lighter hanging around where it could cause a fire."

"Thanks, that would be great," Guido answered, fingering the lighter in his left pocket. "My name is Guido. Nice to meet you."

"And I'm Marco, the manager on duty tonight. Why don't you start at one end, and I'll start at the other, and we'll see if we can find it. If not, I'm sure the gift shop would be happy to sell you a new one. Too bad all the kids are at dinner. They'd probably find it in a flash."

The two of them were leaning over the bushes, pushing and pulling the branches to inspect the ground. By the time Hook returned, they were almost side by side.

"You guys having fun?"

"Hook, longtime no see. What brings you here tonight? Thought you'd be out on the high seas with your celebs this time of year."

"We just got off a cruise and are spending our tips from the last few days. I just got us a nice table for dinner and came to fetch my partner."

"Well, we still haven't found the lighter, even though both of us were looking," Guido answered as he looked Hook straight in the eye.

"Did you look in the foot-washing pool? Maybe it took a dip in this heat."

"Very funny, captain," Guido snapped back.

"How about I order some drinks while you boys finish up? Marco, can I get you anything?" Hook offered as he headed toward the bar.

"No thanks. I'm on duty tonight. Maybe another time. Enjoy your meal."

By this time, Guido was sure that the memory card was not in the bushes. He'd gone over the area twice, including his search with Marco. Thinking it might be a better plan to find the lighter, he slipped it out of his pocket and placed it up against the back of the foot-washing pool.

"Hey, look at this!" Guido shouted. "Hook was right. It almost took a dip in the water here. Thanks for helping me search. This lighter was a present from a little barmaid downtown. I'd hate to go in and see her without it. You saved my skin, Marco."

"No problem. Glad to help."

As Marco turned and walked away, Guido congratulated himself on his fine acting. At least he didn't have to tell Jacks the bad news personally. He didn't want to be around when the reporter found out they'd come back empty-handed.

"Any luck?" Hook asked, returning from the bar. "No pun intended." He was holding out a cold beer for Guido.

"Yeah, we found the lighter. Just like you said. It was hiding behind the edge of the foot pool."

"Good. Now we can have dinner and enjoy ourselves."

"Yeah, you mean our last supper, don't you?" Guido wisecracked.

"Oh, don't get your wig out of shape. We did our job. And you even have a witness. Come on, let's enjoy our meal. Lucky is paying, remember?"

It was late when the two men motored the yacht back into its slip and tied up for the night. Jacks and Wanton were probably just touching down in Boston. When Guido opened up his laptop, Jacks had already emailed him.

Did you find it?

Guido sighed and answered the email. *Jacks, we looked everywhere. Even the manager on duty helped. There was nothing on the ground except roots, bugs, and dead flowers. It's just not there. Are you sure that's where you dropped it?*

Guido wasn't expecting an answer from Jacks until morning. But later, when he went to close his computer, there was a message from the reporter.

As sure as you said that you looked.

Guido could feel Jacks's anger. Boy, was he glad he didn't have to deliver the news personally. Let Wanton calm him down. Shaking his head, Guido came up topside for some air.

"Man, am I glad Lucky's back in Boston."

"Guido, you take life too seriously. Look at it this way. We got a free dinner and beat Lucky at his own game. And this time tomorrow, we'll be out of email range."

But Guido couldn't hear the conversation between Jacks and Wanton in the cab on the way downtown from the airport.

"So, Lucky, are you giving up? Is that why you came home with me?"

"No, I'm not giving up. We'll just find another opportunity when the Keas return to Boston. And yes, a gentleman always accompanies his wife home from vacation."

Fourteen

The person on the other side of Becki's door was not waiting for a response, pressing her doorbell repeatedly.

"Ms. Kea, I know you're in there. You might as well answer, or I'll print something you won't like about you and your mother."

Looking through the privacy hole, Trish turned to her friend with a stunned look and whispered, "Becki, I'm pretty sure it's the reporter from the *Boston Flame.*"

"Trish, I'm not doing any interviews with reporters."

Lucky, however, was not dissuaded. He kept up a coarse stream of expletives, demanding an interview.

Walking to the door where Trish was, Becki shot back, "How did you find this apartment? Get out of here. I'm not talking to you."

"Look, why don't I come back at a more convenient time?" Lucky said with the charm of a serpent. "Here's my number where you can reach me," he said, holding up a small notebook with a phone number scribbled on it.

Trish opened the door cautiously with the guard chain still on. Then, without warning, the reporter thrust his arm and foot through the opening, still holding the notebook.

"Wouldn't you like some publicity for yourself? If your mom isn't guilty, why wouldn't you like your name in the news?"

With one swift motion even Trish didn't see coming, Becki slammed her body against the door, catching the reporter's left arm. Unfortunately, in pulling his arm out of the door, he dropped his notebook inside the apartment. Trish swooped it up and headed for the kitchen table. Angrily banging on the door, he screamed, "Let me in! Give me back my notebook!"

But Trish had found a list of names and the directions to Becki's apartment, so she wasn't about to give up her treasure. Regardless of how insignificant the data appeared, she would lose none of it now. Carefully moving through his notes, Trish took photos of the contents. "He's going to get this back in his face," she murmured.

Jacks had not left the door even though Becki had now closed it. "Let me in or give me back my notebook. Your mother steals photos, and you stoop to stealing personal property. Great family you have. If you've nothing to hide, open the door."

"Yeah, and face me like a man," Trish barked out in a deep voice. Oh, it felt so good to be on the winning side against the press.

"I wouldn't open the door if you were giving away money," Becki added.

"Maybe we should spill some coffee on his notebook and blur the ink," Trish suggested.

"No, he'll be mad enough when he gets it back. Let's not give him the satisfaction of charging us with damaging personal property. It *is* tempting, though," Becki said, a smile edging up the corners of her mouth. She was peering through the privacy hole, watching the scene in the hall. "Trish, hurry. I can't wait to shove it down his throat."

Trish was up from the kitchen table and at the door in no time. "Becki, wait. Don't open the door." She peeked through the privacy hole to see where the reporter was and then shouted, "Okay, Mr. *Boston Flame,* you can have your notebook back under one condition. Walk to the end of the hallway and stop in front of the elevator. I'll toss it to you. But if you try to harass my friend again, I'll sic more than the police on you."

Lucky glared at the door for a few seconds. His face was still red from the struggle, and he held his left arm as if in pain. Carelessly dressed, he looked like he'd slept in his clothes, which he had. Turning around, he skulked down the hallway. Trish thought he looked more and more like Colombo in his rumpled raincoat.

Stopping before he got to the elevator, Jacks turned around to watch Becki's door. Silence. No movement, so he continued until he reached the elevator. Just as he turned around, Trish threw the notebook down the corridor. It fell to the floor within a few feet of him. He heard the locks click on Becki's door.

Picking up the notebook, Trish heard Jacks mumble, "Well, I know one thing. They read my notes. Too bad they weren't smart enough to leave the door open longer. We'll see how long Ms. Botany can stay silent."

"Scumbag, wretched, ugly scumbag," Trish said, finishing up her watch at the peephole to make sure that Jacks took the elevator and left the floor.

"Scumbag is too nice for the likes of him. Poor Mom."

"Oh, Becki, I'm so sorry. But you handled him like a trooper. I'm so proud of you."

But Becki was back at the kitchen table, staring into space. "Who would have thought? What am I going to tell Mom and Dad?"

"Tell them the truth. There's already a lack of that in this town. They wouldn't expect you to hold back. This affects them as well."

"Okay, let's look at the notes. Maybe we'll find out who gave him the trick to finding this loft. Now I know how Mom feels. No wonder they went to the Club."

"Look at this," Trish said, picking up her phone and pointing to a list of names for Becki to see. "I know this name. Didn't this guy buy some of your mom's photographic prints last year?"

"Yeah, I think so." Walking over to the kitchen, Becki picked up the coffeepot and put her finger through the handles of two fresh mugs. She had just finished pouring the coffee when the phone rang.

"I'll get it."

Trish watched Becki cautiously, praying it wasn't bad news.

"It's Stephen." Listening and responding, Becki sat down on the couch and put her coffee on the glass-top table. Underneath the glass, she had displayed pictures of the family on Nantucket. There were even some old black and white photos of Priscilla and Marci in Taylor's corral. After she hung up, Becki turned to Trish.

"Stephen just spoke with Rachel, his lawyer friend specializing in environmental law. He thought maybe she could advise him on how to share the discovery with Justin."

"And?"

"I guess because we were in a foreign country, it's more complicated. But it may help us in the long run. Earsom has to comply with the country's environmental laws, if there are any, as well as pass the island's engineering standards, even without the orchids."

"What about his botany colleagues?"

"Stephen called two mentors who are top botanists in the world. Both are excited and want to see the photos he took and my botanical paintings of the flowers. They are tentative about a new species until they see the details on the botanicals, but they share his enthusiasm. There are enough new species discovered each year to make them hopeful."

"I hate to ask this, but did Stephen tell them that Earsom doesn't know about the discovery?"

"He told the Major, whose real name is Yana Rumfold. No one could pronounce his name, so they nicknamed him the Major, and it stuck. He's one of the foremost scholars on orchid reproduction in the world."

"And what did he say?"

"Stephen needs to relay the discovery as soon as possible. Withholding it could jeopardize Stephen's standing among the botanical and environmental scholars."

"So, what is Stephen going to do?"

"First, he's going to—oh, there goes the phone," Becki said, looking over at the coffee table. Checking the caller ID, she saw it was the Foundation. "Oh no, it's the Foundation. Should I answer it?"

"No. Let it go. We'll listen to the message. Then you can call back if you need to."

Becki waited a few minutes. Then, listening to the message, Trish watched her friend's expression change. "They want me to present the Madeira work this week."

"How can they expect you to complete it so fast? You just got back two days ago," Trish exclaimed.

"Now I'm stuck in the same place as Stephen. Do I share what I know about the orchids?

Good thing Stephen will be here any minute. Maybe he can help me figure out what to do."

Fifteen

After turning around at the Taylor house, Jake carefully maneuvered his pickup back down the rough sandy track that served as Taylor's driveway.

"You know, nobody builds a house on this island as fast as this guy plans on doing. I don't care who you are," Jake sputtered. "It's not like I don't need the money, but another Jurassic Park house just isn't what this island needs."

"I'm with you. But this is how we make our living. What bothers me the most is Taylor selling without knowing what happened to Priscilla. Her family has owned this land for almost two hundred years. I can't see her ever selling it, especially to someone who wants to build a McMansion."

"Maybe Old Man Taylor tumbled for cash," Jake said, not withholding the disdain in his voice.

"But how can he sell the property without declaring Priscilla dead?"

"Wow, I didn't even think of that. I hope we don't get started and end up in a legal fight. I've had my headache quotient for the year."

Josh was gazing through the windshield, lost in thought. Something just wasn't right about this whole deal. Typically, Marci was the one he'd turn to for insight. But in this case, Marci had been so rocked by Priscilla's disappearance that he didn't think it would be fair to broach the subject with her.

Josh was quickly brought back to reality by the sound of sand, pebbles, rocks, and other debris spinning out from the truck's tires as Jake tried to get back onto the Wauwinet Road. A sizeable chunk of macadam had broken off in the last pounding rain, leaving a small cliff and a gaping hole. They'd rolled right over it on the way into the property. Getting back up onto the road was a different story. Stopping the truck, they both got out and started filling in the hole with rocks. But their efforts didn't provide enough leverage for the truck's tires. Somehow, they would have to straddle the hole to get back onto the road.

"I wonder how the realtor and Mr. Moneybags got through this with their Jeep. Or maybe they're the ones who left this mess for us," moaned Jake.

"Let me look at the bushes and see if we can go around the hole by cutting back some of the scrub oak. It's not as if we won't widen this road."

Josh started whacking bushes with Jake's machete. He jumped on a branch or bush, leveling it to the ground, and then chopped it off at the base. He was having difficulty with one scrub oak that wouldn't budge. Scratching the dirt away from its base, Josh called over to Jake. "Hey, check this out! I've never seen anything like it. This scrub oak has grown right around a cement marker. No wonder I couldn't make any headway."

Coming around to the other side of the pickup, Jake stared at the marker. "Man, that's old. Someone put that there a million years ago."

"Well, not quite a million. But it could be one of the original markers. Do you think it's the original property line? Another mystery added to this deal. I wonder how far back the title goes for this land. Did they even do titles two hundred years ago?"

"Boy, I don't know. Let's hope this doesn't pose a legal wrinkle with the property sale. I don't want Ole Man Taylor's neighbors messing up this sale."

Finally, after taking a saw to the scrub oak, Jake's pickup went over the hole using the primitive path Josh had cut. Heading back to town, Josh considered how to tell Jake about his morning in the marsh. Jake had built one of the missing houses just last year.

"Say, Jake, have you been back to see what the landscapers did to that McMansion you built in Pocomo last year?"

"No, I've not been able to fit any house tours into my work schedule this year."

"Since we head back that way, why don't we go check it out? We could see if the other two lots have sold, do a little prospective building?"

"Okay, but then I've got to drop you off, get over to the Madaket job and pick up some flowers for Lovey's birthday."

"Jake, when did you become Mr. Romantic? I've not seen you in this mode for quite a while. I think it becomes you," Josh teased, thinking back to the days when he and Marci fixed up Jake and Lovey on a blind date.

Jake turned into the macadam entrance to Pocomo Road and headed west to find the new road leading into the private development. When the truck hit the dirt road, he turned and looked at Josh. "Did they change the entrance? Guess I missed the road. I'll have to turn around. Don't tell the women we did this. Getting lost in front of Lovey is about the most humiliating thing I've ever experienced."

Turning the truck around, Jake slowed down when they hit the macadam. The road they wanted should have led off to the right. But too soon, they were back to the Wauwinet Road.

"Come on. We couldn't have missed it twice. Do you think the owners put it back to dirt to keep people from gawking at their mansions?"

"No, I don't think so. That's way too logical for what's going on here."

"Come on. Let's just go back to town. I'm tired of looking at dirt roads."

"Jake, just back up a few hundred feet. Then turn into that break in the scrub. *This* dirt road is one you're never going to forget."

"Josh, what's gotten into you? Ever since we climbed the hornbeams, you've been fidgety. Finding strange markers, insisting we sightsee. You're acting weird, man."

"Just humor me. You'll see my point when we get there."

"What? This road looks like the original one we bulldozed five years ago. Where's the Conner's house and Murphy's? Josh, is this some kind of a trick? You took me down a bloomin' rabbit trail. Ha, I'll get you back big time for this one."

But as he spoke, Jake looked straight at Josh's face. It was deadly serious. Come to think of it, a little pale. "Josh, are you okay? You look sick. You're not going to throw up on me, are you?"

"No, Jake. But you better stop the engine. I think you're going to want to take a short walk." He was not relishing the outburst of horror when Jake realized that the houses they'd built had vanished, as well as the others that surrounded them.

Sixteen

"Josh, I'm off to the studio. If you need me, don't come to get me," laughed Marci as she headed toward the wall of scrub oak that bordered their backyard. Tucked into the scrub and *Rosa rugosa,* Marci's studio was nearly invisible from the house. She liked it that way.

Marci had wanted a separate place of retreat all her life, so she could paint her life-sized landscapes. Growing up on a farm in a small New England town, her spirit and soul needed separation from the daily world to release her creative gifts. She wanted a serene and beautiful place so her landscapes would reflect the sense of pristine beauty that God had created all over the island with His paintbrush.

But this wasn't only her painting studio. It was also where Marci spent hours on her knees, interceding for people around the world. While she and Josh traveled the globe on their sailboat, they both had made many special faraway friends. She began praying for the needs they expressed through letters and email. They wrote back about the miracles that happened when Marci prayed.

The couple had designed the one-room studio so that light filled the space year-round. Marci could paint any time of the day, assured that the island's pure, bright light would illuminate her work. The offshore breezes and ceiling fans kept the air moving through the two-story French windows lining the studio's four walls.

One corner of this retreat held a cozy reading nook, complete with an oversized chair covered in vintage floral chintz. Beside it was an endless pile of storybooks that she'd collected on their journey around the world. The children Marci taught loved the chair because of its soft, goose-down cushions. Flopping onto the chair, the cushions puffed up around the child, forming a nest among the fabric flowers.

The studio had a small kitchen, its own Franklin stove, and even a steep staircase leading to a small widow's walk, where there was room enough for a chair, ottoman, and umbrella, or on rare occasions, two chairs. Marci could watch the weather change or gaze at the night sky and watch for shooting stars sitting there in the breeze.

Josh was invited into the cottage studio, but only when the hand-painted sign, Visitors Welcome, was up on the Dutch door. Josh had his truck, and she had her studio. Two years of living on a sailboat had taught both of them the luxury of having their own space.

Guests entered the studio through a trellised doorway covered with roses, clematis, and any other vine that struck Marci's fancy. Her small studio was magical in June, snuggled in among the blueberry, bayberry, and *Rosa rugosa* bushes. Multicolored roses scrambled alongside the windows and over the roof. Twelve different varieties of clematis kept a colorful display all summer long. Blue, purple, and pink morning glories bloomed alongside the white moonflowers. The bright red cardinal vine and Japanese honeysuckle splashed bits of red and yellow amid the tangle of vines.

Marci set aside one day each week to teach a small group of children how to paint. Today was their first day. Upon arriving at the house, the children stood on the deck to see if they could spot the studio. Only the keenest of eyes would find it, often a sign of that child's gift of observation. Marci gave the first child who saw it the oversized key that opened the Dutch door into the studio. The door was round, like the hobbits' houses in Middle Earth.

She rarely taught children over the age of ten, enjoying the fresh, creative minds of the younger children. Knowing how curious children are, she allowed each child to sit at an easel, look at the paints and soft paintbrushes, and choose the colors and brushes for the first painting. Having collected numerous brushes made of sable, rabbit hair, and other materials, she would take one of the big brushes and show how soft it was, sweeping it over the children's palms and the back of their hands. Each child chose a brush to examine, feel and try painting with their favorite colors. The most tactile of the children would put the brush's bristles to their faces just to see how it felt. The more rambunctious of these little ones would try this stunt on their friends, sometimes with paint. She gave each child a painting smock and then sent them off to find an easel or table on which to draw and paint. They were playing, painting, singing, and laughing by the end of the afternoon.

On rainy days, Marci went into the antique jelly cupboard and took out the special powder that made the magic hot chocolate. Each time a child took a sip of the chocolate, a tiny marshmallow popped up onto the surface. There would be a layer of dark chocolate at the bottom of the mug that they scooped out with their hands, or sometimes even a spoon.

If the day was cloudy and cool, Marci invited the children to walk through her garden. They found chocolate-covered cranberries hidden in birds' nests, tufts of grass, or sometimes gum drops hung from tree branches by gossamer strands of the ladybug spiders.

She encouraged the children to explore the various nooks and crannies of the studio. Often, they accidentally overturned jars of paintbrushes. Coming over to the scene of the crime, she would show the children how to play the game Pick-up Sticks to straighten out the mess.

She gave every child an eraser to mold and knead into whatever shape he or she desired. The erasers would often fall off the easels during class, bouncing in different directions. Dropped erasers were fair game, so there was always a quick dash to catch someone else's eraser. Once captured, the child would throw the eraser into the bucket Marci kept explicitly for this purpose. If the eraser landed in the bucket, the child received a special prize. Every day was a new adventure. The children would tell their friends how Mrs. Marci taught them to paint in her "magic" studio.

Marci would often take them out on the moors or beaches to collect specimens to sketch and paint. One particular day ushered in another strange occurrence on the island.

Seventeen

Stephen waited anxiously at Becki's door, wondering why it was taking her so long to answer. Dressed in his formal black suit and power tie, his shaggy blond hair, as usual, was out of control. Impatiently, he swept it off his forehead.

"Oh, Stephen, thank goodness it's only you," Becki said as she opened the door.

"Thanks a lot. Who did you think it was, for heaven's sake?" he said, striding into Becki's spacious loft and studio.

"Stephen, we've had a harrowing morning. Just before you got here, we threw out a *Boston Flame* reporter. When you rang the doorbell, both of us thought he'd come back."

"We fixed him," Trish interrupted. "I grabbed his notebook when Becki slammed the door on his arm. We've been able to piece together who tipped him off to her address."

"Yeah, most people can't find this place even when Becki gives them directions," Stephen laughed.

"Ha, ha, ha," Becki retorted, sounding a bit like Lucy responding to Charlie Brown.

"What's a reporter doing here this early in the morning? Was it about your mom?"

"We're not sure. We didn't give him a chance to ask questions. Becki almost broke his arm when she shut the door. But I got a good look at the notebook he dropped while pulling his arm out of the doorway."

"Stephen, we know that one of the persons in his notebook recently bought some photos from Mom. Trish remembered the name from searching through Mom's customer sales file when we were trying to figure out who might have wanted to steal the antique Nantucket prints and then go to the trouble of planting stolen photos in her studio."

Walking back toward the kitchen, Becki tried to change the subject. "What did your botany colleagues have to say? Did they agree we may have discovered a new species?"

"Any more coffee?" Stephen asked, ignoring Becki's question.

"Always for you. Here, help yourself to milk and sugar," said Trish, pouring him a mug of coffee and placing it before him.

"Okay, here's the story. The Major said there is a definite possibility of a new species. It happens in the Amazon a lot, so he felt it was worth pursuing. He said that they need your detailed botanicals and my photos to be certain."

"Tell him to get in line. What is it with these botanicals? Everyone wants them yesterday. Since when did I become so famous? The Foundation is also pressing me to deliver. Kind of weird, don't you think?"

"I'm not sure. It seems more likely a coincidence," Stephen said, brushing off her question.

"But Stephen, what about your lawyer? Did Rachel say what to do with the information we have? By the way, I called Mom and Dad. They're pondering this as they dine alfresco in the Caribbean. They're going to call back in a little while."

"Rachel wants to meet with us today, so we don't lose any time. She's assuming that the finding is a discovery. I hope she'll tell me how to protect the orchids legally. Unfortunately, she needs you to update her on the investigation about the robbery in your mom's studio. Sorry, but at least you'll be telling it to someone who doesn't want to write a news article."

"Becki, I need to pick up my little one at preschool, and I still have errands to run. Why don't I call you later to see how you're doing? Don't open the door to anyone but us, okay?"

"Don't worry. I've got the botanicals to finish, remember?"

"And don't leave the apartment without Trish or me."

"Stephen, if I'm to meet you at Rachel's, I have to leave the flat. Or are you sending Superman for me? Don't you want to stay and see what Mom and Dad have to say?"

"As long as it's in the next ten minutes. I still need to get to work on a full presentation to the executives."

"I thought you did that?"

"No, that was only the informal briefing with Justin."

"Wait, I'm confused. Didn't you say he took you off the project? Why another presentation?"

But before Stephen could respond, the phone rang. Using that as her cue, Trish got up, mouthed a quick goodbye, and was out the door. Becki ran to her phone.

"Hello, Mom?"

"Yes, darling, your dad is right here. I'm going to put you on speaker."

"You've got both of us. Stephen is here. Hope that's okay." Becki said, hitting the speaker button.

It wasn't okay. Keta could see Lyrica's face. One more person drawn into the publicity vortex of the investigation was not what Lyrica wanted. But Becki was old enough to make her own decisions.

"Becki, your dad and I feel strongly that the press shouldn't harass you. He called our private investigator and alerted him to the incident this morning with the reporter. He'll probably want the information you and Trish found in the notebook."

"Mom, what's the Private I's name?"

"Daniel Keelan. He's going to call you as soon as he can. If you want to call him, Dad will text you his cell number."

"Oh, that would be great. But Mom, isn't he your bodyguard?"

"Yes, darling. But I'm giving him to you. They're providing me with another one. Please don't open the door for anyone and check the caller ID before answering your phone. If the harassment continues, we can get a restraining order."

"Stephen, I called some contacts through my import-export business. I think you may have some protection about the discovery under international law and trade restrictions. But you need to disclose the finding as soon as possible, or it could appear as if you're hiding something for personal gain. Your lawyer can brief you more on the definition of full disclosure."

"I'm sorry we're not there to offer more personal support, darling. But it's probably better for you we are out of the country," Lyrica added.

"Mrs. Kea, Becki and I are meeting with my lawyer this afternoon. My botanical experts are doing the classification search, but the detail in Becki's botanicals will tell us if it's a new species."

"Man, here I was, an unknown artist. Now everyone wants my botanicals," Becki exclaimed. "I thought our trip to Madeira was to paint flowers and spend time together. Little did I know that this would turn into such a big deal."

"Darling, can we call you this time tomorrow morning and see how you're doing?" Lyrica asked.

But just as Becki was about to agree, the doorbell rang. "Mom, hang on, the doorbell just rang."

Taking her phone, she went to see who it was. Stephen followed, shushing her silently. This time, the peephole revealed a sexy, sunburned blonde standing a few feet from the door.

"Who's there?" Becki barked.

"No one you would know. I have some information about your mother's case. I think I can help you," Wanton cooed.

"We're not taking any information. Give it to the police," Becki responded. "Go away, or I'll call the police."

"Suit yourself. You'll have to come out sometime. I'll see you later, perhaps."

Turning around and walking down the hall, Wanton stopped and waited for the elevator. Becki turned to Stephen. "That was easy."

"Mom, there was another person at the door, a young woman."

"What does she look like?" Keta pressed.

"Well, you're going to think this is kind of crazy, but if I said Wonder Woman with bleached blonde hair, would that help?" Becki answered.

There was a long pause at the other end of the phone. "Dad, what's wrong? Who is she?"

"Nothing, baby. It's just that we had a run-in with her yesterday at the resort. Don't, under any circumstance, speak or pay any attention to her. She's working with the reporter you saw earlier today. They're scavenging for information to do another piece for the *Boston Flame.*"

"Okay, but I do have to leave my studio sometime. You know, lead a normal life?"

"Baby, we know. Just try to be more aware of who is around you. I'll alert Daniel about the blonde," Keta warned. "I'm texting you his cell number."

"Darling, we'll call you tomorrow morning. Love you. Bye." Lyrica put down the phone and sighed deeply.

Becki turned toward Stephen. "What a day."

Meanwhile, Lyrica and Keta returned to their meal on the patio in the Caribbean. "I can't believe they got back that fast," Keta said, a frown creasing his forehead.

Keta's long years of big game hunting in South Africa had honed his hunter instincts. He could sense the electricity when prey and predator came within reach of each other. It had happened at the restaurant just a few seconds before he saw Jacks and his partner. Unfortunately, Lyrica had learned to read his change in demeanor. Whoever planted the stolen photographs in her studio tried very hard to ruin her reputation. It wasn't the robbery of her photos that concerned him. The perpetrator's malicious intent to plant stolen photos and have Lyrica take the fall had set his blood boiling. He had seen the intense harassment Lyrica had taken following the robbery. It was going to be a long haul with the press. He had determined nothing would invade their vacation. And now it had. Unfortunately, even the bright Caribbean sun couldn't ease the pain inflicted on their family.

Eighteen

The children looked forward to going on adventures in the moors with Marci. Promptly at ten in the morning, they started dancing through the gate to her studio. The first to arrive got to pull the bell and open the gate, so most came on time. Once through the gate, they were in the magical land created by Marci.

The moms were supposed to stay on Marci's deck and watch their children disappear down the grassy path to the studio. Every so often, she'd see a mom peeking through the rose trellised windows into the studio. Usually, upon seeing this, Marci would smile, silently musing that maybe she would run a class for adults this year. Perhaps they could rediscover the creative, childlike spirit they once had.

After checking into the studio, the budding artists piled into Marci's Jeep and they headed toward the middle of the island. On each expedition, they scouted out a different place. Once she chose a spot, the kids went off in pairs to sketch and find treasures they could bring back to paint and study. This day, two of the girls came back with daisies they'd picked in a small kettle hole. But she could see as they approached that something was bothering them.

"Mrs. Marci, there are hardly any daisies in the kettle hole this year. And we only found two violets growing in the middle of the road. What happened to them? Did they die?"

"No, I don't think so. Maybe we didn't get enough rain to bring the daisies this year. Last summer was beautiful, but we had a lot of rain in the spring. Maybe the daisies are sleeping until next year, hoping the rain will make their seed shells pop so they can bloom. What do you think about that?"

"I think it stinks. How are we going to paint the flowers if they refuse to bloom for us?" little Katharine said, looking quizzically at Marci.

"Oh, I don't think that they're refusing to bloom. You can make them bloom on your canvas. They know you love them. Look how their happy petals surround their yellow smiles. Perhaps next time when the ranger goes with us, we can ask him. He's knowledgeable about this sort of thing. Why don't you two go down by the pond? There'll be other flowers and berries to find. I'll put your daisies in water."

Intent on treasure, they'll soon forget the disappointment and come back with something new, Marci thought. She watched the two girls run down the dirt road to the pond, their blonde and red pigtails flying. Their bright-colored clothing fluttered against the blue sky reflected in the pond. Marci loved these outings because the children were so expressive when they discovered treasures outside. It was deeply satisfying to watch them revel in the same world she loved to paint.

Her favorite place for these adventures was the middle moors, where kettle holes, sculpted out by the glaciers, formed small ponds hidden in the rolling hills. As a young girl, she and her parents often picnicked on the cushion of bearberry that cloaked the hillside above the largest pond or in the soft field grass by the pond's edge amidst the fragrance of sweet pepper bush and honey-suckle. Her dad had named the largest body of water the donut pond because the inner section had slowly turned into bog and cattails.

The blueberry bushes rimmed the pond with flames of fire in the fall as they turned out their last colors. If the sun was out, the ponds glistened and caught the azure sky in their arms. The ponds rippled and sparkled as if diamonds were dancing on the surface when caught in a breeze. Marci had chronicled the subtle changes each pond displayed over the years. Her collection of paintings from this area were probably the largest on the island. Using oil, watercolor, and pastel, she had documented the seasons and the topographical changes that time had wrought. Lyrica, her mom, had a similar series of photographs dating from the late 1960s to the present.

Marci put on her teaching hat while watching the boys throw pebbles into the pond. "Boys, what color do you think a ripple is?"

"Today, it's blue, Mrs. Marci. It's reflecting the sky," said one boy.

"Are you sure the ripple is blue? Even though the pond appears blue when you throw your pebble in, look again and see what you think."

The boys now took small rocks and threw them into the pond. The commotion flushed a mallard and his mate from the reeds to the boys' right.

"Look, there's that fluorescent duck again," Nathaniel exclaimed. "Wow, I'd like to paint him. What a neat green. I wonder why the other duck isn't pretty."

"Maybe it had to get its feathers at Take It or Leave It," laughed James.

"Or maybe it just likes brown," Nathaniel quickly retorted, not to be outdone by his friend. "My mom likes brown."

Marci stood a few yards away and listened intently. "So, boys, have you decided what color the ripples are?"

"Yeah. We think they're ripple-colored, like at the ice cream store. Ha, ha, ha," responded Nathaniel.

"Well, maybe God took his inspiration from this pond to make ice cream," added James, getting in on the imaginative story they were concocting.

"Ice cream, yeah, that's the color. I'm going to paint ice cream when we get back. I'll make the pond ice cream, with chocolate ducks on top," Nathaniel laughed to himself.

"Nat, you're a silly billy. We have to paint what we find out here. There's no ice cream in the pond."

"Oh no? You just wait and see," Nathaniel responded emphatically. "Mrs. Marci says we can paint what we see, and I see ice cream over there."

Too soon, it was time to go back to the studio. Arriving home, the boys and girls raced from the Jeep into the studio, carrying their treasures in little linen sacks, jars, and paper towels. Dropping their shoes in a muddy pile, they dashed to their canvases. Often, the treasures had to be kept alive long enough to paint.

"Okay, let's see what we can paint from today's discoveries. Remember, you don't have to paint what you see with your eyes, but what is in your heart and spirit. Think about why you saved your particular treasure and paint what it means to you."

With paintbrushes in hand, some children mixed their paint colors. Others sat and thought. Others, like Eric, talked to the green striped bug he'd captured.

Racey was still talking about the daisies. "I'm going to paint that kettle hole the way it's supposed to be," she said triumphantly. "That will make all the daisies very happy and make that old kettle hole look like it did last year."

Onto her canvas went green, brown, white, and yellow paint. Racey even glued a few daisies onto her canvas and covered them with clear enamel.

Watching their little minds create from heart and spirit was heaven for Marci. Sometimes one child had difficulty shedding the urge to paint exactly what he or she saw. This year, it was Eric. As Marci wandered toward his place of creative energy, she approached slowly.

"Now, mister bug, I need to paint you, then I can let you go in Mrs. Marci's garden. I know you'll like it there. But what color do you want to be? Hmm."

"I know." And from that point on, he and the canvas were one. Most of the white space became the giant green and red striped bug. But surrounding the bug was Eric, with both arms hugging it. Both the bug and Eric grinned ear to ear. Eric even painted his shirt green to match the bug.

"What have we here?" whispered Marci. "I like it very much. Is that your bug?"

"Yes, Mrs. Marci. We're good friends now. He's telling me all about where he lived. I told him he'd make new friends in your garden, and he was happy. It's a dangerous world out there for a bug," said Eric, using a serious adult voice.

"Oh, you bet," said Marci, "But he'll be safe in my garden."

"Do you think it would be all right if I let him fly on my airplane in the garden? He's never flown on one. He wants to see its wings."

"Sure. Whenever you're ready, we'll take him out for a spin."

Marci's day was filled with laughter and discovery, looking through the children's keen eyes. This kept her own art engaging, spontaneous, and often whimsical. Her oversized landscapes were famous on and off the island. She thought of them as "windows" in the homes of her patrons, offering the serenity of God's creation through the seasons of the year. Her first show of the season was coming up soon. It would be wonderful to have her parents and twin sister Becki together for the show.

The children's laughter and creativity had softened the harrowing memory of their kayak journey into Pocomo Meadows. Flopping down into her worn chintz chair, she dropped her head back and just gazed up at the timbered ceiling. Nantucket had always been their shelter in the storm. But now, it seemed the storm had found them. At least the ponds hadn't disappeared. Yet.

Nineteen

Stephen and Becki left Poodles coffee shop and headed toward the lawyer's office. It was a beautiful spring day in Boston. The long winter was finally over, or at least temporarily put at bay.

"Stephen, what is Rachel like? My experience with lawyers has not been reassuring. Even those that are helping Mom and Dad are somewhat esoteric for me."

"I think you'll like her. I've known her since graduate school. She has single-handedly built up her environmental practice to where people now call and ask if they can work for her."

"But I know nothing about environmental law. Why does she need me in this conversation? I was just your traveling partner."

"Becki, as much as you hate to talk about this, I know Rachel will want an update on the investigation into the robbery at your mom's studio and why someone would plant photos known to have been stolen from Earl Morston six months ago. She understands the tough place you are in."

"Well, that would be a pleasant surprise."

"Becki, she needs to know, so the press doesn't blindside her. The tabloids have already linked the two of us together. Justin Earsom could make this morning's brush with reporters look like child's play."

"Thanks for the encouragement. You certainly know how to make me feel better." snapped Becki. She was wondering whose side Stephen was on.

Finally reaching the new glass skyscraper where Rachel worked, Becki and Stephen took the marble-lined elevator and quickly arrived at her office. Unexpectedly, Rachel walked into the waiting room just as they entered.

"Hello. I was just getting a cup of tea for myself before we began. Would you like anything?"

"Maybe some water. We just filled up on coffee at Poodles," Stephen responded.

"Oh, that's such a fun place. If I'd known you were stopping there, I'd have put in an order for a double chocolate brownie."

"We'll let you know next time," Stephen quipped.

"If there is a next time," Becki mumbled.

"Why don't you come into my office instead of the conference room? We'll leave that for when the papers pile up."

After making them comfortable, Rachel began her questions about the situation with Stephen's journals and Becki's role in the discovery.

"Becki, I'm looking forward to seeing your botanicals. Your mom is such an accomplished artist. It looks like you follow in her footsteps and may be famous one day as well."

"Or infamous," Becki said. "Depending on what happens here, I could join that rank."

Rachel took this opening and gently led into her line of questioning about Becki's mom and the investigation.

"Stephen has filled me in on your role with the Foundation and your professional reputation as a botanical artist. While I've never seen your artwork, it must be excellent. The Foundation only funds top-notch work."

"Thank you, Rachel," Becki responded.

"If I understand correctly, part of your concern about the orchid discovery is the connection with Earsom. It's unlikely, but your professional reputation could be affected if there is adverse publicity about Stephen stemming from the discovery."

"That's true. But I'm more concerned that the recent publicity about my mom doesn't get injected into this and affect both our jobs and personal lives."

"Rachel, she's already had a close call with a reporter who showed up on her doorstep."

"He must have followed me home or had inside information. Even people who have directions have difficulty finding my loft."

"Becki, would you be willing to tell me in your own words what happened with the robbery at your mom's studio? I've read the news reports, but I'd rather hear it from your perspective."

Heaving a sigh, Becki sat back on the couch, looked at Stephen, and started the story. When she finished, Becki once more posed the question that no one had answered. "The weird part of this is that someone would break into my mom's studio and only steal two antique black and white photos of our friend's barn and paddock on Nantucket. There are tons of photos in mom's collection that are extremely valuable. And why did the thief plant the stolen Morston photos in her studio?"

"Becki, clearly there is more to the robbery than meets the eye. I'm sure the detectives are looking for the motive to help find the thief."

"We still aren't sure who is her enemy." Becki sat back and sighed.

"Do you believe the publicity about your mom has affected the Foundation's view of your work? It has a prestigious group of donors."

"Rachel, honestly, I'm not sure. All I know is what I've told you about the Foundation shortening my deadline and requesting a presentation of the Madeira trip long before it's due."

"The fact that Becki and I were in Madeira together cannot help but come out in the press eventually. She painted a botanical of every orchid we saw, new and old species."

Turning toward Stephen, Rachel asked, "What do you think will happen when Justin and the other execs find out about the orchids?"

"I'm hoping that the execs will pour some sense into Justin. It's dangerous to talk to him alone. He'll want to withhold the discovery to save his building plans. I need to know what to do if I lose my job because of this situation."

"You two have woven together some very complicated legal issues. But I think I can help. First, Justin is subject to international laws and any land preservation restrictions in Madeira as a UNESCO World Heritage Site. There are also country environmental restrictions by which he must abide. However, if you withhold the discovery much longer, it could compromise your case and appear like you are only interested in personal gain."

"So, what do we do?" Stephen asked, watching Becki as he listened to Rachel.

"I suggest you send a summary of your complete report to all the execs before you meet with Justin. If you can get them in the same room, you'll at least have witnesses for what you present. Do you have their support?"

"The majority of them. One is hungry politically, so you never know which way he'll swing."

"Your personal notes are your own. However, you cannot present a new plant species to the botanical world without saying where and how you came upon the plants. And if you normally use these notes for your business reports, they belong to the Earsom Corporation."

"So you're saying I can't keep my personal journal separate from the field notes?"

"Yes and no. Regardless of what format you keep your notes in, you discovered the orchids on company time. Thus the discovery belongs to Earsom."

"But what if Justin hides the discovery so they can build without concern for the orchids or the ecosystem?" Stephen was quickly losing control of his emotions.

"In a court of law, your personal journal and related discovery would be material evidence. But I don't think this will get to court. Justin is too smart for that."

Becki's body language was telling. Stephen knew what she was thinking.

"Court? Rachel, that will get messy when Becki's involvement comes out. We've got to stay out of court."

"I'm not saying that court is inevitable. I'm reviewing potential scenarios. If Justin okays the discovery and amends his construction plans, the press coverage might benefit him. In that case, the worst you could suffer would be the personal loss of the discovery."

"But what about Stephen's job?" Becki pressed. "We don't know how long Stephen will stay on the project. If the execs vote to hide the discovery, what do we do?"

"Quite frankly, the land belongs to a foreign government or person. You're going to be required to reveal the environmental findings at some point. We're talking not only about orchids but also about habitat. Correct?"

"Yes, unfortunately," Stephen moaned. "Rachel, won't Becki be drawn into this because she went with me to do the botanicals? Justin won't appreciate any link with her mom, with the investigation still open."

"Wait a minute, Stephen," Becki snapped, her irritation rising fast. "My botanicals are the best evidence of a new orchid species. I'm sorry you've been drawn into my family's affairs. It didn't seem to bother you before we left for Madeira. Now I'm a liability to you?"

Rachel could see a storm brewing. "Becki, I think for now it would be wise to follow the advice of your mom and dad. I'm sure they also have attorneys working for them."

"Rachel, it's gone farther than that. We know that—"

"Wait, Stephen, we don't know for sure," Becki interrupted.

"Okay, we think a reporter followed Becki to her loft. Her dad has now hired a private investigator as a bodyguard. We think—" Stephen never got to finish his sentence because a knock on the door interrupted them.

"Let me see what's going on." Rachel said, carefully shielding the two of them from the messenger.

Rachel returned to the office a few minutes later and sat down again. "That was my administrative assistant. It seems a reporter just called asking for information about Madeira's environmental law."

"Did you get the caller ID? I bet we know who he is," Becki said. "He probably followed us here. Maybe my dad's right. I do need a bodyguard."

Twenty

Finishing up her morning devotions, Marci stood up from her chintz-covered chair, determined to complete the series of landscapes she was painting for her upcoming show. She loved the early morning before the world's noises and colors started competing for her attention.

The morning sun streamed through the windows. The fragrance of roses outside melded with the familiar smell of oil paint. Donning the smock made of flowered material scraps from her childhood, she opened several tubes of paint. Squirting different size dabs on her palette, she stared at the landscape on the canvas before her. Several months ago, she painted a series of morning landscapes of the small ponds scattered throughout the middle moors, many of which were tucked away beyond the reach of tourists. Over the years, Marci had chronicled the subtle changes in these ponds, and she wanted her paintings to capture those changes and the seasonal display of colors on the moors.

Secretly, she hoped that only one buyer would want this newest set of large panels. She designed them as landscape "windows" for the walls of an estate house. Left unframed, they would create a mural. Marci had read *The Lion, the Witch and the Wardrobe.* She wanted her paintings to be like the wardrobe, a doorway into a magical place like Narnia. Not just anyone who opened the wardrobe saw the door. Marci wanted her works to evoke the viewer's senses, feelings, and memories, pulling them into the landscape itself. She wanted them to see not just what she painted but the beauty and grandeur of God's creation.

Marci was Lyrica's daughter and Becki's fraternal twin. The love of art and nature seemed to overflow in their family. Living on an island thirty miles out to sea had kept the publicity and press hounds away from her door. The island had become very protective of her. In a small community, most people knew each other or knew someone who did. Many people moved to the island to escape the rat race, so they were careful not to let it intrude on anyone's life.

The two years Josh and Marci spent sailing around the world gave their work extraordinary life, color, and form. Josh trained as an architect, but he learned the building trade by working construction to earn money in the various ports where they stayed. He'd integrated some of the unique architecture they saw into his construction business on the island. Marci often left her paintings to be sold at some of the more popular ports of call. Starting the painting school was a dream birthed in her travels.

Priscilla Taylor had been a great inspiration to Marci. She missed their painting forays in the moors and on the beaches. Priscilla shared Marci's love for the hidden places on the island that seemed to be slipping away. They had drawn a map of endangered wildflower locations and kept it in Priscilla's tiger maple desk. Each year, they would return to the areas. While Marci painted the landscapes, Priscilla would paint the wildflowers.

Priscilla was one of the few people who could arrive unannounced at Marci's studio. Gazing out the tall French windows, Marci remembered how Priscilla had surprised her one morning, popping her head through the open Dutch door and insisting that Marci come with her to paint a new place she'd found while riding her horse.

"Come on. We have to go *now*. The blooms will be gone tomorrow," Priscilla insisted. "Leave your canvas as is. I've got everything we need, including some hot tea."

So dropping everything, leaving a palette of paint, brushes, and a wet canvas, Marci climbed into Priscilla's vintage Willys Jeep, and they set off on another adventure. Leaving the Longmeadow's driveway, Priscilla turned onto the Wauwinet Road and then quickly swung onto another dirt road. They pursued this track for about ten minutes until her friend suddenly pulled the car off the dirt road onto a soft plot of grass. Priscilla wouldn't tell her what she'd found or where they were going. Marci loved the mystery. Priscilla jumped out and gathered the art materials while Marci brought along the blanket, tea, shortbread, and mugs.

"Come on. It's just over that hummock."

And it was. A group of bright red wood lilies stood like British soldiers posing for a portrait at the base of the hill. These plants usually grew as solitary redcoats. They became endangered because visitors had picked or dug them up, often out of ignorance. Only a few people knew where the survivors were, and Priscilla was one of them.

"Oh, Priscilla, I'm so glad you brought me here. This is more than beautiful. I've never seen so many together. I can't believe they're all here, blooming their heads off just a few yards off the dirt road. We've got to repaint them. Last year's portrait doesn't come close to this brilliant display."

Twenty-One

Trish mentally reviewed the reporter's encounter while she and Becki unloaded groceries onto the kitchen table. She wished Becki had a man who was more sensitive to her needs. Frankly, she didn't think Stephen was good enough for her friend.

"Becki, I think you're making more of this meeting with Daniel Keelan than you need to. Sure, you're going to lose some privacy. But isn't it worth it to have peace of mind?"

"How is having a strange man around me going to give me peace of mind?"

"Look, he must be a nice guy if your mom and dad hired him. I should think you'd be touched that your mom gave him to you. Now she has to start all over with a new bodyguard. Besides, you have to meet him eventually."

"I hope he has a badge of some sort. I'd hate to find out that I'd been entertaining a reporter or a stalker in my living room. Maybe I should ask Stephen if he can come over. It's around his lunchtime."

"Becki, we don't need Stephen. Look how we took care of that reporter."

"Oh, you mean you can stay? That's wonderful!" Becki exclaimed.

"Of course, I'll stay. In the meantime, why don't I unpack the groceries so you can whip up some of your famous chocolate chip cookies? It always helps to feed a guy when you want to make a good impression."

"Isn't he supposed to be making the good impression? Besides, I'm kicking everyone out at one o'clock. I've got the botanicals to finish. I'm working toward a new deadline, remember?"

A half-hour later, Daniel Keelan rang the doorbell at Becki's loft. Peering through the privacy hole, Trish saw that Keelan already had out his ID. She still opened the door using the chain lock.

"I'm Daniel Keelan. Are you Becki Kea?" he said, flashing his ID.

"No, I'm Trish. But come in. We've been expecting you. That's Becki over there in the kitchen with cookie dough all over her hands."

Daniel Keelan was over six feet tall and drop-dead good-looking. He was sporting a yellow polo shirt with aviator sunglasses hanging from the placket on his shirt. You could tell he worked out. His Dockers were professionally pressed, and his shoes Trish knew even before she looked down that she'd find tassels on his loafers. Even though he had light brown hair, his eyes were Paul Newman blue and sparkled when he smiled. Not bad, Trish thought. I should be so lucky.

Holding up her sticky hands, Becki greeted Keelan cautiously. "I'll be with you in a minute. I'm just finishing up making chocolate chip cookies to hold us over until lunch. You can tell us what you've been doing for my mom and dad lately. Too bad they didn't take you with them to the Club."

"From what I hear, it might have helped if I'd been there. The paparazzi tried to get to them, but the Club quickly turned the intruders out on their heels."

"Have a seat, Mr. Keelan," Trish said as she pointed toward the couch and two chairs that made up Becki's living room. The kitchen extended into the living room. The skylight windows on the ceiling sent streams of sunlight onto Becki's coffee table. Watching the early dynamic between Becki and Keelan, Trish mused about Stephen's reaction to this recent addition in Becki's life.

Becki walked into the living room, put a fresh plate of warm cookies on the glass-top coffee table, and then sat down in one of the oversized club chairs. Under the glass, Keelan noted a collection of watercolors and photos of Becki and her family on Nantucket.

"Becki, this is a beautiful place. It's a little sanctuary amidst the concrete and steel. No wonder you were surprised and irritated that the press found you. Your dad told me about your studio loft, but I never expected it to be so lovely. You've done a wonderful job of making this home."

"That's nice of you, Mr. Keelan. I appreciate the compliment," Becki responded, wondering if he was already schmoozing her. She decided to put on her business demeanor. Trish saw the switch and was waiting for her response. Becki was a sensitive, creative artist, but she'd worked long enough in the business world to discern when compliments were genuine or not. Today, she looked unsure and confused.

"Please call me Dan. Your parents do."

Not a good tactic, thought Trish. Strike one. For a private investigator, this guy is all thumbs when it comes to face to face. I wonder if he's nervous. Trish waited for Becki's next comment.

"Mr. Keelan, since our relationship is so new, I'd prefer if we stick to last names for a while. I know my parents have known you for many years, so maybe we'll work up to that familiarity," Becki finished with a bit of a frosty stare.

"Another cookie, Dan?" Trish offered, passing him the plate, trying to soften

Becki's cold welcome.

"Thank you, yes," he replied, wondering if he should tell her how incredible the cookies were or back off. Becki was as skittish as her father had described her.

"So please tell us what you know about these reporters. And also, I'd like to understand better how you intend to protect me from them."

Keelan pulled out two photographs and handed them to Becki and Trish. "Are these the two that came to your door?"

"Yes. Who are they?" Becki asked with rising irritation.

"These are the same reporters from the *Boston Flame* that were trying to get pictures of your parents at the Club Bougainvillea. Fortunately, Robin intercepted them."

"Now, do you recognize any of these men?" Keelan handed them several other photos.

"No, I don't think so," Becki responded.

"I'd have to agree," Trish added.

"Think about the last week or so. Did you notice if anyone was following you?"

"Not that I saw," Becki answered. But Trish picked up on the question.

"Becki, what about the time you thought someone was trying to get onto this floor through the stairwell?"

"I guess I'd forgotten about that. But why would someone other than a reporter decide to follow me? What do I have that someone would want?"

"That's the question I was about to ask you."

"Mr. Keelan, I have nothing worth stealing in this loft. It's not as if my paintings are world renown like my mom's photos."

"Sometimes, when thieves look for something, and they aren't sure where it is, they cover all the bases." Keelan did not want to broach the danger she could be in. He'd have to let her warm up to him a bit.

"According to your mom, you may have two of the photo series that we think the thief wants." He waited, carefully watching her expression. The comment seemed to startle Becki.

"Oh, I didn't know that. I wonder why Mom said nothing about me having photos the thief might want."

"Becki, perhaps they only recently realized that the thief wanted the *series* of photos, not just the three he took from your mom's studio," Trish responded.

Keelan silently thanked Trish for her effort to smooth the way with Becki. He knew that one of the photo series was in Becki's living room, and the other was hanging in her bedroom. Today would not be the day he'd ask to see her bedroom.

"Trish, you are spot on. Becki's mom thinks the thief may be looking for several more old photos of the Taylor property. We still don't know why, but we know that the property is up for sale."

"What? Priscilla would never sell that land. It's been in her family for generations. How can Old Man Taylor sell the land when she's still missing?"

Dan was gazing at how Becki's long, platinum blonde hair folded into a thick braid. I need to watch myself, he thought. She's a beauty. Trish, however, was not missing a bit of the tension between Becki and Keelan. She wasn't sure whether to be happy or worried.

"Dan, what exactly are you doing for the Keas, and specifically, what will you be doing for Becki?" Trish was subtly trying to change the subject. So relieved that Trish asked the question, Becki sat back, a cookie in hand, and waited for him to answer.

"Becki, your parents hired my firm, and me specifically, to ensure reporters do not harass your mom. Also, our investigative office is doing the detective work on the robbery. We've worked with your dad over the past twenty years. I'm going to be tailing you to protect you while we wait to see if the thief drops any clues."

"Too bad you weren't here the day someone followed Becki and tried to get into the hallway from the staircase outside her door," Trish responded.

"You mentioned that earlier. Can you tell me any more about it?"

"Only that I saw a man go into the building about a hundred yards ahead of me. I didn't think about it as people's friends come and go."

"Someone came out of the building just as he arrived. So he may have slipped through the open door," Trish added.

"Did you enter the building after that?"

"When I got to the door, no one was in the entranceway or waiting for the elevator. It wasn't until I got to my floor that I heard someone walking up the back stairway and then jostle the door into the hallway as if trying to get in. But it could have just been someone who didn't want to wait for the elevator and tried to walk up instead. You can't allow yourself to get paranoid."

"True, but it's a bit suspicious." It was more dangerous than he wanted to reveal at the moment.

"Tell me about the photos stolen from your mom's studio?"

Becki sighed deeply. "Mr. Keelan, they were part of a photographic study of Nantucket Island. My mom took them many years ago when my sister, Marci, decided to paint landscapes. She used them in one of her studies of the island's ecosystems. She had Mom shoot black and white to better define the light and structure. Mom kept some of them in her historical archive as provenance for the paintings should Marci ever decide to sell the murals. I kept two photos because I liked the memories they evoked."

"Can you think of anyone who would want these photos?"

"Not really," Becki laughed. "Several were of the Taylor's old barn and paddock. Hardly a stunning landscape compared to the rest of the island."

"Marci never finished the murals because her best friend, Priscilla Taylor, disappeared a month ago," Trish added.

"What's strange is that the thief not only stole Mom's photos, but also left in their place some photos stolen from Earl Morston's private collection. So my question is, was the thief really after Mom's photos or just wanting to smear her reputation?"

"Well, I hoped you might lend some insight into that." Keelan noted Becki had the same soft smile lines around her eyes as her mother. "What was in the collection of the Nantucket landscape photos?"

"I know little about the other photos. I only saw them briefly when my friend Stephen set up an inventory system for us to use. Marci's the one who used the landscape photos. You could ask her. I just have the barn and meadow photos."

Trish noted Becki had now relegated Stephen to the friend category. This could be interesting, she thought. I wonder how Stephen will react to having a potential rival.

Picking up a stack of art books, Becki pointed to the photo of Priscilla and Marci saddling their horses by the old barn. "This is the barn photo, except this is the old barn. They built a new one recently. The meadow scene is in my bedroom."

Replacing the books, Becki turned to Keelan. "Why anyone would want these photos is beyond me. Mom's photo archives hold much more expensive pieces. That's all I know."

Keelan was reading Becki's last comment as a signal that it was time to leave. "I think that's enough for today." Rising from the soft down couch, he reached inside his jacket. Becki visibly jumped, but Trish was pretty sure he didn't see it.

"Here's my card and two phone numbers. The second number is for emergencies; it overrides my first number. Your father asked that our firm post a bodyguard around you. At least for the time being, you're looking at him. In the meantime, you won't often see me, but I will be near you at all times."

"Thank you, Mr. Keelan," Becki said, offering him her business handshake.

"Yeah, stop by anytime. There are always cookies in this house." Trish felt sorry for the icy reception Becki had given him.

"It was nice meeting you," Keelan said, giving Trish a warm smile.

"My pleasure as well."

Becki opened the door, not even checking the hallway. "Goodbye." She closed the door so fast that it almost caught his heel on the door.

"Becki, why did you close the door so fast? What got into you? Why so stiff and cool a reaction to him? Your dad hired him to protect you, remember?"

"Was it that obvious? I was trying to keep it businesslike. He is a man, after all."

"Yeah, I'll say he's a man. I wish he were following me. I'd find some nice place to get lost."

"Okay, I'll be nicer next time." Becki was already concerned about her reaction to his looks and friendly manner. "Maybe I should ask for a female bodyguard."

"What, are you kidding? Get a grip, girl."

"I guess it's okay. I'm just tired of people asking me questions about mom's robbery." Becki grabbed the empty plate of cookies and walked over to the kitchen counter.

Noticing the empty plate, Trish turned to her friend, "I guess you know one thing about him. He loves your cookies. But seriously, Becki, if you're so worried about his character, why don't you talk with your dad? Keelan was guarding your mom, so your dad must trust him. Would that make you feel more secure?"

More secure, she thought. Should I tell Trish that I am attracted to him? I hoped a cool reception would mask my feelings. Boy, it's a good thing Stephen wasn't here. He'd see right through me.

"Trish, how am I going to tell Stephen about him? And what am I going to tell him?"

"You might want to think about that."

Twenty-Two

Marci remembered the last day she'd painted with her friend. Priscilla had laid out the familiar patchwork quilt on a grassy knoll in the Middle Moors and set out their painting materials, tea, and homemade shortcake. Handing Marci some brushes and canvas, they shared a palette of oil paints, each creating their version of the red wood lilies.

Marci painted free form in an atmospheric and luminescent style. The brilliant red of the lilies stood in stark contrast to the light blue sky. Priscilla's style was more photographic. Taken from all angles, she would capture the plant's essence in a beautiful botanical, not unlike the ones Becki created. When both were far enough along to finish at home, Priscilla broke out the tea and Scottish shortcake that she was famous for on the island.

"What a special day this is. I'm so glad we could share this beauty," Priscilla sighed.

"I'm going to mark this day in my journal as one of the best days of this year," Marci responded.

When the sun had worked its way to noon, they packed up to go home. Marci had wrapped the still oiled brushes in wax paper and covered the palette with plastic wrap when she realized that they both would need the palette to finish their paintings.

"Pris, I guess we are going to have to finish these together so we can both continue to use this palette."

Priscilla pressed Marci to keep the palette, brushes, and paint. Always a planner, she had carefully edged her portrait of the lilies with each of the colors she would need to finish.

"We really should do a show of our paintings. We're such opposites in brush technique and color. It would be fun to see them together," Marci suggested.

"Let's do it!" Priscilla was always up for a challenge.

As they packed up their supplies, they chatted about identifying the pieces they'd painted together and plans for a show. The opening of their gallery show would have been this coming weekend, except Priscilla had disappeared. Now

Marci was in her studio preparing to do the show alone.

It was quite a while before she could face going back to the hidden glen of red wood lilies. When she did, they rewarded her with a more spectacular sight. Almost twice as many lilies were blooming. Sitting down on the spongy bearberry, tears fell down her face. She still ached about how much she missed her friend. Marci was the only one who insisted that Priscilla was still alive. Everyone humored her because she seemed so emotionally fragile, an unusual trait for her typically buoyant disposition.

Now she realized that she'd been staring at the large canvases for quite some time. The studio was a permanent reminder of Priscilla and the encouragement she'd brought to her life. Resolutely, she picked up her paintbrush and began work on the final landscape panel for the show. Only this time, Priscilla wouldn't be there.

The large mural was a view from a high hill on the Taylor land. It looked down across the meadow and up the dunes to the sea. She sketched in the old barn and the worn cedar hitching post with its heavy iron rings where she and Priscilla bridled their horses, then threw blankets on their backs and took off riding bareback into the moors.

On and off for the next several hours, Marci painted the panel. Remembering the red lilies, she tucked some of Priscilla's crimson paint into the landscape. Standing back from the piece, she sensed Priscilla's presence in the brilliant color of the lilies set against the moors' subdued colors in mid-summer. The panel worked well with the explosion of colors in her fall panel of the hornbeams standing above the meadow that bordered one of the property's marshes.

She'd heard a rumor from Charlotte that Earl Morston was looking at real estate on the island. Marci was also thinking about Josh and Jake and the land deal they were negotiating. Technically, Josh and Jake weren't supposed to know the owner who had bid on the property. But on a small island, everyone knew the skinny on everyone else, especially when money was involved. If Morston was the buyer, how would Josh feel about working for him, knowing that he'd accused her mom of stealing some of his famous Boston photographic collection?

Josh and Jake were finishing their lunch when Marci came up the path heading toward the deck. Josh was probing Jake about the Taylor deal while sitting back in his director's chair.

"So Jake, what's with Old Man Taylor? Has he really accepted a bid on the property?"

"Yeah, Charlotte told me that some big wig in Boston will pay cash. You'll never see his name in the real estate listings. He hides it behind a trust with some innocuous name, like Morstonia Import and Export Business, also known as MIEB. He's supposed to be a large real estate owner and an art collector extraordinaire. They'll probably rename the airport after him by the time we finish building his houses."

"If he's that busy, how will he have time to vacation on the island?"

"Josh, you still don't get it. This is purely an investment property for him."

"But I thought you said that he was building an estate house and several cottages for his family?"

"I did. But I'll bet you a hundred dollars that business friends occupy them."

"You know, that name seems very familiar."

"Forget it, Josh. You and I don't play in those circles."

"Holy mackerel," Josh exclaimed. "I wonder if it's Earl Morston of Boston fame. He's the guy trying to take down Marci's mom by framing her for the robbery."

"No way, Josh. That's too bizarre a coincidence."

"Jake, how can we work for the guy who's trying to ruin Marci's mom? What will I tell Marci?" Josh said, staring in disbelief at his friend.

"Let's cross that bridge when we come to it."

"It's okay, Josh. I know it's Morston," Marci said as she stepped onto the deck.

Twenty-Three

Becki felt strange leaving her loft to go to the gym, knowing that at least two people could be watching her. *I guess I'm supposed to feel more relaxed because I have a bodyguard,* she thought. *A lot of help he'll be so far away from me I can't even see him.* She turned the corner out of the Mews and headed toward the gym.

Maybe I'll see just how good he is. Stepping into a doorway, she flattened herself against the wall and waited. Several people walked by, but not Keelan. Just as she was about to give up and continue walking, she heard his voice.

"Ms. Kea, you'll have to do better than that if you want to trick me."

"Oh, I wasn't trying to trick you. I—"

"Then what are you doing in this doorway?"

"Well, I stopped to see if I could find some gum in my purse. I didn't want to stop in the middle of the sidewalk. Someone could run into me and grab my purse."

"Or mug you since you had your head down. One thing I want to offer you is some basic visual self-defense."

"And this is your classroom?"

"You might say that. I don't stay right behind you. I move back and forth, so hiding in this doorway was obvious from across the street. Also, when I see you in gym clothes, which look very nice, I have a good idea of your destination. Now anyone who is tailing you might draw the same conclusion."

"Isn't it your job to tail me regardless of my destination? Or am I allowed to have a life?"

"Yes, my job is to keep you in sight regardless of where you go."

"Yeah, that's what I was afraid of."

Turning around to face Becki so she couldn't move forward, Keelan tried one more time to get on her better side. The intake interview didn't go as well as he had expected. Keta had warned him about the bristles on his daughter, but he wasn't expecting this level of defensiveness. Most clients were grateful to have a bodyguard.

"Ms. Kea, I know we didn't get off to a good start, but I *am* trying to protect you."

"Oh really. I thought maybe you were protecting your paycheck." Becki was getting annoyed with this guy. And she didn't like being cornered on the street where everyone could see them. She was anxious about him standing less than a foot away. Becki could smell his musk aftershave. His wonderful but disconcerting blue eyes poured out warmth, trying to get her to show a little less chill. But she was determined not to give an inch.

"Mr. Keelan, go right ahead and do your job. But I don't find it amusing to be startled like that on the street. And I think it's inappropriate for you to be standing where you are. If you don't mind, I'd like to get to my aerobics class."

Stepping to the side, Keelan let her go, wondering what made her the warm, loving person her father had also described. He waited a few seconds and then followed her.

But Becki kept the upper hand. Turning around quickly, she said, "Even *you* should know a setup." If it weren't for the flash of her blue eyes and swish of her platinum blonde hair, he would have missed the dash of a smile showing him that two could play this game.

Keelan slowed his pace to drop back from her. She will not be a straightforward case, he thought. She is hard to read, petulant, and unhelpful. But I still don't believe that this is her usual persona. She's afraid, and she doesn't want me to see it.

Keelan knew that someone else was following the two of them. But he didn't have time to detour. He had to follow her into the club. Guess I'll have to get a membership here, he thought to himself, pulling open the door to her club and spa.

Walking up to the front desk, he inquired about membership. The receptionist was stammering and stuttering over Keelan's good looks. Finally, a young man approached and offered to help Keelan. Glancing at the young receptionist, he rolled his eyes and took over the registration. It wasn't hard to figure out what was happening. Keelan was knockout good-looking. The ladies in the club would be glad when he started pumping iron.

Before filling out the necessary paperwork, Keelan asked where they held the aerobics class. Satisfied that Becki was reasonably safe, he asked for a brief tour. She would realize that he was in the gym at some point, even though the women's equipment was separated from the men's section on the second-floor loft. But the transparent, four-foot-high partition didn't stop the men gazing below to the gym floor where the women's classes were held. It certainly made lifting weights a bit more enjoyable. Keelan noticed that as soon as Becki's class started, several men sauntered over to the partition with their hand weights so they could watch.

Becki wore simple black leggings and a pink Boston Red Sox T-shirt that came down to about mid-thigh. She had pulled back her hair in a ponytail, except short curls kept popping out as she exercised. Even with how she dressed, Keelan could see her beautifully shaped body. Her arms showed muscular definition from weight training, and she moved with the assurance of a dancer. He wondered if she ever went ballroom dancing or out to clubs at night. Maybe he could cut in and ask her to dance. He quickly stopped his mind from wandering into dangerous territory.

Walking back to the desk with the trainer, Keelan filled out the paperwork and then stepped into the club's café. Becki would be out in about fifteen minutes. The café would give him a direct view of her when she exited.

His mind went back to the other person following Becki. Keelan knew almost instinctively that someone was shadowing him. He strongly suspected that the man was tracking Becki's movements. What he missed was the shadow turning back toward Becki's loft.

This shadow belonged to a slight, spry man in his early fifties who moved like quicksilver. He had been following Becki for a few weeks and knew her routine. His first attempt to enter her loft had failed miserably at the top of the stairs. Both the stairwell door and Becki's residence had a double locking system. It wouldn't be easy breaking into the loft through the door. He hoped the rooftop would lend itself to that task. He was pleasantly surprised to find that skylights covered most of the roof. Glass was messy, but he'd go in when he was sure she wasn't home. He was banking that the photos he needed were somewhere in her studio. Morston didn't like him coming back empty-handed, so he'd have to be sure of her routine and Keelan's before he made his move. He wanted Becki and Keelan to get comfortable with their relationship. He needed both of them occupied before he made his move.

Becki came bursting out of the gym and into the café, laughing about something with several other women in her class. Sitting on the opposite side of the coffee bar, Keelan didn't think they could see him. But now he was trapped. Leaving the café might startle her. That would only increase the personal tension between them. Choosing to sit and wait it out, he slowly sipped his latte and read his book.

The women were laughing and kidding around. Keelan listened until he could pick out Becki's laughter. Even with the ambient chatter of the café, he recognized her flighty, trill-like laughter that was very engaging. After about half an hour, two of the young women got up and headed toward him. One of them was Becki. He'd temporarily forgotten that the restrooms were behind him. The women were still laughing as they rounded the corner of the bar where Keelan had taken a small table. Becki was behind the other woman, so she hadn't seen him yet.

Rather than try to hide his presence, he casually looked up as they passed by. He saw Becki stiffen and then try to cover her surprise. Keelan smiled at her gently to soften the blow. Becki met him with a steely glare, a touch of anger on her face. She'd forgotten that he was tailing her. Wait until she finds out that I've joined the club, Keelan thought. Boy, this case got complicated fast. Everywhere he turned, he felt like a blundering idiot with her. He couldn't get a handle on her, and every encounter seemed to make it worse.

Keelan debated whether to drop the case or send her some roses when the women emerged from the ladies' room. Trying to appear fully engaged with his book, he didn't look up as they passed. He was pretty sure she wouldn't allow eye contact again.

Sitting down, Sally, one of Becki's friends, leaned down close to the tabletop and whispered, "Did you see that guy over by the ladies' room? Wow, who cut him out of *GQ* and left him here? Connie, let's take another trip to the ladies' room. Maybe we can get him to join us for coffee."

"No!" Becki fired back.

"No? What's with you, girl? You're the most eligible of us all."

"This might be your lucky day," Sally said excitedly. She was hoping she'd get to meet him. She was fresh out of a messy divorce. But who would turn down an introduction to someone as handsome as Keelan?

"Will you guys cut it out? Can't we just have coffee for once and forget about my love life? Anyway, I've got to be going. I have a deadline to meet, remember?"

"You go along, Cinderella. Leave him to us. We'll find out his details and report back," Connie replied.

"Look, I'm not interested in—" But before Becki could even get the sentence finished, Keelan strolled by their table and out the door. She heaved a sigh of relief as he exited to the outside.

"Well, there goes Prince Charming, right out from under our nose. Darn Becki, now you'd better leave. Maybe you can follow him."

"Will you please stop? See you on Thursday." Becki put a ten-dollar bill on the table, exited the café, and turned in the opposite direction of Keelan.

Fortunately, he had not turned toward her studio. He waited until she'd gotten another block away before pursuing her from the other side of the street. Two encounters in one day were more than enough. Her adrenalin needed a rest. He strolled up the sidewalk when he was sure she wouldn't look back.

Twenty-Four

The island paper still didn't carry any news about what caused the homes to disappear. But the police were busy. The people who owned the houses weren't demanding help at the station. But that was the problem. The police considered owners missing until located. Calling to seek the status of family members was proving to be difficult and unnerving. Several owners had threatened lawsuits against the town and state. Husbands whose wives and children were missing were either overcome with grief or hostile and angry. There was a numbness that even the police force felt. It didn't seem real.

Josh and Jake found out how real it was upon their return to town. The police had an arrest warrant out for them as the home builders. But it was hard to pin a charge on them since there was no precedent and the evidence had disappeared. After an hour of questioning, the police let Josh and Jake go with orders not to leave the island. Of course, there was always the chance that they would disappear.

Marci was finishing one of the panels for her show when Josh raced through the door into the studio and skidded to a stop a few feet from her.

"Marci, I just came back from downtown. Jake and I got arrested trying to get a cup of coffee at the Donut."

"What? Arrested? On what charge, overeating?"

"Marci, I'm not kidding."

"Then, what for? You weren't speeding again, I hope."

"It's the houses. They really are missing."

"No kidding. Who reported it?"

"Jake and I never found that out. But the police came after us because we had built the houses. They thought we might know how or why they disappeared. They questioned us for over an hour."

"What about our kayaking in the marsh? Did you tell them?"

"No, Jake and I didn't have to. One owner had flown in on his private jet to be with his family. When he arrived in Pocomo, he had the same experience we did. Only for him, it was a little more personal," Josh continued with a chuckle.

"Josh, it's not funny. Houses are one thing, but missing people are serious."

"I know. It's sounding like one of Trish's mystery novels."

"Josh, at some point, you're going to have to tell Don about this morning, or your nose will grow," Marci chided, lifting her paintbrush and touching his nose with fresh oil paint.

"Marci, cut it out. Now, who's being silly?"

"Okay. But you look sweet with a blue nose."

"Hey, were any of the kids in your class among the missing?"

"No, they all were *very* present. We had a great time in the moors. Only one child lives over by Pocomo, but I'm not sure exactly where her home is. I expect we'll find out soon enough."

"Don said they wouldn't know for sure if people are missing until the police can't contact them here or on the mainland. So what's for dinner?"

"Good question. How about we call Jake and Lovey and see if they want to go out? It might be an interesting night to be in town, provided you don't get arrested again. I've almost finished this last panel. I could take a break tonight."

"Marci, is this a solo show?"

"Yes, why do you ask?"

"No particular reason. I was thinking this morning that it would be fun for you, Becki, and your mom to do a combined show. Your mom could provide the old and new photos from her collection. You could show the varied landscapes, and Becki could show her Nantucket wildflower botanicals."

"I don't know. I'm not sure Mom is up to the publicity it would bring."

"But maybe it would boost her reputation. She's so loved on this island. With Priscilla gone, the islanders might enjoy seeing the family's work. Who knows, maybe some other artist will appear and offer to paint with you as Priscilla did."

"Now you're exploring territory where I'm not sure I can go. Thanks, hon. Not a terrible suggestion from an old house painter. Right now, I just need to get ready for the show," Marci responded, putting a dab of paint on Josh's hand.

But Josh didn't give up. He thought Marci was much too humble. Wiping his hand on Marci's smock, he asked, "Are your mom and dad coming for the show?"

"They were as of two weeks ago. I can't predict what will transpire once they're home from the Caribbean."

"Oh man, this is not the best timing. Not only do photos disappear and reappear in your mom's studio, but her daughter's husband builds houses that disappear. So much for our quiet life."

"Josh, I'm hoping not to make a big deal about Mom coming. If no one knows until the actual day, we might even have a calm, pleasant show."

"Well, disappearing estate homes won't help my business much. I hope it doesn't affect the sale of the Taylor land. That's an enormous job. We could afford to go with your mom and dad to the Caribbean next year if this comes through."

"That would be fun. I'd love to paint in the tropics." But as she closed the door to the studio and began walking with Josh toward the house, she stopped with a thoughtful look on her face.

"Do you think I should call Mom? Or at least call Becki before the Boston newspapers carry the story?"

"Yes, I do. How about I call Lovey, and you call Becki and your mom?"

But Becki was not home when Marci called. Little Cliffey, Trish's preschooler, answered the phone.

"Heh-woe, Auntie B's house."

"Cliffey, is that you? Where's your mommy?"

"Right here," Trish answered gruffly, not knowing who the caller might be. "Who is this?"

"Trish, it's Marci."

"Oh, Marci, I'm so sorry. I thought it might be a reporter. Cliffey got to the phone before I could read the caller ID. Becki had some problems with the press lately. What's up?"

"Not to add to Becki's worries, but I wanted to alert her to something that's happened on the island that will be more fodder for the Boston reporters."

"What now? We practically threw the last reporter out of her loft."

"I'll tell you, but you need to let me tell Becki myself. Have her call me on my cell." Marci then related to Trish Priscilla's disappearance and the missing homes. She skipped the adventure in the marsh.

"Marci, this may throw Becki. Not only does she have reporters clamoring for an interview, but she's also fed up with the bodyguard your dad got for her, and he's only been on the job one day."

Quickly dodging that subject, Marci asked, "Hey, are you and Paul coming for the opening?"

"Are you kidding? I wouldn't miss it for the world. Paul will be out of town. But that's just his poor planning. Besides, you know I never turn down free champagne and hotel accommodations on Nantucket."

"Well, this season may have just hit its all-time low even before it gets off the ground."

Trish expressed disbelief until Marci told her about Josh and Jake getting arrested. But she was worried when Marci relayed the rumor about Morston investing on the island.

"Trish, will you be there when Becki gets home?"

"Yes, Paul is going to pick up Cliffey and me on his way home from work."

"It might be good for you to call Becki later on tonight after I tell her the story. If you need to talk with me, I'll be with Josh, Jake, and Lovey having dinner on the pier. We want to see what the buzz is downtown."

"You mean to see what the gossip is, don't you?"

"Well, yes. But we're keeping a low profile. None of us wants to spend the night in jail."

"I should be here when Becki comes back from the club. Paul's picking us up at six, and Becki said that she'd be back around five-thirty."

"Just have her call me as soon as possible. Hopefully, it won't hit the Boston papers until tomorrow morning."

Twenty-Five

Stopping at a flower seller, Becki bought a bouquet of peonies and a newspaper. She smiled and chatted with Max and his dog Spott, her longtime friends at the corner newsstand.

Keelan waited until she was a block away before he approached. Forking out a dollar for the newspaper and trying not to look too dumb, he picked up a bunch of peonies and asked the man what they were. Max was no fool.

"Those are peonies, sir. Why don't you buy that bunch for your lady?" he said, playing with Keelan a bit.

"Well," he paused. Keelan was now wondering what he was doing with a bunch of peonies in his hand. "How much are they?"

"Ten dollars, sir."

"Wow, they must be special flowers. I didn't know flowers came that steep."

"If you were here about three minutes earlier, you would have seen a young lady as lovely as the peonies. This time of year, she buys them from me every couple of days. I think they're one of her favorites." Max watched Keelan's face for a reaction as he started to wrap the flowers in newspaper.

"Mmm, thanks," Keelan said, handing Max a ten and taking the bunch of peonies. Now, what in the world am I going to do with these? I must be out of my mind. Or maybe this is a way to her warmer side, Keelan thought, always up for a challenge. Putting the bunch of flowers to his nose, he inhaled their pungent fragrance.

"Wonderful smell, isn't it?"

"Yeah."

"Well, so long. Oh, you might want to wipe the pollen from your nose before you get home." Max smiled as Keelan turned to go. He and Spott always enjoyed a little romance. There seemed to be so little of it these days. It must be the warmer weather.

"Thanks," Keelan said rather sheepishly as he reached in his pocket for his handkerchief.

By this time, Keelan had lost Becki. He would have to hurry. But he didn't want the newsman to see him racing down the block. Fortunately, Becki was strolling along the sidewalk, oblivious to what was going on around her. Keelan was pleased to see her relaxed and happy.

Becki skirted the edge of a small park that bordered the Mews where her loft was located. She often came here to sit in the sun, watch the kids playing ball, or people watch. It was one of the Boston parks open enough to be safe. She sat down on one bench and put her face in the peonies. Then she just stared up at the sky and over the park, enjoying one of the first spring days in Boston.

Keelan slowed his pace, checking for the man tailing him. No one was in sight. Becki seemed lighthearted and even had a little spring in her step. Amazing what aerobics and peonies can do, he thought. Maybe there was hope for a working truce between them. Settling down on a bench out of sight, Keelan contemplated how he could improve things with Becki. He ran through several scenarios as he watched her. None of them seemed right. Maybe it's best to leave well enough alone. But if that's the case, I'll have to ditch these peonies. Deciding to take them home, he waited on the bench until Becki got up and headed down the Mews to her loft. Perhaps they would inspire him with how to get on her good side. He wondered if Max would say anything to her tomorrow. Probably not. A reliable customer was worth some silence.

He waited most of the afternoon. Finally, Stephen popped out of a cab and walked toward Becki's building. Keelan wasn't sure if Becki had told Stephen about him. There it was again, that awkwardness. I wonder how Stephen will react when Becki tells him of their encounter on the street today. Will he be sympathetic or jealous? Maybe she won't even tell him. One more unanswered question. And what about Becki and Stephen's relationship?

Just as he was picturing how he'd introduce himself to Stephen, a short, stocky man turned into the alley and headed toward Becki's building. Quickly getting to his feet, Keelan followed the man as far as possible without being discovered. He could just see the entrance to Becki's building from the street. The man walked confidently up the brick stairs and stood at the door. Keelan couldn't tell if he'd pushed a call button, but about thirty seconds later, he entered the building. Now Keelan wanted to know who he was and to which loft he was heading. Sprinting toward the steps, he put his key in the lock and raced into the hallway. The man was getting into the elevator but had heard the outside door close.

"Yo, dude, need a lift?" The young man popped his head out the elevator door, his tattooed arm holding it open. "This one's leaving any minute."

From a distance, Keelan hadn't seen the tattoos or how he dressed. "Not a likely stalker," he thought, but he'd check, anyway.

"No thanks. I'm going to check the mail first."

"Got it," he heard the young man say as the door closed. Stepping out into the hallway where the elevator was, Keelan looked to see what floor the man left the elevator. He waited until the elevator came back down to ensure that it didn't stop at other floors.

Walking back to his park bench, he checked his watch and made some notes. Then he sat back to read his newspaper, or at least appear to be reading it. Becki and Stephen could see him from the loft. He'd have a long wait until someone could relieve him for the night.

Keelan wasn't alone in his wait. Still lurking behind him was Becki's stalker. Satisfied that she would stay awhile in the apartment with Stephen, he took up a post far enough away to watch both Keelan and Becki. She rarely had visitors in the late afternoon. Stephen came after work or picked her up in a cab. Tonight, he needed the loft to be empty to determine how easy it would be to enter unnoticed and disappear just as quickly. He had only one aim: find the remaining photos. Hopefully, they'd be on a wall so he wouldn't have to rummage through files. Her mother had made his job tough, but he'd found what he was looking for, or at least most of it. The rest would come tomorrow. Slinking out of the park, he gave Keelan another passing look and disappeared into the evening darkness.

Twenty-Six

Josh and Marci met Jake and Lovey at Seaman Cook's on the fishing pier. They all liked the fresh catch of the day, and this was the place to get it directly off the boats. The islanders patronized this restaurant as the food was excellent and reasonable. It wasn't fancy. The tables sat out under awnings, and everyone used paper placemats. You didn't have to ask for water. It would be there thirty seconds after you sat down. And usually, you didn't even have to put in a drink order. The servers remembered the locals.

On a weeknight, islanders and longtime summer residents filled the place. Yes, you could smell the hot grease. But fried potato strings and onion rings were two of the specialties. And yes, when the wind was right, you could smell them filleting the fish. But that's what set Cook's apart and kept it going for sixty years. Most of the summer yachters had never set foot in it, which was probably for the best as sometimes the brawls at the bar also took out visitors. You had to stay sharp and know when danger was brewing.

Knowing what had happened at the police station and Pocomo Meadows, there was bound to be some spouting off about the missing houses. Josh instinctively chose a table away from the bar, tucked away in a corner and lit by Seaman's funky fish candles. He was only interested in observing tonight. He'd already had more participation in the event than he wanted.

The décor may have been from the 1950s, but the green and deep red marbleized vinyl seats were much more comfortable than some of the other restaurants around town. The tables were also vinyl or old wood, depending on who had donated them or what was available at Take It or Leave It.

"You know, I think Cook's gained some bar stools when the pharmacy closed. They look great," Josh commented, sitting down next to his wife.

"So what's everybody having?" Marci asked, warming her hands over the fish candle. "I wonder how many of these candles Seaman bought from The Seven Seas when they went out business. He seems to have an endless supply."

"Let's hope he's not special ordering them," Lovey piped up as she disappeared behind the oversized menu.

"Where else in New England can you get hand-carved fish candles?" Josh asked, smiling at Jake.

"In multiple colors and stripes," Marci chimed in. "Come on, Jake, we know you secretly have a stake in their manufacturing. I've seen them on your picnic table at home."

"Ha, ha, very funny. Just wait until the next power outage. You'll come crawling to me for my stock."

"Have you folks decided?" the waitress asked, looking around the table. "Oh, hi, Lovey, I didn't see you behind the menu."

"Hi, Marina. I'm sure Jake knows what he wants," she said, looking toward her husband. All of them knew Jake changed his mind at least two or three times before the order finally left the table.

"Just to turn over a new leaf, I will order first. I'd like the fried calamari, please." Jake piped up. Lovey rolled her eyes.

"I'll have the sea bass," Marci said.

"Oh, maybe I'll have that instead," Jake added.

"Okay, no calamari and two sea bass."

"Make that three," Josh added. "How about you, Lovey?"

"I'll have the fish and chips with the lobster."

"Good, now what can I get you all to drink?"

"Marina, I'd like to change my order."

"Sure, Jake. Let me guess, fish and chips, but no lobster?"

"How'd you know?"

"Oh, it's a waitress thing. By the way, we're out of calamari. Now, how about that drink order?"

"Say, is your name really Marina, or is that just for the job?"

"Jake, what's come over you? That was flat-out impolite," Lovey snapped at her husband.

"Don't worry, Lovey. I get it all the time. It's Italian."

All three of them were laughing so hard it took a while to get the drinks ordered. When Marina got to Jake, she just paused politely.

"He'll have an Australian beer on tap," Lovey said, grinning.

"Okay, I'll be back with your drinks in a minute."

"Lovey, how do you stand it? It's a good thing he doesn't do this at home," Marci chided.

"I do the decision-making in the kitchen," Lovey added. "Besides, on all other decisions, he's swift and decisive. Ask Josh."

"Can we talk about something else, please?" Jake asked.

But before anyone could answer, a police officer entered the restaurant. Sitting down at the bar, he ordered a cup of coffee and chowder.

"Okay, everybody, just keep a low profile and pretend we're not here," Josh whispered.

"Josh, stop it. You'd think that you were on the run. You guys did nothing wrong. Arresting you was wrong. They even admitted it. If we act like normal people, we're less likely to call attention to ourselves than if we whisper through the entire dinner," Marci pleaded.

"Agreed?" Lovey asked, looking around.

"Agreed." Everyone nodded.

The two couples were busily enjoying their salads when some tourists wandered in. They looked startled at the casual dress and décor and seemed to sit down reluctantly at a table near the bar.

Their meals came, and Jake immediately started inspecting everyone's plate before diving into his own. Lovey tried to change the subject by asking about Marci's upcoming show.

"Are you excited, Marci?"

"No, you know me. I don't get worked up about it until the first person walks into the gallery."

"Maybe that will be Becki and Trish," Lovey answered.

"I hope so. They planned on coming. But things are getting a little more uncomfortable for Becki with Mom out of the country. Josh and I are trying to get a hold of her to give her a heads up in case the *Boston Flame* publishes something about the missing houses."

"Do the Boston reporters know that you're Becki's sister?" Jake asked.

"I'm not sure. But it only takes one reporter to start a domino effect in all the newspapers," Marci responded. Her body language showed the toll she was paying for being part of the family scandal, even on Nantucket.

"All right, no more talk about problems," Josh said quickly, looking over at his wife. "Marci, why don't you tell us about the show?"

"I am excited about showing some of my new landscape panels. Josh even suggested that Becki, Mom, and I do a show together. He thinks it might bring some positive publicity for Mom."

"I think that's a great idea. Your work would be a wonderful collage of expression, even if you all weren't related." Lovey had picked up on Josh's cue and was also trying to keep the conversation light.

"Here's to Marci's show," Josh said, raising his beer and clinking glasses with the others.

Little did they know that at that very minute, another person was tapping on the glass windows of Becki's loft to see how easily they would break. Perched on the roof in the shadows, he studied the loft below. Just like the great blue heron of Pocomo Meadows, he was still, waiting for the precise moment to strike.

Josh and Jake didn't realize they were making enough noise to attract the police officer's attention at the bar. He had finished his day and was busily downing a bowl of chowder and a basket of fish and chips. Lovey sized him up as part of the summer contingent. They knew most of the permanent force.

He appeared to be well over six feet tall based on how he wrapped his legs completely around the barstool. His shoes looked to be at least a size twelve. He was young, maybe in his twenties, and clearly worked out. He had a buzz haircut, and his uniform might soon have to go up a size, but he packed all the standard police garb.

The officer was off duty, enjoying his dinner and chatting with the bartender. But he could hear the laughter and quietly wished he was part of the fun. Without moving an inch, he turned his head around to see what they were all toasting. Lovey faced the officer, so she saw him study them over his shoulder and smile generously.

"Guys, settle down. That officer is checking us out."

"And so are a few other tables. Why don't you two tell us about the land you looked at today?" Marci asked.

But that was not a safe topic either. The Taylor property wasn't far from Pocomo Meadows.

"Uh, oh. He's watching us," warned Lovey. "Nothing is ever easy with you two guys, is it?"

Jake continued. "The title searches reveal conflicting lot lines. Some are on paper, and some have stone markers. The Taylor family has been buying property out there since Adam and Eve took their first vacation here. It's a pretty safe bet they own all of it. But that will ultimately have to be proven in the title search and survey work. The remains of the original house and barn are still visible in the ground, if you know where to look."

"Only their house and barn didn't vanish," Josh quipped with a childlike grin on his face.

"Josh, cut it out. You two are in enough trouble already." Marci gave Josh her killer look. The officer took a second glance.

"Here's something that will disappear, our dinners. Boy, am I starved," Jake announced as the waitress handed out their meals.

"What do you mean, starved? You finished Marci's chowder and my salad," Lovey exclaimed.

"How do you keep this man fed?" Marci asked.

"I think he eats his second meal at your house. That's why Josh is so thin, and Jake is, shall we say, robust?"

The dinners were delicious. Everyone was chatting over cappuccinos while Jake finished Lovey's dessert. They all had finally relaxed and forgotten the houses when the officer swung himself off the barstool and headed in their direction.

"Oh, boy. Here comes tonight's entertainment," Lovey remarked, watching the officer close in on their table.

"What entertainment? I didn't know they have entertainment here. When did—" Josh didn't get to finish his sentence.

"Are you folks enjoying this fine evening? It's a quiet night for my favorite restaurant."

"We are, officer, especially after a hard day's work." Marci quickly responded, hoping to stop what Josh was about to say.

"You know, it took me a month on the force before I discovered this place."

"Well, it's been here for sixty years, so I think it's safe to say that it will be here a few more," Lovey added.

"Say, aren't you the two guys they arrested today about the houses?"

"Yes, they are. Lovey and I are chaperoning them. By the way, I'm Marci, and this is my husband, Josh."

"I'm Lovey, and I'm married to the one over there who's still eating."

"Hi, I'm Jake. Nice to meet you," Jake said, holding out the hand without food in it.

"They let you guys go free right before I returned to the station, so I missed all the excitement."

"Did they arrest anyone else after us?" Jake asked between spoonfuls of pistachio ice cream.

"Jake, cut it out. You know he can't talk about that," Lovey said, interrupting her husband. "Besides, he's off duty."

"Well, there seems to be plenty of fodder for the newspapers. Can you believe that one explanation is that aliens beamed up the houses like on Star Trek?"

"That would take a pretty big transporter," Jake commented. "Although, do you remember the movie where they beamed up the whales?"

"Hey, are you a Trekkie?" the officer asked.

"Oh no, here goes our evening," Lovey sighed, putting her head in her hands. "Marci, maybe you and I should leave now."

"Mam, I'm sorry. I didn't mean to interrupt your dinner. My days are usually so filled with problems that I enjoyed hearing you all having such a good time."

"Why don't you sit down and join us?" suggested Jake.

"Okay. You guys talk Star Trek while Lovey and I go to the ladies' room," Marci said, getting up from the table.

"Ever notice that women always go to the ladies' room together?" Jake asked.

"Yeah, what's that all about?" the young officer asked innocently.

"Trust me. You don't want to go there. You'll only dig yourself in deeper," Josh responded.

"So what role did you two play with the missing houses?" the officer probed.

Twenty-Seven

S tephen and Becki strolled toward the harbor. They had just arrived at the restaurant when Becki's cell phone rang. Checking the caller ID, Becki looked at Stephen with a worried face.

"Who is it?"

"Stephen, it's Marci. She never uses her cell unless it's important. I wonder what's wrong."

"Answer it, babe. Maybe there's nothing wrong," Stephen said, mentally preparing for the storm that was about to hit.

"Marci, are you okay?"

"Sure. Lovey and I just came into the ladies' room to get away from the Star Trek conversation going on at our table."

"Oh, I thought maybe something was wrong since you used your cell."

"I wanted to call and double-check that you'll be at my show. But there is something else."

"It's not about Mom and Dad, is it?"

"No, not directly. But it affects you and me."

"Oh, great. I can hardly wait to hear this. Go on, tell me. And yes, I am coming over for your show, though I'm not sure about Stephen."

Lovey was worried about the men getting into trouble. She signaled to Marci that she was returning to the table. Marci sat down on the comfortable couch and prayed that Becki wouldn't get too upset over the news.

"Great. I'm so excited you are coming. Now for the news. It's actually kind of hard to explain, but this is what happened on the island today."

By the time Stephen had ushered Becki to the outside waiting area and then gone off to the bar for their drinks, Marci had time to tell her sister some of what had happened, leaving out the arrest Josh and Jake experienced that day. Becki took it pretty well, mostly because she was in the restaurant and not at home. But the news hit the gnawing pit in her stomach that she'd had ever since Keelan confronted her on the street. Bringing Marci up to date on that part of her life would have to wait as Stephen headed back from the bar.

"So I guess I better get ready for more newspaper reporters?"

"I'm afraid so. It's right up the *Boston Flame's* alley. We're hoping the news doesn't hit the press for a few days, but you need to know. When you come out for the show, we'll talk some more."

"Are Mom and Dad coming to the show?"

"Yes, as far as I know. But I haven't spoken to them since they left for the Caribbean. We'll all be able to catch up on what's happening here on the island and any progress they've made in Mom's robbery case."

"Marci, Stephen is coming back from the bar. I've got to go."

"Fine. I just didn't want you to be surprised if you saw something in the newspapers."

"Okay, bye."

Making their way through the crowded tables, Becki and Stephen finally sat down at the edge of the deck overlooking the harbor. The sparkling city lights surrounded them as they watched the harbor cruise boats pass back and forth.

Boston's harbor was one of Becki's favorite places, second only to Fenway Park, watching the Red Sox play baseball. Becki grew up near Boston, while Stephen was raised in New York. She'd never dated a man who wasn't a Red Sox fan, but they'd agreed to keep the rivalry to a minimum. When new seats in the Green Monster section of the stadium went on sale, Becki had grabbed two of them so she and Trish could go to the games. Stephen was not interested. He wished there was a game tonight. Becki needed something to distract her from the stress of her mom's investigation and the uncertainty of their jobs. He missed the light-hearted person he knew so well.

"Do you think you'll be able to go to Marci's show?" Becki asked. They had talked briefly about it before they went to Madeira. But with all the issues they'd encountered upon arriving home, Becki had put off pressing Stephen for an answer. It was now down to the wire.

"Becki, I'd planned on it—"

"*Now* what?" Becki interrupted.

"I want to go, and I'm planning to go, but I have to leave open the possibility that Justin will want me to close the deal in Madeira."

"Oh, I see. Maybe some other time," Becki responded, staring at her wineglass, not looking him in the eye.

He'd been trying to keep the conversation light, but Becki was proving to be more of a challenge than usual. He'd gotten used to the artistic temperament of her family, but something was bothering her tonight. She was locked up tight. He knew better than to press her. More conflict would not help.

"How about we say that I'll do my best to come, even if Justin has to fly by himself on the private jet? There are many people on the engineering and construction team that would love a free ticket to Europe."

"I'm not sure that Europe is worth eight hours enclosed in a plane with Justin," Becki joked. Finally, at last, Stephen thought. Now maybe we can have a better evening.

It wasn't long before Becki turned to see one waiter approaching with more wine and appetizers. "Stephen, here comes Kurt. I'll bet he's surprised to see us on a weeknight."

"He'd better get used to it. I think this is our place. We should come here more often. The water and city lights are soothing."

"Not to mention the wine," Becki said, holding up her glass. "What shall we toast to tonight?"

"How about just being alive?" Stephen answered.

"Sounds good to me," Becki added, sitting back and looking at the skyline. "Stephen, I know we love natural settings, but there is something extraordinary about the city lights sparkling on the water."

"You know, I think you can almost see your loft from here."

"No way, Stephen. Where are you looking?"

"Over there behind the brick building on the harbor. Aren't you right behind it?"

"Okay, Superman, your X-ray eyes can see through the brick?" Becki teased, looking at him with her deep blue eyes and puckish grin.

"But if the brick building weren't there, it would be a straight shot."

"Yeah, and I would pay more than a mortgage just to rent it. No thanks, I'll take my view, limited as it is."

Little did they know that Lyrica's thief was inspecting her view as he deftly picked his way across the rooftop opposite Becki's loft. It would make his escape tricky if discovered, but he prided himself on never getting caught.

Measuring the distance between the rooftops with his eyes and then, using a rope line, he calculated the leap between the two buildings. It would be a hard landing in the alley if he missed, but that's why he had a tie line attached to his belt harness. He hadn't been a champion long jumper and pole vaulter in high school for nothing. Not bad for a short guy.

Drilling a few holes in the roof to anchor his line didn't take long. No one would hear him with the echoes of traffic below. He speculated that the roof was about eight inches thick, including several inches of tar coating. The people in the apartment below were not home. He'd memorized the schedules of the various dwellers until he knew their habits precisely. Tonight was not the night to break in. But even the dry run had made his forehead sweat. He ran and leaped like a cat over the alley, quickly and skillfully, taking his rope in hand. Humph, he thought. That was easier than I expected.

Becki's loft was the only one with rooftop conservatory windows. She had added even more to take advantage of the light for her painting. Hunching over, he made his way to the first row of windows. He could hardly control his delight when he saw an entire panel of windows across the loft. Three panels were open tonight, giving him a choice of entry. He hoped the weather stayed clear, so he didn't have to break the glass getting in.

Peering over the side of the window panel closest to him, he saw it was an easy drop into the loft. He chuckled to himself about how simple this was going to be. He'd have to cut the screen, but that was child's play in his book. The real challenge was in the studio. He didn't know how easy it would be to find the photos. Artists were often messy. Nothing was ever in the right place. For many thieves, this was an added challenge. For him, it was a tedious annoyance.

Carefully lowering his line into the loft, he calculated the drop. Isn't that nice. A soft couch just where I need it. How convenient, he thought. This girl makes it easy. Her mother's studio had been unmercifully hard to break into. He saw Becki's homemade cookies on the table in the kitchen. Maybe for Keelan? He was looking forward to besting Keelan.

Twenty-Eight

antucket's fog was legendary, and tonight was no exception. Standing at the departure gate, Josh and Marci couldn't even see the end of the runway as they waited patiently for Lyrica, Keta, Trish, and Becki in her dad's private plane. Usually, they used the jet for business. But security had become so tight the Keas flew only in their aircraft to avoid the press.

Standing outside in the fog, Marci and Josh could hear the engines winding down for a landing. Just when they thought the jet would touch down, the pilot gunned the engine, pulled up, and flew off into the thick fog. Marci turned to Josh, a stricken look on her face. "Josh, why did they pull out at the last minute?"

"I'm not sure. Maybe they couldn't see the runway to land. It's pea soup out there. Let's wait and see if they come back and try again."

After what seemed like an eternity, they heard the whine of jet engines again.

"Okay, hon, here they come again," Josh said, turning to Marci. They were both looking up into the thick fog, mentally figuring out how many more seconds it would be before they heard the screech of the wheels burning rubber on the tarmac and the back whine of the engines as the flaps slowed down the plane.

But it was not to be. Once again, the plane tried to land, checked, and then gunned its engines to lift off again.

"Josh, they can't find the runway," Marci gasped, panic in her voice.

"I don't think it's that. Maybe they can't tell their placement on the runway and if there is enough space to land." Marci was staring at him, her face ashen with tears spilling down her cheeks.

"This is going to be just like Casablanca. We'll never see them again."

"Wait, let's go inside and see if we can find out what's going on before we jump to any conclusions. They have an experienced pilot. If it's not safe to land, they'll fly to the Cape."

"We're cursed."

"Marci, don't say things like that, or you'll curse us real-time."

"I'm sorry, Josh. But nothing seems to be right. First the houses, and now a missing plane."

"Oh, I didn't even think of that. But we heard the plane. It just didn't land."

"Maybe the reason they didn't land is that there's no runway."

"Marci, there's a scientific explanation for everything, even if it's weird. Just because some homes disappear doesn't mean that other things are vanishing. Why didn't we vanish? We were in the marsh."

"But those houses didn't vanish before our eyes. They were gone before we got there. Maybe Nantucket has vanished, and that's why the plane can't find the runway."

"Stop it, Marci. You stay here. I'll go inside and see what's going on." But as he turned to walk inside the small private jet building, he heard a plane engine starting its descent once more.

"Oh no, they're going to try again. What if they crash right here in front of our eyes?"

But before Josh could answer, they heard the screech of burning rubber and the back whine of the jet's engines.

"They made it, Josh! They made it," Marci screamed. "Let's go."

"Marci, you know you can't go out there until the stairs come down and the engines are off."

"But it's *our* plane."

At that moment, the spotlight from the jet terminal focused on the plane, and the stairs came down. Lyrica was first, followed by Keta, Trish, and Becki. Then two guys emerged that neither Marci nor Josh recognized.

"Mom, Dad, we're here. We're here," Marci shouted, running to the stairs. Plowing right into them, she hugged Lyrica, then Keta and Becki. "Mom, we were so scared. What happened up there?"

"Why don't you ask the pilot? Here he comes down the stairs," said Keta, turning everyone's head toward the stairs.

"You both look a bit green," Marci said. Then, eyeing the two men who had reached the bottom of the stairs, she hesitated. "Who are those dudes?" she whispered to Keta.

"Let me introduce you to Daniel Keelan and Matt Rossby, our bodyguards."

"Bodyguards? Can I have one too?" Marci was quick to comment.

"Well, I guess we'll have to see if you need one."

Now walking across the tarmac, the two bodyguards dressed in khakis and polo shirts reached out to shake hands and introduce themselves to Marci and Josh.

"Matt is taking care of Lyrica, and Daniel is guarding Becki. We'll chat more when we're back at the house. You'll see a lot of them over the next few days."

Walking back to the private jet lounge, Marci pulled alongside Becki and whispered, "Becki, your guy is *so* good looking. I'd like the job of guarding *his* body."

"Marci, cut it out. He's annoying to have around."

"What's with the attitude? I'd be elated to have someone like him around."

"Marci, it doesn't work that way. I'll fill you in later after we've had our family get-together."

"I don't know. If I were single and had a guy like that following me, I'd be ecstatic. I wonder what happens if you date your bodyguard. Does that mean that you get another one, and what if—?"

"You're hopeless, Marci. Come on. Let's go make sure they get the luggage into the right vehicles."

Josh pulled up to the curb in Marci's forest green Jeep and handed her the keys while he went back to the lot to find Keta's Land Rover. They would need both cars for the luggage. Keta was still chatting with the pilot as Dan and Matt went to rent a small Jeep.

"Lyrica, why don't you and the gals go ahead? Josh and I can take the Land Rover and pick up the beer. Matt and Dan can follow in their rental Jeep."

"Don't forget to tell them they're invited to the opening of Marci's show," Lyrica piped up.

Matt wasn't too happy about leaving the women unescorted. "Mr. Kea, shouldn't someone go with the ladies?"

"I think we're pretty safe on a night like this. There's pizza at the other end, so I don't think anyone will dawdle. It's a tradition that all arriving guests get to taste Marci's famous pizza sauce."

Marci drove off with Lyrica, Becki, and Trish, the Jeep's taillights quickly disappearing into the fog.

At least Dad didn't suggest Dan come with us, Becki thought. She wasn't sure how it would feel sitting right next to him. Oh, how she wanted to share her feelings about him with Marci. At least if he wasn't right next to her, she could take some time to sort out what she felt. Becki was sure Marci would pick up on her nervous tension. She probably already knew. Marci had a sixth sense about things between the two of them.

As Becki struggled with her feelings about Keelan, her mind went to Stephen. A small part of her was happy he wasn't here for the show. Now, what's that all about? And it wasn't because of all the stress she and Stephen faced at home.

No, something had changed inside of her. Daniel Keelan had lit a spark in her life. Nantucket would be a good neutral ground to see if something was starting between the two of them that wasn't part of the contract with her father. She wondered if Dan felt it as well. Maybe Marci would have some good advice.

"Marci, even in this fog, it's good to be back on the island," Lyrica commented as the car slowly made its way toward Wauwinet. They could only see the dotted line down the middle of the road, and not much of it. The fog was so heavy an oncoming car's headlights didn't even appear until they were right upon them.

"Marci, are you excited about the show?" Becki asked.

"Yes, to be truthful, I am. It's the first solo show I've done on the island. This is a big yachting weekend besides the film festival going on with its normal swarm of visitors. I'd like to sell some paintings if I can."

"Maybe we should put sold signs on a few that you don't want to part with just to spur your guests to buy," Trish suggested.

"I thought we could subtly spread the rumor that a famous mystery writer was interested in one painting for the cover of her next book. How does that sound?" Becki added as she raised her eyebrows at Trish with the question.

"Trish, have you two been scheming on the way over from Boston?" Marci asked.

"Don't look at me. I'm innocent," pleaded Trish. "It's all Becki's idea. But it has a nice ring to it."

"Mom, have you ever thought about the three of us doing a show together?" Becki asked. "Trish suggested it the other day, and I think it would be fun. What do you think?"

"I'd love to do a combined show. I'm just not sure this is the best time to do one."

"We thought about that. Maybe it could bring you good publicity and get people's minds off what's in the *Boston Flame*," Trish answered. "If you're going to be in the news, you might as well get good press."

"I know you're right. But I have to be concerned about the legal aspect too. Let me talk to your dad. We'll see what he says."

"You know, there are never enough good-looking men around. I'll bet Josh and Jake would love a break from hauling canvases back and forth, now that we have Dan and Matt around," Trish added.

"Speaking of bodyguards, where did Dad find those two? I'd like to have one," Marci joked. "What do you think of them? Is it weird to be followed everywhere?"

"Yes," Becki said emphatically.

"When you all hear the story about what happened to Josh and me in the marsh, Dad might want to hire another one. Or maybe you'd trade me Keelan, for my new one?"

Zing. That hit Becki right between the eyes. Tears started to well up, and Marci saw them in the rear-view mirror. Looking back at her sister, she noticed her wiping away the tears to prevent them from being seen. Pulling over to the side of the road, Marci brought the Jeep to a halt.

"Okay, Becki, out with it before we get to the guys. What's going on?" she asked. Marci and Lyrica turned from their front seats to see Becki wiping the tears off her cheek.

"You guys will think I'm crazy if I tell you," Becki choked out the words.

Sensing that it must be about Keelan, Lyrica put her head through the two seats and caressed Becki's cheek. "Come on, baby, what happened that you're crying? You were fine on the plane. A little sick, but not crying," Lyrica said, trying some humor to break the tension.

"We'd better have this out before we get to the house. It will be too crowded to talk," Marci added.

"I don't want you carrying this all night. What's going on that's making you cry? Is it because Stephen can't come to the show?" Lyrica asked, gently looking into Becki's sky-blue eyes.

This brought on more tears and sobs, so the three of them let her cry for a while until she could regain enough composure to talk. Trish had put her arm around Becki to hold her.

"Oh, you're going to think this is so immature. I'm not even sure what *is* going on."

"Going on with Stephen?" Lyrica guessed.

"No, well, sort of. Oh, it's all so icky trying to say this."

"Becki," Marci shushed Lyrica and Trish. "You know we girls don't keep secrets from each other. Whatever happened that would cause such a reaction, I can guarantee it's not immature."

"Becki, does this have anything to do with Daniel Keelan?" Marci had now put two and two together. Becki's attitude toward him at the airport was entirely out of character. She was usually outgoing and cheerful. Marci thought it was the scary flight, but now she saw there was something more profound.

Becki responded with a soft, "Yes."

Now the lioness in Lyrica arose. "Has he done anything to scare you or hurt you?" she asked, trying to keep a lid on her own emotions.

"No, it's quite the opposite," Becki said, regaining some of her composure now that the secret was out.

"You mean you like him? As in, want to date him?" Marci asked. Trish was keeping quiet. She'd seen this brewing, but was waiting to raise the issue when Becki was ready.

"I feel so disloyal to Stephen. And it messes up Dad's plans to protect me."

"Oh, forget Dad's plans. If you like him, we can always get another body-guard instead of Keelan," Lyrica said.

"Yeah, I'll take Keelan," Marci was quick to jump in. "He's the best-looking man I've seen in a long while."

"That's just because you and Josh are always in some marsh or woods where the good-looking guys don't go," Trish joked.

"Seriously, honey. Are you attracted to him, and that's what this is all about?"

"Yes," Becki said and began to cry again.

"Well, this is the right place to find out how you feel. Stephen's not here, and you've got us girls. I say go for it, and we'll do all we can to help or stay out of your way."

"Then you don't think I'm disloyal or crazy to like someone I've only known for a week, and even that's from a distance?"

"No," Trish remarked. "I think this all started when you called his bluff on the street and faced him down. Am I right?"

"Yes," Becki answered softly, as if that would diminish the impact of what she had just admitted.

"Okay. I think we'd better be on our way," Lyrica broke in. "Becki, are you okay to leave? I just looked at my watch. We've been here fifteen minutes. The boys will wonder where we are. I'm surprised we didn't see them."

"I think they went to get some liquid refreshment before going to the house," Trish piped up.

"Or maybe that's them in the car coming up behind us," Marci pointed, seeing the headlights coming closer.

"Mom, I don't want him to see me like this."

"If that isn't proof enough, I don't know what is," Marci exclaimed. "This is a guy who's been following you in all kinds of weather and activities. Now, suddenly, you don't want him to see you crying?"

"Girls, we have a fun weekend coming up. Let's go before they have time to stop and ask why we pulled over. I'm not good at lying," Lyrica proposed.

Marci checked the rear-view mirror and saw that the lights behind them now flashed blue and white. "Oh great, it's the cops. They're probably coming to put Josh and me in jail."

"What?" Lyrica gasped.

"Mom, it's a long story. We'll tell you later."

"Here he comes. Put on your beautiful smiles, girls."

"Hey, we did nothing wrong. We just pulled off the road," Trish said, ready to defend her friends.

"Yeah, but you don't have to live on this island. I do," Marci said as she pressed the button to lower her window.

Twenty-Nine

"Good evening Mrs.—Oh, hi, Marci. What are you ladies doing out on a night like this?"

"Hi, Ben. We just pulled over to talk about something. We were about to get back onto the road when you came up behind us. I picked up these three at the airport tonight. They've come for my art show," Marci explained.

"This is a terrible night to be on the roads. We've already had two cars go into a ditch, so we're keeping a close watch, making sure everybody makes it home okay."

"That's where we're heading," Marci said, putting on her best smile for the young man.

"Good, 'cause I wouldn't want to be the one to arrest you, seeing how your husband was with us this afternoon."

"Thanks again for stopping. We've only got a mile or so to go," Marci smiled, trying to get the officer to leave.

"Sure you don't want an escort to the Wauwinet turn?"

"No thanks, we'll be fine."

"Okay, but be careful."

"Yes, sir," Marci replied as she raised her window and started the car.

"Well, that was sure weird," Trish plunged right in. "Marci, what did he mean Josh was arrested? You're holding out on us."

"What was Josh arrested for? Jaywalking while bird watching?" Becki asked.

"Very funny. That story has to wait until we have our pizza. Josh and Jake had a little adventure with the police."

"Come on, Marci, tell us the secret. You just heard mine. It's time for true confessions," Becki chided her sister.

"How about this? When we pull into the driveway, I'll fill you in. How's that? Josh probably has already told Dad, Matt, and Dan."

"Sounds good to me," Trish said. Lyrica and Becki echoed in agreement.

After plowing through the fog for what seemed like an interminable amount of time, Marci swung the Jeep onto the sandy track leading to their home.

Judging from the tire tracks and mud splashed everywhere, at least one car had already arrived. For some reason, it wasn't as foggy out at this end of the island, but the track leading to Marci and Josh's house was long and filled with puddles and glacial rocks erupting from the sand.

Waiting until she pulled the car up alongside the house before shutting off the engine, Marci turned and said, "Okay, here's the deal. You're going to hear more from Josh tonight, so try to act surprised when you hear it. It's so unbelievable you might benefit from hearing it twice."

As Marci reviewed the missing houses' tale, she told them about the marsh incident, quickly mentioning that no one but she and Josh knew about their kayaking. All three of the women were completely silent. Then she dropped the bombshell about the Taylor land possibly being sold.

"Marci, I still find this hard to believe. Houses don't vanish in real life, only in the movies. I could understand them being hidden in the fog, but not completely disappearing," Lyrica said, looking closely at her daughter. It was not like Marci to joke about something so serious.

But Becki, who'd shared the same womb with Marci for nine months and the same room for as many years after, knew that as ridiculous as it sounded, it was true. Meanwhile, Trish was contemplating the opening chapter of her next mystery.

"Is that why Josh and Jake got arrested? They built those houses, didn't they?" Becki questioned her twin.

Then Lyrica, suddenly aware of the time, turned and said, "Ladies, we have quite a night going for us here. Vanishing houses, disappearing photos, new paintings, and—Oh boy, here comes Dad. He probably timed our ride down to the minute and was ready to call the cops. Speaking of which, I see Dan and Matt just pulled up.

"Fine bunch of bodyguards we have. They can't even keep track of two women on an island that's only fifteen miles at its longest point," Becki said, seeing Keta. Lyrica, lowering her window, saw the genuine concern on his face and was now sorry that she hadn't called to tell him they'd be late.

"Where in the world have you been? I was worried, Lyrica. What happened? You could have run off the road or been in an accident. We were just about to go looking for you."

"Darling, it's okay. We're all safe. I'm sorry. It's my fault for not calling. We got into an intense conversation. Marci pulled off the road so we could finish talking. I didn't realize how much time had passed."

"You could have waited until you got home. You scared me."

"I'm sorry. I'll fill you in later." Lyrica tried to communicate with her eyes that there was more going on than just being late. But she knew it would have to wait.

"Dad, would it help if I told you that a police officer offered to escort us part of the way?" Marci asked.

"What? Don't tell me. I don't want to know. Just come in the house where we can keep an eye on the four of you. The guys are starving. I wouldn't let them make the pizza until Marci got here."

"Right, boss," Lyrica said, looking at Keta, hoping that he understood this wasn't just a roadside chat. He got it. But she knew he'd have plenty of questions later.

"Okay, gals, let's head for the house. The guys can get the luggage after we've eaten." Josh was standing in the doorway with the glow of firelight behind his silhouette. Marci was going to have some explaining to do.

Entering the warm house, the women could smell the wood fire crackling in the fireplace. The kitchen was already a mess. Josh must have ransacked the pantry. He'd spread out every box of crackers and bag of chips they owned on the kitchen counter and living room table. They'd piled the gear by the front door.

"Josh, I hope you left some cheese for the pizza," Marci said testily.

"Oh, we knew better than to touch your mozzarella," Josh replied sheepishly. The two bodyguards were enjoying the family banter.

"Okay, we have sausage, pepperoni, mushrooms, and olives," Marci told the group.

"Becki, go get their orders, so I don't have four hungry bears to feed instead."

Staring directly at her sister, Becki's eyes pleaded with Marci to let her stay in the kitchen and not go into the living room and be near Keelan. Trish caught it and jumped down from one of the bar stools. "I'll take the orders, Becki. You're more useful in the kitchen helping with the pizza."

The men were gathered around the fire, sprawled on the couches. Josh and Keta were sharing fish stories, trying to impress the two bodyguards with their prowess.

"You know, if the women don't have our schedules completely booked with art and food, maybe we can sneak off and fish one morning before breakfast or take out the boat and see what we can catch," Josh offered, looking around to see if anyone was interested.

Matt was quick to respond. "I'm not a deep-sea fisherman, but if anyone wants to fish in the surf, I'd be glad to join in. If Dan can watch over the ladies for a while."

"So, Matt, that means I get your pay for doing your job?"

"What? Isn't following four beautiful women reward enough?"

"How about we see how the day goes? Maybe all of us can go," Keta said, taking charge of the agenda and his two bodyguards. It would be a challenge to have a fun weekend and keep track of everyone, especially the ladies.

The pizzas came steaming hot out of the oven. Marci and Becki filed into the living room, a pizza in each of their hands.

"Okay, men, dig in. But please leave a few bites for the chefs, okay?" Marci teased. Like hungry little boys, each seized a piece.

"Anyone want a refill?" Josh asked, holding up his beer bottle.

"How about the ladies, Josh?" Marci chided.

"Oh yeah, sorry, I forgot."

"That's okay, Josh. I have everything under control," Trish said, pointing out the drinks and ice at the bar. "Help yourselves, boys. There's plenty."

"Keta, save me a spot by the fire. I'm not used to this damp weather." Lyrica was hoping for an opportunity to whisper a few snippets about their late arrival.

When the men had devoured the first round of pizzas, Marci, Trish, Becki, and Lyrica came back into the living room to join the men, each carrying a slice of pizza and a drink. Dan and Matt immediately stood up and offered their seats to the ladies. Beckoning to his wife, Keta pulled a wool throw off the back of the sofa to wrap around her. The fire was warming them. But this was a long way from the heat and soft breezes of the Caribbean.

Dan and Matt had retreated to the bar stools that flanked the kitchen island. Used to keeping their distance, they watched the entire scene. They were more comfortable as observers. But as expansive as the family room was, it was pretty hard to keep a distance.

Tomorrow will be the real challenge, Keta thought. Marci, Becki, and Lyrica will be issuing orders to set up the show. At this late hour, I doubt the men will rise with the sun for early fishing.

He saw Lyrica studying Keelan and then watched Lyrica's eyes protectively meet Becki's. Becki looked uncomfortable, even in this setting, a rarity for her. Something wasn't right in this gathering, and it wasn't just the late hour. Looking at Becki and then again at Keelan, Keta wondered if that's what delayed their arrival. It wasn't like Lyrica to be so dismissive of him. There must have been something significant that would make her forget the time.

"Hey guys, Marci says that they almost had a police escort. What was that all about, my love? Come on, fess up," Josh joked.

"Well, at least we didn't get arrested. Lieutenant Ben Michaels came to offer assistance because we parked on the side of Polpis Road. I explained why we'd pulled over, but he was concerned about us driving in the dense fog."

"Josh, what's this I hear about you and Jake having a run-in with the police?" Keta was now even more worried than before.

"Oh, we just had a little excitement. It's kind of a fun story," Josh lied.

Marci rolled her eyes. They were all sitting around a crackling fire spread out on floor cushions and the two couches. True to form, Marci brought out the marshmallows and sticks to roast their dessert.

"Okay, Josh, out with it," Keta said, knowing full well that he would not like the story. Lyrica glared at him.

"We could all use a good story before we go to bed. How about it, Josh?" Lyrica asked, trying to deflect Keta's impatience.

"Well, it was like this." Marci watched Josh maneuver his body on the barstool and settle into his storytelling position. "Last week, Marci and I went early morning kayaking in Pocomo Meadows. While we were there, we discovered a mysterious change in the hillside overlooking the marsh."

"Josh, get to the point. We're all tired. Just the facts so everyone can prepare for what buyers might say tomorrow," Marci pleaded.

"Okay, I'm getting there. I just wanted to set the stage. Jake and I got arrested downtown because we built the McMansions that used to dot the hillside above the marsh."

"Didn't you guys just finish those houses last year?" Keta wasn't buying the story.

"We did. But the houses we built have vanished."

"The hillside looks just like it did before they built the estate houses. Empty," Marci added.

"The cops arrested us thinking we'd know how and when they disappeared. And not just the houses, people, cars, and driveways, poof, vanished."

"Yeah, right, as if you hid them someplace in the moors," Becki kidded.

"Look, no one knows that Marci and I were the first ones to see the empty hillside. The police somehow got word of it later that day. I guess some of the family members are a bit upset. There's even a reward posted for finding the houses."

"Then, as if that wasn't trouble enough, a new buyer asked Josh and Jake to build an estate house and cottages on Old Man Taylor's land," Marci added.

"What?" Keta said incredulously.

"Darling, remember I told you that Priscilla Taylor disappeared?" Lyrica responded.

"Dad, all this just happened. And if that isn't enough, the buyer for Old Man Taylor's land is none other than Earl Morston."

"You're not joking, are you?" Keta's face had turned to stone.

"No. I wish we were," Marci replied.

"Oh, Lord, help us," Lyrica whispered.

There was a numbing silence in the group. Marci finally broke it. "We know tonight wasn't the ideal time to tell you, but we had no other choice. Tomorrow we'll all be running everywhere to help with the show. You'll likely hear about this in town or at the show."

The group was again silent.

Standing up, Keta took his wife's hand. "Lyrica, I think it's time we went to bed before our bedroom disappears."

Thirty

After the late-night pizza and troubling news, only a few brave souls were up early and moving around Marci's kitchen. Keta and Dan had the same idea as they'd made the coffee, brought a thermos and two mugs out onto the deck, and were admiring the view. The fog had lifted, and the day looked like it would be clear and sunny for the show.

Both men, dressed in their sweats, busily wiped off the dew from the rest of the deck furniture so it would be ready for the others. The coffee tasted wonderful. Keta had even found the sugar bowl, which was now almost empty between the two of them. After his conversation with Lyrica last night, Keta grabbed the opportunity to ask Dan how it was going with Becki.

"So, how are you and my blonde daughter getting along?" He poured himself a little more hot coffee and settled into one of the deck chairs.

"I'm not sure how to answer that. I pretty much know her routine, but she's not the easiest person to guard. To say that she's not happy about having me around is an understatement. However—"

"I noticed a bit of tension between you two last night. Did anything provoke it? Or is Becki being like her mom and resisting any help that might make her look weak or vulnerable?"

"That's it in a nutshell. I think my presence somehow threatens her independence and freedom. However, someone tried to access her loft floor by climbing the stairwell. Fortunately, he failed."

"I've not told her about the other person shadowing the two of us. My concern is that it might make things worse. I hope this doesn't disappoint you. I know we talked about it on the phone, but—"

"That's fine, Dan. It's a good sign if she's prickly. It means that she likes you. Becki doesn't bother with people she doesn't respect. She ignores them. Lyrica is rather like that as well. It's funny because Marci, even though she is Becki's fraternal twin, has none of these characteristics at all."

"Don't get me wrong. I'm enjoying both her and the assignment. I think we'll get a rhythm worked out." That was an understatement. I wonder what

Keta would do if he knew how I actually feel about her.

Both men then reviewed the latest developments in the case against Lyrica. The evidence that Morston was behind the robbery was mounting. They hoped he would get cocky enough to make a mistake. That he'd offered cash for the Taylor land just might be that move.

"Why would he go to the trouble of stealing two old photographs of the Taylor land unless there was something on it he wanted? A man willing to pay cash has something specific in mind." Keta knew Morston was plotting something.

"Did Becki share with you the notes that Trish copied from the reporter's notebook? She is pretty fast on the draw and very protective of Becki. Trish was the one who remembered Morston's company buying several of Lyrica's prints in the last year."

"Trish doesn't miss much," Keta continued. "That's what makes her such a good mystery writer. You could do worse than hire her to do some sleuthing for you."

"Hire me for what?" Trish asked, standing in the doorway. "Man, you can smell the coffee all the way down the hall."

"Grab a mug and join us."

Trish picked out one of the colorful mugs Marci had collected from their travels. "So, hire me for making breakfast? Is that what you two were plotting?" Trish looked at Dan and Keta. "Forget it. The best I'll do for you is The Donut. Anyone have a spare set of keys?"

"Don't bother. Dan and I have things under control. Take a seat and enjoy the view. We'll make some more coffee and start in on the breakfast. Right, Dan?" Keta didn't miss the sheepish look on Dan's face. "Dan's an old pro at making breakfast. Come on, let's show them the proper way to make pancakes. I wonder if Marci has any frozen blueberries."

"You sure you don't want some help?" Trish asked, not believing their story.

"Nope, we're fine. Relax. We've got a busy day before us," Keta answered as he and Dan stepped back into the kitchen.

"Okay. Give a holler if you need me."

Now inside, Keta turned to Dan. "I was only kidding about the pancakes. Why don't you make some more coffee while I get out the pancake mix?"

"Pancake mix? How about I show you how to make them from scratch?"

"Ah, holding out on me? Behind that austere exterior is a chef. You're probably going to tell me you were the executive chef in some exclusive restaurant or for some celebrity's yacht."

"Keta, I wish my past was as exciting as you make it out to be. But I enjoy cooking, and breakfast is my favorite meal. Probably because I hardly ever get to eat it."

"I'm surprised you even know your way around a kitchen with the hours you keep."

"Actually, I find cooking very relaxing. Now, did you say something about blueberries?"

"They're probably in the freezer downstairs. I'll go look."

Dan eyed the spacious kitchen. Marci must also enjoy cooking. There were two islands of black marble in the center of the room, one with four barstools waiting for occupants. Both had deep drawers with every kind of bowl and pan. One island hid a second oven and a wine rack. It took him a few glances around the kitchen to find the refrigerator well hidden behind the pale birch cabinets. Pulling out the skillet and bowls he needed, Dan headed for the frig to get the milk and eggs. He was contemplating where the flour and sugar would be when Lyrica showed up carrying the blueberries.

"Need some of these?" she asked. Placing them on the counter, she headed to the coffeemaker. "Can I share some of your coffee?"

"Yes, Trish is out on the deck. We just made it a few minutes ago."

"You look pretty official with Josh's apron. Keta told me you were making pancakes, but I didn't believe him. He'll be back in a minute. He went over to the cottage to see if the girls were awake. Becki and Marci were probably up until all hours talking."

Dan was wearing the apron Marci had given Josh for his birthday. It was black with Piazza de Navona printed on it. They'd had lunch there on their honeymoon. Marci had found the apron at Take It or Leave It, known for having some great finds, including housewares, furniture, and clothing.

They both remembered their lunch on the Piazza. The rain started just after they were seated under the canopies. Soon it was pouring, and little rivers of water were running under the tables. But it was a warm day, and they didn't have a care in the world. Little did they know what life was going to hurl at them.

Keta came back just as Dan finished the first pile of pancakes for the table. Lyrica and Trish were enjoying watching him.

"I couldn't find the girls," Keta said, looking puzzled. "Do you think they might have gone for a walk?"

Dan almost dropped the batter bowl onto the hot griddle. "Oh no, I'm supposed to be on duty this morning so Matt can sleep, and now I've lost my client. Here, somebody take over for me. I'll go hunt for them," Dan said hurriedly, untying his apron.

"Relax, Dan. They're probably walking the dogs or in Marci's studio. I didn't check there. They may have gone over to organize for the show." Lyrica noted Dan's overreaction to Becki being missing.

"I'll go look. Which way is the studio?"

"Straight out from the deck into that hedge of *Rosa rugosa* and scrub oak. You can't see the opening from here, but you'll see it when you get there. The path takes a few twists and turns until you get to the gate. Give the old ship's bell a few rings so you don't startle them."

Lyrica glanced over at Trish during this dialogue. Was she thinking the same thing? Dan seemed more than upset about misplacing his client. Maybe there was something to what Becki was saying. Maybe Dan also had more than a client's interest in her. This could prove to be an interesting weekend.

Making his way across the lawn, Dan found the winding grass path that led to the studio. Rambler roses tumbled over the scrub oak, the bees hovered for their breakfast, and Marci's English garden bloomed outside the studio's windows. Becki was bending over some flowers, taking cuttings for a bouquet. She'd not heard him arrive. Turning to head back to the studio, she paused, seeing him standing there.

"Oh, my goodness. What are you doing here?" Once again, he'd taken her off guard.

"I'm sorry, Becki. I didn't mean to startle you. Your dad didn't find you and Marci at the cottage, so your mom sent me here to look for you."

Recovering a little, Becki walked toward him and opened the studio door, turning her head to look over her shoulder. "You do have a way of appearing in the most unlikely moments. Do any of your clients die of heart attacks?" she said, looking at him with a puckish grin.

Sheepishly Dan was also trying to hide his surprise. He was genuinely relieved but not prepared for the vision of her startling beauty among the garden flowers. Her long, platinum blond hair was spilling over her shoulders, and she had on a billowy top of colorful flowers that settled over her faded and torn jeans. Seeing her in this setting was heady for him.

Inside the studio, Marci had seen Dan approach. She was now watching the two of them from behind one of her canvas panels. She could hear most of what they said with the windows open, but she didn't need the words. Both were trying to recover their composure. *I wonder if they both know they have feelings for each other,* Marci thought as she ducked behind her panel.

Still at a loss for words, Dan mumbled something about the flowers and Lyrica wanting them to come for breakfast. "Blueberry pancakes are waiting your arrival back at the house."

"Tell Lyrica we'll finish up and be right there. But don't wait for us."

Dan was turning away when Becki called him back. "Would you like to come into the studio before you head back? You can see some of the canvases Marci is using for the show today."

"Sure, that would be great. I'd love to see them."

"Good, because you'll be carrying some of them this afternoon. You might as well see the task you have ahead of you."

Dan was at the studio door with Becki in front of him. The combination of the flowers around him and her soft talc fragrance was enough to lessen all his resolve. He was falling for her. What he was going to do about it was the question. But he'd have plenty of time to think about it this weekend. There must be something about this island that makes you want to drop your defenses. Or maybe it's just the lack of pretense and ease with which this family relates to one another.

Marci saw the look on Becki's face as she stepped through the door. "I think we've marked enough for the exhibit. We'll see once we get downtown if I need to add any more."

"Marci, Dan came to tell us breakfast is ready."

"Great. I'm starved. Let's finish putting the canvases in order, and then we'll go back up to the house. Maybe Dan would help us move those three big ones onto the dolly."

Dan walked over to the back of a ten-foot canvas panel. Then she pointed Becki toward the painted side.

"If you and Dan gently lift the canvas, I'll scoot the dolly underneath." Both Becki and Dan grabbed the canvas from opposite sides. Marci watched their faces as Becki's hand accidentally overlapped Dan's. Neither one of them could control their expressions. Marci had seen enough.

Satisfied that they'd finished the work, Marci dismissed the two of them and said she'd follow along. But Becki protested, telling Dan to go on ahead and keep their plates warm. When Dan disappeared through the shrubbery, Marci turned to Becki with a gleam in her eye.

"Unless I'm losing my touch, Dan is as flummoxed over how to keep his emotions down as you are. I think this is great," Marci said, grabbing Becki's shoulders, then hugging her. "All you have to do now is get lost a few more times so he can find you. Only when you do, I won't be at the end of the maze, just you two."

"Marci, he's my bodyguard, not my date for the weekend."

"Yes, but we have two bodyguards available, so one can always have free time. Now get going before he gets to the gate."

"Marci, I will not run after him. If he's truly interested in me, he can tell me on his own."

"Would you like him to be interested in you?"

"Yes, I think so. But how crazy is that, dating your bodyguard? Isn't that giving sticking close by a new definition?"

Behind the shrubbery, Dan could hardly believe his ears. She likes me! Who would have thought after the way she treated me? Now I'd better high tail it out of here, so they don't catch me eavesdropping. He quickly retraced his steps and soon was climbing the stairs onto the deck.

Keta was the first to tease him. "So, did you find my girls?"

Great, thought Dan, *his* girls. "Yes. I found the two of them getting paintings lined up for the show."

"I hope you told them to hurry. You may have to make some more batter. The pancakes are disappearing quicker than Josh and Jake's houses."

"Hah, you won't think it's so funny when we show you what the hillside looks like," Josh laughed.

"What's this about houses and pancakes disappearing?" Marci spoke as she came up the last step onto the deck.

"Not just any pancakes. Chef Daniel made them from scratch. How's that for a houseguest?"

"You can stay as long as you want in this house." Marci gave him a big smile. Dan was already pouring the last of the batter into the iron skillet.

"Yeah, and he makes a mean cup of coffee," Lyrica added.

"Hey, knock it off, you guys. He'll get a big head and be impossible to live with," Matt said, strolling into the kitchen.

"It's about time you showed up. We were just about to send the dogs out to find you," Dan teased. "You'll have to wait in line. The ladies have returned from the studio. They get the next batch." He looked over toward Becki and Marci, but he couldn't read anything on Becki's face.

"Matt, have some coffee," Lyrica offered. "This is a tough crowd. It's better to wake up before getting into the middle of the fray."

"Thanks, I think I will."

"So, Marci, what can we do to make it easier for you today? You have an eager crew here. Just say the word, and we'll get to work," Trish offered for all of them.

"My top priority is to get the paintings downtown to the gallery. Then we have to mount them. After that, we need to set up some areas for people to sit and stand while having hors d'oeuvres and champagne."

"Matt and Dan need to scope out the place to see where they want to station themselves," Keta added.

"At some point, before we all get going on the show, Lyrica and I want everyone to sit down with Matt and Dan to review the investigation. Trish, that includes you if you'd like. We need to be ready for whatever might happen tonight or tomorrow at the show."

There was a sudden silence. Dan flipped the pancakes; the only sound was the grease spattering in the frying pan.

Thirty-One

I t took four hours to set up and position the paintings for display. Hopefully, the number of visitors wouldn't prevent anyone from viewing the panels from a distance. Marci wanted them to get the full impact of the landscapes. Each mural was life-size, so the series took up every display wall.

Bright afternoon light streamed through the tall windows in the gallery. During the day, she needed only a few spotlights on the paintings. One tribute to Marci's talent was her ability to make the panels take on different moods, depending on how the daylight moved through an owner's home. While each mural had a mystical quality of color and mood, viewers could sense a definite life force present in the landscapes.

Marci imagined the latest series hung on the walls of the large estate houses Josh built. She'd visited several for commission work. But this newest set of panels seemed to carry an exceptional vibrancy. When positioned correctly, they displayed a one-hundred-eighty-degree view of Nantucket's rolling, colorful landscape.

Standing before the panels was like sitting on your deck with the entire island in front of you. Moors, hidden ponds, and dirt roads filled one wall, complete with seasonal wildflowers indigenous to that island area. Other landscapes captured the dunes, the *Rosa rugosa* bushes, and the various beaches surrounding the island. Other panels caught the quietness of the inlets, salt ponds, and marshes, broken only by the coming and going of the water birds. Pocomo Meadows had been one of the peaceful marshes, at least until she and Josh had discovered the missing homes.

In the loft area of the gallery, Marci displayed some of the original studies for the panels. More affordable, these paintings still reflected the beauty and translucent light. The level of detail she achieved gave her smaller paintings a photographic quality.

"Marci, I knew this was going to be beautiful, but these panels are powerful," Lyrica broke the stillness that had come over them when they had placed all the paintings on the walls.

"You've done it again, honey. I'm so proud of you," Keta added, putting his arm around her. He was glowing with pride over his daughter's achievement.

"What's so amazing is that you can see the combination of Mom's photographic gift combined with your impressionistic style." Becki was one of Marci's biggest champions. Though exceptionally talented herself, Becki was genuinely proud of her twin.

"How about we have some champagne and toast the artist before the mob destroys this beautiful atmosphere?" Keta picked up the Moet from the table and was about to pop the cork.

"Dad, wait," Becki shouted. "Pop it toward the door. You might blow a hole through one of Marci's paintings," Becki shouted.

Pow! Too late. But Keta had aimed the bottle toward the loft, so nothing was damaged. The cork took a couple of bounces on the upstairs floor, and Dan retrieved it as it bounced down the stairs.

"Who would like the cork as a memento of the show?" he asked the group.

"You keep it. It's not every day you get this close to a famous artist. Who knows, maybe you can sell it on eBay someday and pay for your kids' college educations," Josh joked.

"I might just do that," Dan smiled.

"Ah, a romantic at heart. I thought so," Trish added, looking from Dan to Becki, who was still finishing the flower displays for the room. She had looked up and was smiling at Dan's comment.

"How about we all go home for a snack and get ready? We need to be here before five." Lyrica looked at the group in their jeans and sweatshirts. A bunch of vagabonds, she thought, a sharp contrast to the beauty all around them. The panels had mesmerized the group. No one wanted to leave.

"Okay, let's go. Whoever is coming with me, I'm leaving right now," Josh said, looking around, jingling his keys.

"Why don't you gals take Marci's Jeep? We'll bring the pickup and Land Rover back to the house," Keta instructed. "But no stopping off to chat, okay?"

"Mr. and Mrs. Kea, Dan, and I will stay behind a while to finish setting up our watch patterns. But don't worry, we'll get dressed in time to slip undercover as potential buyers," Matt promised.

A brief rain shower greeted them on the drive home. The women were quiet as they turned onto the Polpis Road. Trish was pondering the mysterious silence once the paintings were in place. "Did anyone notice how different the atmosphere was when we left the gallery?" she asked.

"You mean like the rain?" Marci quipped.

"No. The gallery has a spiritual presence now that the panels are up on the walls. I felt it build each time we placed a panel."

"The only spirits you sensed were the bubbles in the champagne. Trish, are you going mystical on us again?" Becki laughed. Her friendship with Trish started in childhood. While devoted to one another, they also enjoyed sparring with each other.

"No, I think Trish is right. It felt like the gallery had been waiting for the paintings. A peace came over the whole place when we finished. I'm not sure I can describe it." Lyrica had noticed the change but had said nothing.

"Mom, I think you all are sleep-deprived and too tired to think straight," Marci responded.

"But Marci, you'd be the last person to notice the difference. You've been around the paintings every day. There is an actual presence in the gallery." Trish loved the sense of mystery.

"Well, let me know if you see anything following me," Marci joked.

"Speaking of following, Daniel Keelan is one nice guy, besides being darn good looking." Trish was starting her campaign.

"I agree," Marci added. "And he can cook. Becki, he's a perfect match for your minimalist culinary skill. I think you may have hooked a keeper."

"Will you guys cut it out? He's just polite because Dad and Mom are both here."

"Becki, Becki, Becki, what will it take for you to see this?" Trish was shaking her head.

"I see it. I see it. But what am I supposed to do? Take him out back of the gallery and kiss him?"

"That's not bad for starters," Trish quipped. "Now we just have to figure out how to do that."

"Yikes, I'm surrounded. Can't we just see what happens? He's paid to be nice and stay near me."

"Or at least follow you wherever you go. Like behind the gallery to get your shawl out of the car?" Marci suggested, looking over at her sister.

"Marci, stop it!"

"Interesting how we always end up on this topic when we're driving," Lyrica commented.

"Any other suggested approaches?" Becki asked as they pulled onto the sandy track that led to the house.

"No, you seem to find enough awkward or tight situations without even trying. Next time, just take advantage of one." Trish beamed at her friend.

"You guys may regret the day you suggested this," Becki said, looking straight at Marci and Trish.

"I doubt it. I really doubt it," Trish said with that Wile E. Coyote look on her face that Becki knew so well.

Thirty-Two

A t six o'clock, the family positioned themselves for the gallery's opening. The team that hauled and hung the art panel transformed themselves from a band of ruffians with dirty jeans, T-shirts, and sweat into an artsy, sophisticated group greeting the gallery's visitors.

The day had been sunny and almost hot for June, but the evening air coming off the water was cool and held its usual moisture. Inside the gallery, with minimum spotlights, the air was comfortable. Keta had assigned each person a designated post throughout the gallery with instructions on what to look for and how to monitor what people said.

Lyrica was sitting behind an antique, curly maple desk near the gallery's large front windows in a small alcove off to the side. She could monitor the foot traffic into the gallery and be out of sight to the casual visitor walking by the gallery. She would handle the purchases and the appointments for buyers interested in commission work.

To Becki's relief, Dan was outside on the brick patio in the back where the tall privet hedges surrounded the owner's parking. Hopefully, no one was going to try stealing any paintings. Dan had found a seat in a dark corner where he could watch the gallery's back entrance. A few times around the privet hedge and the gallery building, and he was ready.

Matt, dressed in chinos and a yellow polo shirt, was floating around the gallery, answering people's questions. This freed up Marci to wander at will among the guests. Keta, of course, was orchestrating and overseeing everyone.

To Marci, the group's designated watch positions were overkill. But she hadn't experienced the paparazzi the same way as Becki and her parents. Plus, it gave her the freedom to move around the gallery and introduce herself to the visitors. Trish and Becki were greeting guests at the entrance, but as the gallery filled, Trish took her post upstairs to ensure that nothing on the walls disappeared, at least by human hands.

The large main room filled quickly as the pre-dinner crowd arrived. They consumed the hors d'oeuvres and champagne with gusto. In the slight lull before the after-dinner customers arrived, they put out new food and drink. The latter visitors were usually the purchasers.

At eight o'clock, a short, robust man walked in with a Hollywood blonde attached to his arm. All he needed to complete the picture was a cigar dangling from his lips. Luckily, it wasn't. Keta recognized Earl Morston at once. Matt had already seen him and was texting Dan. Of the family, only Keta and Lyrica would know him by sight.

Morston headed directly to the champagne and food. After chugging one glass of champagne, he took another and strode over to the three colorful panels of the middle moors that Marci had just finished. Marci sensed he was on his first round of looking, so she held back from addressing him.

As Morston headed upstairs, the open staircase shuddered with his weight as he mounted each step. Trish got a good look at him and the blonde, who seemed to be cut from a Jayne Mansfield mold. She wore a tight-fitting sundress with a halter top that dipped down to her waist. She'd been trying to impress Morston and anyone else who listened with her interior design skills.

When Morston reappeared downstairs, he walked directly over to the three panels. Marci was conversing with some guests about the wildflowers in the paintings. Matt saw Morston's deliberate move toward Marci. Quickly, he signaled Keta, who had dropped back to stay unnoticed. Knowing that Morston would recognize Keta, Matt deftly placed himself between Marci and Morston.

"Good evening, sir. I see you've been studying these panels carefully. Is there something I can help you with?"

"Who are you? You work here?" Morston growled.

"Yes, sir. I'm helping tonight. Are you enjoying the show?"

"Oh, very much," the blonde squeaked. "I'm helping—"

"She's my interior decorator. We're furnishing a new house on the island. I heard the artist did large-scale paintings, so we thought we'd see if any fit the design scheme for the house."

Design scheme, right, Matt thought. Design and scheme are both words that fit Morston's modus operandi.

"Where about on the island is your house?" Matt decided to have a bit of fun at Morston's expense. "Besides the work you see displayed here, the artist is well known for her commission work, if that would interest you."

"Yeah, we were hoping to talk with her when you intercepted us."

"How about I introduce you to her?" Matt suggested as he slowly ushered the couple toward Marci. She had finished with some other visitors and was scanning the room.

"Marci, let me introduce you to someone interested in buying your panels for his new house on the island," Matt said, looking at Marci, who politely offered her hand for a handshake.

"Glad to meet you. You're a popular lady this evening. My name is Morston, Earl Morston. You may have heard of me."

Marci, startled, recovered herself quickly and thanked them for coming to the show. The blonde unhooked herself from Morston and held out her hand in greeting.

"I'm Celina, Mr. Morston's interior designer. Pleased to meet you."

Marci noticed that Matt had stepped back from the couple, but was keeping a close watch on her.

"Mr. Morston, are you interested in these panels, or did something else spark your interest?"

"I'm only interested in large paintings for the house. Celina makes sure the art pieces fit with the rest of the décor. I'm interested in this set of panels for one of the living rooms. And possibly those over there of the beach and marsh, for the dining room. Got any more than what's here?"

"Mr. Morston, these series are all I have at the moment. But if you want more, might I suggest some commission work?"

"Now you're talking my language. How about I buy both series tonight, and you start on some more for the house?"

"When would you like me to come out and see the house? I'll need to see your lighting and window views surrounding the artwork." Marci had deftly entered into the game.

"Oh, it's not ready yet," Celina piped up.

"I see."

"I'm just waiting for the land contract to go through. We're drawing up the architectural plans now. But I'm still interested in having more of your work."

"That's fine, Mr. Morston. It might be a good idea to purchase the paintings tonight if you want to ensure that they have a sold sign on them for the rest of the show. Why don't you enjoy looking around and have some more champagne? Stop by the desk as you leave. Have you seen the paintings behind the champagne and caviar?" Marci asked, pointing to a second room off to their left.

"Oh, thank you," Celina cooed as she looked at Morston. "Let's go find the champagne again. Then we can do the second room."

Marci immediately headed toward Matt. "Matt, tell Becki she needs to come quickly to cover for Mom. Morston will recognize her."

"I think Becki just went to the Jeep to get your mom's shawl. It's getting cool as the temperature drops. I'll find her if she's not back in a few minutes. She may be talking with Dan."

"Fine. Trish can relieve Mom at the purchase desk," Marci said as she hurried toward Lyrica.

But Becki didn't reappear in a few minutes. She had gone out the back door, across the patio, and headed down the white shell driveway. They'd parked the Jeep on the street just beyond the driveway and privet hedge. She was happily listening to the crunch, crunch of the shells as she rounded the corner of the privet hedge to the street.

Swiftly, before either could dodge, Becki crashed into Dan, coming around the corner of the hedge from the opposite side. He'd heard someone on the driveway and wanted to see who it was. Becki let out a startled cry and automatically pushed herself away from him. Dan, who had the advantage of knowing that someone was coming, had stepped out to block the person's passage.

"Becki, it's okay. It's just me," he said as he reached to grab hold of her shoulders so she could face him. He didn't let her go until she was looking straight at him. But Becki was hot with anger, frightened, and ready to fight.

"Just you? Why didn't you warn me as you came around the corner if it was just you? Did you think I was stealing a painting?"

"No, but I wasn't sure who it was, and all I had time for was to block your passage. I'm sorry I scared you. Are you okay?"

Becki glared at him. "No! Don't ever do that to me again. You scared me to death. Maybe you should swap with Matt. He and Mom don't seem to have this problem."

That hurt Dan. But he put on a pleasant face. "If that's what you want, I'll talk with your dad." He hoped she didn't hear the tremble in his voice.

"I was only joking," she lied. Or was she? That was the question. She liked his firm but gentle touch on her shoulders. She enjoyed being close to him, inhaling the scent of his aftershave, but it was messing up her brain, let alone her heart. Before she knew it, she started to cry.

"I'm sorry, Dan. It's not you."

Dan pulled her toward him, cradling her in his arms, letting her cry. She choked out a few words about not handling the stress from everyone and everything. But in a few minutes, when she'd finished crying, Dan could feel her backing away and see her putting on the confident face she tried to wear around him.

"Becki, you're allowed to be stressed and scared. I'm your bodyguard because you're vulnerable. You don't have to be tough around me." He was still holding her arms, looking down at her.

"What am I going to do?" She was looking at him as if he had the answer.

"Going to do about what?

"You know. About you. You confuse me every time I'm with you."

"How about we just allow you to be confused and see what happens?" Now Dan felt caught between wanting to share his feelings and being afraid of her reaction. Using his fingers, he wiped away the tears still on her cheeks and gently kissed her forehead.

"Now, Miss, what did you come out here for? Were you headed for the Jeep?"

"Yikes, I almost forgot. Mom wanted her shawl. She's getting cold sitting by the door."

As Becki retrieved Lyrica's blue cashmere shawl from the Jeep, they both could hear the crunch of shells on the driveway behind them. But before they could say anything, Matt appeared. "Becki, we've been wondering where you were. We need you to take over the purchase table. Someone wants to buy some paintings."

"Is it that portly man with the debutante?"

"Yes. Only that man is Earl Morston, and he'll recognize your mom." Matt didn't see Dan look toward heaven. That's all Becki needed now to induce another bout of crying.

"I thought something was up. I saw Dad move out of sight and signal you, so I figured it might be him. How come he's showing up on the island?"

"Becki, he doesn't know that Marci is your mom's daughter. If he did, I doubt he would have exposed himself, especially sporting Celina, if that's her real name."

Quickening her pace, Becki wiped her eyes and turned toward the two bodyguards. "Do I look okay?" Not having a better answer, they both said yes.

When they got to the patio, Dan stayed to resume his watch. Becki wanted to help her mom, but she felt an almost imperceptible reluctance to leave Dan.

"Come on, Matt. Let's go rescue Mom."

Thirty-Three

"**B**oy, that was a long night," Marci said as she walked into the kitchen and headed straight for the coffeepot. "Thanks guys, for making the coffee. Does anyone want a cinnamon roll?"

"I'll take one," Dan said, looking over at Marci. He was freshly shaven and dressed in a light blue polo shirt and jeans.

Marci banged open the cylinder and deftly placed the rolls on the baking sheet, sprinkling them with a bit of cinnamon and confectionary sugar. She then tested out some icing on her finger.

"Looks like you've done this before," Dan said, coming over to the kitchen bar stools and taking a seat. "Not only can you paint, but you can also cook."

"I'd hardly call this cooking. But I'm weary from last night, so easy is the call of the day. Did you guys cook bacon? Or do I just smell the fragrance, and the real bacon has already vanished?"

"Guilty as charged, Miss Marci," Josh confessed from his chair on the deck. "We couldn't wait. We were starving."

"Hmm, I guess we didn't have enough food for you last night," Marci joked as she reached down into the freezer. "I'll just have to go into my private stash. But you three need to keep your mitts off this batch, okay?"

"Got it," Josh said quietly, smiling at Dan and Matt. "I'll trade you a cinnamon bun for some bacon, Marci."

"Such a deal maker. Watch out, guys. He may give you the slip and eat your pastry before you know it. Josh doesn't waste his sleight of hand on poker. He saves it for the kitchen."

"Has anyone seen the girls this morning?" Marci asked, looking up from the frying bacon. She wore her pink terrycloth robe, deep purple, boiled wool slippers, and floral chef's apron. Her spirit was buoyant.

"No, Marci. They're always the stragglers to this party," Keta reminded her. He poured a mug of coffee and settled down on the couch to read the morning newspapers. "Remember, we went to bed only a few hours ago, and you know how slow Becki is in the morning. We may have to send out a search party for them soon."

"That was a great show, Marci," Dan said, breaking into the conversation.

"Agreed. Marci, you outdid yourself. I'm excited to see how today goes." Keta was pleased to see his daughter seem more relaxed.

"Josh, it's a cloudless morning. Why don't you take Matt and Dan up on the widow's walk and orient them to Pocomo, the Taylor land, and the rest of the island? You guys can come back for your second breakfast and then roam wherever you want. But I need you back by noon." Marci was eager to get some time alone with her parents.

The three guys stood up and headed for the upstairs. When Marci was sure they were out of hearing, she turned toward her parents.

"Mom, Dad, what do you think is going on between Becki and Dan?"

"Are you asking if there is a relationship forming?" Lyrica questioned her daughter.

"I'd hardly call it a relationship at this point. But your mom and I discussed it last night. So far, we don't think it's interfering with his job if that's your concern."

"I agree with Marci. There's more than meets the eye."

"Based on what Dan said, she's barely tolerating him right now. I warned him about her prickly side. The stress she's under is making it surface. Stephen's job has certainly made the stress worse."

"Frankly, I think it's good for her to get out from under Stephen's thumb," Lyrica responded. "He's a little too controlling."

"I don't think he's good enough for her," Marci added.

"I don't doubt your women's intuition," Keta added. "But for now, how about we relax and concentrate on enjoying your show? Becki and Dan will work it out."

"If something is going on between them, this is the safest place to let it happen," Lyrica responded.

"I agree. Stephen may be in for the surprise of his life," Marci cautioned.

"What are your plans this morning, Marci?" her dad asked, quickly changing the subject.

"I thought I'd paint a little. I can't explain it, but I feel like I need to get outdoors and paint a bit before I face the maddening crowd again this afternoon."

"As long as you don't consider us part of that crowd," Trish said as she and Becki strolled into the kitchen.

"Hey guys, you missed the proper breakfast. But there's still some raisin bread from the bakery, cinnamon buns, and fresh coffee. I'm making more bacon since Josh ate the first batch."

"Anything better than Cliffey's alphabet cereal sounds good to me," Trish joked.

"Marci, do you want me to come and paint with you?" Becki asked.

Marci was donning her worn, paint-spattered linen jacket, her straw sunhat dangling down her back on its leather strap. Becki strongly suspected another motive for her twin's outing.

"Why don't I get my sketchbook and go with you?"

"Becki, it's unnecessary. I'm only going over to the Taylor land. I thought I'd paint the hornbeams in the morning light. The leaf patterns and lighting are spectacular this time of day."

"Josh said Taylor's driveway is pretty grim at the entrance. It might be better to wait until they put down some heavy gravel. I don't want my artist missing her show because she's stuck in the sand," Keta said with a grin.

"I'm not using the driveway. There's a shortcut to the hornbeams. I know Josh thinks he's got every inch of that property covered, but there are a few corners and hiding places even he hasn't discovered yet. Priscilla and I painted every inch of that land."

"If that's what you want to do, why don't you take Becki and Dan with you now that we know Morston is roaming the island?"

"Dad, all I'm doing is painting. I don't need an entourage with me. I doubt the paparazzi have made it this far out at sea."

At this comment, Becki looked sharply at Lyrica and Keta. Lyrica was uncomfortable, and Becki seemed on edge.

"Marci, let me go with you," Becki repeated. "That way, the men won't imagine something dire happening while you're gone. Matt and Dan can relax for a while. We're not going out in public, so there's no need for a bodyguard. Where *are* the guys, anyway?"

"Matt and Dan are with Josh on the widow's walk, casing out the island's geography," Keta responded. "You two go on ahead. I'll tell them where you are. Lyrica and I will go down to the gallery and make sure everything is ready before the show."

"Dad, Mom, you don't have to do that. We left it in good shape last night. My friend Jane is doing the day shift. She'll clean up anything we left undone. You could use a peaceful morning. Why don't you occupy those lounge chairs on the deck for a while?"

"We spent several weeks in the Caribbean lounging around," Lyrica added. "But if that's what you want, we'll stay and hold down the fort. How about we all rally at eleven o'clock for lunch? Then we can get to town at a leisurely pace."

"Sounds good to me. I'll grab a mug of coffee and two cinnamon buns, and Marci and I are out of here."

Marci checked her linen bag for paints and brushes. She'd already put one small canvas in the bag. Becki grabbed her coffee, cinnamon roll, sketchpad, and the old quilt as they headed out the door.

"See ya later." The two walked out the doors to the deck and headed for Marci's Jeep.

"Marci, thanks for taking me along. I wanted to have some time without Dan by my side."

"Yeah, I could see the tension last night. Try to let it go if you can. We're all a little jittery with everything that's been going on. It will work itself out. It always does on this island."

"I'm trying, Marci. But he's not making it easy."

"Sounds to me like neither of you is making it easy. Try to forget about the mainland and have some fun. You're safe here even with Darth Vader on the island."

"You know, it's been a long time since we went out to paint and sketch together," Becki said, changing the subject. "I think I like this little adventure. Lately, I've been feeling like the walls were closing in on me, squeezing the life out of me. I need some time outdoors. Ever since we got back from Madeira, my rhythm has been off. It seems like every move and word carries emotional overtones. Even Stephen and I are a bit off our rhythm."

"I wouldn't worry about it. A few days here in the sun and fresh air will straighten out that complicated brain of yours. Hey, why don't we go to Pocomo Meadows, and I'll show you the latest news item?"

"As long as there aren't any reporters there. I've had my fill already."

"We'll go in by the dirt road. I doubt any reporters have found that one yet. But can you wait until we're on our way home? It's much easier to get into Taylor's land by skirting the Cox's place."

"Sure."

"Is that what you meant this morning? I wondered where your shortcut was to the Taylor land."

"Remember, Priscilla and I often picnicked on the hill with the hornbeams. From that vantage point, we could paint the ocean and dunes, turn to the left to paint the marsh, and then paint the meadow on the right. It's just through there," Marci pointed, pulling the Jeep onto the side of the road.

"Where? I only see scrub oak," Becki said, exiting the car.

"Aha. I'll show you the trick. Here, you hold the stuff." Getting down on her knees, Marci crawled through a "rabbit hole" in the brambles and scrub oak until she was almost out of sight. Then, popping her head up, she signaled to Becki.

"Okay, hand me the canvas bag. Nice. Now give me your things, unless you want to take them through the rabbit hole."

Becki looked stunned. Marci was only five feet from her, but there was a dense bramble between them. No one would ever have known that there was a path anywhere. Getting down on her hands and knees, Becki crawled through the tunnel.

"That's a regular Alice in Wonderland rabbit hole. How did you ever find it?" Becki was looking at Marci in astonishment.

"We didn't. We made it from the inside. The regular path starts here." Peering around her sister, she saw a narrow pathway that led toward the hornbeams.

"You have to promise never to tell Josh. This trail has been here since Priscilla and I were kids. We created it to get to the blackberry patch. But it was such fun that we continued until we had a regular maze of tunnels and small rooms to play cards, paint or tell secrets where no one could find us. The path will bring us out in the meadow directly below the hornbeams."

And sure enough, within a few minutes, they were at the base of the meadow. Marci spread out the tattered Shaker quilt they used for picnics and began unpacking her linen bag.

Becki immediately ran into the meadow, spreading out her arms, running in circles, and dancing as if she was a sunbeam landing on the meadow grass and bouncing up again.

"I love this. I'm free." Becki exclaimed.

Marci smiled at her sister, picked up her paints, and set out her canvas. Taking out a piece of charcoal, she sketched the scene, then quickly began applying paint, trying to capture the meadow's light before the sun changed the vision she had in front of her. Sitting in the warm sun, her mind traced back to when she and Priscilla painted together. In more recent years, they had a standing date to paint together one afternoon a week. She missed Priscilla's eye for composition and color. The gallery show should have been hers. Priscilla was the master.

Putting down her paintbrush, Marci gazed out across the field. Becki was still dancing, swinging her arms, and singing. I'm so glad she came, Marci mused. She needs this as much as I do.

Unlike Becki, who lived in a city, Marci wasn't used to having a lot of people around her. She needed the quiet of the moors. The rolling hills and crest of the dunes relaxed her. She drank in the cool breeze off the ocean, smelling not only the salt, but also the heady fragrance coming from the sun on the pink *Rosa rugosa*.

Her thoughts went back to the fun she'd had with Priscilla riding bareback around this field. The grassy part was the size of a football field, so they had room enough to set up jumps and a barrel racing course. The scrub was so thick around the meadow that Priscilla could open the paddock door and let the horses find the only trail to the field. There were no other exits except the tunnels. Priscilla could let the horses graze in the area all summer, using the hornbeams for shade when they needed it.

In the fall, the eastern end of the field became a blanket of goldenrod. The black and chestnut horses vividly contrasted the gold and green landscape and the brilliant blue sky. Moving away from her usual style, Marci painted the horses and riders into the scene. Priscilla was putting a blanket on the black horse while Marci placed a bridle on the chestnut. In recent years, Marci had stopped doing portrait work and changed to landscapes. People brought complex emotions and history to a painting. Marci wanted her viewers to feel a sense of peacefulness from the scene's beauty.

Today, the horses and riders were standing waist-high in the field's tall grass. No one had mowed it since Priscilla's disappearance. But her memory brought back the smell of the horses, their velvety muzzles, and the sound of their tails swishing back and forth, swatting the flies. It also brought tears. Like it or not, the art show had made Marci sentimental and renewed her sadness. As the painting came to life, so did her tears. Before she knew it, two wet spots appeared on her linen jacket. For the first time in months, she ached with the despair she'd not allowed herself to feel. The memories stirred up her heartache, and she stared off into space. Her paintbrush had fallen into the tall grass of the meadow.

Unbeknownst to Marci, a figure at the edge of the hornbeams emerged in a stream of early morning light. Marci ignored the sound of footsteps behind her, knowing Becki was wandering around sketching. Suddenly, she heard a strange voice.

"Are you almost finished painting so we can open the hot chocolate?"

Startled, Marci spun around to see who had found the hornbeam pathway into the field. The answer caught in her throat. "Priscilla, what are you doing here?"

Thirty-Four

"What do you mean, what am I doing here? Girl, you've had too much sun."

Marci stared at Priscilla, not knowing what to say. "But, but you're supposed to be missing. I mean, where have you been? People have been looking all over for you."

"Well, they certainly didn't look in the right places, now, did they? Why were they looking for me?"

"Priscilla, it's really you, right?"

"Of course, it's me. Don't you recognize me? Look, I even have on the sunflower socks you gave me."

Staring down at Priscilla's feet, Marci saw the sunflower socks peeking out below the old khakis in which she painted.

"Are you sure it's you? You're not a ghost, are you?"

"Will you knock it off? You'll give me a complex. Marci, would a ghost wear these clothes?" Priscilla had the inveterate twinkle in her eyes that Marci knew so well.

Putting down the thermos of hot chocolate, Priscilla sat down on the quilt, waiting for her friend to join her. Marci was shaking. She scanned the field for Becki.

"Why don't you pour the hot chocolate? I'll get out the homemade raisin bread."

Thinking that a ghost wouldn't be carrying real hot chocolate, Marci stopped devising an escape plan. Surely there wouldn't be hot chocolate in the thermos.

"Marci, I see you brought the wrong cups again. Why don't I run to the house and bring us a few mugs? Oh, look at you. You're painting Bullet and Champ. Would you like me to let them out of the stable so you have some actual models to paint?"

"Yeah, that would be great. I'll wait until later to finish the horses."

"You got it. And Marci, take us out of that painting. You know how I feel about landscapes with people in them. It will sell much faster without us.

People like to look at horses and meadows. They don't want to be reminded of their riding experience or lack thereof. I'll be right back."

"Okay. I'll finish up here." Marci desperately scanned the meadow to find Becki. Her heart was pounding so hard she could feel the pulse in her temples. Spotting Becki sitting on one of the large rocks sketching wildflowers, Marci ran toward her. "Becki, come here."

Turning around, Becki asked, "What's going on?"

"Come back here, please." Marci was frantically motioning for her sister.

Becki jumped to her feet and ran to Marci. "Marci, what's wrong? You're as white as a sheet."

"Becki, I just saw Priscilla."

"You what?"

"I said, I just saw Priscilla."

"Marci, I know the show has stressed you out. But really, you couldn't have seen her. She's still missing. Don't you think you would be one of the first to know if they'd found her?"

"That's just the point. Maybe she's not missing anymore. And if she isn't, who was that person who just left this thermos of hot chocolate on our quilt?"

"Marci, you mean you saw a person leave hot chocolate here? Are you sure you're not having a flashback? Maybe we shouldn't have come here so soon."

"Becki, I'm telling you the truth. Look, it's right here. Did we bring hot chocolate? Didn't Priscilla and I always have hot chocolate here after we rode the horses?"

"Yes, but that doesn't mean—"

"Becki, she went up to the house to get two mugs. She's coming back."

"Marci, thermos, or no thermos, I think we need to go home. You don't look well. Come on, let's get our things and go back to the car. Too many weird things have happened recently. I think it's too stressful for you to be on this property. Your memories are so strong."

Becki was unsure what to do about the thermos of hot chocolate lying on the quilt. Reaching down to pick it up, she expected her hand to pass right through it. But the thermos was real. Opening it up, the wonderful smell of double dark chocolate rose to her nostrils. Okay, I'll let Josh figure this one out. Urging Marci along, Becki gathered their supplies, canvas bag, and quilt and headed back to the car.

"Wait. We can't leave yet. Priscilla is coming back with the mugs."

"Marci, are you sure you saw her?"

"Becki, I wasn't hallucinating. Can't we wait just a few minutes and talk with her when she comes back?"

So they waited five minutes, then ten. When it was pushing twenty minutes, Becki's patience ran out. "Marci, I don't think she's coming. She could have been here and back twice in the last twenty minutes. I think we'd better let the guys figure this out."

"No. I'll call her cell phone." So Becki waited again, only to see Marci's shoulders crumple and tears fall. This was going to deteriorate rapidly if she didn't get back to Josh and Lyrica, Becki thought as they trudged through the scrub and dragged themselves through the rabbit hole to the car.

Becki grabbed the keys from the linen bag and opened the door so that Marci could sit in the front seat beside her. She still had an ashen pallor, but her breathing seemed better. Becki closed the side door of the Jeep and jumped up into the driver's seat.

"Oh, great. I forgot this was a stick shift. Lord, if you are out there, I could use some help. Please get us home." Turning the Jeep around was difficult, but she avoided getting stuck. As she headed for home, Marci bent over and began to sob.

"Becki, I know I saw her. I'm not crazy. She's not missing. Why did you make us leave? What will she say when she comes back and finds we're not there?"

"Marci, she'll call you. Maybe she got delayed at the house. She knows you wouldn't leave without a good reason. We can call her again when we get home."

"No, let's call her now. We're on the main road where there's better reception." Marci reached to the back seat where she'd thrown her tattered linen bag. Fortunately, the cell had fallen to the bottom of the bag, so it took some time to find. Becki kept driving as fast as she could to the house.

"Found it." Great, Becki thought to herself. This ought to be interesting if Priscilla answers.

"She's not answering. She's probably in the field wondering where I've gone with her hot chocolate."

"Thank you, Lord," Becki whispered. "Now get us home where hopefully we'll find some answers."

"Marci, we can call again when we get home. We're almost there."

"Becki, don't you think we should go back and talk with her?"

"We can do that, but not now. You need to get ready for the show this afternoon. Maybe we can send the guys over to see if they can find her."

"Yes. That's a good idea. Dan and Matt will find her."

"Whatever," Becki mumbled.

Mako leaped off the front porch and raced to greet them as they pulled up to the house. No one was on the back deck, so they went inside to the kitchen. Lyrica, Keta, and Trish were sitting by the fireplace reading the newspaper.

"Hey, how'd the painting go?" Lyrica asked, looking up from her reading.

"Mom, I saw Priscilla."

"What? How could you have seen her? She's still missing," Lyrica responded, and looked quizzically at Becki.

"Where did you see her, Becki?" Keta asked, a worried look on his face.

"I didn't see her, but Marci says she had a conversation with her in the meadow."

"Dad, she went back up to the house to get some mugs for the hot chocolate and—"

"That's it. The hot chocolate," Becki exclaimed. "Marci, show them the hot chocolate."

"You mean this hot chocolate?" Marci said as she pulled the thermos out of her canvas bag. "Priscilla left it with me while she went to get some mugs from the house. This is her thermos, and the chocolate is still hot."

Keta and Lyrica were now at full attention. "You didn't take hot chocolate with you when you went out to paint today?"

"No, Dad. That's what I'm trying to tell you. This is Priscilla's chocolate. I tried to call her from the car so she wouldn't be mad at me for leaving before she got back with the mugs. But no one answered. Maybe we should try her again now."

Keta stole a look at Becki. She confirmed Marci was not making this up.

"Okay, let's call her." Pulling out his cell phone, Keta walked over and handed it to Marci. They stood in silence as she waited for Priscilla to pick up.

No answer. Marci sat down on the couch and cried. "I feel like such a terrible friend to up and walk away. She just went to get the mugs. We should have stayed."

"Marci, we stayed for almost a half-hour, remember?" Becki looked over to her parents for help.

"Marci, we don't doubt what you and Becki are saying. With houses disappearing, why can't something that's disappeared reappear? Maybe the chocolate and Priscilla have now reappeared. Why don't we gather up the group and go back and see if we can find Priscilla? Then you can explain why you had to leave so abruptly. Does that sound like a good idea?"

"Yes," Marci said quietly.

"Let's do it. I think Dan and Matt went to town. They should be heading back by now,"

Keta said as he hit Matt's speed call number. Matt answered before the second ring.

"Guys, we need you back here, pronto. Becki and Marci say they saw Priscilla in Taylor's field. I think we need to get out there and see what's going on. Can you meet us there?"

"We're more than halfway there now," Matt replied.

"Find Josh and tell him to meet us there."

"You got it."

"Thanks." Keta placed the phone back on his belt and took a long, worried look at his daughter. He could see the tension in Lyrica and Becki. He was concerned about how this might affect Marci right before her show.

Thirty-Five

Keta, Becki, Marci, and Lyrica piled into the Land Rover. Becki tried to convince Marci that Priscilla was too good a friend to be offended by their leaving the meadow. Keta gunned the engine and prayed. Marci was still trying to reach her friend, with no success. Trish was holding down the fort in case Priscilla called.

Josh was driving above the speed limit. He'd known Marci for twenty years, counting their friendship before marriage. It wasn't like her to crack under pressure. Perhaps having the family visit and the art show was too much. They'd already had one strange event in the marsh. Was Priscilla's disappearance part of the same phenomenon?

To Josh's credit, he'd been a good sport about the publicity around the Kea family. Unfortunately, thirty miles of the ocean didn't keep the scandal from Nantucket. But it was more controllable where they were so well known.

"Why, oh why, does there have to be a mystery on the property Jake and I want to develop?" Josh said to Sandi as they flew down the Polpis Road. "Maybe Old Man Taylor does have a secret he's hidden from the world. But then why would he sell the land? Wouldn't we discover the secret when we tear up the land for development? My excitement about this job is waning rapidly. How about you, Sandi?" The dog looked at him quizzically, put her muzzle on his right arm and sighed.

Josh and Jake were scheduled to show the land to the prospective buyer later that day. Marci wasn't happy about the appointment's conflict with her show. But she knew that their income might also vanish with the other homes disappearing. A new job would be a blessing.

With Keta's driving, they were back at the Taylor place in no time. Eating the dust from the driveway, the two bodyguards were right behind them. Keta brought the Land Rover to a halt and suggested that Marci and Becki go onto the front porch and knock on the door. He and Lyrica would stay at the bottom of the steps while Matt and Dan circled the rear of the house to make sure no one left unnoticed.

Marci ran up the steps and onto the Taylor's gracious, welcoming porch. It spread across the entire front of the home, then wrapped around the northern and southern sides. She didn't see anyone through the windows, but that didn't mean Priscilla wasn't there. After knocking and waiting, Marci called out to her friend.

"Priscilla, it's me, Marci."

After another try, Marci looked at Becki in despair. Lyrica, however, was ahead of them as usual. "Marci, why don't you see if the door is open? They never lock the house. I don't even think there's a key."

"Isn't that breaking and entering?"

"Not when it's your best friend, darling. Besides, why would five people break into a house in broad daylight? Maybe she's in her studio and doesn't hear us."

Issuing a weak "okay," Marci tried the door. It opened easily. Looking back at her mom for encouragement, she and Becki stepped inside the house. Lyrica and Keta followed.

The house was silent, dead silent, as if no one had been there for a long time. The only evidence of someone living there was the pile of breakfast dishes in the sink. Priscilla always cleaned up after a meal. Wandering around the house, calling her name, the family searched every room and cubby in the rambling structure, including Priscilla's studio. Nothing had been touched. The dust and acrid smell testified to that. Returning to the living room, they sat down in silence.

"Well, shall we wait until she comes back?" Lyrica said, hopefully looking at her husband.

"Marci, why don't you write Priscilla a note that you stopped by and hope to see her at the show?" Becki suggested.

"I think it might be better to call her again when we get home," Keta interjected. "If Priscilla is not here, and we leave a note, we might hurt or frighten Taylor. It might seem like someone is playing a grim joke on him."

"Marci, you need to get focused on the show today. Maybe she'll appear at the gallery this afternoon. You could straighten things out then," suggested Lyrica. "I think we all need to get home, have a quick bite to eat, and get downtown."

It was a sad-looking party that filed out of the Taylor house. Dan and Matt were waiting for them. There was only one backdoor, and no one had used it while the family was inside. They'd even checked the outdoor shower.

"Mr. Kea, one of us can stay here and come back with Josh. He'll be pretty upset if he gets here and you've all gone," Matt suggested.

"Matt's right. He's going to be very distraught if he finds no one here."

"I need to stay too," Marci piped up.

"Okay, sweetheart," Keta agreed. "But don't linger. I don't want you to be late for your own show."

That would not be a problem. Marci saw Josh's pickup racing down the last section of Taylor's driveway. She could tell how far he was just by the plume of dust that followed him.

"Dad, don't leave. That's Josh on his way up the driveway. Look, you can see the dust he's kicking up with the truck. I hope his tires survive."

The group stood by their vehicles until Josh pulled alongside them. Fortunately, with the breeze off the water, the dust cloud didn't envelop them. Stopping his pickup abruptly, Josh jumped out of the cab and ran to Marci.

"Honey, are you okay? What's going on? Matt said you saw Priscilla?"

"Josh, I saw her, *and* I talked with her. We have her famous hot chocolate to prove it."

"Marci, are you sure it was Priscilla?"

"Josh, we have the thermos at home. We all came back to find her. But no one's home except the spiders and mice."

"At this time of day, Taylor is at the Hub with his bench buddies," Josh added.

"I know it was Priscilla. She had on the crazy socks I gave her and that awful pair of pants she wears."

"Darling, we wouldn't all be standing here if we didn't believe that she was back." Lyrica was already concerned that this would affect Marci during her show.

"It could be a good sign. Maybe the houses will come back too." Josh was stalling for time. If Priscilla was back, maybe Taylor wouldn't sell the land. Unless it was already a done deal. He'd find out this afternoon.

"Marci, I have to meet Jake and the buyer this afternoon, right where we're standing. Maybe I can find out something then. Come on. We've got to get you home so you can get ready for the show." Josh reached over to take her hand.

"No, wait, Josh. I'm not going home until you tell me you believe what I'm saying."

Josh looked at his wife. Then he looked at the others standing around, who were nodding their heads. Getting Marci home was more important than proving Priscilla's presence. There would be time to do that. She looked tired and sad, not good on the biggest night of her show. More and more, a rational explanation for what was happening just wasn't possible.

"You know, Marci, with the houses disappearing, I think I can believe almost anything. Let's go, hon. Maybe Priscilla will make a surprise appearance at your show tonight."

"Thanks, Josh. It would be wonderful. I hope she won't be upset that I did a solo show. We were supposed to do this together."

"Hon, I think she'll be proud of you."

Thirty-Six

Saturday night held the best prospects for any art show on Nantucket. Visitors moored their yachts for the weekend, and the other tourists came downtown to eat dinner and stroll by the pretty shops that lined Main Street and the yacht basin. Marci's show was a stone's throw from Main Street and close enough to the yacht basin to produce a lot of foot traffic.

Her friend Jane had cleaned up from the previous night, so the family was more than ready to greet the first visitors. Dan was patrolling the outside while Matt was helping answer questions the visitors asked. Lyrica was guarding the cash box and sales. Keta and Trish readied the champagne, caviar, and crackers the visitors would enjoy.

Marci was wandering around, looking at the paintings. The triptych on the far wall was holding her attention. Priscilla had done the first painting only a few weeks before she disappeared. She and Marci had painted all afternoon in the meadow high above the Taylor house. Standing on top of the hillside near the hornbeams, they could see the rolling hills of the moors. She vividly remembered the mornings when she and Priscilla saddled up and rode into the middle moors, following dirt roads that meandered like ribbons through the heath. The horses loved the moors. After a hard gallop, Marci and Priscilla would let them graze freely in the meadow or drink from a pond.

Marci laughed to herself as she remembered Priscilla having to give her a leg up to get on Champ. He was fifteen hands high, and Marci was barely five feet. She could tether her horse to the hitching post at the barn so Priscilla could help her step up into the stirrups. Priscilla was six feet and could almost vault onto a horse. She was up on the saddle so fast sometimes Marci wondered why she didn't fly off and land on the other side.

The hitching post had been around for a long time. Its metal rings had weathered to a deep brown, aged and bumpy with corrosion. Like all wood exposed to the elements, the post had finally weakened and fallen over. Taylor and Priscilla probably burned it in their enormous stone fireplace one cold night. Maybe she would ask Priscilla if they could get a new one and have Josh build a set of steps to mount her horse. Her friend had probably stuffed the iron rings into one of the barn's cubby holes. Priscilla never threw out anything that could be useful later. She'd have to ask her where to find the cement post's foundation, as it would be buried under the soil they overturned for the new barn and corral. With a new post and the old rings, the corral would look much like it did before they rebuilt the barn.

A soft touch on Marci's shoulder broke her daydreaming. Keta was standing behind her, wondering what was holding her attention.

"What's up, darling? Are you having regrets about selling the triptych to Morston?"

"No, Dad. I was reminiscing about the days when Priscilla and I rode the horses together in the middle moors. Actually, I will be glad to have the triptych gone. It always made me sad Priscilla didn't finish it. I wonder what she'll think if she comes tonight and sees it. I'm still hoping she shows up."

"Don't get your hopes up too much. I'd hate to see you disappointed when the show has gone so well. Maybe tonight our visitors will buy up the place, and you'll have a whole new batch of commissions.

Turning around, they both saw that Morston and his companion had returned for a second night. "Remember, we have the place covered," Keta said and then slipped into the background away from Morston's sight.

Marci walked over toward Morston, who was eyeing another painting. Fortunately, several other tourists were in between, so Marci got waylaid by a couple wanting to know where she painted the triptych.

"We'd like to go walk there if we can. You've made it so beautiful. We've not seen the rolling moors on the island."

Marci never liked to reveal her painting spots to the public. The vehicle traffic had already wiped out many wildflowers that grew alongside the dirt roads or down their grassy centers. Becki, overhearing the conversation, hastened over to help Marci.

"Hi. I overheard your conversation. What are you both looking for? Maybe I can help." Marci gratefully stepped backed from the couple and their questions.

"We're naturalists from Scotland. I'm Alex McMure, and this is my wife, Joy. We only arrived yesterday and have been exploring downtown today. But we really would like to see the entire island. We've heard it looks a bit like Scotland, but it's hard to know exactly where to go." The sandy-haired young man was still in his wrinkled cargo pants but had put on a new Nantucket T-shirt.

"We're more comfortable out in the wild than downtown. Alex saw the ad for the show," his wife continued. "We came to see the paintings, hoping that the artist or someone could tell us where to find the wild places on the island. We're also photojournalists when we're not out exploring. Joy is the writer, and I'm the photographer."

"I'm from Boston, but my sister Marci is the artist and lives here year-round. I'm also an artist. Only I do botanicals of rare plant species from unexplored areas."

"I think I've heard of your work," Alex stated. He was trying to place the name. Becki was hoping they would not bring up the robbery scandal. She was relieved when Joy said, "I know where we've heard of you. Haven't you recently done some work in Madeira?"

Becki was stunned by the question. Seeing the change in Becki's demeanor, Joy quickly explained the connection. "Alex is a Harvard graduate. We've done several photojournalism tours and consulted for the Botanical Design Foundation."

"But how did you know about Madeira? I only got back last week. The botanicals are not even ready to show to the Foundation."

Joy smiled and responded, "We are two of the people who supported your grant. We did not know we'd meet you here. We didn't connect you with Marci's last name."

"Yes, we're sisters, twins. I'm here helping. We're having a family reunion. But don't worry, the botanicals will be ready for the showing next week. Will you both be there?"

"Joy will be there. I'll come if I don't have to finish up another project in Boston."

"But you must come," Becki insisted. "There is so much I can tell you about the ecosystems on Madeira. I know you'll enjoy the botanicals. Why don't you wander around and leave your business card with the cashier? Maybe I can spend some time with you tomorrow afternoon."

"That's very generous of you. We'll do that."

"And now I can see that I'm needed over there. It was great talking with you." Becki turned and walked over to check on her mom, still managing the sales desk.

"Becki, who are they? I heard photojournalists, but I didn't get the rest of the conversation as someone stopped by to purchase Marci's painting of the hornbeams."

"They are Alex and Joy McMure from Scotland."

"Becki, are they really photojournalists? Even on Nantucket, we need to be cautious."

"Mom, it's okay. Do they have the paparazzi look?" Becki seemed surprised at her mother's comment.

"How about you have a conversation with Matt or Dan and ask them to check out the McMures? Let's see what they dig up before you spend any time with two strangers."

"Mom, they're going to leave their contact information with you before they leave." Lyrica still looked worried.

"I know, I know, Mom. I'll talk to Matt. He looks like he needs saving from that gorgeous blonde decorator that Morston brought with him tonight."

Leaving Lyrica, Becki walked toward Matt. She caught his eye about halfway across the room and an almost imperceptible "no" movement of his head. Turning around, she headed for the back door to find Dan. "What a life these guys have," she murmured under her breath. "Maybe this will give them some actual work."

Pushing open the screen door that led to the small patio and parking area, Becki stood still for a moment, knowing Dan was outside somewhere on his watch. She wasn't sure she wanted to bump into him again or if she just wanted to give him the message. While she was thinking, a shadowy movement behind her caught her eye. Whirling around, Becki was face to face with Dan. He'd been sitting in an Adirondack chair in the patio's dark corner, so she hadn't seen him when she first walked out of the gallery.

"Hi. I was wondering when I'd get to see you tonight. How's it going in there?" Dan said, nodding toward the window into the gallery. "I see Matt is making eyes at Morston's blonde. Do you know what they're talking about?"

"Dan, don't get jealous. He's not hitting on her. I went over to warn him about some visitors, but he signaled me to stay away. So maybe it's work-related?" she said, smiling with mischief in her eyes.

"Why would I be jealous when I've got you here?" But Dan shifted gears when he saw the quick change in Becki's body language. "I take it you didn't come out here to chat with me. It was a nice thought while it lasted."

Becki didn't like him teasing her. She never knew quite when to believe him. He seemed to have an uncanny way of knowing her feelings a few seconds before even she did.

"Why don't we walk down the driveway where we're less likely to be overheard? Unless that makes you uncomfortable?" Dan said, making her very uncomfortable.

"Okay. This won't take but a minute." Becki turned toward the driveway that led out to the street. They were heading for the exact spot where they had collided last night. Except this time, he wouldn't be able to surprise her. Becki couldn't decide if that disappointed her or not. Why does this guy have such a hold on me? Why isn't Dad doing this? He was the one who hired these guys. Why am I always the one thrown together with Dan? Becki's thoughts were racing ahead to the end of the driveway and the information about the McMures she would relay to Dan.

When they got to the Land Rover, Dan put a hand on Becki's shoulder and said, "Why don't we stop here? I think we're far enough away. Tell me what brought you out here."

Becki's whole body reacted to his touch. She was grateful for the car to lean on. She looked up into his aquamarine eyes, hoping he couldn't see the heat she felt creeping up her neck and onto her face. When she finally could talk, Becki relayed her conversation with the McMures, noting that Lyrica requested that Dan or Matt check them out before anyone spent time with them.

Dan reached for his phone.

"How fast do you think we can get an answer? They want me to show them the island tomorrow."

"It depends who's on the research shift tonight in Boston. If it's who I think it is, we'll have an answer tonight." Finishing up the call, he put the phone into his pocket and turned to walk back toward the gallery. As Becki turned, she felt Dan's gentle hand on her back. It was an innocent enough gesture to guide her back in the right direction, but Becki could feel her body respond to his touch. Dan felt it as well.

Turning toward her once again, Dan stopped walking. He was looking deeply into her eyes. "Becki?"

"What?" she said, trying to be businesslike but failing.

"Becki, I'd like to kiss you. I think you are fighting as hard as I am to suppress your feelings. Am I right?"

Why is he always right about my feelings? Even Stephen wasn't this in tune with her emotions, she thought. But then maybe Stephen didn't cause such a powerful reaction in her anymore. But this guy did, and she knew it.

"Yes," was all she said.

"Yes, you want to kiss me, or yes, you are fighting to cover your feelings?"

"Yes, to both."

Thirty-Seven

The fog bank was slowly creeping across Boston's Back Bay, muting the city lights. A small, wiry man wound his way through the narrow streets, making his way to Becki's studio. Getting onto the roof of the adjacent building hadn't been difficult. His practice run went so well he considered trying the break-in then. But he knew he had to wait until Becki was not coming home for the night. Stealthily, the thief climbed the six flights of stairs to reach the doorway that led out onto the roof of the building next to Becki's loft. He had to do the job swiftly, as the incoming fog could easily make jumping from one building to another impossible. He'd only had a few inches to spare when he jumped it the last time. Silently, he thanked Morston that all he had to carry were photos.

He carefully opened the door to the rooftop. It was always possible that someone was up there, but unlikely given the weather. Any sunbathing was over for the day. He silently crept over to the edge of the roof. The tar was still hot from the summer sun. Hopefully, that wouldn't affect his grounding stakes.

He planted a stake by the eight-inch brick wall surrounding the rooftop, driving it deep into the roofing material. Then, tugging hard on it, he checked its strength. Not so bad, he thought, but he hammered in two other stakes for security. He quickly attached two tie lines to his belt, one to jump and one to lower himself into the loft. I wish I'd asked Morston for more money, he thought. His jobs were getting steadily more dangerous. But that was the way with Morston. He'd squeeze every drop of blood out of you before he'd set another dollar on the table.

The thief's past attempts to gain access to Becki's studio had met with defeat. But he would soon forget that once he was in the loft and had found the photos. He backed up, took a running leap across the small alley between the two buildings, and landed on his feet near the glass windows of Becki's studio. He was on her roof. The eight conservatory windows that made up the studio's ceiling spread out before him. Four were open, two directly above the couch.

"How convenient, a soft landing," he said out loud. "But I'll have to make fast work of this place. The fog is growing denser by the minute." Cutting the screen that covered the window, he slipped on some shoe covers, hooked his harness to one of the steel beams that crisscrossed Becki's ceiling, and slowly lowered himself through the open window to the floor. The landing went smoothly except for a stack of books on the glass coffee table that he accidentally kicked onto the floor.

Unhooking his harness, he headed for the prominent architect's desk and file cabinet. Quickly going through the three file drawers, he said a silent thank you to Becki for not locking them. Her desk drawers were underneath the drawing station. Lovely flowers, he thought to himself as he passed by the latest botanicals from Madeira. Why can't Morston send me to Madeira or Nice?

Becki had filled the drawers with unfinished work, paper, and ink supplies, but no photos. He stood and surveyed the room. None of the images on the walls were black and white. Directly across from him was the kitchen. There wasn't room for wall art, but he saw a plate of cookies on the countertop covered with plastic wrap. Walking over to the counter, he deftly swiped two cookies, rearranged the pile, and re-secured the plastic. He was heading for the rest of the studio when he noticed the books he'd knocked off the coffee table.

Munching on a cookie, he reached over and repositioned the stack of books. Not a bad collection of flower and bird art, he thought. Maybe some of Becki's botanicals were in the books and even worth stealing. But he didn't have time to look. Then, to his delight, under the art books, he noticed that the glass top coffee table had a collage of photos and art prints. Cursing that he hadn't started here, he lifted the large books from the table to check the photo collage.

There were a few black and white snapshots of the family. Some photos appeared to be from Nantucket, but they were of the beach and a sailboat. Morston's description didn't include the beach. But under the stack he'd knocked over, there was a photo that seemed more to Morston's specifications. It was a faded black and white print of a barn, horses, and one very tall woman putting a bridle on a horse. "Now that's more like it," he chuckled to himself.

However, removing the photo would be a challenge, and he was running short on time. It was glued in place, then covered with the glass top of the coffee table. Checking underneath, he saw that decorative brass clamps held the glass in place on each corner. Whipping out his wrench and screwdriver, he quickly tried the corners nearest him. They had rusted in place. Cursing his stupidity for not seeing this first, he looked around for something with which to break the glass. He was starting to smell his sweat.

Flinging open the kitchen drawers, he found a wooden mallet. Grabbing a dish towel, he headed for the table. Hopefully, no one would hear him. He positioned a screwdriver to protect the photo and brought the mallet down hard. Several nice cracks in the glass appeared, but nothing moved. Another whack and glass fell to the carpet on two sides.

Clearing off the shards with his gloved hand, the thief inspected the photo's mounting. It was taped in two spots. Quickly lifting the photo from its cardboard backing, he rolled it, put a rubber band around it, and stuffed it inside his jacket. Then he carefully put back the large pieces of glass and pushed the shards underneath the table. The weight of the books appeared to hold the broken glass in place. He stood up, ready to search the bedrooms. But he hadn't counted on Becki's neighbor coming to feed Rollo.

Ellen lived in the flat at the end of the hall. She and Becki took turns cat-sitting for each other. Closing the door to her flat, she walked down the hallway to feed and play with Rollo.

Great, all I need is a witness, he thought, hearing Ellen's footsteps come closer. He swiftly climbed back up through the window just as Ellen unlocked the two deadbolts. Without looking back, he leaped across the alley as Ellen opened the door into Becki's studio. He'd left a line tied to one of the steel rafters of the studio. Sloppy job, but he had to escape fast.

When Ellen entered the studio, she couldn't find Rollo. "Hmm, that's funny," she said out loud. "She's usually here waiting for me. Maybe she's napping on Becki's bed." Sure enough, Rollo was in the bedroom under the quilt.

"Rollo, what's up, girl?"

Rollo didn't move. Ellen peeled back the Shaker quilt. Rollo looked at her suspiciously. Usually, she'd get up, stretch, jump down and head for the kitchen.

"Hey girl, are you okay? Missing Mom?" Rollo jumped down and raced down the hallway toward the kitchen. But instead of positioning herself on the cushioned chairs, she hid under the table.

Ellen pulled up the tablecloth and got down on her knees to coax her out of hiding. Then she saw some shards the thief had missed. She looked at the coffee table. Becki's books were still there, but she could see that someone had broken the tabletop and patched it together.

"Oh, my gosh. Someone's been in here," Ellen said out loud. "That's why you were hiding." Then she saw the tie line hanging above her. She'd been so focused on looking for Rollo that she'd missed it when she first entered. But now she saw it and froze. What if the thief was still there? Quickly grabbing Rollo, she dashed out the door and raced down the hall to her loft. Slamming her door shut, she locked it, put Rollo on the couch, and dialed 911.

It wasn't long before a police officer called up through the intercom. When he appeared at her door, she cautiously opened it with the chain still on. She was about to ask for an ID when the officer asked her, "Are you Ellen Duffy? You called 911, something about a break-in?"

"Yes, officer, down the hall. I can show you if you show me your ID." Smiling, the officer complied. Ellen grabbed Becki's keys and walked the young officer down the hall.

"I think it would be better if you stayed outside until I know the thief has left." Taking Becki's key, he went inside, looked around the open-air studio, and then walked down the hallway to check the bedrooms. Returning to the door, he told Ellen to come in.

"Miss Duffy, is this exactly the way you found the studio? Have you touched or moved anything in here?"

"No," Ellen responded. "I went to the bedroom to look for Rollo, Becki's cat. She was hiding under the quilt. After I coaxed her off the bed, she hid under the kitchen table. I was going to pull her out from under the table when I saw broken glass on the Oriental rug, right there," Becki pointed. "I grabbed Rollo and ran out."

"Thank you, Miss Duffy. Why don't you sit down while I have another look around?"

The officer called for backup and the detective on duty. Ellen sat on the chenille couch staring at the broken glass, trying to figure out how the table got damaged. Then she noticed a photo was missing. The enormous books covering most of the space were askew, but she could see the photo's mounting board. She motioned to the officer and pointed to the table. Ellen was about to lift the books to show him when he stopped her.

"We need to check for fingerprints before we move anything."

The officer asked Ellen to walk around the studio and see if anything else was disturbed or missing. He also wanted to know who else had a key to the flat. She knew Stephen had a key, but there was zero chance it was him or Trish. When it was all said and done, the only evidence of the break-in was the coffee table and the line still tied to the steel beam below the open window.

It didn't take long for the police backup to arrive. When they'd checked the studio and the roof, the officer instructed Ellen to call Becki and tell her that a detective would call her tomorrow for more information.

"Officer, is there any way you can keep this out of the newspaper?" Ellen asked.

"That will not be easy. Why?"

Ellen hesitated to mention the robbery at Lyrica's home, but she decided they'd figure it out, anyway.

"Officer, Becki's mom is Lyrica Kea. Do you remember the robbery at her home a month ago? The press made an enormous deal about it. This won't help."

"Yes, I know about it. I'll see what I can do. One more question, Ms. Duffy. Do you think that the two robberies are related?"

"Anything is possible, I guess. But how did the thief know Becki was away?"

"This was a professional job. He probably cased the studio for several weeks to learn her habits."

"What about Rollo?"

"For now, I'd keep the cat in your flat. The likelihood of the thief returning is small. But since it looks like you interrupted him, we shouldn't leave out that possibility. Hopefully, the thief got what he wanted. Now, unless you have any other questions, how about I walk you back to your flat?"

"Sounds good to me."

Once inside, with the doors locked, Ellen plopped down on her couch with Rollo beside her. She picked up her cell phone and called her friend.

Thirty-Eight

awn came too quickly after the late night at the gallery. The show had been a great success. Marci sold many of her paintings and had several invitations for commission work. Everyone gratefully tumbled into bed without any discussion of breakfast.

Only the men knew it was going to be a short night. Josh, Keta, and the two bodyguards quickly gathered their things and piled into the Land Rover at dawn. Mako and Sandi lifted their heads, took one look at them, and curled back up in their warm beds. Hopefully, starting up the engine wouldn't awaken the women.

Three hours later, they arrived home. Their mission to the Taylor land had been successful, but disturbing. Lyrica, the only one aware of the plan, came outside to meet them.

"Josh, Marci wasn't too happy you left her behind. Becki wisely escorted her to the studio and got her mind focused elsewhere."

Lyrica put the cinnamon French toast on the table. She then made her way through the rose hedge to the studio.

"Hey, you two. Come and get some breakfast before the guys devour your French toast."

"Okay, be there in a minute," Marci replied. Lyrica noticed her mood seemed to have lifted.

When she got back, the French toast had diminished significantly. But Keta was at the stove making more. The smell of maple syrup and bacon wafted through the screen doors onto the deck.

When everyone was finally together at the table, Keta opened the discussion about what they'd found at the Taylor place. Everyone paused eating their breakfast, eager to have the news. Only Josh kept eating.

"Marci, we went to the Taylor property this morning to look for evidence of someone walking up behind you and Becki and then later walking toward the house. We wanted a clean trail to look for Priscilla's footprints. Thanks to our super sleuths, Matt and Dan, we found potential evidence of someone being there when you two girls were in the meadow." Then, turning to the two body-guards, Keta handed the story over to Dan and Matt.

"Josh showed us where you'd been in the meadow. You could see where the grass was flattened by the quilt and trodden down where you'd entered the meadow," Matt continued. "It's possible that someone used your trail to enter the meadow. But since you told us that Priscilla went back to the house, we looked to see if the grass showed evidence of being walked on as you head toward the house and corral."

"Whoever was there, and we believe there was someone else in the meadow with you, didn't take time to cover his or her tracks."

Marci cut in impatiently. "Guys, I know you're trying to be scientific, but it *was* Priscilla who appeared in the meadow. It wasn't an imposter or a hallucination."

"Okay. Let's assume it was Priscilla. Based on where you both were in the meadow, someone still could have entered the area from behind you, Marci. If you had been farther up the hill by the hornbeams, I would have guessed something else."

"Grasses were bent from yesterday, and the morning dew on them had not been disturbed," Dan continued. "We walked a parallel path between you and the other entrance to the meadow. While deer could have been there, we didn't find any tracks in the muddier parts of the trail. We did, however, find some footprints."

"Footprints?" exclaimed Marci.

"Yes. I'll get to that in a minute. We found a trail to and from the house. There were footprints, or rather parts of footprints, in the muddy places of the meadow and by the barn," Dan finished.

"Whose footprints?" Marci shouted.

"We don't know. But Dan took some measurements and drew out the pattern from the shoe's sole. We didn't get a full print. But it's likely someone in town may can identify what kind of shoe it is."

Silence blanketed the room as they processed what the detectives had just related.

"I knew I wasn't crazy," snapped Marci.

"Darling, no one thought you were crazy, just maybe scared and confused," said Lyrica.

"Here's what the footprint looks like." Dan pulled out a large sketch.

"What we don't know is why someone came to the property when you two were there."

"Marci, do you remember what shoes Priscilla was wearing?" Keta asked.

"Of course, it had to be her beat-up running shoes for me to see her socks. I don't think she owns another pair of shoes except for flip flops and some rubber boots to muck the stalls."

Passing Dan's drawing across the table to Marci, Keta asked his daughter, "Marci, do you think these prints could have been Priscilla's?"

"This is a pretty big size shoe," Dan commented.

"Ha, you guys never saw Priscilla," Josh joked. "She was six feet, and her shoes were probably as big as yours."

"Josh is right," Marci agreed. "She has big feet. What size, I don't know."

"Would you like to go downtown with us to see if we can find out what shoe this is?" Matt asked Marci.

"No thanks. I'll let you guys explain your way out of asking questions like that. I'm going to the gallery to drop off some bakery items with Jane for this afternoon's visitors. Maybe Morston and Celina will come back."

"Marci, why don't I do that for you?" Trish asked.

"No. I'm okay by myself. I'm only going to town."

Thirty-Nine

ut Marci didn't go to the bakery. Determined to find her own evidence of Priscilla, she headed back to the Taylor property. "Men. They think they're the only ones who can solve mysteries. Trish could teach them a few things," she muttered to herself.

Marci was grateful not to see Taylor's car by the house. But just as she pulled up to park, she saw Priscilla cresting the dune on the path to the beach. Beeping the horn, she shouted out the window. But the sound of the surf and wind drowned out her calls. Marci leaped out of the Jeep, not even taking time to close the door. She ran toward the path to the beach. Puffing as she approached the dune's crest, she saw Priscilla settling in on the beach.

It startled her at first. Then she had time to become a little frightened. Maybe she should have brought Trish or Becki with her. There was no sense in yelling against the pounding surf. The wind and water would take her voice, so she walked closer. Yes, it was Priscilla. When she was within a few yards, she called out her name. Priscilla turned around and greeted her as if they were picking up from the day before. Still a bit stunned, Marci walked over to her and sat down on the soft old quilt Priscilla used as a beach blanket.

"Priscilla, where have you been?"

"What do you mean, where have I been? I just saw you yesterday."

"Priscilla, remember that I said everyone thinks you're missing? You disappeared a month ago. Taylor is a mess. Some people are saying you're dead."

"What? You've got to be joking."

"No, I'm not. Really."

"Marci, I saw you painting in the meadow with Becki. Don't you remember?"

"Yes, I do. That's why I came out here. I had to see if I could find you. I'm sorry we left. We waited for you to come back, but we finally had to go."

"Well, you've found me, girl. What's on your mind?"

"Priscilla, you don't seem to understand. The entire island thinks you're dead. Taylor has put the property up for sale. Josh and Jake are talking with a prospective buyer today to build an estate house on it."

"What? Taylor wouldn't do that. What kind of joke are you trying to play on me?"

"Priscilla, it's no joke. If you come home with me, I'll show you. Or better yet, I'll take you to Pocomo Meadows and show you what else has happened."

"Okay. Let's get this straight. You and everyone, including T, think I'm dead or missing. What else is missing? Is my car gone, my paints, the barn, and my horses?"

"I'm not sure about the horses. I haven't seen either recently. And we were in the meadow yesterday."

"They haven't disappeared. I mucked the stalls this morning."

Suddenly Marci saw that this conversation was going nowhere. "Priscilla, have you seen this week's paper? There's an article about some missing houses in it."

"Marci, there wasn't anything in the paper about missing houses. Anyway, houses don't vanish overnight," Priscilla pronounced in her matter-of-fact manner. "Wait, I'll show you. I have the paper in my bag."

"Great. Let's have a look."

"Okay, you show me where the article is on the missing houses."

"It's on the front page in the lower right corner. There's a picture of the Pocomo hillside from the air."

Holding the newspaper so they both could scan the front page, Marci checked for the article. All she saw was an article on the local debate about wind energy.

"Are you sure this is this week's paper?" Marci asked.

"See for yourself, girl."

Marci looked where Priscilla was pointing to the date at the top of the paper. It *was* the same week. The headlines and articles were the same, except the lower right corner had the wrong piece.

"Priscilla, there's got to be some mistake. I'm telling you, this is not the same front page as the one we have at home."

"Maybe you're a week behind. You know how slow you read."

"Pris, everything else on this front page is the same as the paper we have at home, except this article in the lower right-hand corner."

"Suit yourself, girl. Why don't you come and join me on the beach for a while? Maybe it will clear your head."

"No, Pris. I can't. You've got to come with me. I need to show you something."

"Marci, I just got here. Can't it wait until later?"

"No. We have to go now. Come on. It won't take long." Marci got up from the blanket and started toward the dune. Priscilla watched her for a few seconds, then shaking her head, got up to follow her friend.

Once in Marci's Jeep, they headed down the driveway and out toward Pocomo. She was determined to show Priscilla the hillside and see what she said. It was eerie to be conversing with her missing friend. Priscilla asked about the new mural painting Marci was doing. The only thing Marci held back was the show and the triptych that she had finished in honor of her friend. How would she break it to Priscilla that she completed her murals?

They quickly reached the dirt road leading to Medouie Creek. Marci took another track that led out to the marsh, where she and Josh launched their kayaks. Pulling to a stop, Marci got out of the Jeep.

"Come on, Pris, this way."

"Okay, I'm coming. But this better be good. You're using up my beach time, you know," Priscilla groused.

"Now, look over there," Marci said, pointing to the hillside above the marsh. "Remember the homes that Josh and Jake built on that hillside?"

"Remember them. How can I forget them? They ruined a beautiful view in both directions. Why people insist on building enormous estate homes on a small island, I'll never figure out." Priscilla was off on one of her tangents about the island. Perfect, thought Marci.

"Pris, look at the hillside. The houses aren't there anymore."

"Gone? Yeah, don't I wish."

"Pris, look."

"Oh my gosh, Marci. That hillside looks just like it did when Taylor and I moved onto our property."

Marci waited for Priscilla to recover from the shock. It didn't take long for her crusty New England pragmatism to take over.

"So, girlfriend, where did they go?"

"Good question. We'd all like to know."

"Marci, what about the people? Where are they?"

"That, my dear, the police are still trying to figure out."

"Look, houses and people just don't disappear."

"Pris, I'd take you to Pocomo and show you that the private drive into the development is gone, but it wouldn't make any difference. The houses have vanished, and no one knows why."

"You know, I like it a lot better without the houses. Now the landscape is pristine again," Priscilla chuckled.

"Well, you and I might like it this way, but there are some people who are hopping mad and mighty worried."

"What I don't understand is why haven't I heard about this? It wasn't in the paper. How could I have missed it? Are you sure about this?"

"Priscilla, it was in the paper. That's what I was trying to show you."

"Well, this certainly beats sitting on the beach."

Marci was slowly realizing it would take some time for Priscilla to believe the disappearances, including her own.

"Pris, I'd better drop you off at home. I've got to get back and change before the show." It was out before Marci knew what she was saying.

"What show, Marci? You didn't tell me you were doing a show? Or did that conversation disappear too?"

"Oh, you've just forgotten, that's all. Let's get you home so you can change and come to the show. It's the last big day."

Marci headed toward the Taylor farm, trying to figure out how to explain this to Josh. What if he showed up with the real estate people while she was there? When she pulled up to the house, Priscilla gathered up her beach bag, with the paper still in it.

"I'll see you later, okay?" Marci said.

"You sure you don't want to come in for some lemonade?"

"No thanks. I've got to get ready. See you later?"

"Sure thing. I'll be there. Maybe you and I could do a show together one of these days."

"Sure. Sounds good to me," Marci sighed. Then, just as Priscilla was about to leave, Marci remembered the newspaper.

"Pris, are you done with your newspaper?"

"Yup, do you want it? Taylor always has a copy around somewhere. He likes to have his own, you know."

"Oh yes. How well I know," Marci responded quietly.

"Here you go, girl. Bring by that paper you had with the article in it, okay?"

"Right. See you later."

"You too." Priscilla turned to walk back to the house.

Maybe if Priscilla isn't gone, things will get back to normal again, whatever that means, Marci thought. Everyone will be so happy. She watched her friend walk across the grass toward the house. It was so good to know she was alive.

Marci was lost in thought watching her friend when suddenly Priscilla vanished. She never made it to the house. One minute Priscilla was there, and the next, she was gone. Marci leaned her head on the steering wheel and began to cry. Priscilla didn't disappear on the path to the beach or the front porch.

She vanished before she even made it to the porch. Picking up her cell, she called Josh.

After several rings, Josh answered. "Hey, baby, where are you? We were getting worried."

"Josh, I'm just leaving the Taylor place. You will not believe this, but I just spent the last thirty minutes with Priscilla."

"What?"

"Yeah, I know. I was excited to find her. But Josh, she's not here anymore. She vanished before my eyes."

Forty

Josh was waiting for Marci when she pulled up to the house. Walking over to the Jeep, he looked at his wife carefully and tenderly. She seemed okay. The past few days, she seemed happier than he'd seen her since Priscilla disappeared.

"Marci, now tell me again. You said you talked with Priscilla, and then she vanished?"

"Josh, not quite in that order. When I got to the Taylor place, I saw her going over the dune to the beach, so I followed her. We had a discussion on the beach about her disappearance, and then I took her to see the empty hillside in Pocomo."

"What did she say? Was she surprised that the houses were missing?"

"Yes, but you know how practical she is. She immediately wanted to know what happened, what else was missing, and what's being done about it."

"But Marci, didn't she know about it? The paper had it on the front page."

"Josh, that's just it. She showed me a copy of her paper on the beach. The article wasn't in it."

"Are you sure it was this week's paper?"

"Yes, I'm sure. Look, here it is." Marci pulled the paper out of her bag and showed it to Josh.

"I don't like the looks of this."

"Josh, I really saw her. I took her to see the empty hillside above the marsh. You've got to believe me."

"Marci, anything is possible. I'm just glad *you* didn't vanish. From now on, don't go looking for her without me, okay?"

Marci didn't answer.

"Marci, you've got to let me protect you. I don't want you to vanish with Priscilla."

"Josh, we don't even know where she goes. Why didn't I vanish when I was with her?"

Before they could finish their discussion, they entered the living room, where the group had once more gathered around the kitchen counter.

"Here they are," Lyrica announced, with a look of relief on her face.

"Marci, are you okay?"

"I'm okay. But I saw Priscilla again, and I have a newspaper from her to prove it."

"She's not joking. She has a copy of this week's *The Inquirer and Mirror* that looks identical to the one on the coffee table, except it's missing the article on the houses."

"Look." Marci put Priscilla's paper on the kitchen table while Matt grabbed the copy off the coffee table. She pointed to the article on the lower right corner of Priscilla's paper.

"Anyone have an explanation?"

"Josh, before you came in, we were discussing the possibility of Matt or Dan returning to the Taylors to see if she shows up again," Keta explained.

"Only this time, Marci, you're staying home," Josh ordered.

"Got it. But Josh, aren't you and Jake showing the land this afternoon?"

"Yes, we are. I'm okay with your plan as long as you stay out of sight while we're there. Remember, we're showing *all* the land. The only place you can hide is on the beach."

"You better get some gear from the Jeep, so you look like a beachcomber. You'll need to keep a sharp watch in case Morston wants to come down to the beach," Keta added.

"I'll take Morston to the beach right before we leave. You can watch us from behind the dune, and then, if needed, head down the beach by the water, and I'll pick you up in Squam."

"Sounds like pleasant duty for one of us," Dan said jokingly.

"I don't know. Spending an afternoon watching three lovely ladies sounds more appealing to me than hot sun and beach grass. Why don't you go? I'll look after the ladies downtown." Matt suggested.

"You got it. Just give me a baseball hat, some suntan lotion, a towel, and I'm ready."

Inwardly, Becki sighed. She was grateful for an afternoon without being under the microscope with Dan, or maybe just relieved that there would be little chance of them meeting as they had outside the gallery. At least, she thought that was what she felt. But when it came right down to it, she wasn't sure.

"Now, let's look through the newspaper Marci brought back to see if we can find any clues," Keta proposed to the group.

❧

Later that same day, the men reviewed the disappearances again. No one, not even Josh, Jake, or the buyer, had seen Priscilla. Dan had garnered a sunburn waiting on the beach. No one had entered the house or property all afternoon except Josh, Jake, Morston, and the realtor. He hadn't even seen Taylor.

What he saw, however, was a strange pattern of compass readings while walking the property, something scientifically unexplainable. He readily found fixed compass points while standing on the hill by the hornbeams. But there were three places on the property where the needle on his compass wouldn't settle on any one direction. The first place was by the house at the base of the path leading to the beach, right where Marci said Priscilla disappeared. The second was in the corral outside the barn. And the third was in the meadow where Marci had been painting. There was nothing notable about any of the sites except wonky compass readings.

Dan, Matt, and Keta were discussing all this when Marci and Lyrica walked into the kitchen. Josh was out on a job. Grabbing a homemade cookie, Marci sat down at the table. Lyrica joined them, peeling the skin off a navel orange. Josh's survey map took up half the table.

"Okay, boys, what's this about wacky compass readings?" Lyrica asked.

Keta answered by asking another question. "Marci, where were you when you saw Priscilla appear and disappear?"

"Which time, Dad?"

"Any or all of them? We had Josh's survey map copied. I think Matt and Dan may be on to something."

"The first time I saw her was in the meadow just below the hornbeams where Becki and I were painting."

"And where did Priscilla come from and go to?" Dan pressed.

"I'm not sure where she entered the meadow, but it was somewhere behind me, either through the horse path from the corral or near the hornbeams where the deer trail disappears into the scrub."

"Marci, can you place yourself on the map the first time you saw Priscilla?"

Marci looked on the map, pointed, and then Dan placed a dime at the top of the meadow by the hornbeams.

"That's where the deer trail and the secret path come in from the road. I last saw her leaving the meadow on the way to the house where the scrub opens up so the horses can go between the meadow and the corral."

"Is there any other place in the meadow where you saw Priscilla at any point?" Matt asked.

"Hey, what's going on here?" Becki said, coming into the room. "Are we looking for buried treasure?" She walked over to the table where the group had gathered.

"Hi, doll. Grab a cookie, and we'll count you in on the treasure hunt," Keta replied as Becki came over and stood by his side.

"What are you doing with Josh's map?"

"Becki, we copied his map. We're trying to pinpoint places where Priscilla appeared over the last few days. Marci was showing us the meadow where you and she painted the day of the show."

"What about the lower edge of the meadow?" her sister asked. "Weren't you painting the horses and Priscilla that day?"

"Yes, but she and the horses weren't there when I was painting. I imagined that part. I took Priscilla out of the picture when I remembered how she lectured me about people ruining a good landscape painting. But she wasn't in that part of the meadow. That's where *you* were that day."

"And where is that on the map?" Matt asked.

"Down there," Becki and Marci answered together. Matt took out a few pennies from his pocket and placed one on the map.

"But Marci, what about when you took her to see the hillside overlooking Pocomo Meadows?" Dan asked.

Once again, Marci explained how she saw Priscilla go over the dune to the beach.

"The needle on the compass read true on the beach," Dan added.

"That's because she disappeared in front of the house." Marci was tiring of the endless questions.

"Where else did you find odd compass readings?" Keta asked.

Dan put dimes on the map. The places where Priscilla was seen coincided with irregular compass readings. But it also included the corral. There were other places, such as the hillside above Pocomo meadows, where Dan hadn't checked the compass yet.

"This is all very interesting, but what is your theory?" Keta asked, interested but impatient to get to an answer.

"Mr. Kea, we're not sure. But we think the unusual readings occur wherever Priscilla disappears and reappears. We're still looking for a pattern," Dan explained.

"Dad, don't be too hard on them. Priscilla is a slippery character,"

Becki laughed.

"Darling," Lyrica spoke up. "I think we need to start thinking out of the box. Let's talk about how Priscilla could have a different newspaper with the same publication date."

"But Mom, there's no way to explain that," Marci added.

"I think there is," Lyrica continued. "I believe it *was* the same date. But somehow, a second time frame runs parallel to ours. That's where she goes. She disappeared before the houses vanished. Right?"

Marci was the only one who answered. "Yes, that's correct, Mom."

"I don't think Priscilla disappeared. I think she is still alive, and occasionally, for whatever reason, she breaks through some type of membrane, separating her time frame from ours. If she *is* living in a parallel reality, I'll bet the McMansions are there as well."

The room fell silent. Finally, Lyrica spoke again.

"Don't you see? What else can it be? Marci said that Priscilla disappeared before she got to the house. And Marci and Becki brought back hot chocolate in Priscilla's thermos. So real people and real things appear and disappear. Why, how, who knows? This may sound like science fiction, but does anyone have a better explanation?"

Forty-One

The group around the kitchen table was silent for several minutes while each processed what Lyrica had said. During the silence, Dan excused himself to take a call on his phone. All eyes were on him when he returned to the table.

"I need to change the subject for a minute to update you on the McMures. Our investigative team traced the post office box on Joy's business card to Kyle of Lochalsh on the western shore of Scotland. Their home location, however, is not in that town. The team is reviewing classified names and addresses as well as taking tips from our operatives in the United Kingdom. McMure is a reasonably common name in western Scotland. So it will take some time unless we get lucky."

"But who are they?" Lyrica asked.

"Alex and Joy are high-caliber photojournalists who freelance for several global nature magazines. Besides being a journalist, Alex is a geologist, and Joy is a naturalist. A marriage certificate using their names isn't on record in the United Kingdom. However, they could have been married abroad. We are hoping to check tax records next.

"They were truthful about their involvement with the Botanical Design Foundation in Boston and Becki's botanical grant. But they could be simply using the McMure name. Their tenure with the Foundation has been only six months. I strongly advise caution when conversing with them until we answer the questions about their identity. If any of you spend time with them, Matt or I need to be with you.

"I have some other information to share. We've linked the McMures with a chain of investigations involving stolen photos and shady land deals. It appears they've been in the same places as Morston, including Madeira, and most recently, Nice, France. At this point, we don't know if they are working with Morston or tracking him for their own reasons. They could be here for a quick vacation, but I doubt it. Their appearance is too coincidental."

"If that's the case, why didn't you warn us before Becki met them at the show?" Keta stated. "Isn't that what I'm paying you guys for?"

"Darling, give the guys a chance," Lyrica said as she gave Keta her "calm down" look.

"Mr. Kea, their link with our investigation wasn't clear until we confirmed that they'd been in the same places as Morston. Our European office is following the McMures under a separate investigation. That office is treating them as suspects and possible cohorts of Morston until proven otherwise. They're not tied to any private investigative firm that we can find. Their business cards lead to dead ends, including the one Alex gave Becki. Before anyone can discover the card is a fake, they move on and create another.

"We know Morston dropped out of sight briefly last month. We found him in Nice, supposedly taking a vacation. But when he filed his return flight plan, the destination was Boston, not Nantucket. We didn't know he was here until he appeared at Marci's show Friday night. His plane is still at the Nantucket Airport. Apparently, the McMures have been shadowing Morston for several months. They knew he had interests in Madeira before heading to Nice," Dan explained.

"What would interest Morston in Madeira?" Becki asked.

"Morston is masterminding several shady, international real estate deals. Madeira and Nice were his latest victims until he landed on Nantucket. And here's an interesting fact. Morston owns the controlling interest in Earsom Technicals, the holding company for Justin Earsom's construction firm."

"What?" Becki shouted. "That can't be true. Next, you're going to tell us he's the one that wants the land Stephen and I surveyed, not Justin Earsom."

"You said it, not me," Dan replied, flashing his enigmatic smile.

"Well, well, well. Sounds as if we have a nasty web of deceit and robbery with Lyrica, only one of his targets," Keta said. "It makes more sense to me now. He was always looking for a way to repay me for exposing him five years ago. He doesn't forget until his revenge is complete. What else do you have for us?"

"Usually, Morston has a front person do his work. But in the past, he has brought down his schemes by showing up in person. Coming to this island was a critical mistake. But it also means he's after something here that trumps a land deal to build a home," Matt continued.

"There certainly is no geological treasure here worth his time," Keta laughed.

"Why does everything in this family have to be so complicated?" Marci put her head in her hands. "I thought Josh and I were safe out here. Now it looks like we're being sucked into this publicity vortex all over again. Excuse me, but I'm going to the studio. I've had enough of this conversation." Getting up from the table, Marci walked out the French doors to the deck and headed down the path to her studio. Lyrica got up to follow her, but Keta held her back.

"Let her go, darling. She needs a break. We can talk with her later. First, we need to find Josh. He and Jake must be very attentive to the questions Morston asks about the land. He obviously wants more from that land than a family compound."

"Maybe Priscilla will show up and scare him to death," Becki jested.

"Or better yet, grab him and take him into her reality and out of our hair," Lyrica countered.

"In the meantime, I think we should invite the McMures here for a seafood grill tomorrow and test the water with them. They may or may not be allies of Morston. They could be following him for reasons of their own," Keta suggested.

"And who, my dear, is going to be the chef for this grill party?" Lyrica looked at her husband.

"I'll do the grilling, no pun intended, if you guys do the rest," Dan offered.

"Now that's a suggestion I'd advise you to take," Matt added. "Dan's the best chef on the investigative staff in Boston. He may be an elite bodyguard, but he's also a master with the grill."

"Sold," Lyrica said. Dan's face was coloring. But Becki was looking at him with great interest.

"I'll get you later," Dan spun back at his partner.

"Darling, why don't you and Matt go to the fish market and stop at the farm to pick up some fresh greens for a salad? I'll check on Marci."

"Becki, why don't you take Dan to the marsh where Josh and Marci first saw the missing houses? It's high tide this afternoon. Dan can keep his eye on you while you paddle. Only don't strand him in that maze of channels. We need him to be chef tonight."

Becki looked uneasy, but Dan quickly accepted. "Let's load the kayaks onto the Jeep and see how we feel when we get there. The beach is right around the corner if we change our minds."

"Sounds like a plan to me," Becki replied. She wanted to accept his offer, but felt torn. Those darn blue eyes get to me every time, she thought.

Marci was wholly absorbed in her painting when Lyrica opened the gate to the studio. The flag wasn't up, so she called out to announce her arrival.

"Come on in, Mom. I knew you'd show up, eventually. What's happening at the house?"

"Not much. Keta and Matt went to the fish market, and Becki and Dan went kayaking in Pocomo Meadows so she could show him the empty hillside."

"What are you painting, darling? It's beautiful. Those yellow and gold hues invite you right into the meadow."

"Thanks. I was missing Champ, so I thought I'd paint his meadow and relive some wonderful memories. Remember how he'd stand in the goldenrod? It was a sea of color."

"Don't tell your father you're painting goldenrod. He'll start sneezing."

"Mom, do you really think that Priscilla is on the island, or were you just challenging us?"

"Marci, I wasn't kidding. We know there's a spiritual realm that we can't see, except possibly on occasions such as angelic visitations or demonic manifestations. But what we don't know is how time and space operate anywhere outside our reality. Anything is possible."

"Don't tell Becki you said that. You know how she feels about the spiritual realm."

"I'm not talking only about the heavenly realm. We don't know enough to rule out other realities than our own. We'll just have to see when Priscilla shows up again. Who knows? Maybe she'll come for her thermos of hot chocolate."

"Next time, if there is one, I'm going to keep her in the Jeep and bring her home."

"That would be fun, if not enlightening."

"So, you sent Dan and Becki kayaking? Isn't he supposed to be guarding her, not dating her? What did Dad say?"

"He's okay, as long as the guys do their job. Remember, Becki has Stephen on the mainland. Dan could quickly revert to pure bodyguard. Frankly, I'm happy she's willing to entertain the idea of dating someone other than Stephen. What do you think?"

But Marci's mind had wandered back to Priscilla. "Mom, do you think Priscilla is alive?"

"I know Priscilla's appearance and disappearance unnerves you. And we didn't intend to bring the mainland with us. Dad and I did not know that Morston would show up here."

"Do you think he knows we suspect his involvement in the robbery? Isn't it pretty arrogant to appear here after trying to pin the robbery on you?"

"Marci, he doesn't know you're my daughter, and he didn't see me at the show. He doesn't realize that he's stepped into a trap. Morston thinks he's invincible. Besides, Morston always has someone do his dirty work. He hardly looks fit enough to break into Becki's studio."

"Why Becki's studio?"

"Dad thinks he wants the other photos of the Taylor land. Plus, he wants to ruin my reputation as part of his revenge against Keta, who bested him in court several years ago."

"Does Becki have the photos? I thought her neighbor said the thief only stole one photo."

"Ellen scared the thief before he finished the job. The other photo in that series was on Becki's bedroom wall. We only have a copy to protect the original."

"I think I'd like to talk about something else. You know how I feel about negative thoughts in my studio. The little feet come here tomorrow, and I want this to be a wholesome place for them."

"Do you mind if I wander around and look at their paintings?"

"Hey, take a brush and start painting. Maybe you can shed some stress, too."

"I might just do that."

Lyrica wandered around the studio, looking at the various scenes and objects the kids were creating. "I love this one with the daisies and real flowers shellacked onto the canvas. How precious. Maybe I will take up a brush and see if I can paint back the houses in Pocomo."

"Now, that would be a miracle."

"I wonder if Becki and Dan are enjoying the kayaking."

"Or not kayaking," Marci responded.

Forty-Two

B ecki and Dan launched the kayaks at Pocomo and made their way toward the marsh. The wind limited their conversation, but Becki noticed how strongly Dan paddled. It was hard for her to keep up with him. She could see his muscles through his T-shirt. Maybe it would get hot enough he'll have to take it off, she thought.

Dan was curious to see the site of the disappearance. He'd only been to the island in previous years before the building boom.

Becki expertly took them through the entrance to the marsh, backtracking only once to find the main channel. Once inside the marsh, they parked their kayaks on a small strip of sand usually occupied by seagulls. There was just enough sand at high tide to stretch out in the sun and watch the birds. The sea lavender was blooming early, and the marsh grasses were fresh with the rain.

"It's beautiful here. I can see why you and Marci have an endless supply of plants and landscapes to paint. Have you ever painted the sea lavender? It gives the whole marsh a rosy hue, and yet it's so finely constructed you'd think its color would fade with the distance."

"Yes. I did a series of paintings on endangered wildflowers. Sea lavender is on the list because people pick it so often. We were hoping to decrease the number of people doing so. I'll take you through the Whaling Museum and the Maria Mitchell Museum if we have time. There are wonderful displays of island history, plants, and animals."

They sat quietly, watching the birds and the wind caress the grasses and ripple across the water. They even played tag with some sand crabs. Dan seemed appreciative of the beauty offered by the vista across the marsh. Like Priscilla, he preferred the many shades of green to a series of houses cut into the hillside.

After a while, Dan got up from the sand, dusted off his shorts, and reached down for Becki's hand. "I think we should probably head back. The tide is starting to go out."

Becki took his hand and let him pull her up from the sand. Her face glanced past his. When she had shaken off the sand, she turned to him and asked with a cheerful smile, "Well, where to now? We still have a little time before you need to start supper."

This is one of those moments that you don't waste, he thought. "How about right here?" he said, putting his hands around her waist and gently pulling her toward him. Becki slipped easily into his embrace and responded to his tender kiss. When he paused to gently stroke her face, she was the one who drew him closer.

It was all he could do not to pull her down onto the soft grass. He knew from her response that she felt drawn to him. But he also knew that they would regret it later when the reality of their lives caught up with them. Finishing up a satisfying kiss, he looked down at her and cupped her chin in his hands.

"I think this is enough, or we won't make dinner without looking disheveled and guilty. Don't you agree?"

Playing back Dan's form of teasing, Becki answered, "Don't I agree, or will we look disheveled?"

Laughing, he kissed her forehead. "Both."

"Mmm," Becki responded. "I thought so. Perhaps the cold water of the marsh will help." She stepped away from him into the water to push her kayak off the sand and splashed water on him. She then positioned her kayak so Dan had room to turn his around. The tide was going out rapidly.

"We'd better put some energy into getting out. I'm not great at portaging my kayak through a marsh. Why don't you lead us out?"

They both were silent as they paddled through the maze of channels toward the opening on Pocomo beach. Each knew what they had just experienced would complicate their lives in Boston. But neither wanted to think about it now.

Not far inland from Becki and Dan, Josh finished up his day. Tired from jousting with Morston, he stepped into his pickup and headed home. He was going over in his mind what the conservation organizations would say if Morston "accidentally" ruined the land's environmental value. How much clout could they bring against him? Was there even time to do so? The more he thought about it, the worse he felt. He needed to consult privately with Old Man Taylor and ask him why he was selling the land before they knew the last story behind Priscilla's disappearance—and reappearance.

As Josh made his way down the rough track that led to his home, Mako and Sandi heard the truck and bounded toward him with their usual greeting. Both were coated with mud from the marsh and smelled like it, too. Josh quickly put up the windows so they couldn't jump in.

Dan and Becki were only minutes behind Josh. Mako and Sandi dashed off to greet them. But Becki was wise to their games. She beeped the horn as Josh opened his truck's door. Shooing off the two dogs, he offered to help them take down the kayaks.

"Josh, I think we'd better let Dan get to the kitchen. He's chef tonight, and we've made everyone wait longer than we expected."

"Fine with me. I'll help you with the kayaks."

"Josh, did you see Priscilla?"

"No, Taylor wasn't there either. How was the kayaking? Did you take Dan to see the hillside where the houses disappeared?"

"Yes, we paddled up as far as we could with the tide, then rested and watched the birds. And no, the houses have not reappeared."

Leaving the kayaks by the garage, Becki and Josh headed for the deck behind the house. Everyone had gathered for drinks and hors d'oeuvres with the McMures. Becki graciously offered them a handshake, but then withdrew it when she saw how dirty it was from stowing the kayaks.

"Josh, let me introduce the McMures to you. They were at Marci's show and asked if we could show them the wilder parts of the island."

"Boy, you picked the right bunch if you want wild. We know every dirt road and deer path on the island. We even know some that have disappeared."

Marci looked very concerned. "Josh, on a more serious note—"

"Uh oh, here it comes. I knew this was too good to be true. What now? Is Priscilla coming to dinner?"

"Josh, why don't you go wash up and change your clothes? But hurry, we're having seafood grill and fresh salad from the farm," Marci said, swatting him on the butt.

With his loquacious son-in-law gone, Keta asked the McMures what brought them to the island.

"While it's true, we want to see more of the island. Our presence is really part of a private investigation. We're following someone in Boston who unexpectedly came to Nantucket this past Friday. It was sheer luck we found out," Alex said. "We thought your family might be a source of information about the island."

"Why our family? There are thousands of people on the island you could ask." Keta was not buying their explanation.

"This man has a vast network. But there is a pattern to the way he operates. He discovers valuable land and proposes a recreational or hospitality complex that will bring business to the location. Then his bulldozers accidentally uncover mineral deposits beneath the surface that are of more value than the original endeavor."

"Why would he come to Nantucket? It's a small sand pile in the ocean. There's no geological value here," Keta sparred.

"That has us stumped as well. But he's followed this pattern in Scotland and most recently in Nice, France. The jury is still out on Madeira, but we're hoping Becki might enlighten us on that front," Alex continued.

"Alex, I'm a botanical artist, not a geologist. I only work with plants."

Sensing that Becki was annoyed and could also be in danger, Matt broke into the conversation before Alex could press her into a discussion of the eco-systems on Madeira. "Looks to me like the shish kebabs are ready. Why don't we all refresh our drinks, grab a plate and start in on the salad Marci prepared?"

Later, Alex returned to questions about the Foundation work Becki was doing on Madeiran wildflowers. This time, it was Dan who came to her rescue. "Didn't you guys say you wanted to watch the sunset at Altar Rock?"

"It only takes five minutes to miss it, especially when it's this clear. Why don't I give you a few markers to make sure you find the spot while I walk you to your car?" Keta headed for the stairs and the McMure's car.

"That would be great," Joy answered. "We can continue this discussion some other time."

When Keta got back to the deck, Josh was chatting with Dan and Matt. "So Josh, how did it go today? Did Morston ask any geological or unusual questions for a new buyer on the island?"

"Dad, it was a beautiful day out there, perfect for a buyer to see the property at its best. The sky was blue, the meadow was ablaze with gold flowers, and the beach was clear of red seaweed. That said, he's definitely in high gear. He asked several pointed questions about the land, wanting to know how easy it is to dig into this soil, the history of the Taylor property, and how fast I thought Taylor would sell. Most buyers are interested in beach rights, the size of the house footprint, and how long it takes to build.

"Bottom line, he skillfully dodged most of my questions by trying to in-timidate me. I'll tell you another thing. Morston's a control freak. He was very savvy about what he asked. When I pressed him if this was the right spot for a family compound, he was not interested in pursuing other real estate. Nor could I get him to reveal how he knew Taylor was selling the land when even Jake and I didn't know until last week."

"Josh, we think he approached Taylor based on private information. It makes sense when you think about the stolen photographs. Morston thinks that there is something in the soil beneath the Taylor property," Matt clarified. "He was just fortunate that Taylor was not in the best frame of mind with Priscilla having disappeared."

"Priscilla would have bitten off his head the first chance she had if he approached them to buy their land," Marci laughed.

"No sign of Priscilla today, I take it?" Lyrica asked.

"None that I know about," Josh answered.

"What did you guys do with the hot chocolate?" Keta asked.

"We drank it," Marci replied to the question. "But if you mean, has the thermos disappeared? The answer is no."

"Son, did you say there was goldenrod blooming in the meadow?" Lyrica asked.

Keta immediately sneezed. "See, I told you, Marci. All it takes is the word to start his allergies."

"Yeah, I'm pretty sure that's what it was. It seems early for goldenrod, but then it's been so wet Marci says some wildflowers on the moors are blooming early."

Lyrica glanced at Marci. Was the goldenrod in bloom when she and Becki were in the meadow? A wet spring was one thing, but goldenrod blooming three months early wasn't normal. She wanted to see the field.

Forty-Three

After finishing up dessert, Keta decided it was time to reveal that the robbery in Becki's studio had made the news. While the regular city newspapers gave the robbery second-page attention, it was the headline of the *Boston Flame:* "Robbery Suspect's Daughter Gets Robbed." The paper positioned an oversized photo of Lyrica and Becki, created by some fast computer editing, below the headline. Fortunately, the photo's background wasn't of Nantucket. But if Morston was the driving force behind the two robberies and discovered Marci's relationship with Becki and Lyrica, it was only a matter of time before the family's presence on Nantucket would hit the press. Fortunately, Morston's inflated ego had kept him from sending a well-informed henchman to scout out the property. This was a mistake he would live to regret.

"How do you think the thief knew I wasn't home?"

Dan was quick to answer. "Becki, before we left Boston, someone was tailing you for about ten days. He knew your routine, so he probably saw you get into the cab with your suitcase. He may even have followed us to the airport."

"Well, maybe you guys should have been guarding my studio instead of me," Becki responded angrily. "What's the use of having a bodyguard if I can get robbed? What if I'd been in the studio?"

"Becki, the robber was looking for the two photos that complete the set stolen from your mom. He would never have broken in if you were home. We just made it more convenient for him by coming to Nantucket."

"But Becki had the fourth photo in her bedroom. Ellen said only the coffee table was disturbed," Lyrica reminded them.

"It appears that Ellen interrupted the thief. He escaped but left his line still attached to the steel rafters. That's sloppy work. It will make him more cautious. He may or may not know that the last photo in the series was in Becki's bedroom," Matt added, trying to diffuse the tension that was building between Becki and Dan.

"Why didn't we know the thief wanted those particular photos?" Becki snapped.

"The photo that hung in your bedroom is now in our investigative offices in Boston. We had a high-resolution copy sent here," Matt explained, trying to diffuse Becki's anger toward Dan.

"Becki, it wasn't clear that the thief wanted the Taylor photos. Until this latest robbery and Morston showed up on Nantucket, we thought he chose them at random after he planted the stolen photos in Lyrica's studio," Dan explained.

"We picked up the man tailing you. But we don't know for sure if he's the thief. Your burglar wore gloves, so there weren't any fingerprints. However, only a few suppliers sell the type of equipment he used. We have a photo that we are using to question the retailers," Matt added.

"If he's such a good thief, why didn't he take anything else? There are far more valuable things in the studio than the photo."

"Such as?" Matt asked.

"Antique, one-of-a-kind botanicals from Europe, jewelry that I left on the dresser, and money I left in the cookie jar."

"Becki, if those items were his target, they'd be gone. But he was after the photos. We are almost positive Morston hired him," Matt continued.

Dan then related that the McMures had reinforced their suspicions about Morston. "He wants something on or in the Taylor land. He may be buying Marci's paintings for his estate house, but you can be very sure that before he puts up any buildings, he'll find some way to check the soil."

"But Dan," Keta interrupted, "there aren't any mineral deposits here that would interest Morston. This island is glacial moraine and outwash plain. Apart from some arrowheads and fossils, there isn't much here. There's no oil underground, only a large aquifer."

"Then there's something else he wants on the Taylor land. And it's in the photos. Ideas, anyone?"

"Pirate treasure?" Josh joked. "No, seriously, maybe I can find out more by going to town and talking with Ralph and Charlotte. They always know more about what is happening than anyone else, and they're good friends with Taylor. If they don't have the answer, maybe I can press Morston to give us information about where he wants to dig to start the town approval process."

"Well, tomorrow, you boys can go sleuthing. I've got kids coming to the studio, so count me out."

"Why don't we sleep on it and see if we come up with some fresh ideas tomorrow?" Keta proposed. "Now, Marci, where are the marshmallows?"

❧

Monday morning arrived sooner than any of them wanted. Marci, the early riser, was already enjoying the view from the deck with a mug of black coffee and a slice of Portuguese bread when Becki and Lyrica arrived. Soon they were making oatmeal with warm blueberry sauce. The rest of the family wandered in gradually.

"Becki, would you like to take our paints and go to Madequecham to see which wildflowers are blooming?" Lyrica asked her daughter.

"Do we have to take a bodyguard with us?" Becki kidded as she smiled over at the two bodyguards. Keta caught the glance.

"No, Dan or Matt can take the rental Jeep and follow you. I want one guy near you," Keta replied.

"It's your choice, fellows," Lyrica teased. "Want to flip a coin?"

"Come on, ladies, let's walk down to the studio and let the men make the big decisions," Marci suggested, taking some of the dirty dishes to the kitchen.

"Sounds good to me," Becki said. "Maybe we'll find the dishes done when we come back." Marci just rolled her eyes.

It was a cool morning, and the warm sun felt good on their shoulders. Marci picked up the pace as she entered the path to the studio. Becki rang the bell at the gate, and they entered through the trellised doorway into Marci's personal sanctuary. After they opened all the windows to let in the fresh sea air, Marci put on her smock, went to her stack of blank canvases, grabbed some paint and brushes, and sat down to paint.

"What are you going to work on next?" Lyrica asked her daughter.

"I think I may do some beach scenes. There are so many kinds of sand and water patterns. And that reminds me. Mom, we never finished discussing all of us doing a show with your old photo collection, paintings to match the old images, and a set of new paintings to reflect the island now. You know, a before and after, Nantucket style."

"That would be fun," Becki said. "I could paint the wildflowers that were so abundant, the wild violets that grew in the sandy moors, and the clusters of red wood lily that you rarely see now. We could even depict some that are extinct to help visitors understand the fragility of the moors."

"What do you think, Mom?" Marci asked, dabbing red paint on her brush and applying it to the white canvas.

"It sounds like a good idea, but we might want to wait until they clear my name from the photo robbery. I wouldn't want to spoil a good show with paparazzi."

"I think it's a *great* idea." A new female voice came from the doorway. "How about I do some of the before paintings since I'm the oldest one here?"

Silence blanketed the studio as each of the women turned toward the visitor in the doorway. Dressed for painting, Priscilla had arrived with her brushes and paints.

"Why is everyone looking at me like that?"

Stunned, Lyrica and Becki were silent. Marci, who'd already seen Priscilla twice, tried to make her voice sound casual.

"Priscilla, have you come to paint with the kids and me?"

"No, I'll clear out before the little monsters arrive. You know how I feel about all that ruckus. Why are you all looking at me as if I was a ghost?"

"Priscilla, how did you get here?" Marci asked, trying to sound calm.

"How do you think I got here?" Priscilla responded with her usual, crotchety New England abruptness. "Marci, you're sure acting weird these days. You were so surprised to see me in the horse meadow, and then you walked off with my hot chocolate."

"Marci told us about that, Priscilla," Lyrica responded. "Why don't I go up to the house and get your thermos before she forgets again? I'm afraid we drank the hot chocolate."

"Only if you bring it back full."

"It's a deal. I'll be right back." Lyrica quickly skirted the kids' easels and practically ran out the door.

"So, Priscilla, what have you been painting these days?" Marci asked, trying to keep the situation under control until Lyrica brought reinforcements. Becki was so quiet Marci turned to see if she had fainted.

"You know, I've been painting a lot of the endangered wildflowers. Not, of course, the way you do, Becki. You're an expert. I'm more interested in painting them in their environment, so people understand their fragility."

"Funny that you should say that, Priscilla. The three of us talked about creating a show using old photos and botanicals to show how the wildflowers have disappeared and the landscapes changed over time. What do you think?"

"Sounds nifty. Why don't we have lemonade on my porch and talk about it this week?"

"That's good for me. Becki has to go home tomorrow, but she'll be back. Unless we can persuade you to stay a few more days?" Marci looked over at her sister hopefully.

"Don't make it any harder than it is. You know I'd love to stay, but I have a strict deadline with some botanicals this week. Count me in on the show whenever we do it."

Back at the house, Lyrica was almost beside herself. "Guys, you've got to come. Priscilla is in Marci's studio. She appeared at the door a few minutes ago."

Keta was first on his feet. "Let's go. Matt, you stay here in case she tries to get away."

"Somehow, I don't think we could stop her. But yes, I'll stand watch."

Lyrica, Keta, and Dan raced down the grassy path that led to Marci's secluded studio.

"Oh no, I forgot the thermos. I told Priscilla I'd bring it back."

"Lyrica, we'll get it later. Right now, we need to get to the studio."

Forty-Four

The gate was ajar, and the studio door was still open when Keta and Lyrica arrived. Breathing hard, they halted at the doorway. Dan had stayed behind to block the path.

When they entered Marci's studio, the three women were painting and chatting as if nothing unusual had happened. Priscilla spread out her paint and brushes as she worked on a marsh landscape in the Madequecham Valley. Marci was painting a seascape of the same valley, looking across the boggy land through an opening in the dunes to the ocean.

"Ladies, I brought Keta. He wanted to see what we were up to and say hi to Priscilla."

"Keta, nice to see you. It's been too long," Priscilla said, wiping her right hand on her smock and extending it to greet him.

"Who's the fellow hanging out by the gate? Too shy to come in?"

"That's Dan Keelan. He's one of the two bodyguards we hired to protect Lyrica and Becki from the press. You'll like him." Keta motioned to Dan to come into the studio.

"Bodyguards, what's all this about bodyguards? Marci didn't tell me about that."

"Priscilla, we've missed you. Where've you been?" Keta asked, changing the subject and pouring on the charm to keep Priscilla occupied.

"I tried to tell Marci that she's imagining things. I've been here. You can ask Taylor. I'm sure some days he wishes I *would* disappear."

"But Priscilla, remember when we drove to Pocomo to see the houses that disappeared? Don't you remember I said that you'd been missing for over a month?"

"Yeah, I remember. And you know what? I took Taylor over there 'cause he thought I was nuts. I made an idiot of myself telling him the houses weren't there. Well, I don't know where we were that day, Marci, but when Taylor and I got there, the private road and the houses were still there. Now fancy that."

Marci looked desperately at Keta. Priscilla, however, seemed undisturbed.

186

She went back to her easel and started painting again.

"Marci, what kind of joke were you trying to play on us? I'll bet it was Josh who thought that one up. Old T and I almost expected Josh and Jake to jump out of the scrub to surprise us. We drove through the loop and then came home. They built some gracious homes there."

"Priscilla, the houses really are gone. And believe it or not, *you* disappeared too. I know this sounds impossible, but it's true. We were worried about you," Marci reiterated.

"I'm one person you never have to worry about. I'm not going anywhere. But I will tell you one thing, Bullet, my horse, has wandered off this weekend, and so far, we can't find her. So if she shows up here looking for a carrot or an apple, let me know.

"Taylor doesn't want me calling downtown as we'll get fined if the police find her munching on someone's lawn. Better that we find her and bring her home. I probably should get home. Is it okay if I leave my stuff here? How about I come back tomorrow and paint when there are no little rascals around? Just keep my brushes and paint away from them, okay?"

"You got it."

"Nice meeting you, young man. You take care of these ladies. They're important people here on this little spit of sand called an island."

"Yes, mam," Dan said, smiling at her as she brushed by him and headed for the gate.

"Priscilla, wait. I'll walk you to the car," Marci said, dashing after her, still holding a wet paintbrush.

Dan turned to follow them back to the house, as did Keta. Both hoped that Priscilla had come in her Jeep and wouldn't disappear. But their hope was rapidly dashed. Priscilla and Marci walked through the gate and headed down the path toward the house. One minute, they were in front of the two men. The next minute, both women vanished. Dan and Keta started running to see if the high bush blueberries and *Rosa rugosa* surrounding Marci's studio had hidden them from sight. But to no avail.

The two men continued up to the house, hoping that Matt might have seen them. When he answered no, Keta turned to Dan. "Let's go. I don't want Lyrica and Becki disappearing." The two men raced back down the path to Marci's studio.

"I don't think Lyrica and Becki could see us from the studio. Dan, tell me you *saw* them disappear?" Keta doubted even his own eyes.

"Unfortunately, yes. But it was so fast. One second they were in front of us, and the next, nothing."

"We've got to tell the ladies."

Stepping back into the studio, a breathless Keta and Dan found the women waiting for them, but unaware of what had happened.

"Dad, *now* what do you think? Wasn't that Priscilla in the flesh?" Becki teased.

"Yes, that was Priscilla. No one could imitate her dry humor and Maine accent. But girls, Dan and I followed them down to the gate. Just as they passed through the gate, they vanished."

"No kidding, Dad. Come on."

"Darling, what are you saying?"

"Mrs. Kea, your husband and I watched Marci and Priscilla disappear before our eyes. They vanished into thin air, just like Marci described Priscilla disappearing by her house. Only this time, Marci went with her."

The color drained from Lyrica's face. "Darling, how could that be? Priscilla was here. They both walked through the gate. I saw them."

"Mrs. Kea, they were here. And I will vouch for Priscilla being here in the flesh. I shook her hand. But the fact is, we watched them vanish. How or where, I don't know." Dan looked at Lyrica and then walked over to where Becki was sitting.

Matt, who had disappeared outside for a few minutes, was now standing in the doorway, compass in hand. "I think we might be on to something here. I just went back to where you said they disappeared. The compass won't settle on a direction. It keeps stopping and starting, spinning and jumping. There must be some kind of power or magnetic field where the disappearances happen. I'm not saying that I buy your theory, Lyrica, but I'm leaning in that direction."

"Keta, what are we going to do? We have to find Marci," Lyrica pleaded.

"Right now, I think the five of us have the best chance of finding where they've gone. It seems reasonable to expect that they will both show up again. Priscilla keeps reappearing. That makes me believe Marci will reappear."

"But she might not reappear soon. Dad, you have to tell Josh. He needs to know."

"What does Josh need to know?" Marci said, walking through the doorway into the studio.

"Marci, you're back," Lyrica said, running over to her daughter and embracing her.

"Of course I'm back. Did you think Priscilla kidnapped me?"

"Marci, are you aware that when you and Priscilla were about halfway down the path, you both vanished?"

"No way, Dad. I just saw Priscilla to her Jeep and came right back."

"That's just the point. Matt was on the deck and didn't see you or Priscilla. Her Jeep wasn't in the driveway."

"But you must have seen us walk by. She parked her Jeep right where Josh does. You know she does that because it drives him crazy."

"Marci, we think you disappeared and then reappeared, not realizing it. The problem is the only evidence we have is the strange compass readings," Matt responded.

"We can check for Priscilla's fingerprints on the canvas and brushes," Matt offered. "But I don't think it's worth the effort. That was a real, breathing human being, not a ghost."

"Then what's going on?" Marci asked.

"I don't know, honey. Somehow, we have to keep Priscilla with us long enough to test Matt's theory. We need to take her and Taylor to the Pocomo hillside."

"But why didn't she come to my show?"

"That's just it, Marci. There wasn't a show in her reality," Lyrica said.

"What? Mom, are you serious?"

"Yes, Marci. I am."

Forty-Five

The group in Marci's studio was silent for several minutes while they processed Lyrica's theory. During the silence, Dan's phone rang. He excused himself to take the call. All eyes were on him when he returned.

"Sorry to interrupt, but that was the home office reporting on the robbery at Becki's studio. The police went back to check for fingerprints. I had them recheck the glass coffee table for any other missing photos."

"When are we going to get the copy of the photo that was in Becki's bedroom?" Lyrica asked.

"The original is in our vault. You should get the copy today. Unless you have a negative of the one stolen from the coffee table, we're out of luck."

"Do you believe that whoever stole the third photo in the series might come looking for the other one?" Lyrica asked.

"Yes, I'm afraid so. The second robbery reinforces our theory that Morston directed both heists."

"If that's supposed to encourage me to go home, thanks a lot. How do we know the thief won't come back to find the fourth photo? He clearly didn't finish his work," Becki responded petulantly.

"That's why you have Dan." Keta watched Becki's face move into its protective, stony countenance. He had hoped that the budding relationship would help Becki feel more secure.

"Thanks, Dad. And no offense, Dan. But I don't feel safe anywhere."

"We'll see what I can do about that." Dan was smiling softly and looking straight into Becki's eyes. He was hoping to see a glimmer of trust. But his comment bounced off of her with no recognition of his effort.

"Becki, you can stay in my studio and finish the presentation here," Marci offered. "Think about it, sis. I'm sure Dan wouldn't mind some extra duty on the island. Right?"

Both were silent.

"Becki, why don't you think about it this afternoon? You could go home, gather up the Madeira botanicals and come right back," Lyrica proposed.

Matt then tried to change the subject. "Dan, why don't you share with us the other information from the home office?"

"You bet. The research team collected more information about the McMures, not only in Scotland but also in the other sites Morston visited. We checked birth and death records, tax records, newspaper articles, police reports, and other sources that we use, including informants on the street. We have some answers, but not as many as we'd like.

"We traced the McMures' birth records to Scotland. That said, we can't find a current address. I was skeptical about their business card when it only had a post office box in Kyle of Lochalsh."

"What about their jobs at the Botanical Design Foundation?" Keta asked.

"Alex and Joy both legitimately consult for the Foundation that holds Becki's botanical grant," Matt continued. "However, according to our British office, the McMures appear each time there is a land acquisition Morston owns or wants to buy, such as in Nice and Madeira.

"Their appearance on Nantucket may seem accidental, but we have evidence that the McMures have been with Morston for several months. They knew he wanted to buy land on Nantucket. Fortunately, no one seems to understand why Morston wants this specific piece of property."

"What would interest Morston in Madeira?" Becki asked.

"Morston is involved behind the scenes in several international real estate deals. But we're not sure who, other than Justin, is on Morston's private payroll. Showing up unannounced may have been a huge mistake. One from which we can benefit. But it also means that there is something he wants on the Taylor land that is more than a family estate," Matt stated.

"Josh, you and Jake need to be very careful. Remember, you are not supposed to know Morston's involvement with our family in Boston. So far, he doesn't know that I am related to Mom, Becki, or you. We need to keep it that way," Marci warned.

"That may be easier said than done. We can't control the gossip that gets passed around a small island." Josh's face had taken on a pallor that was uncommon for him. "I think the best way to track what's said is to bring Charlotte and Ralph into this discussion. They seem to have their finger on the pulse of the island. They were the ones that knew Morston was interested in the land."

"I'm fine with that. Just don't discuss any of the disappearances and our theories about them. Let's keep that to ourselves until we know what we are dealing with," Keta said with concern written across his face. He was sensing danger closing in on them.

Forty-Six

L ate Monday afternoon, everyone in Nantucket was driven inside by pelting rain. The family gathered in the living room around the fire, sharing information and theories about the disappearances and the robberies. Earlier in the day, the guys had made more maps of the surrounding Wauwinet and Pocomo areas, so they could chart all the disappearances and reappearances. Matt was holding his compass, studying the maps.

"Marci, did you feel any differently when you were in the studio with Priscilla or after you disappeared and reappeared?" Matt asked.

"I hate to say it, but everything seemed very fluid. If you're saying that somehow I passed through a time or space membrane, then I have to say there was no sensory feeling. Priscilla even looked and acted the same."

"Honey, we all believe it was Priscilla. But there's got to be a reason homes and people are disappearing," Lyrica encouraged.

"Since Nantucket appears to be Morston's next game, the photos are the only evidence we have that points to his interest in the Taylor land. Can any of you remember what the stolen photos portrayed?" Matt asked, turning first to Lyrica, then to Becki.

"Why don't Becki and I sketch what we remember of the photos? A clue might appear when the sketches are together. Otherwise, why would Morston go to so much trouble to gather all of them?" Lyrica asked.

"Then, let's get to it. I've got a plane to catch tomorrow."

"So you've decided to go back to Boston?" Keta asked.

"For now, although I'll see how I feel when I'm home. It might be less distracting to work here. I still have to give Stephen copies of the orchid botanicals."

Lyrica was watching Dan as Becki spoke. When she mentioned Stephen's name, there was a subtle change in Dan's body language, and he clenched his jaw. She wasn't sure why Dan appealed to her more than Stephen. The two had different body types, personalities, and careers. Perhaps it was more Dan's gentle but persistent effort to understand Becki rather than Stephen's more authoritative, controlling nature.

Lyrica was trying to decide if this emerging romance was good for the two of them or if Dan and Matt should switch jobs. She knew Becki had resented Dan's intrusion into her life at first. Now on Nantucket, the tenor of their dialogue had changed, despite Becki's hesitancy. But then again, Dan's blue eyes were enough to melt most women.

"Becki, I think it would be safer not to share the disappearances with Stephen until we are sure what is happening with the Taylor land and Morston's role in all this. Do you think you can do that?" Keta was pressing his daughter hard. He had his suspicions about Stephen based on his private conversations with Dan and Matt. But he wasn't at liberty to discuss them yet.

"It's okay, Dad. I'm not sure Stephen is interested in anything on Nantucket, anyway. He's shown no interest in visiting here. I'll just bore him by talking about the show. And I won't mention Morston's presence at the show, I promise."

"Mom, why don't you and I do some sketches now? We may have to take a trip to Taylors to capture all that was in the photos."

"Remember, we took those photos before they tore down the barn and expanded the paddock. It's too bad we don't have Priscilla here to help," Marci sighed. "She has a great visual memory."

When Tuesday dawned, Becki found herself self-conscious traveling with Dan. Stephen planned to meet her at the airport in Boston. Dan let her board with Trish and then followed several of the other passengers onto the Cessna, so his presence wasn't so obvious.

The goodbyes had been bittersweet. Ultimately, Lyrica and Keta would come home to Boston. But for the time being, they'd stay until they could reach some closure about the Taylor estate, Morston, and Priscilla. Lyrica hoped Becki would see Nantucket as a safe haven compared to her loft in the city.

When the plane taxied to a stop at Logan Airport and the door opened, Dan could see Becki tense up. True to his word, Stephen was waiting for Becki at the gate with a bouquet. Trish's husband and kids were also waiting. Dan tried to be discrete as Becki and Stephen embraced, but he couldn't help watching Becki. He was ready for Stephen's adverse reaction to his taking Becki home. But he had no choice with Morston on the loose. After safely depositing Becki at home, Dan planned to meet his colleague, who'd been monitoring Becki's flat. They could sit in the pocket park and still monitor her flat.

"I hope you don't mind, Stephen, but Dan needs to come with me to the studio before he turns in his badge for the night."

"What, you don't trust me to get her home safely?" Stephen asked jokingly, but with a harsh tone Becki recognized. So much for a peaceful transition.

"Stephen, I'm working for Becki's dad. I'm sure you know by now he's a stickler for doing the job right. I need to be there the first time she enters the studio after the robbery. She may notice something that we missed. It can be very unnerving to see that someone has violated your personal space. And while the broken glass is gone, I still need to check the rooms before I can say good night."

"Stephen, I also invited Dan to stay for dinner. Trish's husband dropped off a homemade lasagna, Caesar salad, and carrot cake, your favorite. Wasn't that nice of him?" Dan missed Stephen's response, but he could guess.

"Come on, Stephen, lighten up. You can tell us in the cab all that's happening at Earsom," Becki continued.

It took a while for the cab to thread through the city traffic. Becki was tired when she finally unlocked the door to her studio. Dan made them wait outside while he checked the rooms. Once inside, Becki quickly had dinner in the oven, the table set, and some candles lit.

"Stephen, why don't you open the wine you brought? We can have some snacks while the dinner heats up."

Stephen was doing a slow burn. Not only had Becki insisted Dan stay for dinner, but now he would drink the wine he'd brought for the two of them. He never quite recovered for the rest of the evening. As careful as Becki and Dan were, they had developed a new relationship that was noticeable.

Back on Nantucket, Matt shared more information about Morston's international deals and the McMures.

"It's challenging to discover what role Alex and Joy have with Morston. The McMures popped up on our radar in London because they seem to travel in tandem with Morston. Our firm has no substantial evidence that they met with him, but Alex spent a lot of time in bars and restaurants talking with Morston's staff and ladies."

"While traveling, Morston always occupies a private villa, one he owns or leases. He posts Doberman pinschers at the gates and throughout the property. He uses local staff, but their contact with him is minimal, preferring his armed bodyguards for company. And of course, there are always gorgeous, engaging, and sexy women around him.

"Morston made his early money selling illegal gems in Africa and South America. Part of his entourage of ladies includes a gemologist and a geologist. We know that Joy once served as a naturalist in this harem. After gems, Morston began buying land in underdeveloped regions of the world. Each purchase ultimately yielded an undiscovered mineral deposit, unbeknownst to the seller.

"While Morston conducts most of his deals under the table, he's launched environmental and preservation publicity as camouflage. Unfortunately, few sellers stay around to ask questions after they collect their cash."

"Matt, you told me earlier that the firm was checking how Morston is using Earsom Technicals. What have you found out?" Keta probed.

"Morston uses Earsom as the environmental company for his front. Justin Earsom is as crooked as they get. Newer information about Morston's strategy is a bit more frightening. While our firm isn't entirely sure, they are confident enough to share with you some information that hits very close to home. It appears Stephen is in business with Justin Earsom. We traced his work history and found that his environmental, legal, and academic contacts have directly or indirectly worked for one of Morston's minions. It's not a coincidence that Stephen went to Madeira.

"Morston has woven a large web of spiders working for him all over the world. He pays well, but there is no escape once in his web. At first, Morston used Stephen to work for him through Earsom in ways even Stephen didn't know. But Morston was quick to see Stephen's innate greed and reeled him in slowly."

"This is going to be so hard for Becki to hear," Lyrica responded. "Matt, is she in danger?"

"She's not in physical danger that we know of. But her loft was one of his targets. We still believe the initial robbery and smear campaign is part of his revenge on you, Mr. Kea, for besting him in court. The photo robberies appear to be part of a new land scheme Morston is hatching. He has a thin layer of patience. He won't be content until he gathers all the photos. But he isn't holding back on his plan until then."

Josh put his head back on the couch and groaned as Matt related this new information. "Great, I suppose now you're going to tell me not to pursue the Morston building contract?" he asked, looking depressed. But Matt surprised him.

"I don't see any reason you should not take the job. It could help us. Morston is so open about his presence on the island that he can't suspect we are on to him. And with you and Jake as contractors, we can keep up with his plans, whatever they may be."

Marci instantly wanted to call Becki to warn her about Stephen. Fortunately, Matt had been in contact with Dan several times that day, making sure that Becki was safe and that he knew this new twist to the case.

"Darling, I think Becki needs to come back here to finish her botanicals. It's too dangerous for her to continue a relationship with Stephen."

"While I agree, Lyrica, we have to let her decide what's best."

"Matt, where is she the safest? Do you think she should be here?" Lyrica asked.

"From a safety standpoint, it's easier to protect you both when we are all together. But Becki needs to decide for herself."

"Stephen's done a brilliant job of covering himself. He has her all hyped up about the orchids," Lyrica commented with a worried look on her face.

"Darling, when Becki finds out that Stephen is working with Morston's colleagues through the threads of this spider web, it's going to be impossible to stay in the relationship."

"I hope Dan won't spring this on her tonight after Stephen leaves," Marci said, concerned about protecting her twin. "Frankly, I think Becki should come back here. It's definitely safer. We can at least track Morston's jet at the airport. Our home is secluded, and she can use my studio."

"How about you call her tomorrow after Dan has had ample time to talk with her?"

Forty-Seven

Tomorrow morning arrived right on schedule in both Boston and Nantucket. It had been a difficult night. Neither Stephen nor Dan wanted to be the first to leave Becki's flat. She finally kicked them out simultaneously and locked the door. However, Dan beat Stephen to the phone to arrange plans for the next day.

The following day, Dan knocked on Becki's door at 10 am. After checking the peephole, Becki opened the door.

"Oooh, you look soaked. Raining cats and dogs outside, I guess?" Becki held out her arms to help him take off his coat. For a fleeting second, Dan almost took the chance.

"Let's put your coat over the closet door to dry out unless you think it will flood the room."

"What's for breakfast?" he asked mischievously. "Any more chocolate chip cookies left, or did the police confiscate them for evidence?"

It was a little early for teasing. Becki was a slow starter, and she'd only had one cup of coffee. Dressed in her painting clothes, she'd casually pulled her long hair into a ponytail. Her second cup of coffee was now getting cold by her drawing table.

"Just because I am sheltering you from the storm outside doesn't mean you can take advantage of my good nature this early in the morning."

"I always want to take advantage of your good nature." He was looking at her with those mischievous blue eyes.

"Are your eyes really that color, or do you wear tinted contacts?" Becki asked, trying to change the subject and put him on the spot while recovering her composure.

"Aquamarine is what my mom always called them, just like the waters of the Caribbean. I was born under a palm tree. There weren't too many cabbage patches there."

"And where were you born? It's time I had as much information about you as you do about me. So fess up. But before you start, do you want any coffee? I can make another pot. I'm sure mine is cold by now."

"Sure. I'm always up for coffee. Even if the cookies are gone." Dan was making a sad face at Becki.

"The cookies are still there. Unless the police ate them when they checked for fingerprints."

"I like that sense of humor."

"Now, what's so important that you had to see me first thing this morning and interrupt my painting?"

Sitting down at Becki's kitchen table, Dan brought out some papers and a pen.

"You're not drawing another map, are you?" Becki was stalling. It was hard being alone with Dan in such close quarters.

"I spoke with Matt and your dad last night. The firm gave Matt new information about the case, or cases, as the case may be. Sorry. I know it's too early for puns. I need to review this information with you and discuss how you want to handle this week."

"Okay, shoot. I'm all ears," she said, sitting down at the table while the coffee finished brewing.

"What we heard last night confirmed our concerns about Alex and Joy. In addition, we now have a handle on Morston's modus operandi. Some of the material is sensitive and somewhat shocking, but you need to know." Dan hoped he could ease into the Stephen issue.

"And that is?" Becki said, moving to get the coffee pot.

"We uncovered some cleverly hidden financial links between Morston and Justin Earsom. Morston's company controls Earsom Technicals, and Justin is on Morston's private payroll. And someone else is also on that payroll, Stephen." There, he thought, I've said it, and the sky didn't fall. He waited for her response.

"So what exactly does that mean? Stephen is a struggling scientist on his way up the ladder. Not that I approve of the ladder. But that's a conversation for another day."

"Unfortunately, I think another day has come. Alex and Joy have been following Morston worldwide for two years, keeping up with his building projects. Each time he goes in proposing a hotel and boutique shops to help the local economy, suddenly his bulldozers uncover gem or mineral deposits below the land he's purchased."

"Okay, we all knew he was a creep, but that still doesn't explain how Stephen is part of this." Becki's defense of Stephen did not go unnoticed by Dan.

"I'll tell you. Just give me a minute more to set the stage. Okay?"

Dan had taken Rollo's seat, so she was now on Becki's lap. The two of them stared across the table at Dan with suspicious looks in their eyes. He knew it would be tricky to convince Becki about Stephen. That was abundantly clear the previous evening. He felt like it was a contest, and Becki wasn't sure which one she wanted to win. His only edge was the relationship they'd shared on Nantucket.

"Morston's ties are with international money. He uses his financial power to get practically anything he wants around the globe. I say *practically* because your dad won a lawsuit against him several years ago. Morston's not used to losing. His plan to smear your mother's reputation is probably only a piece of the revenge he's been waiting to carry out. This was the initial reason your dad hired me as your mom's bodyguard."

"So then, why are you *my* bodyguard if this is really about Mom?"

"Good question. We'll get to that."

"No, I want to know now. I'm tired of playing catch up because you guys think I'm so fragile and need protecting."

"Becki, this isn't about anyone thinking you're fragile. It's about your dad trying to protect you from an evil man."

"Well, you guys struck out with the robbery. I only hope you're better at being bodyguards."

That line was an excellent opener for another time, Dan thought. Right now, this was not going well. He could see Becki's anger resurfacing to cover her vulnerability.

"We are all playing catch up, you, me, Matt, your parents, Marci, and Josh."

"Okay, fine. Spit it out. I'm halfway through my second coffee. I think I can take it."

This was killing Dan. He knew what he was about to say would hurt her deeply. He didn't know how intimate a relationship Becki and Stephen had, but he could guess. It would have been a lot easier if he didn't have his own feelings for Becki, ones that were intensifying every time he was with her. He so wanted to reach out and hold her hand while he revealed the information about Stephen. But that was hardly professional. Nor had he earned the right to do so.

"Becki, Stephen has worked for Earsom for what, four years?" He waited for confirmation from her.

"Correct."

"And his skills are in environmental and botanical science, right?"

"Yes."

"Are you aware that besides his scientific acumen, Stephen is an expert in rare mineral exploration and identification? And that he's primarily working for Earsom in this capacity?"

Becki was silent.

"Morston owns the mineral rights to several of Earsom's so-called environmental endeavors. The botanical and scientific knowledge that Stephen has is real. But unfortunately, it's also his cover. He's a key player in Morston's empire."

"What? What do you mean, Stephen's cover?" Becki's body language conveyed her surprise. She stiffened up, and Dan saw the fear on her face. Again, he wanted to comfort her, but he had to keep going.

"What I mean—and this is going to come as a shock to you. Stephen is not who you think he is. He's not just a young guy struggling up the ladder at Earsom. He's already up the ladder. He's a kingpin in Morston's empire worldwide."

"If I didn't just spend the last few weeks around you, I'd say you were out of your mind or just making this up. But you're not kidding, are you?"

"No, Becki, I'm not. I'm so sorry. And I mean that sincerely. We didn't know the full extent of Stephen's involvement until yesterday. And last night wasn't a good time to tell you. He would not leave you alone with me and go home."

"I can't believe it! How could I have been so stupid? I believed Stephen and his struggle to climb the corporate ladder. What an idiot I've been."

This time, Dan reached over the table and picked up Becki's hand. It was a relief just to know she trusted him enough to admit her mistake.

"Becki, these guys are experts. They fool most people or intimidate them, whatever works best. You have no reason to beat yourself up because of this. Just trust nothing Stephen says or reports to you from his colleagues. And don't give his lawyer any more information. We're not sure of her role in this, but we suspect collusion."

Becki didn't know whether to get angry or cry. It was too much for her to take in. Pulling her hand away from Dan, she put her elbows on the table, covered her face with her hands, and peeked out at him.

"Dan, what am I going to do? Morston knew I wasn't at home, so he robbed my studio. If I break off with Stephen, will they try to kill me?"

"I doubt it would be that dramatic. But you have to decide whether you can continue your work here or go back to Nantucket. Your parents are staying a few weeks longer. You could stay with them at Marci's. If you stay in Boston, however, your dad wants someone here twenty-four-seven until we're sure about Morston's plan. He didn't get the fourth photo, so he may try to come back again."

"What am I going to do about the botanicals? I don't even want to finish them now."

"Becki, try to separate your work and talent from Stephen and Morston. If I know you, once you get working on the paintings again, you'll be able to distract yourself from the stress. It will at least give you a mental break from all that's going on. For now, Morston's target is the Taylor land. We don't know what he thinks is on or below that tract of land. But hopefully, we will know before his bulldozers find it."

"What would you do if you were me?"

"I'm not sure I know you well enough to say. But I know you need to feel safe mentally and physically to do the intensive, detailed work you create. At the moment, I'm not sure Boston is that place, as much as I'd enjoy bunking here in your spare room." Dan watched Becki's face as she received his last comment. A slightly embarrassed smile crept over her face before she once again tried to appear calm and independent.

"Well, I'd have to take Rollo. I don't want her kidnapped in my absence."

"I don't think that would be an issue unless she scares Mako and Sandi." Dan was teasing again, but Becki blew right over it.

"I hate giving in to fear."

"Becki, there's nothing wrong with fear when it's warranted. Here, the danger you're in is real. If you stay here, you'll not only have me guarding you, but the firm will expand the day and night force."

"And if I go back to Marci's, will you stay with me?"

"Yes, but only if that's what you want. I know we have more than a professional relationship, so I could ask to be taken off the assignment and return to Boston. Or I can stay on the case. Matt and I have already considered swapping places. How would you feel about that?"

"It's too much for me to decide. I feel so confused about this whole thing. I want to run away and hide."

"If that's the case, your best choice is to stay with Marci. How about I leave you for a few hours, give you some breathing space, and I'll come back this afternoon around one o'clock? That way, you'll have some time with your botanicals. You might even want to call your folks. Sometimes it just takes a little while to settle on what you want to do."

"I guess that would be the best. The sooner I get painting, the better I'll feel emotionally and physically."

"In the meantime, two things: don't answer the phone or the door, especially if it's Stephen. That will begin to distance you. And second, I need one of your house keys. Do you have a spare one?"

"And what, Mr. Keelan, would you need that for? Do you think that I just hand out my key to anyone?" Becki asked as she got up to fetch the key from a kitchen drawer. But her tone was teasing, so Dan knew the battle was temporarily over. Even if she didn't like what was happening, she was regaining her sense of humor and trust in him.

"Well, if I need to rescue you, it's easier to come in the front door than break all that glass in the skylight," he said puckishly.

"Seriously, we're installing an electronic key system in your parent's home, so only the keys we have made will work. Even hardware store copies of the existing ones won't work. We plan to put the same system here."

"I hope Dad's paying for all this. Remember, I'm a struggling artist."

"Not to worry. You won't get a bill from me. Now, how about I grab my coat and leave you to your work? If you want to go to the gym when I come back, we can go together. I've eaten enough blueberry pancakes to deserve a few hours there."

Dan got up from the kitchen table and grabbed his coat where Becki had left it drying. It was still damp, but wearable. Becki got up to walk him to the door. Stooping to peek through the privacy hole, he checked the hallway. After he gave her the okay sign, she unlocked the door and looked up at him.

"I know I'm not the easiest person to take care of, but I thank you for all you've done for my family and me. It's made a difference even though I struggle against the entire process. And I enjoyed my time with you on the island."

Dan put his hands on her shoulders and gazed into her eyes, trying to read her last comment. He leaned over and quickly kissed her forehead. "This will work out. I promise you."

"Thanks, Dan. For both," she said, with a twinkle in her eye.

"Same back at you. See you in a little while." Dan smiled and opened the door.

Forty-Eight

While Dan and Becki were talking, little hands were painting new scenes of Nantucket in Marci's studio. When the kids first arrived, two boys rang the bell, each claiming to have reached the gate first. There was much laughter floating down the path. Marci was standing by the door donned in her flower-covered painting smock, welcoming each child with a pat on the head or a playful comment.

"Today, I want you to finish your paintings from the trip we took to the moors last week. Go to your easels and get to work. I'll be around to see how you're doing. If we finish up today, we'll go to the bigger ponds on the other end of the island next week. Would that be fun?"

Happy cheers echoed throughout the studio.

After the intensity of the show weekend, Marci was glad to be with the kids and immerse her spirit in a cheerful, calm environment. As they got started, Marci sat down to finish the painting of the field of goldenrod and Champ.

Each of the kids put their treasures on the lower edge of their easels. Although some of the treasure had to be coaxed out of their pockets. Sometimes, the children put them right onto the painting using glue or shellac like Racey with the field of daisies.

"Nicolas, I see you have quite a varied group of treasures from the moors. I recognize the acorn and the bumblebee, but what is that little black and red box? I don't remember that from last week."

Nicolas, a skinny kid with light brown hair and long eyelashes, beamed up at Marci. He was creating a bird's nest out of sticks and paint. After painting the sky vivid blue, he'd glued half of a bird's eggshell into the nest with the other eggs he'd painted. A bee poised over the nest. Nicolas had drawn a red wood lily right beside the tree with the nest.

"The bee is interested in the bird's nest, Mrs. Marci. But he's pretending to be looking at the lily. This acorn hasn't fallen off the tree yet. I've glued it on so it will stay on forever, even with the wind and weather."

The thought, creativity, and story each child's painting revealed continually fascinated Marci. She was innately curious about how their little minds came up with such creative art. These days filled her with joy.

"And what's that red and black box?" Marci asked.

"Oh, that's the cargo that got ejected from the plane when it went down in the Caribbean. The pilot had to eject, too. This cargo landed in the bird's nest. The bird likes it because it's red like the flower."

"I see. Can I look at the cargo before you glue it into the nest?"

"Sure. But be real careful with it. It's carrying lifesaving supplies to the islanders."

"Okay." Marci picked up the little box and inspected it. It appeared to be a memory card from a camera. It didn't look damaged even in the fall it had taken out of the airplane. "Nicolas, would you mind if I borrowed this for a few minutes? I'd like to look at it under my magnifying glass to read what's printed on the other side."

"I think I better come with you, Mrs. Marci. As the pilot, I don't want to report I lost my cargo."

"How about we both go back to my desk and have a look at it?" Nicolas jumped happily off his stool and followed Marci to her desk. Picking up her magnifying glass, she examined it carefully.

"Nicolas, I think this box may have some pictures in it. Let's see if I put it into my computer. Maybe the landing site is recorded." Nicolas was wide-eyed as Marci inserted the memory card into her laptop. There were about a dozen pictures. The rest of the card was blank or damaged in the fall.

"Nicolas, look at that nice beach where the cargo landed."

"Yes, Mrs. Marci. I've been there. Great sand crabs and lots of colorful fish. Are there any fish in the photos? I don't think it fell into the ocean, but you never know."

"I don't see any fish, but I'll save the pictures just in case any fish show up. Here, you can take it back now. I think the bird's nest is a great place for it. I'll be around later to see how it looks."

"Okay, see you later," Nicolas chirped as he turned and skipped back to his easel.

Marci was dumbfounded. There were pictures of Lyrica and Keta at the Club Bougainvillea. They'd been taken from a distance, but there was no mistaking why someone had taken the photos. How was she going to wait until the kids disappeared to tell Keta? Quickly saving the file, she sat back in silence. This must be what Robin tried to get from the paparazzi at the resort. But how in the world did it end up in Nicolas's pocket, and now glued onto his painting?

To keep herself from running out the door and back to the house with the photos, Marci decided to finish the painting she'd started the day Priscilla appeared at the studio. The Madequecham valley was still one of the wilder places left on the island. Long swaths of beach, dunes, *Rosa rugosa,* and beach grass created vistas as far as the eye could see. The colors of the valley changed each day as one set of wildflowers bloomed, and a new group replaced them. Clusters of white daisies appeared like confectionary sugar sprinkled across the meadows. Some grasses tufted red, so there were soft patches of red and green that moved like the waves with each ocean breeze.

Marci had already mixed fourteen shades of green. A patchwork of color was now emerging from her paintbrush, blending color and motion into one. The textures of the grass, sky, clouds, and roses all added to the valley's wild, open beauty. The *Rosa rugosa* was brimming with deep fuchsia flowers, contrasting with its vibrant green leaves. The pink and purple beach pea spread out its tiny tendrils in the sand. Fractured segments of fences appeared silvered and relaxed with age.

She put down her paintbrush to check on the children and study one of Priscilla's interpretations of the same valley. Walking past Priscilla's canvas, she saw the valley display a bright mixture of flowers with colors stolen from every season of the year. The gray shingled cottages were small and low to the ground, with just enough room to sleep, eat and take an outside shower. Bathing suits hung outside on the clothesline like multi-colored nautical flags.

Looking around, she saw Nicolas had added sticks and moss to his bird's nest. He was humming as he moved the black and red box around the painting, searching for its permanent home. Finally, he painted a small hole in the tree with a woodpecker below it. Inside the hole, he glued the box with a red ribbon painted around it.

Racey was gluing daisies onto her canvas. She'd painted the kettle hole in the moors the way she remembered it, full of white daisies, as if someone poured out the flowers into vast swaths of color—no bare spots, no sadness for their lack of an appearance this year.

Returning to her desk, Marci pondered how Keta would respond to the photos she'd found.

Forty-Nine

Becki turned off her phone and curled up in the corner of her soft down couch. Stephen was not taking the separation lightly. But Becki had also noticed that he seemed less interested in her botanicals and their discovery. And he appeared overconfident that Justin and his execs would approve the land purchase—quite a change from the previous week.

She had reluctantly agreed that Stephen would be off-limits unless Dan was present. This annoyed Stephen no end, as she had just experienced by his phone message. Besides Becki's safety, Dan was hoping to trap Stephen into making a slip that would connect him with the photo robbery at Becki's studio.

When Stephen wanted to come for lunch, Becki didn't tell him Dan would be there. She'd texted him back, giving him an arrival time. Even though Stephen implied they had taken him off the Madeira project, Dan was curious if he was working on the Nantucket land deal.

Dan arrived at Becki's at about 11:30 am to discuss their strategy with Stephen. Promptly at noon, the doorbell rang. Becki rose to get it. Checking the peephole, she saw Stephen with a bouquet of deep red, pink, and white peonies.

"Oh, Stephen, thank you. They're beautiful," she said as she let him in.

Stephen was looking and waiting for a kiss, but he didn't get one. He had no sooner taken off his coat to sit down on the couch when Dan appeared from down the hallway. There was a quick flash of anger on Stephen's face, but he recovered quickly.

"Dan, what brings you here, or are you bunking in with Becki now?"

"Stephen, that's unkind. Dan has set up a temporary workstation in the guest room. He's not bunking in with anybody. Why don't you guys both get yourself something to drink while I finish the Panini?"

"Oh, Becki, no onions, remember?" Stephen was teasing her.

"Stephen, stop acting like you haven't seen me for years. I was only gone five days."

"It seemed like a lot more. You get all the enjoyable jobs. I have to stay home in crowded downtown Boston."

"I thought you and Becki were in Madeira recently," Dan said, deliberately sparring. "I've heard that's a pretty luxurious island or will be when Earsom builds his hotel and spa."

"True. But I was referring to Nantucket, home of the rich and famous."

"I would hardly include Marci and Josh's house in that category. Actually, we worked our tails off getting ready for her show and then entertaining buyers at the gallery. Ask Dan. He'll tell you about his aching back from lifting and holding seven by five-foot murals while Marci hemmed and hawed over their placement on the wall."

"Stephen, have you been to Nantucket?" Dan asked innocently.

"No, Becki keeps saying, let's go, but it never seems to be a convenient time for me to get away," Stephen lied.

"It's geologically and environmentally quite a diverse island with probably more ecosystems than even Madeira. Are you interested in geology, Stephen?" Dan was trying to see just how many lies Stephen could fabricate.

"Oh somewhat, but only what pertains to my work. The firm has several geologists."

"Here you are, boys, lunch in the art studio. There's plenty of salad and chips, and if your taste ranges to pickles, watch out for Rollo. She loves dill pickles."

Hearing her name, Rollo jumped onto the top of the couch, where she could watch the food. Stephen shooed her off and sat down at the coffee table. Rollo quickly circled the couch, waited until Dan sat down, then curled up right beside him.

"So, how is the investigation going?" Stephen asked Dan.

"Which one are you referring to, Lyrica's or Becki's?"

"Becki's? I thought that was just a straight robbery."

"Thanks for your compassion, Stephen," Becki said acidly as she walked to the other side of the coffee table.

Dan couldn't tell if Stephen was bluffing, but there was one quick way to find out. "Here, let's just move some of these enormous books so we can eat our food."

"Careful Dan," Becki warned, "I only duct-taped the glass pieces at the end of the table."

Dan turned toward the kitchen table, grabbing the two oversized art books that covered the empty photo space. "Hey, does anyone want more chips?"

As he turned, Dan caught Stephen quickly scanning the table. He knew, Dan thought. He probably helped mastermind the job. Good thing we're changing the locks.

"Stephen, what are you going to do about the botanicals and your presentation? Do you need digitals of all the orchids or just the one we think is a discovery?"

"Justin is only interested in the ecosystems for advance publicity. I'm pretty sure we can save the orchids, so I won't need the botanicals."

"Why the sudden change in Justin? Did you schmooze him into saving the forest?"

"Not exactly. But I got him to order some geological tests just to make sure caves or underground springs aren't hiding below the surface."

"Oh, I see," Becki replied, suddenly taking more of an interest in her sandwich.

"What made Justin think there might be underground issues?" Dan pressed.

"Even though we know the island is mostly volcanic, its geology is uncertain. We need to ensure that the construction site can withstand the digging and weight of the building complex."

Smooth, pretty smooth, thought Dan. He's done this before. But this time, we're going to catch him in his own web. Looking at Becki, Dan could see she was miserable. Her face was tight, her body tense, and she was watching Stephen every time he looked down at his sandwich. She's beginning to see, Dan thought. But it's killing her to admit that she was so fond of a traitor.

"Will you be going back?" Dan asked.

"Perhaps, but not right away. The geology and survey team go next."

"But Stephen, what about the orchids? If you don't go with the team, they could be damaged. All our work will be for nothing."

"When the Major has seen your botanicals, I can exert pressure before the team leaves. We have a few weeks. Most of these guys come from other jobs in Europe. We have to give them a few weeks' notice."

"The botanicals of our discovery are done. It only took two sheets."

"Great. Any chance I can borrow them for the afternoon so I can take digitals to send to the Major?"

"Stephen, you know how I feel about moving originals. I can take the digitals and email them to you this afternoon. I'd rather they not leave the studio since they belong to the Foundation. My digitals can give the Major enough detail. Would you like to see the botanicals?"

"Sure, babe. Where are they?"

"On my desk, but no touching with carrot cake icing on your hands. Finish your dessert first."

After they'd all taken their plates into the kitchen, Dan could tell that

Stephen was waiting for him to leave. He'd provided the required compliments on her paintings, then headed for the couch. This time, Rollo jumped off and hid under the kitchen table. However, Becki was the one that ended the gathering.

"Stephen, it was great seeing you for lunch, but I've got to work on the rest of the botanicals. I have a tight deadline."

"What about him?" Stephen said, pointing to Dan. "Are you kicking him out too?"

"No, she doesn't have to. I've got about an hour of computer work to do, and then I also need to leave."

"Okay, but how about dinner tonight?" Stephen asked, turning to Becki.

"If I get the work done, okay? If not, it will have to wait until the deadline is over."

"I can have dinner with you, Stephen," Dan joked.

"Uh, that's not what I had in mind."

I'll bet that's not what you had in mind, thought Dan. And you will not get it on my watch. This visibly irritated Stephen. Getting up from the couch, he grabbed his coat and headed for the door without even a hug or a goodbye. Turning around as he opened the studio door, he looked first at Dan, then Becki.

"I'll talk with you later."

And with that, he was out the door. Dan silently reopened the door and watched him walk down the hall. Standing by the elevator, Stephen punched in a number, then lifted the cell phone to his ear.

"No, I found out nothing. That goon she has tailing her has set up camp. It's going to be a lot harder to get back in. We may have to—" The elevator door opened, and his conversation ended.

Dan turned to Becki. "We need to be out of here this afternoon. I'm sure Stephen just talked with someone about coming back here to look for the other photo. I don't want you here. Why don't you pack your bags and your paintings? I'll see if I can get us tickets on the five o'clock plane. Okay?"

"No, it's not okay. Do you think you can just order me to leave my home? Do you know how much trouble it is to pack up everything and get it safely to the island? And then, how long am I going to stay? I still need to do the presentation at the Foundation. Don't you think you're being a little paranoid?"

"Call it what you like. My job is to protect you. Whoever comes back to the apartment won't want you here. We stand a much better chance of catching the thief if your home is empty."

"Is that what this is all about? Catching the thief? Who cares about me?"

Dan walked over to Becki and put his hands on her shoulders. He recognized the anger, but that didn't make it any easier. He wasn't even sure that Becki knew how transparent she was. Now, his only thought was to get her safely away from whatever might break loose in Boston.

"Oh, don't get cozy with me, mister. I don't know who to trust less, Stephen or you. How do I know you're not some undercover agent for some other group who wants the photos? Sometimes I wonder what in the world I was doing to accept you as a bodyguard." And with that, Becki stomped down the hall to her bedroom and slammed the door.

Fifty

Twenty minutes later, Becki emerged from the bedroom, threw her duffel on the kitchen floor, and headed for her easel and paints. Her face was red and swollen, and she looked exhausted. Dan had heard her crying, but was reluctant to invade her privacy.

He was sitting on the couch working on the computer when Becki walked by. Still not saying anything, she opened her black leather portfolio case and carefully placed the botanicals into a protective sleeve with padding to keep them clean and safe. She gathered up her paints, brushes, and other supplies, wrapped them in a soft chamois cloth, then put them in a small case. Returning to her room, she came back out and dropped her backpack behind where Dan was sitting.

"Okay, let's go. I'm ready. I called Dad. He said you're legit. So, for now, I'll keep you around. But don't push your luck."

Dan could tell she was coming out of her fear. She was regaining the sense of humor and spunk that he enjoyed so much.

"Got it. I'm glad you called your dad. I hope that settled your mind."

"Let's just say I was feeling a bit like Audrey Hepburn in *Charade*, not knowing whom to trust."

"Hey, I'm happy to be compared with Cary Grant. I'm ready whenever you are."

"Good, because you have all the way to the airport to think of how to persuade the pilot to allow me on board with this portfolio. There's no way it's getting stored in the wing."

"Not to worry. I've seen them board a Great Dane. Your portfolio should be a piece of cake. Is there anything else in the studio you'd like to bring with you?"

"Yes. You can help me get Rollo into her carrying case. I'm not leaving her here. She's the most valuable possession I own, except, of course, my diamond jewelry. But I've hidden that in the freezer."

"And how does Miss Rollo find traveling?"

"You'll know in a minute. Or more like a flash." Rollo wanted no part of the carrying case. All Dan saw was a blur of black fur headed down the hall to the bedroom. Becki was right on her tail, but Rollo made it to the bedroom closet first. Becki pushed back the closet's sliding door, and another flash of black fur leaped out from among Becki's shoes, slipping through Dan's hands.

"Nice try, but you'll have to be quicker than that. She won't bite or scratch, but she will give us a merry chase."

Almost an hour later, Dan and Becki were exiting the cab at the airport with Rollo crying mournfully from her carrier. Dan flashed his enigmatic smile and blue eyes at the woman checking their bags at the ticket counter and made sure Becki's portfolio had its own seat.

Becki had changed into her threadbare jeans, flip-flops, and a short tank top with a colorful scarf around her neck. She'd pinned up her hair with what Dan thought were chopsticks, but wisps of platinum blonde hair kept popping out around her face. Rollo, now reconciled to the case, poked her front paw through the opening, playing with the cord on Dan's sweatshirt jacket.

"Becki, do you want to read the Nantucket paper while we wait? I picked one up on the way into the airport. I can read the second section while you peruse the headlines."

"Sure, why not? Maybe they've found the missing—"

"Houses," they exclaimed simultaneously. Both were staring at the headlines.

Madequechem Homes Vanish. Early this afternoon, several residents stormed into police headquarters demanding to know what happened to their homes. The owners had arrived on a recent flight. Not knowing when the homes vanished, the police called in the two island builders involved in the Pocomo investigation.

"That's crazy. Josh and Jake only built some of those houses," Becki exclaimed.

Dan leaned over Becki's shoulder to read the article. Becki could smell his aftershave, but she was determined to keep up a stony attitude. She didn't dare look him in the eyes, or she'd lose her composure altogether.

"Why didn't Matt mention this to you earlier today when you guys talked? Do Mom and Dad know that Josh and Jake have been called in for questioning again?"

"It's possible they haven't gotten today's paper. Maybe your dad didn't go downtown for the paper thinking they'd pick one up at the airport."

Becki picked up her phone and texted her dad. When he called back, she jumped on it. "Dad, we're in Boston waiting for the plane. Have you seen what's on the front page of the Nantucket paper today?"

"No, we haven't read the paper. But the police called looking for Josh and Jake, so we heard the news. Your Mom and I plan to stop in Madequecham before we pick you up. What time are you arriving?"

"We're scheduled for a 6:30 arrival. How's the weather over there?"

"Sunny enough to see that some houses disappeared."

"Maybe we'll fly over it on our way down. How many disappeared, Dad?"

"The police either aren't sure or aren't saying. That's why your mother and I thought we'd drive over there on the way to the airport."

"But Jake and Josh didn't build all the houses in Madequecham. What about the other builders? Did the cops arrest them, too?"

"I'm not sure. I'm hoping to hear more by the time we get to the airport."

"Dad, can we drive over to Madequecham on our way home?"

"I don't see any reason we can't. See you soon."

"Poor Marci. I hope the police don't come to the house while her kids are painting. Or the parents come to take their kids away," Becki groaned.

But Marci was sitting at her computer, studying the photos she'd downloaded from Nicolas's memory card. It had to be from the reporters they caught at the private club her parents frequented. Picking up her phone, Marci texted Keta. Hearing the text, Keta whisked his phone out from his pocket and read Marci's message. Texting him while she was still in class was enough to alarm him.

Showing the text to Lyrica, they both stared at each other in disbelief. How in the world did those photos get here? And was that why Robin didn't find photos in Lucky's cameras? They both simultaneously checked their watches to see how much longer Marci had the kids in her class.

"How about I text her? She can send the photos to my phone."

"Great idea. I think it might calm her down until we get back home from the airport."

Becki and Dan's plane was on time. They came down the stairs with Becki passing her portfolio to Dan while returning to the plane to retrieve Rollo. By the time she emerged, Dan was carrying both their duffels and her portfolio as they walked toward her parents.

"Darling, they look like everything's okay. Maybe Becki just had to let off some steam with Dan. You know how she gets if she thinks someone is trying to control her life."

"Why do women always make everything so complicated?"

"Because we feel and notice everything. You guys just process and proceed."

Their conversation ended as Dan and Becki arrived at the baggage area, despite Rollo pawing and meowing in her carrying case. Becki ran to hug her parents, tears now flowing down her face.

"Honey, it's so good to have you back."

"Becki, I know you did this for me. But I think you'll be happier here and safer," Keta added.

They piled the luggage into the back of the Land Rover. Once everyone was in the car, Becki opened Rollo's case. She dashed out, looked left and right, and then jumped onto the pile of beach towels in the back of the car.

"We'll take you to Madequecham on the way home. Matt's downtown somewhere, probably trying to get Josh and Jake out of jail," Keta jested.

"Honey, I'm sure they won't keep them there. How can you prove two builders made houses disappear? They don't have a leg to stand on."

It wasn't far from the airport to Madequecham. The dirt roads were pretty good, except for the layer of mud splashed on the scrub from the deep rain puddles. Pulling up on one of the higher places near the beach, Keta parked, and they all got out. Leaning against the Rover, he picked up his binoculars and scanned the meadows for houses.

"Whoever made the houses vanish did a thorough job. The landscape looks like it did twenty years ago."

"It's stunning," commented Dan. "I had no idea there was so much open meadow stretching to the beach."

"It's always been beautiful here, even with the houses," Lyrica remarked.

"Look down there," Becki said as she pointed toward an area filled with reeds and soon-to-be cattails. "That bog is full of tiny flowers that no one knows about. You have to get down on your hands and knees or wade into the bog to see them. And look at the meadow. See how the colors are in a patchwork? The wildflowers are rampant this year."

"You can paint these meadows every day for a month, and each painting will be different. I'm so glad the daisies didn't vanish," Lyrica sighed.

"What's so fascinating is that the missing houses took the landscaping with them. The valley looks much like it did when we first came here," Keta commented. "There aren't even any driveways left."

"I much prefer this view," Lyrica added. "Whoever or whatever is making the houses disappear must want the island to return to an earlier state."

"At least whoever is gobbling up houses is environmentally conscious. Although if he takes away the new golf club, you might not appreciate the gesture, Dad," Becki teased.

"Wait a minute," Keta interrupted. "Who says it's a person doing this? And why does it have to be a guy?"

"We don't know if the disappearances are intentional," Lyrica commented as she admired the view.

"Are you ready to head home?" Keta suggested.

"Dad, I don't think we're going to get there soon. Look over there. Isn't that the police?"

The police had parked two SUVs across the entrance to the road leading to the small bluff where they stood.

"Let's go back through Nobadeer and leave these guys to their work," Keta suggested.

"Honey, I don't think that's a good idea. We're quite obvious up here. I don't want them to think we're running away."

"Aren't we? Let them come to the house if they want to discuss anything. They can cut us off by the airport if they're interested in us."

"Okay, let's get going before they decide to come any closer," Lyrica said, walking around to her side of the Land Rover and getting into the front seat. Keta waved at the police as they drove off.

When they arrived home, Josh and Marci were sitting on the deck talking with Jake. Mako, Sandi, and Lucy were piled in a heap, sleeping. Hearing the cars, all three dogs went on alert. There was a wild scramble to see who could welcome the family first. Marci got up and walked onto the front porch to greet them.

Once they put the travel bags away and settled Rollo on her pillow in the guest house, everyone took a seat on the deck where Marci had put out some homemade salsa and chips with a bottle of wine. It was a beautiful summer evening.

Becki popped open two beers and headed to the front porch where Matt and Dan were standing, both on their cell phones. Holding up the cold beers, she lured them back to the deck. It was nearly sunset when they finished their meal and conversation about the vanishing houses.

"Anyone want to watch the sunset?" Keta asked the group.

"I don't think we'd make it, Dad. It'll be down by the time we get to the beach."

"I wasn't talking about the beach. I meant the widow's walk up on the roof. Anyone care to join me?"

"Sure, I'll go," Becki answered, picking up her plate to take it to the kitchen.

"Matt, you and Dan go too. It's quite a sight from up there," Lyrica said, motioning for the two guys to leave.

The clouds had settled slightly above the horizon and off to the north. The sky was turning a spectacular gold and pink with lavender clouds. Becki pointed out the lights at the Taylor home and the marsh where she and Dan had kayaked.

"And that's a police car that just turned off the Wauwinet Road into our driveway," Keta remarked as if he were finishing Becki's visual tour. "I'd better go down and warn Josh and Jake."

Fifty-One

Matt quietly followed Keta down the sharp descent of the hanging stairway to the second floor. Becki and Dan stood in the sunset's afterglow, watching the lights come on in the houses below.

"We seem destined to meet in small spaces," said Dan as he looked down from the sky to Becki. He was hoping they might have a few minutes together before the investigation pulled them downstairs.

"Mmm," Becki murmured. "I think I'll stay up here and watch the stars come out. Would you like to join me?"

"Sure. How long does that take? We might freeze to death up here if we stay too long."

"Josh has a stash of blankets, sleeping bags, and pillows in the second bedroom where you and Matt are staying. We can go down and get some. But we'll have to be quiet, or we'll get invited to the police party downstairs. I want no part of it."

"Agreed. And your bodyguard has to stay with you, right?"

"Let's go." Becki slowly and carefully climbed down the narrow stairway and headed for the bedroom. Once inside, she opened the larger of the two closets and pulled down two sleeping bags and some pillows.

"It's a good thing we made our beds this morning," Dan kidded.

"Here," Becki threw a dark green sleeping bag to Dan, followed immediately by another. "Good show. I'm glad to see you are up on your passing game," she whispered as she headed back toward the drop-down stairs.

The twilight was almost gone as they rolled out the sleeping bags on the widow's walk. Climbing into her bag, Becki zipped it up and propped the pillow behind her back. "Bet you never did *this* on assignment before."

"No, I admit, this is a first. Not that I haven't camped out on a few jobs. But never on top of a house or with such splendid company."

"Thank you. Now let's see who can see the first star or planet to appear," she whispered. "We'd better not talk too loudly. Sound carries easily here. I can tell they're all out on the deck."

The two of them sprawled out, gazing up at the stars. A perfect moment, but what to do? Dan waited to take the next cue from Becki. It didn't take long. Turning her head, Becki looked directly into Dan's eyes.

"I'm sorry if I've been so emotionally erratic. There's just too much going on. I need intense focus to create detailed botanical work. Too much external distraction unbalances me, so I clam up or get irritable, which you've probably noticed by now. Thank you for pushing me to get out of Boston."

"Becki, I have to admit that I enjoy being with you. Your moods are part of your charm. And I think I'm getting pretty good at reading some of them. But my job is to make your life easier, not more complicated."

"I'm not sure you've achieved that goal. But we can work on it."

"Thanks, I'll remember that." Dan reached over and planted a soft kiss on Becki's lips. Then he gently put his hand on the top of her head and stroked her hair. Pulling her toward him, he embraced her with another kiss. Both of them were tentative at first, but the kiss itself seemed to release them to each other. When they came up for air, Dan leaned back with his head propped on his hand and elbow on the pillow facing Becki.

"That, Mr. Keelan, does not make my life easier or less complicated."

"Oh, maybe we stopped too soon." Dan leaned forward and placed another kiss on her lips, lingering just a while before pulling back and looking at her. "How is that?"

"You're a smooth operator in tight places," Becki teased.

"I don't think I'd have it any other way."

"Dan, I don't think I'm ready to take this any farther on a wood floor, regardless of our sleeping bags and how wonderful it feels."

"You're right. But you can't fault me for enjoying my time with you."

"Not at all. But we better go down soon, or they'll wonder what's happened to us. See if the police car is still there."

"I don't see it, and it sounds like they've gone inside."

Becki took Dan's outstretched hand and stood up. "Man, it's cold up here. Let's go see what the police wanted. We can always come back up. It's such a great night for stars. There should be some shooting stars later."

"You're not proposing we sleep up here, are you?" Dan asked tentatively.

"Guess you don't know me as well as you think." Becki paused for a moment. "If you think I'm going to sleep on this cold floor, even with you beside me, you're crazy."

"Hey, you two. Are you ever coming down, or are you camping out for the night?" Keta's head popped up through the trapdoor opening.

"Good timing. We're coming down now. It's getting too cold up here, even with the sleeping bags."

Tossing the sleeping bags and pillows through the hatchway to her father, Becki turned and started down the ladder to the second floor. When they were back in the living room, she headed directly toward the fire.

"So, what did the police want?"

"They thought we might know how the houses on Madequecham disappeared. They did spot us earlier on the dune, but were polite enough not to accuse us of evading them. The news is spreading like wildfire around the island. Many people were on the beach today. The police were hoping someone might have seen what happened."

"Do they think we're hiding the houses on our property?" Becki asked.

"Actually, I think they may suspect all of us since we were at the scene of the crime earlier," Keta added.

"But not when it happened. Didn't you say that the homes were gone when you got there?" Marci asked.

"They suspect us because out of the seven houses that vanished, Jake and I built four. Not recently, I will add. We were the first to build there," Josh added.

"But what motive would you have for taking houses you labored so hard to build?" Becki asked.

"Why do people intentionally burn down their houses?" Jake asked.

"The police don't seriously think you stole them to gain more business?" Marci gasped.

"The thought had crossed my mind." Jake winced. "I hope they don't think we're holding the people hostage somewhere."

"That's ridiculous!" Becki fired back.

"Sis, in this world, anything is possible." Josh had slumped down into his chair and was looking pretty beat.

"Wait. Are all the houses gone?" Matt asked.

"No. There are still a few houses in the valley as you head toward Tom Nevers. But other than that, it's a clear view across the valley to the ocean," Keta answered.

"I have to say," Becki admitted sheepishly. "I like the valley with just the grasses, marsh, and a sprinkling of beach cottages."

"I'm enjoying the island looking more like it did when we were kids," Marci added.

"Yeah, but we could be next. This *thing* might come over here," Josh warned.

"Wait, guys," Lyrica interjected. "I don't think this is a thing. Maybe whoever is responsible is tired of the growth that has spoiled so many beautiful vistas on the island. I have to admit. I'm rather enjoying regaining the past."

"Mom, you don't really think a person is doing this intentionally? It's not just houses that are gone, but the people too." Becki gave her mother a puzzled look.

"I do not know who or what force is causing this. But it seems like there is intelligence behind what is happening. And I'm not convinced that the people are dead. More like transferred to another realm, like when Marci disappeared with Priscilla."

"Dan, Matt, what do you think? Have you ever encountered anything like this before?" Keta looked at both investigators intently.

"Mr. Kea, this is as unique to us as it is to you. It seems more like science fiction than reality. What's different is that we've witnessed it ourselves."

"Except, what about Priscilla?" Lyrica remarked. "Marci, didn't you say that Priscilla drove Old Man Taylor over to Pocomo and that the houses were still there?"

"Yes, and to quote her, 'Taylor was mighty angry for dragging him on a wild goose chase.' We might want to go back to the property and see if we can find any clues."

"And while you're doing that, Jake and I can chat with Old Man Taylor and hear his version of their drive to Pocomo."

"Careful Josh, remember Taylor still thinks Priscilla is missing. You might upset him and jeopardize your new job," Marci warned her husband.

"Well, as long as Jake and I don't disappear when we're building this compound, I guess we'll just keep going forward, as stumped as the police."

Fifty-Two

The next day brought brilliant sunshine and warmer air. According to Becki and Dan, who'd been on the widow's walk to check the wind and weather, the only fog was over the south shore.

"It's a good thing the fog didn't settle in yesterday, or we might have missed seeing the Madequecham valley revert to its original state," Becki quipped as she and Dan walked into the kitchen where Lyrica and Marci were preparing breakfast.

"Good morning, everybody," Dan said cheerfully, walking toward the coffeepot.

"Where are Josh and Dad?" Becki asked.

"They went downtown to scout gossip and pick up the papers," Marci laughed.

"Is Josh coming back before he goes to work today?" Lyrica was like a hen gathering her chicks.

"Mom, I'm not sure. It kind of depends on what they find downtown. He and Jake were supposed to meet the realtor in his office this morning."

"I was hoping to check with Josh to see if we can go to the Taylor land to paint on the beach," Lyrica said, looking at her daughter.

"I don't see any reason we can't go there. But I thought you wanted to paint by the ponds today?" Marci asked as she poured coffee into mugs for the two bodyguards.

"I want to take a walk in the moors with the dogs. Then we can spend the rest of the morning on the beach." Lyrica took her beach bag off the hook in the hallway and grabbed the dog's leashes. "We'll need to take one guy with us. I don't think your father will risk the two of us falling into a portal and disappearing with Priscilla."

"Yeah, better to let Dan or Matt disappear. They might find their way back more easily. This is sounding like Alice in Wonderland," Becki laughed. "You all go. I have a deadline to meet. If anyone needs me today, I'll be in Marci's studio." And with that, Becki bounced out of the kitchen and headed for the studio.

"Dan, why don't you come with us for a change of pace? Give your buddy a break." Lyrica sensed that the combination of Dan and Becki might not be the best for her getting work done.

"Marci, I'll make some sandwiches if you load the beach things into the Land Rover and round up the dogs." Lyrica was already laying out the Portuguese bread and cold cuts.

Within twenty minutes, the two women were bouncing along the rutted dirt track that served as the Longmeadow's driveway. Dan followed in his Jeep. Pulling out onto the Wauwinet Road, they passed the Pocomo sign and headed for the Polpis Road. Then, turning right, they headed west toward town.

Some of the roads into the moors had taken a beating from the rainstorms earlier that month. But Marci knew every dirt road on the island. The Land Rover took the giant puddles in stride, while Dan found taking a lightweight Jeep through the rocky, puddled tracks left more than one splash of mud and sand on his jeans.

Taking the road to Altar Rock, the women followed a roller coaster, sandy track to the bottom of the hill. Straight ahead was what the family jokingly called the "Dairy Queen," a white tracking tower that sat at the bottom of the slope below Altar Rock. While the crest of this hill was one of the best painting sites for the middle moors, Marci headed in the opposite direction toward the ponds.

Taking a right turn, they rode down the well-worn track to the foot ponds. The road diminished in size and became wilder as they approached the ponds. In the distant past, the town had regularly cut back the scrub. With more visitors on these roads, it seemed like the island had stopped that practice. Some of the dirt roads now were so closely wrapped in scrub oak that they were more like tunnels.

"I took my kids treasure hunting here last week. That's what you saw on the easels in the studio," Marci remarked to her mom. "Racey was the one who painted a kettle hole filled with daisies. She was so crushed at their absence that she even glued her fresh daisies onto the canvas."

"They look somewhat sparse for this time of year. But I love how the kids paint with reckless abandon whatever they see here or conjure up in their minds. I only wish adults could be so free. This is my favorite part of the moors. The kettle holes left by the glacier are lovely every season of the year. Where do you want to park the cars?"

"How about the dirt road that used to come in from the Polpis Road? We can check the donut pond and see if the bog has finally taken over, or if it's still a donut," Lyrica suggested.

Opening the Land Rover door, Mako and Sandi sprang out, glad to be let loose to run. Dan parked off the road and donned his Red Sox baseball cap as he joined the ladies.

"Marci, will the dogs run off?" he asked.

"Nah, I trained them here with my whistle."

"Let's head east up that hill for a better view of the ponds and then walk down into the glacial kettle hole Racey painted," Marci said, pointing to a hill off to their right.

There weren't any Jeep tracks here, so they forged ahead, enjoying the spring-like cushion of the bearberry under their feet. At the top of the hill, they could see all three ponds, and the rolling moors the glacier had carved.

"I thought Racey and Sally said there weren't any daisies in the kettle holes this year. Look at that one over there. It's almost solid white. I've never seen anything like it," Lyrica exclaimed.

"Wow," Dan remarked. "I'd forgotten the island held such wild beauty."

"Are you sure this is where they went?"

"Yes, I'm sure because I saw them running up the hill toward that lone scrub pine, their red and blonde pigtails flying in the wind. It was so windy that day I was afraid I'd lose them."

"Marci, do you remember when Priscilla came back and reported a stand of red wood lilies over there where the two roads intersect? Hadn't she just finished the wood lily paintings that she hung in their dining room?" Lyrica asked.

"What are you getting at, Mom?" Marci was frowning as she tried to interpret her mother's question. "Do you think Priscilla can make flowers appear wherever she wants just by painting them?"

"If that were the case, wildflowers would cover the island," Lyrica laughed. "You know how much she loved to travel and paint wildflowers from every mountain range and valley around the world. Her enthusiasm inspired Becki to become a botanical artist."

"Yeah, but painting flowers into life is a bit far-fetched."

"Maybe," Lyrica said tentatively. "How about we go check for red wood lilies before we walk the beach by the Taylor house?"

After parking their cars in Squam, Marci, Lyrica, and Dan headed for the beach below the Taylor's house. Morston, however, had sent two of his minions to the property. He might have succeeded with the secret visit if Marci and Lyrica had not decided to see if Priscilla was home. As they crested the beach path to the house, they saw the two men in the corral.

"Mom, get down," Marci whispered, pushing on her mother's shoulder so they couldn't be seen. Dan instinctively dropped down behind them. "Look at that." Marci pointed to a strange piece of equipment in the middle of the corral. "What in the world are they doing?"

"It looks like he's taking core samples of the soil," Dan said, handing over his high-power binoculars to Marci. "The equipment isn't big enough for a well. My instinct says they're trespassing. The tall guy keeps looking around as if he's the lookout."

"Aren't they worried Taylor will show up?" Marci asked incredulously.

"They probably checked the house but didn't think to check the beach. Not too smart."

"Brazen is more like it." Lyrica did not like the danger they were in.

"Dan, can you capture them on your camera from Priscilla's front porch?"

"I can try, Mrs. Kea. But Marci, while I do that, call Josh and see if he knows this is going on. It seems premature for soil sampling. Morston's a fool if he displays his hand this early in the game."

Watching the lookout man, Dan crept down to the back of the house where the wrap-around porch started and slowly crept to the front of the house. Positioning himself behind one of the old wicker chairs, he pulled out his camera and binoculars. Then, returning to the dune, he rejoined the women.

"They're clearly taking core samples. I didn't see Morston, only two guys. One is drilling, and the other is transferring the core samples into a large canvas bag. That equipment looks like Morston crafted it for his mineral work. I'd like to come back later and try to find the drill holes. Marci, were you able to raise Josh?"

"Not yet. I'm trying Jake now."

"Can you tell how far along they are in the process?" Lyrica asked.

"Usually, when they have enough samples, they fill the holes with sand and replace the top layer, so it's barely noticeable that they sampled the soil. That technology is made for stealth operations."

"Jake, it's Marci. Is Josh with you? I need to speak with him."

"Hold on a second. I think he's still jawing with Charlotte and Ralph. I'll go back inside."

Marci could hear the screen door slam behind Jake. Men, she thought, they stay noisy little boys all their lives. She listened to the exchange between Jake and Josh.

"What's up, hon? I thought you guys were going to the beach."

"Josh, we did. But on our way back, we thought we'd look for Priscilla. We spotted a piece of drilling equipment and two guys taking core samples in the corral. Dan's got photos of them. What's going on?" Again, she could hear muffled voices as Josh and Jake conversed.

"Marci, can I talk with Dan for a minute?"

Marci handed the phone to Dan and took his binoculars. The two workers were now kneeling on the ground.

"Josh, it looks like they're filling the holes with sand. They're finishing up. If this is an illicit visit to the land, I don't think it's a good idea to surprise them with the ladies here." Marci just rolled her eyes. "I'll try to follow their truck when it leaves the property."

Dan handed Marci her phone and took one last look with the binoculars.

"Okay, we need to get going. They're packing up, disassembling the drill. I want to catch them as they emerge out of Taylor's driveway. We've got to hoof it down the beach to get to our cars. You ladies take the Land Rover and head home. I don't want you meeting up with them."

Meanwhile, Josh was politely trying to extricate himself from Ralph and Charlotte. With a hasty goodbye, he grabbed Jake and headed for their pickups.

"What's going on that you don't want anyone to hear?" Jake quizzed his friend.

"Morston's up to something. Marci, Lyrica, and Dan saw some men taking soil samples in Priscilla's corral."

Fifty-Three

The three of them raced down the beach to the path that led out to Squam Road. Even the dogs were panting when they got to their cars. Dan went ahead of them and waited in the Jeep on the side of the dirt road, watching for the men to emerge from Taylor's property. Lyrica waited until they saw Dan take off to follow the truck.

"How far are we going to follow Dan?" Marci asked her mom.

"I say we follow both to their destination. I don't like the idea of Dan being alone with those guys."

"Mom, don't you think it would be better to call Dad and have Matt do this?"

"Probably, but I suspect Josh has already called Keta and Matt. They couldn't catch up now, anyway. We'll be fine. I'm curious to see where the truck goes."

Waiting until Dan's Jeep was almost out of sight, Lyrica steered the Land Rover out of its hiding place and picked up the chase. "Now, when we hit the macadam, we'll slow down. Maybe Dan will think we've headed home."

The three-car parade continued straight into town. Dan saw that Lyrica and Marci were still behind him, but he would not sacrifice his prey. The drill truck took a right at the rotary and proceeded straight to Washington Street and the piers. But which pier?

The truck quickly turned and headed for where the larger yachts moored. It slowed down and pulled up by the pier. Dan made a swift decision about which guy to follow. Putting on the flashers, he slid out of the Jeep and pursued the man as he headed down the pier. He was still carrying the canvas bag they'd used at the Taylor land. Dan hoped Lyrica would follow the other guy to his destination.

He watched the man run a short distance down the dock. He pulled out his camera and took photos of the man and his shipmate. The yacht started its motor the minute the captain saw the runner with the canvas pack. He quickly started casting off his lines. The runner tossed the bag to the captain and leaped onto the deck. Only minutes passed before they headed out into the harbor. Dan got part of the yacht's name, but it would be enough with the photos.

Lyrica and Marci followed the drill truck to Steamboat Wharf, where the driver showed his ticket and pulled in line to wait for the next boat. Avoiding the Steamship employee, they drove across the empty car lanes close enough to catch the truck's license plate. Coming alongside the truck, they stopped beside the driver.

"Hey, do you know when the next ferry gets in?" Marci asked, smiling at the driver.

"It should be pretty soon."

"What's that funny piece of metal you've got in the back? Are you a sculptor? I've never seen anything quite like it."

"Yeah, something like that."

"You must be an experienced craftsman. This island is a great place for artists," Lyrica commented.

"Yeah. Where are you ladies headed?"

Marci was about to answer when the man's cell phone rang. Turning from his conversation, he grabbed the cell. Marci could hear the caller on the other end say, "Where are you?"

"I'm waiting for the ferry with some lovely ladies," he answered, winking at Lyrica and Marci.

"I'll meet you back at the office as soon as I get in."

"Well, it's going to take a few hours, you know. This isn't the fast ferry. Not all of us get to travel first class."

"Okay, see you in a few." The man put his cell back on the seat and turned toward the ladies.

"That was the boss. Where are you ladies headed?"

"Same place you are, but we couldn't get on this boat. We can't go until tonight. It was nice chatting with you." And with that parting comment, Lyrica pulled the Land Rover out of the car line and headed to town.

"Marci, you were fantastic."

"Thanks, but I think he was flirting with both of us."

"Well, we got an excellent description of him and his license plate. Too bad he was driving a rental. But that's child's play for Dan and Matt."

"Yeah, I'd say we put in a good day's work, walking in the moors, sunning on the beach, and chasing criminals."

"Dad won't like the fact that we took such a risk."

"But he *will* like what we found out today. Marci, get Dan on the phone and see where he is now."

Lyrica made a right at the Whaling Museum and then turned toward

Cliff Road.

"I'm going to stop at Something Natural. If Dan wants to meet us there, we'll wait for him."

Dan had made it to the ferry parking lot just as the boat was rounding the Brant Point lighthouse. Several other cars had pulled up around the truck. Dan was about to call Lyrica when his phone signaled Marci's call.

"Hey, where are you?"

"We thought we'd do a little sleuthing on our own since you had to follow the other guy. We saw you park, so we tailed the truck until it parked at the ferry terminal. The driver had a friendly chat with us."

"Tell me you didn't," Dan said in a worried voice. "Now he has a description of you all."

"Don't worry, Dan. I don't think he suspected a thing. We only chatted for a few minutes because his cell phone rang. Besides, we had the dogs in the car."

"Did you find out his final destination?"

"No, but we know he's meeting someone on the Cape. He didn't specify where. Maybe you can get a tail on him. You can tell he was driving a rental by the license plate. I'll text you the number and state. You've got at least two hours before either of them reaches land."

"Does Marci know where Josh is?"

Lyrica answered without skipping a beat. "We talked with Josh and Jake right after we left the Taylor land. They headed back to check out the holes in the corral, but only if Old Man Taylor wasn't home."

"Mrs. Kea, I think you all need to head home. But I would like to know what you found out about the driver."

"How about we meet at Something Natural?"

"Sounds great. Get some Portuguese bread if there's any left."

"And a few hermits?" Lyrica chided.

"Hermits are good, or chocolate chip. See you in a few minutes."

Lyrica parked the Land Rover a few steps away from the building. Marci got out and headed inside. The dogs were whining in the back seat.

"Okay, girls, settle down. If you're good, maybe I'll give you a cookie."

Dan pulled up next to the Land Rover while Marci was still inside. He got right into the front seat to chat with Lyrica.

"You know, you three just about gave me a heart attack when I saw you following me. Matt's going to think I don't take care of you."

"No. Matt will be jealous that he didn't get in on the fun. We weren't really in any danger."

"Probably not. But you left a lasting impression on that guy. If he talks about you with his buddies, they may identify you. Hopefully, he's so far down the food chain you're safe. But thank you for taking up the chase."

"We enjoyed it. At least I did," Lyrica replied.

Marci exited the house with three bags in her arms. Reaching the car, Dan got out of the driver's seat and helped her put the bags on the floor. He then climbed in the back seat with the dogs, who were already on to the scent of freshly baked cookies.

"Want a cookie, Dan?" Marci asked.

"Sure, what have we got?"

"They only had one hermit left, but I got some chocolate chip, so take your pick," Marci said, holding back the bag away from Mako's nose.

"Thanks for getting the license plate of the truck. That will make it easier to find these guys unless they used aliases." He was busy digging in the bag of cookies, trying to keep the dogs at bay.

"Absolutely. You don't think we're amateurs, do you?" Lyrica said, grinning. She opened the center compartment and pulled out the paper on which Marci had made notes. There was even a quick sketch, including the funky piece of equipment in the rear of the truck.

"Unfortunately, I couldn't get a close-up shot of the first guy, but the guys at the lab can work wonders with very little. I got a photo of the lookout guy in Priscilla's corral and the captain of the boat. I'll download the digitals when we get home, but you can look at them now if you'd like."

"Wait until we are home? Are you kidding?" Marci laughed and put her hand out to Dan for the camera. Mako took a long sniff, thinking it might be another cookie.

"Did you get a parking ticket at the wharf? We noticed you'd parked in a loading zone," Lyrica asked.

"No, for once, I didn't. So far, my nose is clean with the Nantucket police."

"That's a good thing because ours certainly isn't," Marci joked. "Well, how about we leave you to rendezvous with Josh and Jake at the Taylor land? We'll go home and tell the rest of the gang what happened."

"I think I need to see you safely home. Remember, I'm your bodyguard today. Keta will want to look at the photos, and I can get the lab started on the identification."

"Okay. See you in a few." Dan got out of the Rover and headed toward his Jeep.

Changing the subject, Marci turned toward Lyrica. "Mom, what do you think of Dan?"

"As a bodyguard or as the man for Becki?" Lyrica answered, her eyes still focused on the road as they drove down the narrow streets.

"You read my mind. Seriously, what do you think of Dan and Becki's relationship? Do you think she can put Stephen aside now that she knows the truth about him?"

"Becki is the mistress of her own heart. While I'm not in favor of Dan being both Becki's boyfriend and bodyguard, I think it's good for her to have a man who protects her and treats her as special."

"Frankly, I never thought Stephen could get outside of his ego long enough to appreciate Becki," Marci added.

With two women talking about men, the drive home went quickly. They soon were heading up the Longmeadow's driveway. Marci opened the car's back door to let the dogs out as soon as she turned onto the dirt track. They were already at the house when Lyrica pulled up, their tongues hanging out of their mouths, waiting at the hose for a drink.

Getting out of the car, Lyrica turned to Marci. "I'd like to go back to your studio after we tell the guys about our latest adventure."

"Sure, Mom. What do you have in mind?"

"I want to check Racey's painting of the daisies and maybe a few others in the studio."

"Any specific reason?" Marci responded.

"Yes. I'll show you when we get there."

Fifty-Four

By four-thirty that afternoon, the entire family, including Jake and Lovey, sprawled out on the deck in lounge chairs and the colorful Adirondack chairs. Keta and Dan both sat at the picnic table with their laptops. They were devouring a large platter of veggies and dip since none of them had eaten lunch.

"Even if we can identify who did the sampling, we still don't know why Morston wants the soil samples. Maybe we should hire the same firm to come back and sample for us," Josh joked.

"That might create an interesting scenario," Lyrica responded.

"This island is a pile of sand and rubble from the glaciers. As far as I know, there's nothing valuable in that. And trust me, there's no oil below us," Jake teased.

"He certainly doesn't need soil samples to build a house. And he's out of line doing so before they sign a contract. According to the realtor, Morston only has the first right of refusal. No one else is trying to buy the land," Josh responded, clearly frustrated by the turn of events.

"I'm disappointed that those two men didn't fall into the portal and meet up with Priscilla. Maybe she's watching all this," Marci added.

"According to the printouts we have on Morston's mineral investments, each time he's bought land, he later found oil, diamonds, gold, opals, and certain types of specialized clay. Any of these seem possible here?" Dan asked.

"Don't I wish," Josh laughed. "If there's gold below his land, let's start digging."

"Josh, be serious. We live on a pile of sand with a few artifacts and glacial moraine." Marci was trying her best to keep the conversation light.

"What about the clay on the cliffs at Gay Head on the Vineyard? Isn't that unusual?" Becki asked.

"It may be unusual for that island, but it's not valuable enough to interest Morston," Keta answered.

"Now, wait a minute. Sometimes there are gemstones in the rock, just below the clay layers. Often you find quartz immediately below the clay. Quartz is valuable when it contains emeralds." Lyrica added.

"Remember how we dug in deep red clay looking for emeralds?" Keta asked, smiling at his wife.

"Emeralds? Then I hope our land connects underground to Taylors," Josh exclaimed.

"Don't get your hopes up, Josh," Marci said, rolling her eyes once more at her husband's childlike enthusiasm.

"Glacial moraine and the outwash plain are unlikely to hold large enough deposits of quartz. Remember, the glacier moved all those rocks and pebbles from north of us and deposited them here thousands of years ago," Keta added.

"The best way to settle this is to go back to the corral, carefully open and clean the cores, then scrape the sides of the channel to see what we find," Keta proposed.

"That sounds nice, but neither Taylor nor the realtor know about this. I don't want the police arresting me for trespassing and robbery over a few piles of dirt. Does anyone have another idea?" Josh asked.

"What about the possibility that Morston knows about the portals and is trying to find one?" Lyrica commented. She was again in her problem-solving mode.

"Old T might be in on a deal with Morston," Jake suggested. "None of us know what he might have hidden from us all these years."

"None of this would happen if Priscilla was here. I'm sure she could shed light on this." Marci was once more looking sad and worried.

"But Marci, she didn't believe you after she saw the empty hillside with Taylor. I don't think she's living in the same reality as we are. She's living in a reality that hasn't changed," Lyrica said.

"What would happen if she saw the Madequecham valley?" Marci asked.

"Sis, the houses probably would be there if she took Taylor, just like Pocomo."

"Then we need to take her into our reality. We just have to find her again."

Lyrica looked lovingly at her daughter and then gave Keta a good stare. "You boys better find your fishing gear if you're going to catch dinner. We'll have the rest of the dinner ready when you come back, say around seven?"

"Gentlemen, that's our cue that the ladies want the house to themselves. Let's get going," Keta barked. Lyrica walked past her husband and smiled.

"I'll explain later," she whispered to him.

"Be careful, okay?" he replied.

When the men finally disappeared down the driveway, Becki said something first. "Mom, what was that all about? I thought we were going out to dinner?"

"I needed to get the men out of here because I want to try something with you all, and I can't do it with bodyguards and husbands around."

"How do you know they won't drop one of them at the end of the driveway?" Marci asked.

"That's certainly possible, and I wouldn't put it past Keta. But I think he knows what I want to do. We were talking about last night before going to bed."

"Talking about what?" Becki asked.

"Come with me. I'll show you what I think I've discovered. We need to go to Marci's studio."

Becki, Marci, and Lovey joined Lyrica as she headed for the studio. The girls were chatting about Becki's paintings and Marci's recent show. Lyrica was silently praying. This would be the acid test for her theory.

Upon entering the studio, Lyrica immediately went to Racey's painting of the daisies in the kettle holes.

"Okay, here's my theory. There is something about this painting that changed the hillside Racey saw from being devoid of daisies to the sea of flowers we saw today at the ponds."

"You don't think that just because Racey painted a field full of flowers, they suddenly appear, do you?" Marci asked.

"Yes, I do. Or something like that," Lyrica said hesitantly. "Now, don't look at me like that."

"Mom, that's just a coincidence. You can't paint flowers into being. If you could, the entire world would be beautiful. It's not so strange that the hillside wasn't in bloom last week. It's still early in the season," Becki said.

"Then what about the corral? Remember Josh reported the other day that the corral was overflowing with goldenrod?"

"Yes, but I still don't understand. What am I missing?" Marci said, looking over at Becki and Lovey for some help.

"Marci, Josh mentioned the field of goldenrod *after* you completed the painting that's over there in the corner."

"But what do daisies and goldenrod have to do with disappearing houses?" Marci asked.

"Wait, Marci. I see what Mom is saying. Daisies bloom in June, but goldenrod blooms in September."

"So maybe it's just a coincidence that they are blooming together?" Becki asked.

"I don't think it's a coincidence. There's something here in this studio that can change our surroundings." Lyrica was like a hound that has picked up the fox scent.

"Why would it have to be in the studio? Couldn't it be anywhere—whatever it is?" Marci retorted.

"Mom, weren't you painting the day you picked us up at the airport? That was the day the houses disappeared."

"Becki, I'm talking about creating things, not having them vanish."

"But what if it works both ways?" Lovey asked.

"Well, don't look at me. I leave the creating stuff to God," Marci said.

"I'm not accusing you or anybody. I'm just trying to see why supernatural or paranormal events are happening on the island. And in this case, things appear *and* disappear."

"Mom, when did you get into science fiction? I thought you were a firm believer in God?" Becki asked.

"Becki, it's possible there is a supernatural action taking place. God does supernatural things. The Bible is full of His appearances and His angels. But some demonic angels followed Satan when God kicked him out of heaven. They are often up to mischief and evil in this realm."

"Well, I don't remember any houses disappearing when Jesus went into them—or fields of flowers appearing," Becki retorted. "It's easier for me to believe that there's a parallel reality than your spiritual stuff."

"Maybe God is in both realities. We can't see Him because He's not made of flesh," Lovey chimed in.

"Okay, then let's put the parallel reality on hold. I want you to think about what was going on when Priscilla appeared in the meadow. Marci, what were you and Becki painting?"

"I was sketching wildflowers," Becki answered.

"And I was painting the horses in the meadow."

"But Marci, you said you were painting *Priscilla* and the horses that day," Lyrica responded.

"Where's the painting?" Lovey asked.

"I stopped painting Priscilla when she appeared. But later, I painted her out because she kidded me about how landscapes have less monetary value if people are in them," Marci said.

"No, Marci, I think Priscilla hated to have *herself* painted," Becki said.

"Or photographed," Lyrica added.

"Some people believe that your spirit will leave if you photograph them," Marci responded. "Mom, do you think Priscilla appeared in the meadow because I was painting her in the landscape?"

"Yes, I do."

Fifty-Five

Marci and Becki both stared at their mom, dumbfounded.

"You aren't kidding, are you?" Marci asked.

"No, I'm not. And I'm not saying I understand all of this. But it sure seems to fit."

"So that means all we have to do is paint Priscilla back, and she's not missing anymore?" Becki asked.

"I'm not sure," Lyrica responded.

"But where does she go?" Marci asked.

"Maybe there is a second Nantucket that she lives in," Becki offered.

"Right. And it has hot chocolate just like here," Marci quipped.

"Now, who's being cynical?" Becki retorted.

"What about the newspaper article? Remember when you ran into Priscilla on the beach? She had an identical newspaper to yours. Only hers didn't have an article about the missing houses," Lyrica added.

"So, does that mean that there are two Priscillas?" Lovey asked hesitatingly.

"I don't think so. We've seen no evidence of that," Lyrica said quietly.

"Well then, let's paint her back and talk with her," Becki exclaimed. "Marci, get a blank canvas."

"What? I'm going to paint Priscilla back to life?"

"Yes," both Becki and Lyrica chimed.

"Do it, Marci. Or I *will*," said Becki, challenging her sister.

"But Marci, paint her here in the studio. If you paint her somewhere else, we won't know if it works," Lyrica instructed.

"I know. I'm just trying to figure out what brushes and paint I used in the meadow that day."

"Come on," Becki said. "Just paint her."

Marci took her charcoal and sketched the surrounding studio, and then she put Priscilla in the doorway. They waited. Nothing happened.

"Marci, try some other paintbrushes."

Marci put a few colors on her palette, picked up a paintbrush, and tried again. They waited. Nothing.

"There goes that theory," moaned Becki.

"Marci, which easel is Racey's? I want to try to paint some flowers. Maybe it's easier to paint wildflowers into being than it is a person."

"It's over here, Mom." Marci walked over to the easel. "But you know the kids pick new brushes each day. Her paints would be the same, but not the brushes."

"How many brushes do I have to go through?"

"There are about fifty in here now," Marci responded.

"Great. How about the brushes we took to paint the Madequecham Valley?" Lyrica asked her daughter.

"But those houses disappeared. We didn't paint them in."

"That's right. But we painted the meadow valley *without* houses the way it used to be, didn't we?"

"Of course. What am I thinking?" Marci said, walking back to her easel and supplies. "The question is, did I take any of the brushes out of my traveling pack and bring them in here?" Going to the front of the studio, Marci rummaged through her things to find her paints.

"Look what I found," she said, holding up two boxes of paints. "One of these, and I think it's this one, is Priscilla's. Maybe we should try hers first?"

"Wait, what if you make one of us vanish instead of Priscilla reappearing?" Becki asked.

"Becki's right. We need to be careful about what we attempt," Lovey cautioned.

"Marci, don't paint yourself out of the picture. You already disappeared once outside the studio. The next time, we might not get you back," Lyrica warned her daughter.

"Not to worry, Mom. I'm only going to paint flowers for the garden outside. If that works, then I'll paint Priscilla right here in the studio."

Picking up the paints and brushes, Marci drew the entry gate and the flower garden outside her studio. Choosing a beautiful periwinkle blue, she painted clematis climbing up the sides of the trellis over the entrance and spilling onto the *Rosa rugosa* hedge. It looked as if the sky had fallen in drops all over the garden. The roses became a patchwork of pink and blue and differing shades of green. Marci kept on painting. Suddenly, Becki pointed to the gate.

"Look, Marci, it's working! Look at the flowers on the gate."

Putting down her paintbrush, Marci walked over to where Becki and her mom were staring out the large French windows to the garden. Sure enough, the clematis was there. But something looked odd about the vines. Walking outside, Marci went over to the gate and *Rosa rugosa hedge*. Picking up one of the clematis vines, she looked at it. All the leaves and tendrils were missing.

"Mom, take some green paint from Racey's station and paint in some leaves and the small tendrils that wind around other plants," Marci shouted toward the studio windows.

Lyrica did as her daughter requested, but nothing appeared. Coming into the studio, Marci took the brush she'd used to paint the blue petals, wiped it clean with a rag, and dipped it into some of the green paint at Racey's easel.

"Now, do you see anything?" Marci asked, holding the brush off the canvas.

"I'm not sure," Lyrica said.

"What do you mean, you're not sure? Either there are new leaves, or there are not," Marci said, frustration building inside of her. Looking over Becki's shoulder, she looked out at the hedge. There were now new green leaves on the vine.

"What?" Marci exclaimed. "Those aren't clematis leaves."

Going out the studio door, Marci turned to the left and walked toward the far side of the garden, where the clematis stopped. She then went back to the gate to look at the leaves. Unlocking the gate, she went to the other side of the rose hedge, where the clematis disappeared. Bending down, she followed the vine to the ground. It was also growing on the scrub oak along the path back to the house. Lyrica and Becki watched her go up the grassy route to the house until she disappeared.

"Oh no," Lyrica cried. "She's gone."

"No, Mom, she only went around the corner," Becki answered. But Lyrica was out the door, through the gate, and down the path. She saw where the clematis stopped, but the only sign of Marci was her paintbrush lying on the ground.

"Marci, where are you?" she cried.

"I'm over here. Come see what I found."

Picking up the paintbrush, Lyrica ran back toward her daughter's voice. Becki was standing in the doorway. Her face was ashen.

"Mom, don't go near her. You'll vanish," she shouted.

Coming to a screeching stop, Lyrica turned toward Becki. "What's going on?" She was standing, looking back and forth between Becki and Marci.

"Marci, how did you get there? The last time I looked, you were at the gate. There's no path to where you are," Lyrica said, wanting to go over and hug her daughter. "You disappeared on the path. I have your paintbrush."

"I know. Stay where you are for a minute. I think there is another portal here, and I don't want to fall into it again."

"Again? What do you mean again?" Lyrica stammered.

"Mom, I didn't walk here. And there were no clematis flowers or leaves where I was. Toss me the paintbrush. I'm going to come back into the studio."

"Marci, you aren't kidding, are you? You went somewhere, didn't you?" Lyrica asked.

"Yes, I did, but only for a few seconds. One minute I was walking down the path, and the next, I was walking here in the garden looking at the tiny blue clematis blossoms littered throughout this part of the perennial garden."

"How do you know you weren't here?" Lyrica asked. "And how do I know you won't disappear the next time you walk down that path?"

"You don't. But I have a theory about this now. I'm holding the paintbrush. You won't disappear. Come on, let's go into the studio and have a cup of tea. I'm tired of traveling."

Becki was standing in the studio crying. Immediately Lyrica went and threw her arms around her and guided her to Marci's comforting floral chintz chair. The two of them sat down next to Lovey and waited for Marci's explanation. The afternoon sun was fading, but the light was still coming in through the French windows that surrounded the studio. Putting on the teakettle, Marci sat down on the arm of her favorite overstuffed chair where Becki had curled up. Then, facing the three women, Marci tried to unravel the mystery that had just occurred.

"Mom, remember you thought there were two realities, one that we're in and one that Priscilla is in?"

"Yes, and you all laughed at me."

"Were you saying that somehow my paint and brushes can paint you into another reality that looks exactly like this one?"

"Yes. I think if we stayed in that parallel reality, we would find Priscilla *and* the houses that have disappeared."

Lyrica was eyeing Becki during this interchange. She still looked like a frightened baby rabbit enveloped in Marci's chair, but she was attuned to the conversation.

"Mom, you've got to be kidding," Becki said. She was regaining her composure, coming back around to her cynical but inquisitive self.

"I'm not kidding. But what I can't figure out is why the paintbrush didn't stay with you, Marci."

"Maybe it can only stay in one reality," Lovey offered.

Pouring the hot water into the teapot, Marci carried it over to the coffee table and put it down. Lyrica retrieved the unique teacups painted in varied chintz patterns. Marci then grabbed the painted tin Becki had made for her when she was a child and offered them some sugar cookies covered with colorful sprinkles and different flower patterns.

"These aren't magic cookies, are they?" Becki asked her sister.

"Not as far as I know. Just don't touch them with that brush."

"In case anyone didn't notice, I feel completely unglued about this," Becki confessed.

"I'm not happy about it either. But there doesn't seem to be any danger as far as I can tell. It's not like Marci was held hostage in the other realm."

"Mom, come on. She disappeared. Isn't that dangerous enough?"

"More to the point, sis, what are we going to tell Dad?" Marci asked. "He'll want to cut a path around the place in the grassy walk, so no one else falls in."

"If I fall in, I'm going to take the Jeep, find Priscilla, and bring her back here," Lyrica responded to her daughter. "She's got a lot of explaining to do."

"But Mom, maybe she doesn't know. Maybe she hasn't figured it out. There don't seem to be any rules governing when you can walk through a portal. If there is such a thing."

"Then the only way to find out is to find Priscilla and bring her back. But we have to figure out how to control what portal we use."

"Oh, great," Becki responded, falling back into her chair and looking up at the windowed ceiling. "What, you think you can control this thing?"

Fifty-Six

Conversation at dinner was lively but sobering. Keta was visibly distressed that Marci had disappeared again. Marci wanted to go back and find her friend. Dan and Matt had already gone to the studio to check for portals. Protecting the family when new portals kept opening was justifiably tricky. Josh, however, thought he had a solution.

"I think it's simple. Let's go to Taylor's property, and Marci can paint Priscilla back into the picture. Then we sit her down and find out what she knows about the mystery."

"Josh, we don't know that the paintbrush I have can do that. And if so, we're taking an enormous risk that whoever does the painting may disappear into Priscilla's realm just as she appears here," Marci warned her husband.

"Then send Dan or Matt. They're more expendable. Only kidding, guys," Josh said, smiling at the two bodyguards.

"We're also assuming that Priscilla knows how to control the passage between the realities," Becki cautioned.

"Having been back and forth, I can attest that there is some other reality that looks very much like this one. I agree with Josh. Let's experiment on the Taylor land with all of us there. If we can identify one portal using Matt's compass, I'll paint Priscilla on a canvas. I can stand close to, but not in the portal, and she should appear without me disappearing."

"You hope," Becki said. "Maybe you should tie a rope between you and Matt or Dan."

"Can you paint out some more McMansions, so Jake and I have more work to do?" Josh asked mischievously.

"Now, that's exactly what we want to avoid," Keta said soberly. "If these brushes and paint really have that power, we are holding a dangerous weapon that has great potential for evil."

"What I don't understand is why now? Why is this happening when these brushes have been around for years?" Lyrica asked. "Marci, didn't you say that the brush you used came from Priscilla's traveling paint set?"

"Yes, but the paint came from Racey's easel."

"But you can't be sure that some of your paint isn't from Priscilla's set. You've painted with her for years. It's likely your paints are mixed with hers," Lyrica answered.

"If Priscilla knows they have this power, I doubt she would have allowed them out of her sight. She may not even know I have them. And she may have some of her own," Marci responded. "For all we know, she may have painted Josh's Pocomo houses out of existence and not realize it. She loves that marsh."

"But we can't ignore the fact that Marci has at least one paintbrush and some paint that has this power. We need to find out what Priscilla knows and if she has more brushes and paints like these," Lyrica said.

"That's assuming the Priscilla we've seen is the person we know," Becki added.

"Since none of us will rest until we solve this mystery, how about we all go to the Taylors tomorrow morning? If we time it right, he'll be down on Main Street chatting with his bench buddies. That will give us a few hours of safety," Keta proposed.

"Depending on what you define as safe, Dad," Becki commented.

"Well said, daughter."

"Josh, would you like me to paint back one McMansion and see what happens?" Marci asked.

"I wouldn't like it one bit. I like the hillside restored to its classic beauty. I'd rather paint a few more houses *out* of the picture. There are several places on the island that would be lovely without them. And it's not because I want to rebuild them."

"I agree with Josh. I love the island in its pristine condition before the building boom," Dan added.

"As long as we aren't killing the people who are in them," Becki commented with a worried look on her face.

"I think that's unlikely," Keta said. "It appears as if Priscilla's world hasn't changed."

"Yet," Becki said. "If she has paints and brushes with her, she could paint us out of existence and not even know it."

"So how about it, everyone? Shall we go tomorrow when Taylor is downtown with his buddies?" Keta asked the group.

❧

The next morning, breakfast was brief. All of them were eager to get going. Keta, Lyrica, and Matt led the way in the Land Rover. Josh and Marci followed in their pickup, and Becki and Dan took the rental Jeep. Matt took his compass and map to see what portals might still be open.

It was a perfect Nantucket day for an adventure. The sun was high, not a cloud in sight, just blue sky and the smell of wild roses in the air. Pulling up by the Taylor house, they rallied at the base of the front porch. Marci set up her paints and easel while Matt carefully walked around with the compass.

"Okay, here goes," Marci said, picking up the paintbrush and tube of paint Racey used for the daisies. "You know, Priscilla's going to hate me for painting her into a landscape."

"I would say that's the least of our worries, sis."

Painting the meadow that ran down to the corral, Marci quickly sketched Priscilla's horse and then picked up the paintbrush to paint her friend back to life. She painted Priscilla in her barn boots, jeans, and old jacket standing near her horse.

They waited. Nothing happened. Matt checked the compass. They were definitely near a portal as the compass needle would not settle down in any one direction.

"Now what?" Marci asked the group.

"Why don't you go down toward the barn? Priscilla might have taken the horse back into its stall, and we've missed her here," Lyrica said.

"Well, if you say so," Marci said, putting down the paintbrush.

"No, honey, take your paints. Matt, you, Josh, and Lyrica follow her. I'll stay here with Dan and Becki." Keta was taking no chances of losing everyone.

Marci didn't know whether to be afraid, excited, or sad. Nothing with her friend seemed to be dependable, least of all her appearances. Approaching the barn, she could hear a voice inside by the stalls. Marci stopped and waited. Yes, there was a female voice talking to the horse. Setting her jaw, she determinedly walked through the open barn door. The horse was there, but Priscilla was not. The family was standing at the entrance to the barn, looking as confused as Marci.

"You heard her voice, didn't you?"

"Come on. Let's go back to the horse stalls." Josh grabbed Marci's hand. "Maybe she's just getting feed and water. Or she could be in the loft." Marci was like a reluctant dog on a leash. She dug in her feet and didn't move.

"No, Josh, I can't. This was a mistake," Marci's eyes welled up with tears.

"Okay, baby, you stay here with Mom. Matt and I will go in and find her."

The two of them disappeared into the inner recesses of the barn. The women could hear them calling Priscilla's name. Then suddenly, just like before, she materialized in Bullet's stall with a curry brush in one hand and the grain bucket in the other.

"Hey Josh, what are you doing here? And who's your handsome friend?" Priscilla remarked, putting down the bucket, wiping her right hand on her jeans, and extending it toward Matt.

"Priscilla, this is Matt. He's a friend of the family who's staying with us for a few weeks."

"Matt, glad to meet you. So what are you two boys doing here this morning? If you're looking for Taylor, he's jawing with his cronies downtown right about now."

"Actually, we were looking for you, Priscilla," Marci said as she came toward the stall.

"Marci, what a delightful surprise. This is a fine thing. Why don't we go back to the house and have some ice-cold lemonade on the porch?"

"Sure, Pris, that sounds good. I have some questions I want to ask you, and Josh has a few of his own."

"Josh, you're not taking up painting, are you?" Priscilla laughed.

"No, not unless you have some hints on how to tame the subjects that Marci paints. Some of them seem to have a life of their own," he laughed. Josh was trying to shake off the eerie feeling as they walked with Priscilla back to the house. It really was her. Or was it?

When they reached the house, Priscilla was thrilled to find the others. Sitting down on the front porch in the wicker chairs, each of them tried to present a calm, cheerful look. After re-introducing Priscilla to Dan, Marci followed Priscilla into the house and returned with a tray of lemonade and some chocolate chip cookies that were still warm.

"Mmm, thanks Priscilla, these are great." And also real, Lyrica thought.

Not missing a beat, Priscilla sat down with her lemonade and turned to the group. "Okay, so to what do I owe this group visit?"

Marci, having regained her composure, spoke up. "Priscilla, we came to see if you could help us solve a mystery that appears to be going on in certain places on the island. It seems to be connected to the paint and paintbrushes from your traveling set. I guess I unknowingly absconded with them, and when I use them, some rather strange happenings occur."

There was a long pause before Priscilla spoke. Putting down her lemonade on the coffee table, Priscilla looked at each of them sitting there. "There is an explanation, but I confess, I had hoped that I wouldn't be sharing it with a group, only you, Marci."

No one said a word. Marci also put down her lemonade, bracing herself for what Priscilla was about to say. "Priscilla, it's okay. Everyone knows that these painting tools have some kind of power."

"We've seen it, Priscilla. We just want to understand it before you disappear again," Lyrica explained.

"I'm not sure I can give you all the information you want. But I will tell you what I can. I knew that something was going on with the paint and paintbrushes, and I was suspicious that you'd accidentally gotten some of them. When you told me I was missing, I started to wonder. I figured that I'd gotten careless with the materials. Unfortunately, when I first disappeared, it was without the paint and brushes."

"But wait, Priscilla. Where did the paint and brushes come from in the first place?" Marci was leaning over with her hand on Priscilla's knee.

"That's a story for another day. Right now, let's just focus on the how and what."

"That's fine. But how do we know you won't disappear on us while we sit here?" Keta was glowering, despite Lyrica's attempts to soothe his impatience.

"For now, we are safe on the porch. But I wouldn't wander too far from the house with me for a while," Priscilla warned.

"Priscilla, excuse me for interrupting. Dan and Matt are bodyguards for Lyrica and Becki, so they're like family. Whatever your secret is, it's safe with them. I hired them because of the two robberies. Are you familiar with that set of events since you disappeared?"

"Yes, I know about the robberies, and I'm glad Keta that you have seen fit to hire some protection. Not that it will help if the paint and brushes get into the wrong hands. But let's not go there for now."

"Priscilla, wait. There seems to be a growing number of things you don't want to talk about," Marci said.

"Yes, I know. But Taylor will return from downtown, so I can't be here. He'd have a heart attack if he saw me here."

"Can you reappear someplace where Taylor can't see you?" Keta asked.

"Yes, but I don't like doing it. It's hard on me physically, and I don't know how reliable or often I can transfer between the two worlds. Marci could come with me and then return with your questions answered."

"Oh no, Priscilla. We're not letting her disappear again," Josh quickly responded.

"I'm not too keen on that either," Marci said. "How about our house? You've been there at the studio. Why wouldn't that be a good place for us to meet? There was a portal outside the studio where you and I transferred between the two realities the other day."

"That might be a better idea. But Marci, now that you have passed through the portal, you'll need to be careful where you go. Once you've built a two-way street, you enter and re-enter more easily. And any of you can accidentally slip through."

"You mean she doesn't have to paint herself out as she did you?" Becki asked.

"That's correct, but it's hard on the fabric of our bodies to do so. We're only meant to be in one reality, not trespassing into another."

"In what way?" Keta asked.

"I will tell you that later. But first, you need to understand why Lyrica's and Becki's studios were robbed. Earl Morston wants this land. And I suspect he knows there is something valuable here. You need to make sure he doesn't buy the land from Taylor. We need to protect the portals. Morston plays a dangerous game."

"Oh great, we move here to get away from it all, and it follows us," Josh said, throwing his hands up in the air in frustration.

"Is there no place that's safe?" Lyrica asked.

"Not at the moment," Priscilla answered.

Fifty-Seven

I n Boston, Morston was smoking a cigar looking out his floor-to-ceiling windows when Stephen opened the door and entered. As usual, the room was blue with cigar smoke. Fortunately, Stephen was giving the presentation, so he didn't have to stand directly in the cloud of smoke. The other five men were not as fortunate.

They'd analyzed the soil samples from the Taylor land. Stephen and several other technical colleagues were presenting the results of the tests and suggesting future action before the sale.

"So, what's the plan, boys?" Morston asked, fixing his eyes on Stephen and his colleagues with an impatient look.

"Sir, you have two choices. Buy the land using our information and analysis. Or do more extensive soil tests to identify the anomaly you believe to be somewhere underneath the soil. We didn't find any stone or quartz vein to indicate the presence of gems. But we only sampled the corral."

"Why the heck did you only sample one place?" Morston barked.

"I believe your intelligence report said that the corral was the primary place to find what we were looking for," Stephen answered, hoping he wouldn't get crushed for reminding Morston something he'd temporarily forgotten. "We had limited time, so we picked the most likely place."

"Don't remind me of the report. Do you think I've forgotten?" Morston hissed at Stephen.

"Sir, it's difficult to sample when we don't know what we are looking for." One of Stephen's colleagues was jumping into the fray. "If you think there is a quartz vein or other gem-laden material, going for deeper and wider samples should give us solid evidence. But that means re-sampling on the Taylor land and possibly other private property."

"Who said you were to look for a quartz vein?" Morston thundered. "Do you believe there's a gem casing in that sandpile of an island? I said anomaly, you idiots."

"In that case," Stephen responded, "do we know what kind of anomaly we are looking for, geologic, topographical, atmospheric?"

"If I knew, do you think I'd be wasting my time chatting with you all? Just get on with it so we can complete the sale before that old codger changes his mind."

"With all due respect, sir, we think the price tag is small compared to the size of your other holdings. You're buying land that will only increase in value. If we're unsuccessful, which we don't think we will be, you can still sell it for a profit later," Stephen added.

"Well, what are you waiting for? And while you're at it, put your brains on those photos. I didn't go to all the trouble of getting those photos for nothing. The tip we got was from an excellent source. How come none of you are working that line?" Morston asked acidly.

"Sir, a specialist is examining the photos to see if there is something that points us in a specific direction. But they only include the area around the barn and corral. Unless the missing photo gives us more clues. And if all else fails, you'll have a private piece of property on which to build another villa so you can escape Boston whenever you like."

"Land to build a house on? There's land all over this planet. Why would I need to buy some on Nantucket? I can have it anywhere I put my foot down," Morston shouted.

"Sir, you need to buy the land for us to do more samples. At a minimum, it was trespassing. Fortunately, our men didn't get caught," Stephen answered.

"Did you somehow develop a conscience in the last few weeks? How do you know what is legal or illegal? Sometimes I wonder why I hired you, Stephen," Morston snapped.

"Yes, sir. The figures you see here today give you several choices. We would welcome moving the project along as you'd like."

"Fine, fine, pick up the land. It's a drop in the bucket. And get that equipment ready to be out there fast. Get me some better figures and maps for the surrounding properties. Maybe we'll make them a deal they can't refuse."

"Yes, sir," Stephen answered.

"Well, don't just stand there. Get going," Morston barked.

As the men filed out of the room, Morston leaned back in his Australian leather chair, gazed out the window, enjoying the view of the harbor out toward the Cape and Islands. Humph, maybe I'll buy the whole damn island, he thought to himself as he puffed away on his Cuban cigar.

Fifty-Eight

*P*riscilla quickly picked up the empty lemonade cups and cookie crumbs to erase any evidence of the meeting. They had agreed to regroup at Marci's studio in half an hour. But Priscilla had shooed them out too quickly. The brief interview satisfied no one. It only raised more questions. Keta was frustrated and angry. He hated feeling out of control, and he especially didn't like the specter of Morston looming over his family.

"You know, I always thought Priscilla was outspoken about her life and everyone else's. I don't understand her being so tight-lipped, especially when it endangers Marci."

"Keta, I think you are jumping to conclusions. I don't think she's withholding information, or she wouldn't have offered to meet us back at the studio," Lyrica commented.

"Unless she doesn't show up."

"Now you're being harsh. Marci has been her friend for many years. I don't think Priscilla is trying to string us along. I think she's trying to protect Marci and not run into Taylor. Besides, we know how to find her."

"Josh better rein in Marci from using the portals. I'm sure he's not happy about this either."

"Honey, none of us are happy. But the reality is—or should I say realities? We're involved whether we like it or not. We have to see this through. With the whole family, we have the best brains around."

Matt sat quietly in the back seat during this discussion. He listened carefully, trying to construct a safety framework for the family. He could feel the tension and fear hovering over everyone. Taking advantage of a temporary lull, he tried to infuse some hope into the situation.

"I know this all seems to get more and more complex. But in my experience, there's always a tangle of interwoven clues that seem to lead nowhere in the beginning. Today we connected several pieces. It's a bit like a jigsaw puzzle. Once you have the frame done and the beginning colors separated, you know you're on to figuring out the puzzle."

"So, Matt, how about you show me the frame and a few colors?" Keta groused.

"Don't take it personally, Matt. Keta hates jigsaw puzzles. But I get your point. Keta and I are two of the color groupings, whereas you and Dan are sitting on the frame."

"Perhaps when we get home, we can create a master list of questions for Priscilla and prioritize them. She has a way she wants to reveal the mystery. But I don't think we can afford to have partial disclosure."

"You're right, Matt. I'm sorry. My protective instinct is in overdrive. I'll try to let you and Dan have more time in the game."

Josh and Marci were having a similar conversation. Only Becki and Dan seemed to dig into what they could conclude from Priscilla's revelations. Becki had let her creative mind work on the mystery instead of just her emotions. She seemed to be calmer than the rest of the group, at least when Dan was around. She still needed a strategy to untangle herself from Stephen without raising suspicion. But after that, what did she want?

Men, Becki thought. They make life so messy. They slip into your life, settle down in your heart, and then pull you with them wherever they want to go, regardless of how you feel. At least that's been my story. But Dan seems to be different. Maybe being my bodyguard keeps a healthy distance between us. Yeah right. The lack of space put my heart and brain on a collision course.

Marci had put on the teakettle and coffee maker the minute the family entered her studio. Everyone flopped down in the comfy chairs or brought out one of the many multicolored futons stored under the window seat for the kids. It looked almost like story time, except the main character was missing.

"Does anyone want to guess where Priscilla will appear?" Josh asked with an impish grin.

"Stop it, Josh," Marci said, turning around to face her husband. "Or I'll paint you back onto the Taylor land."

Keta was eager to get started on the questions for Priscilla. He explained what he and Lyrica had discussed. The group then quickly made a list of questions. The vote was unanimous on finding out where the paint and paintbrushes came from and why Priscilla had them. Each thought of several things they'd like to paint in or out of existence. Morston was number one.

There was an undertone of anxiety based on what Priscilla had said about

Morston. And the dangers of traveling back and forth between the two realities still hung over them. They were debating what part the photo robberies played when Priscilla appeared at the door in the same jeans, T-shirt, and flip-flops she'd had on while seated on her front porch.

"Have you been waiting a long time? From what I heard, you have a lot of questions for me. I wasn't trying to be mysterious. It's just hard to accept that so many of you now know the secret. Usually, the trust gets passed to one or two people, and that's it. That's why we've been able to keep it secret for so many years."

"Let's start with how you became the steward of the paint and paintbrushes," Keta suggested, still impatient to get the mystery solved.

Priscilla sighed heavily and walked over to a futon that Matt had just vacated for her. "I can tell you what I know, what was passed on to me, and what you'll need to understand. But know upfront there are some questions even I don't have answers to."

"That's fine, Priscilla," Marci said, trying to make her friend feel more comfortable. The tone of her dad's questions embarrassed her. He was usually so calm in a crisis.

"Every Scottish ancestor has held the secret of the painting materials as far back as the 1600s. I never traced the family before that time as there was no need. This is the first breach of the family trust that has happened in a long time."

"Are you saying that this is the first use of the paint materials that you know of?" Keta pressed in.

"Darling, let her finish," Lyrica said, trying to reign in her husband. "Priscilla, can I get you some tea or coffee?"

"I'm fine, thank you. To my knowledge, this is the first time the materials created such dramatic changes—enough to create separate but parallel realities. There is no written record of these materials, only the oral history handed down through the generations listed in the trust box. Taylor doesn't even know. Until the houses above Pocomo Meadows disappeared, I didn't know any of the brushes and paint were missing."

"Priscilla, how did you and your family keep from using the brushes for personal gain or power?" Dan asked.

"This is a well-guarded trust. Inheriting the materials is a weighty responsibility. We were all given the fear of God for using or abusing them."

"So do they come from God?" Becki asked.

"Their origin and purpose have been lost in time. For some reason, God has allowed their supernatural power to exist. Man gets tempted to use such control for personal gain because of his inherent sinfulness. As far as I know, that has never happened within the trust. That's why it's critical to choose carefully who the next trustee is. For whatever reason, the materials still exist. But remember, God ultimately controls all power—natural and supernatural."

"Why doesn't He destroy it?" Becki asked.

"God will ultimately destroy it all at the end of time. But until that day, we must keep it from being used for evil.

"I think we should destroy them," Lyrica added.

"Well, that will be your choice," Priscilla said, looking at Marci.

"Oh, thanks. Make me the scapegoat."

"We've handed down the trust through so many generations that the original designer's intent has been lost. And the materials only work where they physically are. For example, you can't make Europe disappear unless you go there with the brushes and paint."

"Oh, thank goodness. I always wanted to go to Paris," Becki said, trying to lighten the deadening atmosphere that had overtaken the group.

"So you're saying there wasn't a plan to remove the McMansions from the island?" Josh asked.

"No. Not that I don't think it was an acceptable use of the power. But to give you and Jake a permanent stream of business? No. I painted that marsh with the wrong brushes and paint."

"Too bad, hon. We could have been rich," Marci said, elbowing her husband.

"So why didn't someone destroy them if they are so dangerous?" Dan asked.

"Or steal them?" Keta asked.

"It is a sacred trust. None of us would destroy them. You can only understand when you own the trust. And yes, they have been stolen, but they were recovered."

"So if I understand you correctly, they are like a trump card that only the owner can play and only in dire emergencies. Is that correct?" Keta continued.

"That is correct. And removing McMansions is not a dire emergency."

"That, my dear, depends on your opinion. I think they're a blight to the land even if they provide Josh with work," Marci commented.

"I agree. Let's get rid of some more," Becki added.

Priscilla was looking very sad. Such frivolous comments proved the reason for holding the trust so secret. Even she didn't know why her clan was chosen. Would she rather not have had the responsibility? You bet. But that wasn't possible, and now more people, including two strangers, were part of the trust.

There was an eerie silence as they watched Priscilla. No one wanted charge over such a trust. But it was impossible now to go back.

"Priscilla, it's clear this discussion has upset you as well as the group. What can we do to help make things right for you?" Lyrica asked. She was so sensitive to people's feelings that the tension in the room was causing her physical pain.

"This was bound to happen. Taylor and I have no children to pass along the brushes and paint. I have to pick someone to hold them for the next generation. But now the job is done. They can now pass to you, Marci."

"Me? Why me?" Marci exclaimed.

"You are the logical recipient."

"But I don't *want* them."

"Now, hold on, Marci," Josh interrupted.

"Josh, be serious for once," Marci snapped, staring at her husband.

"We don't have to decide today. But we need to talk about Morston and the danger he represents," Keta warned. He was still afraid that Priscilla would disappear before she'd finished their questions.

"Are you saying that Morston knows about the paint and brushes, and that's why he wants your land?" Dan asked.

"Morston only knows that there is something about the land that is valuable. How he found out, I don't know." Priscilla's face was showing the strain.

"But he thinks it's in the soil as far as we can tell," Matt said.

"He's not far from wrong."

"We think he got several pieces of the puzzle from my studio and then Becki's. He stole the old black and white photographs we had of your property," Lyrica said. "We surmised that there is something in the photographs that shows what is valuable on your land."

"What was the subject of the photos he stole?"

"The thief took two old photos of your house and barn about a month ago. Then he stole one of the new barn and corral from Becki's studio."

"What we can't figure out is why they were stolen. In and of themselves, they seem innocuous," Keta related.

"Did the photo of the new barn have the old hitching post and rock in front of the barn?" Priscilla asked. Everyone turned to Becki to see what she would answer.

"Not that I remember. It looked almost like it does today, without the hitching post."

"What's the significance of an old hitching post?" Matt asked, uncertain where Priscilla was going.

"We set the hitching post into a cement base. Marci, do you remember the two iron rings we used to tie up the horses? We knocked the post down when we built the new barn. We didn't bulldoze the corral, so it should still be there."

"Why is that so important?" Keta asked, trying to see where Priscilla was taking them, hoping it was not on a wild goose chase.

"Inside the cement base, there is a lead box. The box holds the original paint and brushes and the genealogy of the inheritance. It's sealed in the cement, so even if someone uncovered the post, they wouldn't see the box."

"But what about the brushes and paint in my studio?" Marci asked. "I have them here. That's what is causing things to appear and disappear. The children have painted flowers back onto the moors, not knowing that the brushes held such power," Marci continued.

"Those brushes and paint should never have left my property or studio. I've always kept them separate. But I've grown absent-minded. We probably mixed them up when we went painting on the moors."

"But there's no reason you and I can't figure out which ones they are and return them to you," Marci responded.

"That's all well and fine, but in which reality do they belong? And which hitching post has the original box? Or are there two cement posts and boxes, so we now have double the problem?" Keta's frustration was growing.

"Priscilla, why can't we go back to your place, dig up the cement base and see what we find?" Josh suggested. "If you know where it was before you rebuilt the barn."

"We could do a lot of digging, Josh," Marci said.

"Not if we laid out the architectural plans for the new barn and how it melded with the footprint of the old one," Josh said, excited at the challenge.

"Pris, Becki, and Mom sketched what they remembered of the photos several days ago."

"I can get the old and new barn plans from Ralph and Charlotte and meet you guys out there later today. But you'll need to show us where to dig, or we'll have a long afternoon ahead of us."

"It's critical that we find the post base in this reality rather than in the one Priscilla lives in. Morston is here now. He's not trying to buy the property in Priscilla's reality. Or will we not find the post base here?" Lyrica asked.

"Good point. I think we need to find that post quickly. We don't know what's being negotiated between Morston and Taylor," Keta replied.

"Well, he'd better not sell the place out from under me," Priscilla growled.

"But Pris, remember you're not in this reality. You're considered missing or dead here," Marci said, trying not to appear too morbid.

"Well, maybe I'll just stay here."

"That would make a lot of people very happy. But it wouldn't solve the problem of whether we've gotten all the paint and brushes from both realities and put them in a new safe place," Keta pressed.

"But in which reality do they belong?" Lyrica asked.

"That is the question we will have to answer soon. Right now, we need to beat Morston to the hitching post, or we could have a bigger issue on our hands. I don't even want to think about what he would do with that kind of power," Priscilla responded.

Fifty-Nine

C limbing into their four-wheel-drive vehicles, the family, bodyguards, and Priscilla headed back to the Taylor property. Jake also headed there from town with a copy of the plans he'd gotten from Ralph and Charlotte. He'd had a hard time explaining why Josh wanted them.

"Priscilla, we need to check the house to make sure Taylor isn't around. Your sudden appearance might just do him in, which would not help matters any way you look at it," Keta advised.

"Unless you've decided to stay in this reality with us," Lyrica added.

"Well, I can't very well abandon you here without knowing where the brushes and paints are. We may have to take a trip to my reality and do the same digging," Priscilla announced.

"Oh, Josh will *love* another day of digging," Marci added, smiling.

"There is no way around it. We have to be sure where the brushes and paints are and then find a home for them once and for all," Keta declared.

Priscilla was frowning. "You guys need to understand that you can't just flit back and forth between these two realities without damaging your bodies. Every time you pass through that membrane, the glue that holds your body together is damaged. I don't know how many more times I can travel back and forth before I'll start to disintegrate."

"What?" Marci exclaimed. "Why didn't you tell us that?"

"Marci, remember we didn't get to that issue," Keta responded, trying to calm his daughter.

"Don't forget, Dad. I'm now partially disintegrated, too. Who knows how many times I can cross over and back before I go, poof!"

"I don't think we are quite at that stage, Marci. However, I don't know exactly how many times anyone can travel back and forth," Priscilla explained. "I've never had to deal with a situation like this. But right now, I'd prefer to stay in this reality with you all."

When the troop of vehicles finally came to a stop at the Taylor place, Keta got out of the Land Rover first and headed to Matt and Dan's Jeep. Marci and

Josh parked right alongside them. Soon they would add Jake to the group that held Priscilla's secret.

Taylor's Jeep was gone, so they could at least look for the hitching post in the corral. They appointed Becki as the lookout while the rest of the group unloaded their tools. Priscilla, Marci, and Lyrica walked ahead of the men to choose possible dig sites.

"We made the barn smaller this time, so the post will be farther out from the building. Also, we shifted the barn thirty degrees to catch the breeze off the ocean."

"I think we should wait for Jake to dig. Oh my gosh," Marci exclaimed. "Now, he will know the secret as well."

"Josh, can you call off Jake before he gets here?" Keta asked.

"I can certainly try, but he's probably on his way. I pressed him to get here quickly. What do you want me to tell him? He's already suspicious because I was so vague in explaining why we needed the two sets of barn plans."

Josh was still waiting for the call to connect when he saw the nose of Jake's pickup coming down the driveway. "Too late, guys, he's here."

"Let me handle this," Keta spoke quickly to Josh as he turned to greet their friend.

"Dad, I think he'll want an explanation from me first. You can tell him about Priscilla," Josh teased.

"Hey, are we having a party? Where's the food and drink?" Jake asked while looking at his friend's face for a clue about the gathering. "Did Old Man Taylor sell the property so we can celebrate?"

"Sorry to disappoint you, Jake. But we're not here for a party. I need to fill you in on a few things after we look at the plans," Josh said to his partner while they walked toward the barn and corral.

"What's with all the shovels, guys? Are we digging for pirate treasure or a body, maybe?" Jake asked. "Oops, sorry, I guess that wasn't too appropriate."

But it was a perfect opening for Marci, who was now standing in the upper doorway to the hayloft.

"Jake, what if I told you we found Priscilla alive and well? Wouldn't that be great?"

"What? The shock would kill Taylor. Don't be funny."

"I'm not joking."

"Great. What if Priscilla doesn't want to sell the land? We don't know if Morston has closed the deal yet."

"Jake, come over here to the barn. We need to look at the plans you brought,"

Josh interrupted. "We're looking for something, but it's not pirate treasure. We need to compare the old footprint with the new one to narrow our digging area. We'd rather not dig up the whole corral."

"But before we do that, there are a few things we need to share with you," Keta said soberly as the others looked on.

"Uh oh. I don't like the sound of this. Josh, you didn't make more houses disappear, did you? I can't even walk from Ralph's to get a newspaper without being accosted on the street and given the third degree. We may not be guilty, but we sure are the resident experts."

"Jake, Priscilla is alive. She's right here with us."

"Marci, don't be morbid."

"No, it's true," Priscilla said, coming alongside Marci into the loft opening.

"What? I thought you were dead—or missing."

"It's okay, Jake. I've gotten used to people saying that."

"Josh, we're coming down now, okay?"

"Sure, hon."

"Great," Marci answered as she swung out of the loft on the rope pulley and slid to the ground.

"Yikes!" Josh jumped back as his wife landed in front of him. "I wasn't expecting you to use the rope."

"Too late. We thought we'd liven up the place. Too much talk about death," Priscilla said, dropping down right next to Marci. Jake was speechless.

Meanwhile, Keta and Matt had laid out the plans on the ground in the corral. They were talking numbers and angles when the rest of the group walked over.

"Priscilla, I think we can be fairly certain that the border of the old barn ran along this line," Keta said, and drew a line in the dirt.

"Good. Then we just need to line up the old barn door minus a thirty-degree angle and walk straight out into the corral. I'd say about thirty-five feet," Priscilla said, walking out into the corral. "I'd start here."

"You got it." Josh was ready to sink his spade into the dirt.

"Wait. Before we trample this area with our footsteps, everyone freeze where you are," Dan cautioned. "Now look around you and see if you can see any evidence of small circles of dirt about four inches wide. Or any place where there is fresh dirt."

"We know Morston sent his henchmen here the other day to take core samples of the dirt. It's possible he came close to our target," Keta explained.

They didn't find any circular holes, but they found a series of spots where someone had removed the dirt. Fortunately, it wasn't even close to where they planned to dig. They could see a line where the perpetrators must have walked back to their truck and tried to stir up the dusty soil to cover their tracks.

"Okay, I think we need to dig here," Matt said, pointing to the area where Priscilla was standing.

"I told you so," Priscilla said, offering him a big smile.

The men dug for twenty minutes and found nothing. But Priscilla warned them that years of dirt would cover the pillar, including what the bulldozers had left when they built the new barn.

It was tough going, and the women were glad not to be digging. The men kept at it for another ten minutes, going deeper and broader into the soil. Just when they were about to give up, Matt's shovel hit something hard.

"Guys, I've hit something. Dig around here a bit, and we'll see if it's a rock or if we've hit pay dirt."

More shoveling revealed the top of a five-inch square cement post. Stopping to rest, they speculated how far down they would need to dig to reach the bottom of the post.

"Sorry guys, you're going to have to pull it completely out of the dirt to get at its innards," Priscilla said, coaching them on. "It will only be another two feet or so."

It took another twenty minutes before the men started pushing and pulling the post back and forth like they were trying to work a loose tooth. Only it wasn't loose. Sand and dirt encrusted the cement post. Fortunately, it was all in one piece. They dug down several feet to reach the base. It took all four men to haul it out, two standing in the hole and two pulling the rope tied around it from the top of the hole.

"If we're going to put all this dirt back before Taylor sees that someone's been here, we'd better get going," Keta suggested.

None of them moved to take up the shovels again. Everyone focused on the post.

"Given how heavy this is, perhaps it would be better if we took it apart here and transported the box instead," Josh suggested.

"Priscilla, unless you have another suggestion, I think the easiest way to crack this open is to use the sledgehammers. Maybe two of the guys can hold down one end while the others hit the cement. Ladies, you might want to step back a few feet in case any cement fragments go flying," Matt suggested.

The first several tries at the cement did nothing except produce some sweat on the men's brows. Josh held the pick and axe. "Looks like we are going to have to use this. I just hope we don't hit the box too."

"Maybe it would be easier to paint it out of existence," Marci said meekly.

"I think we've gone beyond that now. And I'm not sure you can even do that, or the trust would have disappeared long ago," Priscilla remarked.

"Who wants to be the first at it?" Keta said, holding up the pick.

Dan, who was by far in the best shape, offered to go first. "If I can't crack it in a few tries, we'll just keep passing it around until we finish."

"Okay, muscle man. Go at it," Matt teased.

Two hits with the pick broke off one end of the cement, but no sign of the lead box. On the next hit, Matt made a significant crack in the post's body. Taking up the axe, Keta placed it on the break. "Okay, now one of you guys hit the ax head, and we'll see if we can open this thing."

Three more hits, and the cement cracked, revealing a hollow chamber.

"Oh no, tell me this was a waste of time," Josh lamented as he fell to his knees in exhaustion.

"Wait. Look down inside the chamber. Maybe it's at the bottom, and we just can't see it," Lyrica urged. "It's got to be there."

Time was moving on, and every minute put them closer to Taylor coming home and seeing the party of vehicles parked in front of his house. Soon everyone had a look, but no one could see a thing.

"I'll get a flashlight from the barn," Priscilla proposed and walked back to the barn.

"We still have over two feet of post left. I say we crack open the remaining post at Josh's place. Maybe there are two chambers, and one is to discourage us," Lyrica suggested.

"Always the optimist, aren't you, darling?" Keta remarked, sweat dripping from his forehead. "Let's just see how heavy this is. Josh, grab that end, and we'll see if we can carry it to your truck."

Picking up the opened end, Keta motioned to Josh, who grabbed the base of the post. They would need several men to carry it to the truck.

"It's rather a good sign that you guys are struggling to pick it up. The heavier it is, the more likely it has the lead box in it," Priscilla quipped. She received only scowls and grumbles from the men.

Marci drove Josh's truck into the corral, and they lifted the post into the back of the pickup. Meanwhile, the ladies began filling in the hole. "I think we should take the remaining cement pieces with us so anyone digging here won't find any evidence," Marci suggested.

"Whatever we do, let's do it quickly before Taylor gets here. Somebody might want to go relieve Becki as the lookout," Josh suggested.

"Priscilla, you may want to pop back into your reality before Taylor comes home. Unless today you're going to explain where you've been. That could get dicey, since he doesn't know about the brushes and paint." Marci's look of concern was visible as she spoke to her friend.

"If Taylor knew, he'd have dug this up before he put the property up for sale. And I'm not eager to tell him either. I'll have to figure out another way of reappearing. This is going to be tricky. Still, I'd like to come back to your house, Marci, to see what we have. If anyone has suggestions about what to tell Taylor, I'm all ears."

"Right now, we'd better fill the hole and get out of here. But before you pop back into your reality, is there a post with brushes and paint in your reality?" Keta asked.

"We'll talk about that shortly," Priscilla answered.

"I hope the realtor doesn't bring Morston to the property until after it's rained," Jake warned.

"He'd be a fine one to talk since his guys dug holes all over this place," Josh retorted.

"Yeah, but Josh, we aren't supposed to know those guys were here," Jake reminded his buddy.

"There's not a chance in a million he found anything in this pile of sand," Josh said.

"What drill holes?" Priscilla asked, looking a bit mystified.

"Pris, we'll fill you in on the way home. I think we should get going," Marci urged the group.

As the train of vehicles proceeded down Taylor's worn driveway, everyone was chatting about what they'd find in the hitching post. At least until they saw Taylor's Jeep pull into the end of the driveway, where he could easily see the line of cars and trucks. Josh, who was at the front of the line, stopped and quickly got out of his pickup.

"Hi, Taylor. Heard any good gossip downtown? Or were you with the realtor?" Josh asked.

"Nah, I was spending time on the bench with Cranston and Wilson, reading the newspapers and comparing the coverage of events. They're still warning me not to sell the place until we find Priscilla, alive or dead."

"I don't like the sound of the last alternative, but I agree with them. I wouldn't give up hope yet."

"Well, it's been a month. I don't know if I'd find a buyer so quickly again.

He's offering a lot of money."

"How much money is he offering, if you don't mind me asking?"

"More than one of your McMansions cost. And that's all I'm going to tell you for now."

"But Taylor, would you sell the property if Priscilla came back? She wouldn't want to sell it, would she?"

"No telling about Priscilla. She's as changeable as the weather. But I'm reconciled that she's gone. Admit it. They did a good job searching for her."

"Yes, I agree. But I'll never give up hope, nor will Marci."

"Say, Josh, what's this parade of cars and trucks blocking my driveway? More buyers?"

"Nah, Marci's mom, dad, and sister are here. They wanted to see the place before you sold it and the new owner put up a gate. The other guys are the bodyguards for Lyrica and Becki. We had a good time looking around the barn and corral with Marci narrating stories about Priscilla. But we're all getting hungry, so we're headed to town for an early dinner. If you back up a bit, we can go around you. I expect I'll see you someday soon with the buyer?"

"Yes, I'm supposed to hear from him this week."

"Okay, we'll be out in a minute." Josh quickly turned and headed down the track to the others.

"Everything okay?" Keta asked.

"It's fine. But Priscilla needs to stay out of sight."

With that, Josh jumped into his pickup, hoping that Taylor wouldn't notice the post and fragments in the bed of his truck. When they'd all passed Taylor and were onto the road, Josh heaved a sigh of relief. Marci looked over at him lovingly.

"You know it's not over, Josh. It's just begun."

Sixty

As the guys lifted the post from Josh's truck, Lyrica, Marci, and Becki went inside to prepare the iced tea and nachos. Priscilla hung out with the men in the backyard. As soon as the food and drinks were on the picnic table, the ladies walked over to check the men's progress. They were all excited when the box was recovered from inside the post. But without a key, they'd have to break the lock.

Dan and Matt tried the keyhole with some tools while the others waited in suspense.

"How'd you guys know that we'd need to pick a lock?" Marci asked incredulously.

"Oh, we grabbed our tools, expecting that the box to be locked."

"There, that does it," Matt exclaimed.

"Priscilla, why don't you open the box?" Marci looked at her friend with great anticipation.

"You bet. I've not seen the contents for a long time. I hope everything is still there."

Matt proudly handed the box to Priscilla. Then, sitting on the ground, she balanced the box on her legs and gently pried it open. The hinges squeaked a bit from their rusted state, adding drama to the scene.

"Well, look at that," Priscilla smiled.

The paint tubes and brushes were all neatly packed into the box. None of the tubes had leaked, and the brushes, although far from new, weren't ratty or even terribly worn. They had the remnants of paint on them. Tucked behind the items was a yellowed envelope, which Priscilla pulled out and carefully opened.

"This should be the history and genealogy of the families who have held the trust." Opening up the paper, she surveyed the names. "I'll be darned. This goes back to the fourteenth century. That's earlier than even I remembered."

"I don't see the McMure's name," Keta noted.

"Maybe they're related to one of the trust families, Dad. Or they might have found out accidentally as we did. What do you think, Priscilla?"

"I'm not familiar with that family name, but it's possible. Now I think I'd better paint myself out of this picture and get back before Taylor becomes a bear when he doesn't see dinner on the stove. What do you say, Marci? Want to paint me out again?"

"Oh, Priscilla, no. Why don't you walk down toward the studio and see if you can walk into the portal? But please come back soon so the men can dig for the post in your reality."

"The studio portal might work. How about I come back tomorrow morning around eleven, and we'll decide about the other post and a strategy to explain my reappearance to Taylor?"

"Sounds good. Josh, you might want to take Jake and follow Priscilla until she disappears. I think this might make the missing McMansions a bit more real to him," Marci teased.

"Just don't paint us out of the picture while we're gone," shouted Jake. "I'd hate to miss Lovey's vegetable spaghetti tonight."

"Well, shall we see if these brushes and paints work?" Marci said quietly.

"Why not?" Lyrica agreed.

"I don't think Priscilla would mind, as long as we don't create a third reality."

"I don't think that's a good idea," Becki responded fearfully. "How about we wait for Priscilla tomorrow? We don't know what might happen. We *could* create a third reality."

"As much as we'd all like to try the paints, I think Becki's right. We don't know the ground rules. We could make the situation worse. And that's something none of us want," Keta cautioned.

"But we're so close to solving the mystery. It kills me to wait," Marci sighed. "I know, I know. I see that look on your face, Dad."

"Thank you, my dear. Now, why don't we take them inside and talk over dinner about how to get Priscilla and Taylor to stay in our reality?"

Returning to the deck, Jake was still shaking his head in disbelief. "Josh, I thought this parallel reality was only in science fiction novels. But I saw her disappear. How did you know she'd disappear at that place on the path?"

"Marci and Priscilla disappeared there yesterday. We're not sure, but one or two portals seem to be near the studio. Let's hope they stay open until Priscilla reappears tomorrow," Josh quipped.

"I'd like to be there when Taylor sees Priscilla is alive. We might even see him smile for the first time in a century," Jake kidded.

"Well, don't get too happy. If Priscilla stays here, we lose out on the land deal and the houses."

"We could always offer to rebuild the McMansions that have gone missing."

"We need to buff up our reputation downtown first," Josh reminded his buddy.

"Oh, I'm not worried about that. I've heard some of the construction guys downtown don't even want to set foot on any land in Pocomo or Madequecham. They're afraid they'll disappear."

"Who's afraid, Jake?" Marci asked, coming out onto the porch with a tray of shrimp, chips, and salsa.

"Jake says that some of the builders are superstitious about building on the land where the houses vanished. They think they'll disappear into some black hole or end up where the other houses are now."

"Good. I hope no one builds on that land. It would be tempting to paint them out again, don't you think?"

"Marci, I'm surprised at you. I didn't think you had it in you," Jake exclaimed.

"If you ask me, there are a few other places on the island that could use my paintbrush."

"So, are you guys planning on recreating the island?" Keta asked, stepping out onto the deck from the kitchen.

"Oops, caught us again. Dad, your timing is still impeccable. You always appear just when I'm about to get into trouble."

"I had lots of experience when you were growing up."

"Guess I can always dream," Marci said, looking over at her dad as he speared a shrimp and dipped it into the hot sauce.

"Marci, all of us have ideas of how we'd like the world to be if we were in charge. But we don't have that option here. That's why it's been a sacred trust for all these years. I'm sure some of our predecessors wanted to make the world to their liking, and for all we know, they may have done so. I don't think it's our choice, as much as we'd like to see the island go back to its pristine state," Keta remarked.

Soon everyone but Dan and Matt had collected themselves and spread out on the deck in the Longmeadow's Adirondack chairs. The shrimp, chips, and peach salsa quickly disappeared.

"Say, where are the Hardy Boys?" Jake asked.

"The Hardy Boys were doing a little sleuthing," said Matt, appearing from around the side of the house with Dan.

"We were trying to get some information on the McMures. Both Matt and I are still suspicious of their story. Neither one of us can tell you why. But our instinct tells us there's something not quite right about their presence here,"

Dan responded.

"I thought they were tailing Morston garnering any evidence they could about his underground dealings—no pun intended," Josh said. "You don't think they suspect the paint and brushes, do you?"

"We don't know. They could have heard clan legends about the brushes and paint," Matt answered. "All we know so far is that they're Scottish citizens. But what they think Morston has found, we're still not sure about."

"We can't take the chance that they know or might find out about the post," Dan said. "It's dangerous for any of you to be with them. Until we know for sure what they're looking for, we have to assume it's the trust box."

"So, how do you propose to get that information?" Becki asked petulantly. "I guess that means *you* can be with them, and we can't?"

"Becki, who put a burr under your saddle?" Keta broke in. "Of course, I'm excluding the guys. And there are now two more men from their firm here to see what they can garner about the McMures at the local pubs and restaurants."

"Sorry, Dad. I'm feeling hemmed in by all the restraints on us."

"Then let's get to work. We have two likely scenarios. Morston knows there's more on the Taylor land than underground mineral or commodity material, but he doesn't know what it is. Or, he knows that something on the land is powerful, and we know he feeds on power," Keta continued.

"And the photos are his map," Lyrica added.

"That's why they took the soil borings from the corral. Thank heavens they didn't hit the post. God must have been looking out for us," Marci said.

"I think it's pretty clear the Lord has a watch over this trust," Lyrica said. "So let's keep it that way when we make our decisions."

"Mom, God's not interested in paint and paintbrushes. He's got more important things to do."

"Don't be so sure of that, Becki. The trust holds the power of the materials and the owner's character. What we decide to do with this box is very important to God, not just Priscilla."

"Thank you for that segue, darling. We need to talk seriously about going into Priscilla's reality to dig up the other post. Remember, no one has painted out the post from the corral, as far as we know. We can't take the risk that there is another set of brushes and paints," Keta said.

"*If* there is another post in her corral," Josh responded.

"We can't take that chance, hon," Marci responded.

"Then how about we look tomorrow after Priscilla comes here in the morning? She can go ahead of us to make sure that Taylor isn't on the property, so we have some time to dig and remove the post," Josh suggested.

"I think we should bring it back here to open," Dan added.

"Wait, guys. There's one more thing Priscilla told me. You can only live in one reality once you pass through a portal. You have to choose in which reality you'll stay. Flitting back-and-forth causes your cellular structure to disintegrate within a short time. Then you won't be in any reality."

"So, does that mean if I want to meet my doppelgänger, I'd better do it now?" Josh asked. "Josh, this is serious," Marci pleaded. "Be nice, or I'll paint you into the other reality."

"It's clear our family will want to be together. But now that Dan, Matt, and Jake know, they may have to make their decisions tomorrow," Lyrica pointed out.

It took several minutes before any group members stirred from their thoughts. Keta watched each person. None of them had counted on making such a decision.

"While we are talking about tomorrow, let's discuss who's going to the Taylor property with Priscilla. Some or all of the men need to dig and haul." Keta was hoping to have the support of all the guys.

"And remember," Dan added, "people in that reality are still the same. Morston exists in that reality."

"Does that mean that Stephen is a fraud in both realities?" Becki asked, turning to look directly at Dan.

"Yes, I'm afraid so."

"Why can't Marci just paint Stephen out of this reality?" Becki asked, with a mischievous look on her face.

"That, my precious, is exactly the point of the trust. These tools weren't intended for personal use," Keta said, eyeing his daughter. "We've already got one extra reality to deal with. We don't know how many the paint and brushes might create."

"That's too bad. I'd love to paint out Morston and his entire crew," Marci stated emphatically.

"But then Dan and Matt would be unemployed," Becki added with a twinkle in her eye.

"Not necessarily," continued Dan. "We still have to solve the robberies, even if the perpetrators are in another reality. You can't get rid of me that easily."

"Okay, you two. Now that we know in which reality you both are staying. Let's talk about how we can get Priscilla and Taylor reunited," Keta began, always the strategist among the group.

"Right now, Taylor exists in both realities. If he passes through the portal, either by accident or on purpose, he and Priscilla will need to decide where they'll live. Priscilla probably will want to stay here as long as Taylor comes too," Marci spoke up. "Then the box, or boxes, can stay here."

"Morston is going to love Priscilla reappearing," Josh laughed.

"Don't laugh too hard, Josh. When Priscilla comes back, your job goes out the portal, so to speak," Marci teased.

"Okay, so how about we talk about tomorrow's expedition? Who wants to go?" Keta looked at the group. Lyrica was the first to jump in.

"Marci, I don't think you should go. You've already crossed through a portal. I wouldn't risk it. And Becki, I know that look on your face, so I guess that leaves just Priscilla and me."

"Tomorrow, Priscilla will have to decide in which reality she'll keep the paint and brushes, regardless of whether there is another set. But Marci, that doesn't imply that you need to be the trustee," Keta added.

"I don't want to be the keeper of the box. I've had enough adventure for one lifetime."

"So how about we talk some more in the morning when we're fresh?" Keta said, trying to bring the discussion to a close.

"Oh, come on, Dad. The night is young. Anyone for popcorn and a game of scrabble?" Becki proposed.

"I'll take you on," Dan replied. "Anyone care to join us?"

Sixty-One

The following day was a workday for Josh and Marci. They were up early enough to see Dan and Matt head to town for breakfast with the two other agents to catch up on information about the McMures.

"Guess there'll be no blueberry pancakes this morning," Josh teased as he wearily grabbed a cup of coffee and gazed out the French doors to the deck. "I must be tired from all that digging. Maybe someone will wait on me this morning."

Marci, cocking her head, eyed her husband. "You'll be doing a lot of waiting if you think I'm making pancakes for you after that remark."

"That's okay. I have to meet Jake at the architect this morning."

"Boy, Morston is sure he's getting this property, isn't he?"

"Guess so. I wonder if there's a way to get his houses built, then have him fall through the portal—"

"Josh, cut it out. Do you have time for pancakes today or not?"

"Did I hear someone say pancakes?" Keta asked, sitting on the couch reading the newspapers with Lyrica and Becki.

"Sure. Have a seat at the table, and I'll wait on you," Marci said, giving Josh a look of disdain.

"How about I scramble some eggs? You guys are going to need your strength to get the other post back here," Lyrica offered.

"And bacon, Marci?" Josh asked wistfully.

"When is our reconnaissance team coming back?" Becki asked hopefully.

"Probably about the time the pancakes are ready," Josh quipped. "They have an uncanny sense when food is being served."

"Hmm, not unlike someone else I know," mused Marci.

"Dan said they were going to eat breakfast when The Donut opened at six this morning. Joy made some statement about hating donuts, so they figured that was a safe place."

"They must look pretty funny in my fishing gear. Two city slickers posing as fishermen," Josh joked.

"Who looks pretty funny?" Dan jested as he and Matt crossed the deck and opened the French door. "Boy, we could smell those pancakes all the way up the driveway."

"That's because she burned the first batch," Josh teased his wife.

"Josh, you're on very shaky ground. I'd quit while you're ahead. Never cross a chef before you're served," Matt warned.

"So what did you two find out this morning besides the local gossip on the chalkboard?" Marci said, eyeing them over her shoulder.

"The McMures are two of the most invisible people we've ever tracked. We know that Joy and Alex don't work for a detective agency. They hire themselves out as private investigators, but they don't advertise. Finding former clients will not be easy," Matt warned.

"Their personal lives come up pretty clean. Both were raised in northern Scotland and schooled in England. We've identified their clan based on the birth information," Dan added.

"McMure is an offshoot of the MacIver clan. To some extent, they were and still are a warring clan with Priscilla's ancestors. That said, we have no proof that they have malevolent intentions or know about the trust. But the coincidence makes one pause and rethink our strategy. They may not know about the box. But they're certainly sticking like glue to Morston."

"And, it looks like they're staying on the island for a while," Matt added.

"Our agents agreed that they're hiding something. There is a pattern to their answers. We also hit a dead end on many casual inquiries about their reason to be on the island. We're hoping that it isn't about the paint and brushes." Dan and Matt seemed equally frustrated with the lack of answers.

"Maybe your undercover guys could seek to hire them and then ask for references?" Becki asked.

"That's not a terrible suggestion," Dan added.

"We need to discuss ideas for Priscilla to explain her disappearance to Taylor. Any suggestions?" Keta asked, changing the subject.

"Yeah," said Becki. "What's wrong with the truth? Taylor can take it. And it's a lot easier to explain where Priscilla has been."

"But what about the rest of the island? This is a tight community. Everyone else is going to want to know," Josh asked.

"Josh, there are some things that will have to remain unexplained. We can't reveal how houses disappear or why goldenrod and daisies are blooming in strange ways," Marci replied.

"Why can't it remain a secret between the two of them?" Lyrica suggested.

"Because everyone in the world will want to know what she was doing for the last month," Becki responded.

"Maybe she was in the witness protection program," Lyrica answered.

"Or she had amnesia," Marci offered.

"Aren't you ladies getting a bit dramatic?" Keta laughed, looking at his wife and daughters.

"That's because you don't watch television much, Mr. Kea," Matt interjected. "Hollywood relies on those two explanations for many of their characters' disappearances."

"We're thousands of miles east of Hollywood," Josh protested.

"Hey, this island looks a lot like Hollywood in some places," Dan retorted.

"But we're not living in a movie script," Keta fired back.

"Who says we're not?" Becki interjected. "I wish this was a movie. Then I could walk out of it."

Quickly changing the subject, Keta pushed his chair back from the table and said, "We need to head out of here shortly. Remember, Taylor won't stay downtown all day."

"Then, let's go. Are we using your pickup, Josh?" Matt asked.

"No, I've got to take it to town to meet with Morston's architect."

"Hon, take my Jeep. Let the men take the truck. One day without your pickup won't tarnish your image downtown. That post is not only huge, but it weighs a ton."

"Marci, we won't need the pickup. We'll crack the post open and only bring back the box," Keta explained. "We're going to bury the cement post in the same hole."

"Let's hope the portal by Priscilla's house still functions," Matt declared.

"If it doesn't, we'll have to find one that does. We can't leave the box there if Priscilla and Taylor choose to stay in this reality," Keta pointed out. "Come on, let's go before we're late for our appointment."

They were right on time for Priscilla. She'd already had a glass of lemonade and was complacently rocking in her favorite weather-beaten chair on the porch as they drove up. Dressed in her jeans and barn boots, she had her shovel right beside the rocking chair.

"About time you guys arrived. I've already downed a glass of lemonade, just sweating out the time before you got here. Taylor left an hour ago, so that gives us less time. We'd better get moving. Everyone ready for a portal walk?"

Dan, Matt, and Lyrica started toward the front porch. But Keta held out a cautious hand.

"I think we should stop here. The portal is somewhere around here, and I don't want any of us to slip through without Priscilla. Why don't you come down here, and we'll all gather around you? When you disappear, we'll follow."

"And what if you don't show up on my side?" Priscilla asked, her eyes sparkling with mischief.

"Hopefully, you'll come back and get us," Lyrica answered.

"Then let's get on with it. Hope you boys brought your muscles." Priscilla grabbed her shovel, danced down the porch steps, and walked toward them. Just as she passed the opening between the privet hedge and the *Rosa rugosa* that bordered the front porch, she vanished.

"That's our cue. Let's go," Keta shouted.

One by one, they stepped through the portal. Popping out on the other side in precisely the same spot was a bit confusing until they saw Priscilla waiting for them with her shovel.

"What are we waiting for? Let's get digging."

The group quickly arrived at the paddock and paced out the distance from the barn to where the post should be. Dropping the pick and axe, the guys took their shovels and started digging.

"Priscilla, I think you should be the first to shovel," Keta said ceremoniously.

"Oh, stop being so dramatic, Keta. It doesn't suit you," Priscilla barked. Everyone grinned.

It took several attempts to find the post, but finally, they hit pay dirt. While the men dug deep enough to pull it out, Priscilla took bets on whether they'd find the trust or an empty box. Except for Lyrica, the vote was unanimous about the contents of the metal box.

A little over an hour later, they hauled the post from its resting place, and it was ready to be broken open. Before Dan took the pick, he looked up at Priscilla. "Okay to go?"

"Yeah, fire away."

It took two men with the pickax to even get a crack in the cement. Cement exploded everywhere after the next hit. The corner of the metal box was now visible.

The women carefully picked up the small cement pieces while the men began putting the rest of the post and soil into the hole. Priscilla went to the barn to fetch a broom and saddle her horse. She would ride the corral for a while to stir up the ground and make their dig less visible.

"How much time do you think we have before Taylor comes home for his lunch?" Lyrica asked Priscilla.

"As much as I'd like to sit with you over an iced tea, I think it would be better to get the post out of here. I want to talk with Taylor about the trust. I can't keep going back and forth. The last two times, my body felt like mush afterward. I don't see any reason for us to stay here. I'd much rather live on the island the way it is in your reality. We'll have to change our will. This land needs to be forever into conservation, so Morston can't buy or develop it. I don't want to leave this reality without that protection. Hopefully, we can do that today or tomorrow. Then if Taylor agrees, we'll come and drop in at Marci's studio. We can change our will in your reality later."

"Priscilla, what if Taylor doesn't believe you?"

"Oh, that's easy. I'll just send him through the portal to you guys, and Josh can take him to see the hillside. Then he can pop back, and we'll take care of the will."

"Won't Taylor object to leaving the other reality?" Lyrica asked her friend.

"Not for a moment. He's a crusty old sailor. Once he sees the box and then Pocomo Meadows and realizes that he doesn't even have to pack up, he'll be here in a snap. The tough part will be to keep him from the brushes."

"Okay, then I guess it's time we headed out," Keta was quickly changing the subject. "We'll see you both sometime in the next couple of days. Lyrica, let's go. I see the boys have already vanished."

"Priscilla, are you sure you're okay leaving us with the other box?"

"Lyrica, I'm fine. Open it up and see who won the bet. At the moment, one box of paint and brushes is enough for me. See you in a few days." And with that parting comment, Priscilla headed for the barn and her horse. A few seconds later, the others had vanished and reappeared in their world. Dan and Matt's Jeep was gone, so the rest of the family headed home.

Arriving at the house, Dan and Matt pulled cold beers from the fridge and waited on the deck for Lyrica and Keta to appear. Marci had seen them drive up but waited until the whole family returned before asking what they'd found.

"Hey, guys. Are you on our payroll? What's this hanging about on the deck?" Marci teased.

Becki was in the kitchen unpacking groceries. "Boy, I didn't know shrimp were so heavy."

"Does that mean we're having shrimp tonight?" Matt asked hopefully.

"Only if we have a volunteer to use Lyrica's scampi recipe," Becki said, looking directly at Dan.

"Hey, don't look at me. I'm the pancake man, remember?"

"Don't let him fool you, Becki. He makes a hot and spicy scampi that will knock your socks off." Matt was grinning at Dan.

"Then that's settled. We'll forgo Mom's recipe."

"What's settled?" Marci remarked, coming from the mudroom with a load of laundry. "Mom, Dad, I see you made it back from the other world."

"Yes, we just left Priscilla riding around the corral to cover our tracks. Then she's going to wait at the house to tell Taylor about the box and vanishing houses."

"If she can get that ole curmudgeon to move on it, we could see them back here in a few days. Priscilla wants to change their will, so they preserve the land for conservation."

"But what about Priscilla's horse?" Becki asked her mom.

"Knowing Priscilla, she'll ride him into the portal after she sees Taylor disappear. She won't risk leaving him behind."

"I think we should wait until Josh is here to open the box. Right now, I'm going to take a shower," Keta announced, heading for the stairs.

"Sounds like a good idea. We need to check in with the home office to see if they've got anything new for us." And with that, Dan and Matt followed Keta toward the stairs. Lyrica and Becki headed for the sink to prepare the shrimp.

"Becki, I meant to ask you. Has Stephen called?"

"Yes, he's called twice in the last few days. But I haven't listened to his messages. He gave up texting me, so maybe he thought I'd respond better to his voice."

"Becki, you might want to listen to your messages. There could be something that Dan and Matt would want to hear about Morston. We're coming precariously close to the finish line of Morston buying the land from Taylor."

"I hadn't thought about that. But then Dan would hear what Stephen says. What if he says something romantic? I'd be so embarrassed."

"A little jealousy sometimes sparks the chase." Lyrica was looking at Becki with a mischievous smile. "Besides, if you two are serious, there shouldn't be any secrets between you."

"Mom, don't start planning a wedding, okay?"

"Who said anything about a wedding? But a tropical one at the Club Bougainvillea would be fun."

"Mom, please."

"Okay, but it would be fun, don't you agree?"

Lyrica never got an answer. The conversation ended abruptly as Matt and Dan had come back for two more beers. Both the women had startled looks on their faces.

"Everything okay, Mrs. Kea?"

"Matt, we're fine. You just startled us. We thought you'd gone upstairs," Lyrica covered.

"We're just getting the shrimp ready for you to make scampi," Becki added, smiling at the two of them.

Unfortunately, they didn't fool the two bodyguards. Not that they had heard anything. But the look on Becki and Lyrica's faces was more like being caught eating cookie dough than hulling shrimp.

Finally, after a long day, Josh and the two dogs arrived home for dinner. The family was once again parked on the deck with appetizers, wine, and beer all around.

"Man, doesn't anybody around here work but me?"

"Hi, hon." Marci walked over to give Josh a sympathetic hug.

"So what did you guys find in the post? I tried to call while the architect conferred with Morston. He must have asked a thousand questions, including some strange ones about what was below the land and who owns the surrounding properties. I dodged those pretty well. But he tried to cross-examine me."

"Josh, we were waiting for you to open the box."

"What about Priscilla?" Josh asked.

"She told us to go ahead. She had enough to tackle just getting Taylor up to speed."

"What are we waiting for? Let's open it now."

Matt pulled out his lock tools and waited for the family to gather.

"What do you think? Will we find paint and brushes or not?" Lyrica asked.

It was unanimous that there would be another set of paints, except for Lyrica. After everyone was staring at her, she announced, "I don't think there will be anything in the box. I think the paint and brushes are part of this reality, or they wouldn't have shown up in Marci's studio."

"Anyone want to recast your vote? Lyrica's not usually wrong. I'm now voting that it's empty," Keta said.

The group was silent. Matt unlocked the box on the third try.

"Who wants to open it?" he asked.

"Marci, why don't you open it? You're Priscilla's trustee."

"No, I'm not. I resigned, remember? But I will gladly open the box."

They stood like statues. No one spoke as Marci opened the lid to view the contents. The box was empty.

Sixty-Two

It was several days before Priscilla and Taylor appeared at the Longmeadow's. He was carrying a mounted fish and his fishing pole. Priscilla was riding Bullet and holding the reins of Champ. Only Lyrica and Matt were on the deck. The others had gone kayaking.

"Here we are, fish, fisherman, and tackle," Priscilla announced as they approached the house.

"Taylor, great to see you," Lyrica said. "But what's with the fish and rod?"

"He didn't believe they'd be in our house here. So now he'll have two."

"You guys missed the gang by about ten minutes. Everyone went kayaking in Pocomo Meadows. Taylor, if you want to join them, I'm sure they'd love to see you. You could take Marci's Jeep."

After the frightened rabbit look washed from his face, Taylor stuttered, "Thanks, Lyrica. Maybe tomorrow after I adjust to this realm. This is not the kind of travel I'm used to."

"Oh, humbug, no backing out now. I'll take you home so you can gaze at your two fish with a glass of iced tea. Is Josh with Morston today? We've got to stop this deal," Priscilla stated.

"Josh is working another job today. But yesterday, he spent most of the day with Morston's architect. Do you want me to text him and ask what the status of the deal is?" Lyrica offered.

"Well, Taylor said he didn't sign a contract. But it might be a good idea to check."

"I told you, Pris, I didn't sign any contract. I only signed a pre-contract agreement." Taylor's color was rising.

"What? You didn't tell me you'd signed anything."

"No, I told you I didn't sign the contract," Taylor responded testily.

"What did it say? Did it commit us to anything?"

"Nah. Just something about the first right of refusal and access to the land for architectural planning and ground testing. No big deal."

"Taylor, what kind of testing does he want to do on the land, and when?"

Lyrica asked.

"I don't remember. He had some engineer or legal beagle with him, and he wanted this agreement, or the deal was off."

"I think we need to text Josh. Why don't you two come up on the porch? Bullet can graze back here."

"Thanks, Lyrica, but I think we need to get home and settle in. Would you mind if Taylor borrowed your Jeep?"

"Taylor, take the keys to the Jeep and go on home. You don't want to stand holding that stuff all day, do you?" Priscilla barked.

Taylor took the keys and headed for the side of the Longmeadow's house where the Jeep was parked.

"So, what was in the box?" Priscilla asked as she dismounted and walked with Lyrica to the front of the house.

"Do you want to guess?"

"No, I don't want to guess. I know what's in it."

"And that is?"

"Nothing."

"Boy, do I wish you were here when we opened it up. I was the only one who thought it would be empty, not counting Keta, who caved to my superior wisdom seconds before we opened it."

"That's because you're smart about these things. Told you so many times."

"But how did you know?"

"Only a hunch. Remember, I've been around these paints for over fifty years."

"Priscilla, you'd better get going. We don't want Taylor to think you've vanished again."

"No chance of that. He'll be waiting at the end of our driveway. He's still afraid he'll lose me again."

"Call if you want to come back for dinner. We're having shrimp scampi."

"You got it," Priscilla responded as she mounted her horse and headed down the dirt drive.

When Lyrica got back to the deck, she already had a return text from Josh. This time, she called him to tell him precisely what Taylor had just told them.

Josh whistled slowly. "That's not as bad as it might have been, but we'd better put a stop to this freight train soon. I'll find Larry and see what I can get out of him. Anything you need from the store?"

"No, just come home with some encouraging news," Lyrica responded. "Matt, how about you call your partners in crime and find out what they know about Morston's movements? We've got to catch that big rat."

❧

Sometime around seven, everyone gathered on the deck to eat and exchange stories and news. The kayakers were sunburned and muddy. Keta had bought the Boston Globe and local papers to check for articles on the robbery and the missing homes in Madequecham. Still in her painting smock, Marci was helping Dan and Becki in the kitchen with dinner. Josh and Matt were enjoying their first beers of the evening.

"Josh, tell us what you found out at the realtor. Did Taylor sign anything at Larry's that obligated them to sell to Morston?" Keta asked.

"Oh no. Are we too late?" Marci exclaimed.

"No, honey. Josh, tell us what you found out," Lyrica responded.

"While I didn't see what Taylor signed, I talked with Larry. He assured me that no legal contract was signed. However, Morston is still pressing to complete the sale. His latest request is to do some digging on the land, which Taylor had agreed to."

"Right now, Larry's principal job is to keep Morston away from Taylor. When I told Larry that Taylor had changed his mind and would not sell, he dropped the cup of coffee he was holding. What a mess. While we cleaned that up, he started asking me questions I didn't want to answer, so I left."

"Hopefully, Priscilla can get Taylor to call Larry tomorrow and formally tell him the deal's off," Keta said.

"There'll be some interesting stories going around once people know Priscilla is back," Josh said. "Maybe it'll take the focus off Jake and me."

"Matt, what's the status on the McMures?" Keta asked.

"That remains an open question. Now that we have the trust safe, I'm less worried about the damage they can do. Frankly, none of us believe their story, so our guys haven't left the island. Matt and I think they know about the trust. We're hoping one of them will slip and give our guys a clue."

"Knowing the McMures should make it less obvious for me to accompany Becki when she interacts with Joy at the presentation," Dan answered.

"Will they let you be with Becki at the presentation?" Lyrica asked.

"Absolutely. I need to stay beside her wherever she goes from now on. We also think it would be safer for her to fly back on the presentation day. We need to keep her from bumping into Stephen. Then we can come back here until things settle down a bit. The safest place for all of you is here until we've solved the robberies."

"Morston will be hopping mad when he loses the property. Isn't it likely he'll take it out on Lyrica and Becki?" Marci asked.

"That's always a possibility. But the photos are useless without the land. Even if we can't recover the photos, we're still committed to pinning the robberies on him. We're just waiting for one of his minions to get hungry enough to take a bribe."

"I hope by the time you're through, you'll have enough evidence to shut his machine down for many years," Keta remarked.

"Forever would be a better outcome," Lyrica added.

"I'll drink to that," Becki said, standing on the doorstep toasting with her glass of wine.

"Say, why don't we have a beach barbeque tomorrow at Pocomo to celebrate?" Keta suggested.

"Now you're talking," Josh responded.

Sixty-Three

*P*riscilla's reappearance was all over town the next day. It only took an hour before a reporter spotted her walking into the grocery store and pressed for an interview and photos. When she refused, the reporter informed her that an article would appear anyway, with or without her consent. Priscilla laughed, grabbed his camera, and threw it on the ground. Then she walked away silently thinking, this young man doesn't know with whom he's dealing. With a flick of a brush, I could paint him and his paper out of existence. Not that I would, of course.

Priscilla and Taylor had to put a gate across the entrance to their driveway to keep out the curious. This irritated Taylor a lot. They also fenced around the portal below their porch after testing it with a few rocks that disappeared. But Priscilla hoped the portals would close once the paint and brushes were inactive again.

While both of them were curious what people in the other reality would say about their disappearance, they'd agreed not to cross over again. Taylor was fearful of losing Priscilla, and they both wanted some peace and quiet. A few weeks to settle back in would be a welcome respite.

The sunset was going to be spectacular. After packing up the Land Rover and the various other vehicles, the group pulled out of the Longmeadow's driveway and headed for Pocomo. The dogs got excited when they realized that they and the food were going to the same place.

As the sun headed toward the horizon, they unloaded onto the beach, facing the harbor. The dogs were racing up and down, splashing in the water, making a sandy mess by rolling in the sand and seaweed and then shaking off.

Dan and Becki sat down on a log by the warm fire. Not content to wait for dessert, Becki was already toasting marshmallows. Marci and Lyrica prepared a plate with avocado dip, salsa, and chips while Josh, Keta, and Matt hauled coolers and logs from the Land Rover. Soon everyone was eating, laughing, and reminiscing as they watched the sparks pop and crack from the fire in the growing darkness. The sun had slipped silently below the horizon, setting off rich streaks of gold, pink, and lavender behind the remaining clouds. The water gently lapped the shore.

"I know we haven't crossed all the t's or dotted all the i's," Keta began. "But I think we've accomplished a lot. It's time to celebrate. We've done a mighty job of preserving the trust. Now it's up to Taylor and Priscilla to determine its future."

"Dad, that's fine for here on Nantucket. But what about the robberies?" Becki interrupted. "They're still open cases. Does that mean I'm going to have to continue hiding from the *Boston Flame,* or do you know something you're not telling us?"

Matt threw another log on the fire.

"If you're asking, am I still going to be your bodyguard," Dan grinned and turned to look directly at Becki's face. "For now, you're stuck with me."

"That's great," Becki said, promptly throwing her arms around him. Quickly realizing what she'd done, she pulled away and looked sheepishly at the circle of family.

"Becki, I think they all know," Dan said, smiling at her.

"Oh. Is it that obvious?"

Everyone started laughing, including Dan and finally Becki. "Okay. But this time, maybe you'll be a little friendlier than you were last time we were in Boston," she teased as she poked her finger into Dan's chest.

"Agreed."

"Matt, what's your plan to protect us from falling into the portals? Who knows when one of us might fall through one we've not yet discovered?"

"Please, Becki. Let's not go there, okay?" Lyrica pleaded.

"Mom, Priscilla led me to believe that the portals would fade once people quit using the paint and brushes to make things and people disappear and appear," Marci said.

"For now, I suggest we keep the places by your studio fenced so we don't lose anybody," Keta responded. "The robberies are still open cases."

"None of us can let down our guard around Morston. He's still dangerous until we can nail him for the robberies. I'd also stay away from the McMures until we have more definitive information," Matt continued.

Josh broke in with another thought. "What are we going to do about the missing houses? Are you going to paint them back in, or let us rebuild them?"

The thought had occurred to all of them, but no one wanted to answer the question. Priscilla wasn't sure you could even reverse what had happened.

"Wouldn't life be a lot easier if I painted Morston out of this reality, and maybe a few other people?" Marci suggested.

"No, Marci," Lyrica jumped in. "We've had enough disappearances for a lifetime. Remember, we agreed no more messing around with Priscilla's brushes and paint. They're back in the box, and she's looking for a new hiding place."

"Who said anything about messing around? I only kept one brush and a small tube of paint."

Reader's Guide

1. When you read the first chapter, what did you think was going on in the marsh?
2. What did you suspect to be the actual cause of the disappearances? When did you come to that conclusion?
3. Do you think Morston knows what he is looking for?
4. What do you think about the McMures? Who do you think they really are?
5. Where do you think this kind of supernatural power comes from?
6. Does anyone have the right to this kind of power? Should it be kept secret?
7. What would you like to do, and what would you actually do, if someone entrusted you with his power?
8. Why do you think they didn't destroy their discovery?
9. Do you believe in parallel realities? Why or why not?
10. Which of the characters did you find the most appealing and why?
11. Marci and Becki clearly have their mother's artistic talents. How much of this talent do you think they inherited versus Lyrica nurtured when they were growing up?
12. Have you ever wanted to paint, but were terrified? Would you go to an art class that Marci taught? Why or why not?
13. How does Josh reconcile his conflict between a successful career as an architect building McMansions on Nantucket with his and Marci's love of the natural beauty on the island and concern about its diminishing open spaces?
14. How do you feel about the development of McMansions in beautiful places like Nantucket?
15. Would you build a McMansion if you had the money? Why or why not?
16. When Becki first met Daniel Keelan, do you think she was right to be suspicious and standoffish toward him? Why or why not?
17. How long would it take you to trust someone like Daniel Keelan? Why?

18. Contrast the relationship Becki has with Stephen and the relationship she has with Dan. Do you hope Becki becomes involved with Dan? Why?
19. When, if ever, did you become suspicious of Stephen?
20. What would you enjoy most about being part of this family?
21. What do you think about Marci's last decision regarding the trust materials?
22. What do you think happens after the story ends? What would you do if you were Marci?
23. Would you read a sequel to this story? What would you like to see happen in a sequel?

Grateful Thanks

Every book is a creation of the author and a tribute to the friends who help bring it to life. This book is no exception. One of the nicest tasks of a writer is to remember those special people. With that in mind, I would like to give special thanks to Donna and Sal, for your creative input to the plot and my sister, Mary, for her input to the Reader's Guide. Thank you to my special friends Eleni, Marilyn, and all those of you who prayed and encouraged me when I most needed it. Special thanks go to Art Busch, the "Computer Doctor," who came to my rescue when I had technical issues during critical times in the process. Thank you to Taryn Nergaard and Sara Ward of Typewriter Creative Co., who patiently worked with me to publish this new edition. If I have missed someone, know that you are still part of this work and always part of my heart.

Soli Deo Gloria.

About the Author

During her career at a major corporation, Rebecca wrote award-winning communications in health promotion and human resources. She published extensively as well as spoke about her work with multiple audiences around the world. Rebecca has now turned to writing fiction and non-fiction. She currently posts a blog on her website, sharing photos with scriptural insights from her observations of nature to inspire readers. She is also a landscape artist.

Nantucket Island provides a profound source of inspiration for Rebecca. Its pristine beauty was the seed for her first book, *The Artistry of God: Devotional Beach Walks to Inspire Your Soul.* She sees nature unfolding stories as gentle evangelism, linking people with their Creator God—those who know Him and those still searching. She set her latest work of fiction on Nantucket but also draws from her favorite Caribbean island and Boston. In this latest work of fiction, her characters are artists who also share a reverence for Nantucket's natural beauty and the need to protect open space. Rebecca's corporate experience, world travels, and personal journey of faith play a role in her characters and writing. She is no stranger to corporate greed, cunning, and betrayal, as well as deep friendship, love, and faith. She weaves a story that challenges readers to ponder their place in the natural world and who really is in charge of the universe.

You can communicate with Rebecca via her website: nature-reflections.com.